QUETZALSONG

QUETZALSONG

St. Wishnevsky

Writers Club Press

San Jose New York Lincoln Shanghai

Quetzalsong

Writers Club Press
an imprint of iUniverse, Inc.

For information address:
iUniverse, Inc.
5220 S. 16th St., Suite 200
Lincoln, NE 68512
www.iuniverse.com

Any resemblance to actual people and events is purely coincidental. This is a work of fiction.

ISBN: 0-595-24185-9

Printed in the United States of America

"Evolution is not a story of an inexorable march toward perfection in form, but a story of continual improvement in the ability of organisms to evolve."

—Gregory Stock

CHAPTER I

▼

Munge was a pretty normal world as such things went. Even a nice world. Perhaps a little on the small side and mildly deficient in metals, but you'd hardly notice. It wasn't wrought into a Mobius Strip, or borne on the backs of six phoenixes (pheoni?), or covered in lichen or anything. It just was. Normal, like I said. Your standard world type world. Mountains in the higher places, salt water in the low.

This particular normal planet was, at this time, enjoying a warm period, with the result that the salt watery places were temporarily a little closer to the mountainous bits. Lots of shallow seas, lots of volcanic islands, lots of coral reefs and archipelagos. Soggy, like; but scenic. Easy.

Nice place to visit, but you wouldn't, as they say, want to live there. Unless you already did, in which case you were stuck with it. Not only stuck with it, but proud of your with-it-stuck-ness-hood. No problem. Except for one teeny little difficulty.

It was the people, you know. A bit of a problem. It always is. People.

About the worst problem a world gets up to on it's own is an over-enthusiastic tectonic plate or a youthful tendency to volcanism. Not really a problem. Just high spirits. Not like people.

It's almost always people. They're just not to be trusted with intelligence. It's actually a good thing most of them never use the little brains that they have and so remain content. And the ones that are forced to actually think....Makes you want to believe in Gods. Or worse.

Take for example, Conway. Young Conway. Young, pimple faced, shy, spindly, top-knot-less, Conway.

Young, etc., etc., Conway has a common problem. He wants to breed. Not really to propagate the species, but merely to go through, as it were, the motions of breeding. Did we mention that Conway is an adolescent male? Perhaps it was unnecessary. Be that as it may, Conway has an obsession, and being a people, he takes every path but the direct one to obtain his heart's desire.

A rational being, and we must emphasize that people are, by definition, decidedly non-rational beings, would simply approach other beings of the class of beings who possess the object or characteristic desired and directly propose a mutually beneficial exchange of fricative interplays. If the first being rejects one, then one simply accosts another objective being. Given equal numbers of objective and subjective beings, then success is only a matter of perseverance.

This was of course an impossible conception for poor Conway to formulate.

He brooded, he pondered, he suffered, he worried, he pined, he cried into his pillow. None of these actions had the slightest effect on his misery. Especially crying into his pillow, as the denizens of this planet slept in hammocks and used sea-sponges for pillows.

He was especially enamored of one particular person, one who was providently of the opposite polarity, or sex, as it was called. She possessed, or seemed to possess, all those character defects that endear each unto the other. She was excessively slender, and flighty, and heedless, and cruel, and was noticeably deficient in computational capacity and melanin. She was lovely. She obsessed poor Conway. He studied her form and features from a distance, and became so familiar with her topology that he was quite unable to accurately perceive any salient feature of her face, body, or personality. He was, as they say, in love.

Unfortunately for Conway, fair Rosialindia was not only immune to his soggy longings, but, being immune to the very idea of love, had taken up company with one Blundoor Kreegah, an alpha lout of the island. Kreegah was large, unlovely, brutish, hairy, and had amassed vast quantities of worldly goods by the simple process of taking them from those weaker than himself. As this included almost everyone in the circumambulant vicinity, he was regarded as quite the up and coming young man about East Angst. Rosialindia and Blundoor had an adult relationship. She knew what she wanted, and he got it for her.

One spring day, (I told you it was a normal planet, didn't I?) Conway, quite worn out with moping, had reached an altered state of consciousness, and was moping in the sun, upon a stump in a dell nearby to the road.

Dragons whirred and squawked in the sky, the sun shining ruddy through their wings, and sordes continued their life long war for carrion against the hordes of hand sized beetles that infested all of Munge.

In this dell, oblivious to the dactyl wars waging around him, his idle hands had plucked a single blade of grass, and his idle lips were teasing flatulent tunes from this simple reed, stretched between his thumbs, while a hopeful beetle nibbled at his toes and the dragons croaked above him. His mopery was increased most pleasantly with this futile diversion and he had managed to coax a recognizable, if melancholy tune from this most rudimentary of all woodwinds. It was, in fact, the aged lament "The Ballad of Fair Elsinor and the Elf Punk."

He knew the words, all forty stanzas, but he wasn't such a fool as to utter them aloud. The depths of his mind were a safe repository for sentiments such as;

"Elsinor was a fair maid fair, her ringlets curled and shiny-oh;
She loved her husband, but not as well, as she loved the Elfin Punk-e-i-oh."

His rendition made him sadder, and that made him happy. He was so engrossed in his pathos, that it took a silvery peal of mocking laughter to open his eyes. It was Rosialindia, complete with lout. He opened his aforesaid orbs wider and perceived the object of his futile desires slinking on the mighty arm of Kreegah. He felt simultaneous waves of desire, rejection, and humiliation sweep his spindly frame. He desired the planet crack open and swallow him. He desired instant doom. He desired Rosialindia. He desired....He didn't know what exactly he desired, but he wanted it with all his heart and soul and several meters of his intestines and a few underemployed glands. And then something happened that changed his entire life. Fair Rosialindia smiled. At him. Smiled at him. Shock-headed, scorned, him. He might have been able to stand that, but then she did something that destroyed his entire shabby lonely life. With great glee, and malice aforethought, she placed her lily-white hand to her ruby lips, and blew him a kiss. A kiss!

He knew it was a mockery, a jest, a cruelty, a jape, but he also knew it was a real live kiss, from a real live woman.

It was a first. He was making progress. He was on his way to the unimaginable bliss of going though the motions of breeding. He was a man!

And he owed it all to music.

He formulated a simple mathematical equation, ignorant of the fact that mathematics is the language that describes reality. He was as ignorant of mathematics as he was of reality, but he had now the beginning of a handle on life and love and everything. "Women liked music."

Now all he had to do was to learn how to make music, and attract a women. Presumably she would be better informed about breeding than he, and could be induced to share her insights with him. The very thought of such induction filled his vitals with a churning sensation, but his obsession was so strong that he had little real choice in the matter. All the rest was tactics.

Tactically he was in deep trouble. His native island, East Angst, had only one claim to fame, and that was its unchallenged title as "Third Hole from the End of the Sanctity Circingle." This proud motto referred to East Angst's allegiance to the most rigorous tenets of the Last And Final Unreformed Original Primitive Purity Church Of Total Wisdom And Holiness Church (Northeast). The LAFUOPP-COTWAHC (NE) was known across the length and breadth (actually Lat. and Long.) of the planet Munge as the ultimate bastion of theological rigidity extant. There had in fact been stricter churches, but they had all eliminated themselves by their own severity. The Pandemic Gnonads, for example, had viewed Flesh as an Impediment to Holiness, and had elevated bulimia to the status of Sacrament. Their last Prelate, Anorexia the Exiguous, had weighed only sixty-two lubbs at the time of his Translation to the Ultimate.

The Vibrators, actually The Society of the Sinful, had realized that carnality was the Sure Impediment to Vision of the All, and had sexually segregated themselves out of existence years ago. In this sense, young Conway was lucky. The Last Church only forbade music. Or, more precisely, forbade fun music. The services of the Last Church were not entirely innocent of song, but the Strictures of Sanctity were firm in denying any Complexity, Adulation, or Accompaniment. These were Bad.

The Thirty-ninth Alphate, Tinnearius the Explicit, had in the last century issued a Primal Dogma limiting Last Church Hymnody to Tritonics. These three sacred tones, La, Lee, and Lu, were deemed Sufficient and Pleasing to the putative Aural Organs of The Last Church's Deity, LLord. Services in the Last Church, therefore tended to consist of drones, interspersed with louder communal drones.

Anything else was viewed with alarm, and could lead to the dunking pond, or even to the impalement postle. Even Conway's grass leaf ballads were close to the edge of danger, and an outside observer might have suspected that Fair Rosialindia's applause was elicited more by Conway's skirting the bounds of custom, than by her appreciation of Art. In fact, she had zero appreciation for anything except her own comfort and bediziment, and she had titillated Conway more in the hopes of encouraging a possible henchman, rather than then from any aesthetic appreciation.

Mature persons realize how important it is to not ascribe motives to others, in ignorance of their true intentions. Many musicians thought that Tinnearius hated music or musicians personally, but he actually could not distinguish one note from another. The poor old man wanted only to snooze off in church and the dynamic variations of normal music made him restless. It wasn't that he hated music, he just liked drones. They hid his snores. Many a musician wasted his last breath cursing poor old Tinnearius, when he should have been concentrating on developing gills.

Similarly Conway thought that Rosialindia actually liked him for his music, when her likes were confined to the contents of her own skin. But this is so typical of musicians. They think other people care. They think this because they lack all communication skills.

Of course they do. If they were able to communicate normally, they would be used draken salesmen, and live comfortably. It is noticeable that used draken salesmen often hire musicians, while the converse is rarely true.

Conway pondered a while, and then rose from the sward. He had learned "Fair Elsinor and the Elf Punk" from his mother, who had come from the heretical, if neighboring, island of Angston Corners. She used to sing the ballad whilst washing the family dish. She sang it softly, it was true, but he had learned all the verses before she died a few years ago. Only one other in all of East Angst had the nerve to admit to any knowledge of foreign parts and that was Old Badmash the Sailor, who eked out a living tanning drake and dragon hides on the outskirts of town.

Badmash had little fear of Rector Charl and the dunking stool, and could be in fact be heard whistling at his work in the tannery. This work, involving as it did, copious amounts of assorted urines and even less wholesome substances, provided Old Badmash with certain immunity. No Older of the Church cared to contaminate his robes with the powerful pungencies Badmash used, and indeed few cared to approach close enough to even hear his whistling. Similarly, his ingrained nastiness served to protect him from immersion in the Dunking Pond, which also served as East Angst's water supply.

Also, there was the obvious problem; if Badmash was submerged in the village pond, some true believer must take his place. Dragonskin was important to the economy of all the Angsts. No dragonskin meant no clothing, nor sailage, nor cordage, no harnesses, nor coracles or jacks or firkins. And the firkins of the Angsts were famous to the very corners of Munge. Actually Munge, being a normal planet, had very few corners, but still it was evident that heretics and outlanders had their uses.

Conway agreed. And having a use for one outlander in particular, he set out to the tannery, past the rows of windmills, while drakes and dragons and iridescent furred wyvverns wheeled and screeched in the sky above and sordes and psallies gamboled on the Village Green. Actually, the grass was as red as a cabbage, but the traditional name still applied (The Omnipotent Author apologizes for the digression, but is forced into such byways by his hatred for footnotes and total detestation of parentheses.)

The tannery was on the downwind side of the island, logically enough, and architecturally speaking, aspired towards the ramshackle. It was a noble, if futile, aspiration. Badmash had fewer aspirations than his edifice, and therefore was not as stylish.

As Conway approached the tannery he was careful to cage a firkin of nut-brown quaff from his nuncle, Bilbeau the brewer, so as to placate Badmash. It wasn't that the ex-sailor was inimical, but he was of large disposition and prone to excess of spirit. Persons taking him unaware and unplacated had been know to suffer certain splashes of vilements to the detriment of their attire. Badmash was at his station under the thatch of the tannery, scraper blade in hand. His diligence level was somewhere between lackadaisical and desultory.

"Hola, Badmash. Got time for a quaff?"

"Boy!" Badmash's personal dialect was perhaps traceable to the reaches of the Caliabu Peninsula, but solitude, and perhaps excess quaffage, had pruned his vocabulary to the minimum. He did usually manage to communicate, however. He beckoned, and hung his scraper on its peg on one of the beams that comprised the structure of his empire. The tannery had even fewer pretenses of walls than the other buildings of East Angst, as the more sea breezes that wandered under the thatch roof the better. Conway ankled up, and breathing through his mouth, poured Badmash a jack of ale. Glugging noises ensued.

"Boy!"

"Good, Huh?"

"Ma-an...Boy!"

"Best on Munge."

"Boy."

"That's what they all say."

"Burrrp!"

"Want another, just ask."

"Man?"

"Sure thing. I'm your friend, and friends should help each other...right?"

"Boy."

Conway poured with a heavy thumb on the firkin lid, trying to judge the exact dose that would gently nudge Badmash over the threshold of polysyllabism, while halting him this side of incoherence. Badmash cast an appraising eye on the firkin, as if assaying its contents.

As everyone knows, a firkin is one eighth of a Mungian barrel, or one third of a demijohn. Therefore it is approximately ten of even the largish jacks Badmash favored. In layman's terms, that's about two good drunks and a gut ache. As Conway drank only to forget, and wasn't old enough to remember much of anything, there was enough ale to impress even an old soak like Badmash. It only took one more jackful to loosen the "Taunt Wound Skeins of Tribulation," as the troubadour Hwaltmein succinctly puts it, and Old Badmash soon had his feet up on the nearest bale of wyvvern hides and his broad back snuggled up against his nominal work bench. His unkempt topknot straggled from its pierced copper band and cascaded over his idle tools. He took another pull.

He belched approvingly; "Good quaff. Boy!"

"Glad you liked it. Here, have another."

"Man."

Conway hastened to pour again, fearing losing ground.

He poured and plunged. "Look, Badmash, I need some information…information about the world." He grimaced and then shrugged. "You're the only one in all the Angsts who's traveled more than to market."

Badmash shook his heavy head, as if wondering at his own daring. "Man. It's….It's vary out there"

"Very what?"

"Not very….Vary…" He grappled through his skull for his traces of language skills. "Man….varied, I mean. It's varied out there."

"What is?"

"Man."

Conway waited, and then started to grow wroth, but finally realized that the monosyllable had been an answer, and not an ejaculation. "Men! You mean men are very varied out there?"

"Man!" Badmash pursed his lips and blew a soundless whistle of affirmation and amazement. He swilled his quaff and peered at the sediments at the bottom of the jack as if there was wisdom slopping about there. Conway tapped the resonant leather side of the firkin, both to estimate the level and to attempt to retack the ex-sailor. He decided to push on to the nub.

"What about music?"

"S' Worse…

"How worse."

"Much worse…" Badmash laid a finger alongside his nose and tried to look wise. Instead he looked thirsty. Conway obliged, lowering the firkin to the halfway mark.

"Not how much worse, I mean worse how?"

"Oh." Badmash lubricated his tongue and scratched his muzzy head. One action or the other produced a coherent sentence.

"What's the difference between East Angst and West Angst?"

"Not much. About two..." Conway counted to himself. Yep. Two. "Two letters."

Badmash didn't get this sally. "No sir. The difference is forty flongs of water. They're islands."

The youngster was unimpressed and began to regret the hop chopping he had promised Bilbeau in exchange for the firkin. Hops stained the hands and smelled badly. "So what else is new? Islands!" He snorted and wished he had brought his own jack, or a piggin. He could use a quaff himself.

"Right. Boy. Islands." The old sailor gave an expansive sweep of an arm. "Islands. All islands. All of Munge...Islands." He reached over and clapped the young man on his knee. It hurt. "And, my boy, do you know what that means?"

"No. What?" Conway tried to conceal the impact to his spindly frame, and olfactory insult to his nose caused by the proximity of Badmash.

"They're all crazy." He nodded to himself. "Ever' damn one of 'um."

"Who, the islands?"

"No, man! The damn people. Each one on their little damn islands and they're all sure they're the only sane ones on the whole plamn danet. All crazy."

There was a lot in this statement that escaped Conway, but he sensed he was nearing the nub, and restrained himself to a simple, "And so?"

"So if you want music, or quaff, or....Or....Or....Whatever, you just go to the island where the damn people think that's the most important thing in the whole damn world, and you get it. See?"

Conway did see. He wasn't stupid, just obsessed and he also saw a definite problem arise. "You need a coracle to travel."

"Yes, you do." Badmash held out his jack and shook it. The boy took the hint.

"I don't have one."

"They're made out of dragonhide, ain't they."

Such was common knowledge, Conway agreed.

Badmash smacked the bale beneath him with his jack and the ale splashed over the soft, iridescent fur of the wyvvern hides. "This here's dragonhide, ain't it?"

Again, agreement, and a dawning hope.

"I got dragonhide unreal. What I ain't got is nobody to talk with." Badmash belched again. The air curdled and slowly cleared. "Tell you what, boy. You bring me slosh, or quaff, or ale, every day, and help me work here, and I'll tell you all I know about sailing and tanning and pay your wages in finest grade dragonhide, enough to build a coracle. A catamaran, or a caique, say, and help you set out. No problem."

"Mariner Badmash, I don't know how to thank you. Why would you do such a thing for me?"

"I dunno, boy. I guess....I guess, it's because you remind me of myself when I was young and stupid."

"Well....Thanks, I guess. Mariner, you got a deal. I'll work half days at Bilbeau's Brewery and half for you. I'll be off, learning music in no time. Thanks a million."

"Boy...Man......"

So young Conway settled into his new life as tanner's 'prentice. There were no relatives closer than old Bilbeau to say him nay, and indeed half a day's work at the brewery was nearly twice what Conway had grudged him before. The tannery work was simple to the point of idiocy, and Badmash had vested himself in his monopoly status so as to actually labor as little as possible.

The noisome hides were delivered relatively cleaned and scraped by the divers divers, stockmen, fishers, hunters and retiaria who harvested them. Then the hides were scraped, soaked, fleshed, scraped again, and split. Then they were actually tanned, in baths of urines, oak galls, or the infusions of the barks of several trees.

The tannery windmill creaked and groaned above them while they worked, and provided a constant background for the instructions Badmash provided.

There was always time for a break or a snack or a siesta or another quaff, and Conway spent many lazy hours listening to Badmash rumble on, and scratching the crest of the tannery's grossly fat sorde, Buster. Buster had become an epicure and fattened upon only the choicest scrap-fed beetles, and the occasional very slow ptigion. Sordes were to be found in innumerable breeds and Buster seemed to contain all of them some where in his gene pool. He had the blue spackled crest of the Oman, and the fringed wing membrane of the Pariclate Rounders from the Pice and the soft curly fur of the Stopwick native to the Angsts. He also had the appetites of all his ancestors combined, and as soon as Conway and Badmash sat down for a moment, Buster would come lurching out from under a bench on his clawed feet and wing wrists to share whatever was available. In this manner, Conway learned more than he really wanted to know about hides, skins, and leathers, but somehow, in his mind, this knowledge was underlain with the murmuring satisfied sounds of Buster getting his crest rubbed.

The wing membranes of the larger flying dactyls, your dragons, drakes, pterigrines, and wyvverns, were split and the aktins variously scraped off and saved for fish spears and snares. The split skins, without the aktins, were used for raiment, and those with the barely visible stiffening rods were mostly used for sails or armor.

Hides with the aktins were dragonhide, proper, while hides without were referred to as leather. The name stuck, even though dragons proper were rarely used for tanning, due to procurement difficulties. Six laminations of dragonhide would stop a steel arrowhead, not that many could afford to use metal, much less iron or steel for an expendable weapon. That sort of thing was left for the Smithers and Hazlens and the other Bigslanders. The Flyers of the Maine used steel points too, in their blowguns, but one tried to ignore the Flyers as much as possible. At least until they actually swooped down on their quetzals on their occasional raids.

They were far enough away to border on the mystical anyway. Way out here in the simple Angst Archipelago, folks made due with draken teeth, or flint, or sting skate spines, like LLord intended.

But that was about all there was to the tannery business. The wind mill drove a laminated bamb shaft that ran the length of the tannery's rafters, and from time to time Conway clambered about these rafters, shifting belts about to agitate, stir, or pummel various vats and tubs of vile chemicals. The same system powered the great wringer rollers that expressed the tanning liquors from the pelts. There were also fast spinning wheels for glossing, brushing, and burnishing the leathers, and the great slow rotating drums for softening the cured hides.

Care had to be taken as the various hides were fuzzed, like wyvverns, furred like sordes, or feathered like drakes, or smooth like dragons, drakens, or psallies. Some applications called for a stay in the retting pool, to defur a batch of hides for jacks, or carefully smoked and dry tanned for luxury leather goods. But still and all it mostly involved scraping. Hour after hour of careful scraping with a big double handed steel fleshing blade, or a single-handed burnisher. Conway had thought that Badmash's broad shoulders were the legacy of years of rowing and sheet hauling, but he began to have his doubts. And as they worked, Badmash talked and when he wasn't talking, he whistled. Conway dutifully quizzed him on every tune, and the old man patiently explained each song, its origin, and elucidated the meanings of each obscure word of every lyric. It developed that each island had developed a separate music, each with its own instruments and conventions, and although Badmash was unschooled in music, and indeed had a voice of no charm whatsoever, he did have a full memory and was more than happy to share it's contents.

And so Conway learned of the pipers of Hazlen's Land and the harpists of Badmash's own Caliabu Peninsula, and the wind organs of

Murka Ahven, and at least a smattering of most of the other musics of the Pancreatic Ocean. Songs rowdy and gay, songs sad or wistful, all the songs and tunes that might stick in the ear of a sailor man were poured into the receptive mind of the youngster. It was a cruel thing to do, but it was meant well. All unaware the youngster was developing the first requisite of a musician, the ability to listen. And he had very good ears. They stuck out too much for beauty, but they functioned quite well.

And Badmash, as good as his word, told Conway all he knew about the wide reaches of Munge and indeed, the young man began to fear for his hearing as well as for his shoulders and his nasal passages.

The smell was bad. No doubt about it. The urines and salt baths were pungent enough, and the ptigions and beetles could barely keep up with the rotting scrapings, and they stunk, but the dung from the sagitaries and psigils that they used to supple the hides was of a whole other order of foulness from all the rest.

They had to trundle a barrow down the shore side cliffs to the rookery once a week or so, to get a new load of nice fresh guano for their work and even the bonus of unlimited eggs scarcely made the trips bearable.

Naturally, they tried to approach the rookery at low tides, when the most of the long tailed psigils, and the short tailed sagitaries, were out fishing. This left only the nesting mothers, but they were a handful. As soon as the men crossed some invisible boundary around each nest, the mother dactyls would attack, lurching across the slick stone on their webbed feet and clawed wing wrists. The psigils were amply toothed and even the spoon beaked sagitaries were quite capable of ripping off a chunk of man flesh. Conway tripped over a scavenger beetle on one trip, and received enough nips and claw scratches and wing buffets from a twenty-lubb granny sagitary, as to make him stiff and sore for a week.

He feared that this misfortune would make him the laughingstock of the island, but as he already had retired this title with honors, there was little apparent change in his status.

Psigils and sagitaries, like most dactyls on Munge, were pisciverous, and like all flyers, had very rapid metabolisms. They ate approximately twice their body weight in fish every day, and only partially digested it. Without going into too great detail, it would suffice to say that their excrement stank. Horribly. And such was Conway's love and devotion that he willingly rubbed this substance into the flesh side of partially cured, that is to say, slowly rotting, dactyl hides every day for the rest of that dry season. He didn't do it uncomplainingly, he wasn't that big of a chump, but he did it. Ah, the things we do for love.

And slowly his escape took shape behind the tannery, under the staggering dock. The frame was made of bamb and withe, split from the silver barked weeping withe trees that garlanded the shores of East Angst. The frames were lashed with rawhide that shrank as it dried to an immensely strong, but flexible, joint. Once dried, it was treated with a concoction of cone tree beetles simmered in moby oil. The resins of the cone trees were incorporated into the cone tree beetle's carapaces, and cooked down to a species of lacquer that remained waterproof for years, in temperate waters. The dragonhide hull of the coracle was similarly impregnated, after being shrunk on over a slow fire.

The plan of the boat was quite simple, as Conway had little energy for anything but scraping, and little imagination for anything but...well, you know. It became an outrigger canoe, what the locals called a 'long coracle'. The outrigger was itself another canoe, perhaps half the length, and one quarter the beam, of the main boat. It was covered entirely with dragonhide, with only a lashed down cover to provide access to the storage cubby and bilges. Both ends of both canoes were bulkheaded off from the sea and filled with the waterproof husks of the almanc nut, for flotation. Conway had enough optimism to insist on two thwarts in the main coracle, as well as a tiny cabin, astern.

There was a latticework main mast, with a balanced lug sail, of seven battens. He made provision for a jury mizzen, and a slanted forespit, if a longer crossings became necessary.

There was no question as to Conway's competence as a sailor, for he was an Angstman. Raised on an island less than ninety flongs in any dimension, the terms 'Angstman', and 'sailor', were synonymous. If he hadn't been such a drippy brained doopus head, he could have had a good living as a retaitius, like his vanished father. But, then again, if he wasn't such a fool boy, there would have been no story here, and you would probably be reading the bible right now. Not that that would hurt you, of course. The only real problem is deciding which bible to be seen reading. It's only a matter of Afterlife and death, after all.

Finally, after working through the dry season, the leaves of the trees had faded to pink, and his coracle was ready. Even the Sigil had been painted on the bleached sail. The Angst colors were sable and azure, but Conway had only used these hues for the base of his device.

His slogan was an uprooted withe tree, its twisted trunk twined up of shades of blue and black, and the drooping branches rendered with all the shades of red, from orange pink to deep lavender, available to his pallet. He wasn't sure what it really meant, but it seemed to reflect how he felt. It would suffice. More than suffice, he thought his colors reflected well in the sea above and below the gold of the lacquered dragonhide hull. It was a lovely craft and Conway began to feel as if he was becoming somebody, somebody real, if still unimportant. This insight was not shared by his fellow Angstmen.

Now, all that was necessary was for him to become ready to leave. This desire became harder to construct than the coracle. The choice became brutally clear. He could remain on East Angst, as a derided, insignificant nobody; or else he could be somebody else, elsewhere. Put that coldly, it was a really scary choice. It wasn't all that simple, and Badmash's tales made it worst.

"This is the way the world is, boy. The Angsts are smack dab in the middle of the Pancreatic Sea, it serves us right, and good riddance to us." He spat and quaffed. "North is Hazlen's Land where they worship goats and play bagpipes and live on haggis. They're Bigslanders and don't know any better."

"Are Bigslanders dumber than islanders?"

"No, but they don't get out and meet people, and so they think they are smarter than everybody else, and that's what makes them dumber than us...well, than me, anyway."

"Thanks. I guess."

"Think nothing of it, boy. East is Smith, where people first landed on Munge, at New Ahven. There they think they are the first people on Munge and that makes them stuck on themselves and that makes them dumber than everybody else."

"We learned that in school. There's Outers at New Ahven, what I hear. You ever see an Outer, Badmash?"

"Never know, they're just like everybody else, unless they're not."

"Not what?"

"Human, boy."

"What else is there?"

"Saw a book once."

"Other than the Bible?"

"Lots of books other than the Bible, Conway. This one was called Barrette's Extrobiology."

"Extro what?"

"Ex-tro-bi-ol-ogy. Means critters. Biology is critters. Extro means furn."

"Furn?"

"Foreign. Alien. Outer. Lots of weird critters in that book. S'posed to be people."

"That's blasphemy!"

"Yeah, and ugly too. But you don't worry about that, boy. Them critters ain't allowed on Munge, Munge is for human folks only. That's why they don't officially allow no Outers on Munge. That's why. Munge is a Preserve. What they call a Primitive Preserve."

"What does that....Who's a primitive?"

"It's part of the Quartonial Pact. It just means that each race is allowed to keep some planets reserved as places to preserve the purity of the race for breeding stock."

"Why would they want to do that?" Conway didn't even notice as Badmash's diction improved and his speech cleared to approximate the language he had used as a youth, before drink and disappointment had taken their toll.

"Space travel changes people, boy. After a few generations, people in the Habitats, or the Free Worlds, or the Dysons, can't even breed with each other. So the Outers, when they find a planet that is like Olearth, where folks can live natural like, save it and keep it simple so that the race will remain close to the norm. What with the Rippertons and the JJjglils and the Umpquas, humans have enough competition, without dozens of human variants confusing the issue. They still got them, but Preserves serve as a source of pure DNA for the Outers. Do you understand?"

"Not a word. How do you know all this?"

"I was an Ahvener. They have real schools, and galactic contact. You can leave Munge, you just can't come back."

Conway understood a little more, but only from hearing the pain and loss in the old man's voice. He did get the "leave here" part. That he understood. "So did you..."

"Try to leave Munge?" Badmash looked down into his jack as if it was a wishing well. "Maybe I did. Once." He raised his saggy head and looked Conway in the eye. "But that's neither here or there. On Smith, they have some of the Olearth records. They can still play real music, Olearth music there. Otherwise, they herd duncows, and axebeaks, and sailbacks and play tarinzas and vithels." He swallowed and shook the daily firkin. It was empty.

"And west of here is the Main. That's the biggest island on Munge. Even you know what they do on the Main."

"That's where the Flyers are."

"That's where the Flyers are. And they drink blood, and play music on harps of dragonhide and flutes of dragonbone, and ride their damn quetzals and do anything normal people can't stop them from doing. And nobody goes there unless they want their killing." Badmash nodded to himself, and stood and reached for his scraper blade.

Conway was puzzled. "I thought you said that people bred true on Munge?"

"That I did, boy. It's just that some purity is purer than other purity."

And that was all that Conway could get from him for that day. And, as a matter of fact, that was all he could get from Badmash for several more days. But the boy barely noticed. He had more than enough to try to digest as it was.

The fact that everything Badmash told him directly contradicted what the Olders had taught him at Fane School was perhaps irrelevant. At least he understood what Badmash was doing on East Angst and why he was willing to help him leave. He did remind him of himself when Badmash was young and stupid. At least he got the young part. It took many a long day's sail before Conway got even an inkling about the stupid part. Also lazy, slack, unlettered and pretty damn ignorant.

Well, it's all just part of growing up. Good work if you survive.

One day, Badmash was waxing profane about the near islands, with special emphasis on the skate racers of the Hastings, when there came an interruption that made several of Conway's decisions for him. The pattern had become pretty well established over the dry season. First, an early morning's work scraping hides, and then Conway would spend a couple of hours chopping hops or cooling wort for his uncle Bilbeau. Then, it would be firkin thirty, and Conway would tote Badmash's daily guzzle over to the tannery for lunch. Conway would gnaw a few grilled beetles, or a barbecued psallie drumstick, and Badmash would hold forth while drinking his midday meal.

Conway wondered, sometimes, why he had thought the old man tongue tied and indeed sometimes wished he would just hush up. Like many recluses, all Badmash needed was an audience, and the wisdom just spouted out of him. Still and all, Conway realized that he was getting an education that was unavailable this side of Smith. Conway did, slowly, come to realize how many different people an adventurous soul could become in sixty or so years.

"Those Hastingers are the worse gamblers on the planet, boy, damme if they ain't. Race them damn skates, and even bet their wives on the races. Some winds up with fifteen, twenty wives, all crowded together in one house, fighting like sordes and ptigions. Wives get all ugly, boy…boy, they get ugly with their men all down at the skate pens, day and night. Handicapping. Handicapping…hah. They're just drinking and telling lies and playing grab ass" Conway declined to point out that this was approximately their own occupation at the moment.

He did appreciate the music in the old man's voice. Conway may not have had much of a head, but he did have great ears. And he was already beginning to miss this tannery, refulgent under its foul thatch, with it's shafts and belts creaking beneath the weeping withes. He didn't know it, but he was beginning to grow up.

"So, here's all these women, just pining away, and here's me, old enough to know better, and young enough not to care, and just off a long line drifter and flat full of piss and vinegar. So I'm strolling down the Reiado, the main drag of Hastington, minding my own business, innocent as a day old sailback, and I see this lady drop her fan on the blockwalk. And, boy, I…"

There came a sudden clamor from the Faneknell, high in the steeple of the village Fane, towering high above even the tallest of the windmills and withe trees. Instinctively, Conway checked the time and date in his head against his ingrained calendar of Last Church Obligations. It was past lunch, on Tressdy. There was no reason to toll the Knell except for…he jumped to his feet and tugged at Badmash's shoulder.

"C'mon, Badmash, maybe there's a fire or a shipwreck, or a sail come lose on a mill! Some excitement for sure! Let's go."

"Excitement ain't nothing but somebody else's trouble, boy. Left well enough alone, what I say." He grumbled, but he followed after Conway.

They hadn't far to go, just up the hill to the Green, where they came upon the ranked shoulders of the rest of the island's population. The population was lined up at a safe distance from the Fane, apparently awaiting inspiration or leadership. The Knell fell silent just as they worked their way into the crowd, their tanyard aroma more successful than their elbows in opening a way for them.

There was little to see; the Green was empty of people except for a knot of Olders clustered around an object sprawled on the purple-red grass. As Conway's mind adjusted his eyes, he discerned that the sprawled object was a clot of white bleached leather, closely resembling the habitual robes of Rector Charl, except for some odd blotches of crimson color. Conway was trying to remember what ranks of the Last Church's Hierarchy wore red on their robes, when the clot on the Green resolved itself into the crumpled body of Rector Charl himself, and the red into a seemingly excessive amount of blood.

Behind this cluster of inaction, the Fane rose, silent and familiar. The Fane was the only building on East Angst with cochina stone walls, and had been built as much as a blockhouse as a house of worship. Times had been hard centuries ago, and the Flyers had been active out as far as the Angsts and even as far as the Knowles and the Fane had been built with them and the perennial pirates in mind. There was little hope of storming the Fane against any resistance at all.

Sometimes a person just has to say something stupid if he wants to know what is going on.

"Rector Charl isn't moving." Nobody lost their eye lock on the scene before them, but the largest man nearby, Obean the diver, spoke out of the side of his mouth.

"Somebody stabbed him, and ran into the Fane."

"Why doesn't somebody go see who it is?" Dumb questions are also enlightening, if answered.

"Fane School's in session. There's a bunch of kids downstairs. They ain't come out yet."

"Do you know who done it?"

"Only one person on Angst mean enough to stab an old man like that." said Obean, quietly. Heads nodded around them at these words. Conway looked around for Kreegah and Rosialindia. East Angst village was small enough that a census could be conducted with one sweep of the eye. No Rosialindia. No Kreegah. No Mistress Sweeneah, the Fane School teacher. About ten children short. Conway added up the numbers and arrived at a sum of big trouble. Rector Charl had been an old man, but the Vice-Rectors and Laym under him were not much younger. They, the total government of East Angst, remained clustered about the body of their leader, muttering unanswered questions in low tones, and making the sign of the double crosses on their breasts.

"Why doesn't somebody do something?"

Sometimes even very dumb questions have no answers. The tableau gave every sign of lasting until the psallies came home, but suddenly the carved logany doors of the Fane slammed open and a spindly figure in a brief kirtle pirouetted down the cochina steps, stumbled and collapsed in a heap. The Olders scurried toward the fallen man, but there was a twang and a sibilant hiss from the darkened doorway, and the lead Older, Fernster, collapsed on top of the first body.

Conway had just about decided that the first body was that of old Soopneit, the Fane Custodian, when the arrow from the dark dropped Fernster. Soopneit was one of the few Angstmen who had treated Conway like even a provisional human being, and Conway, unthinkingly rushed through the crowd to the old man's side.

"Soopy...are you..." Conway never did know how he was going to finish that sentence, because it was very evident that Old Soopy, and Fernster atop him, wasn't much of anything any more. Both arrows were driven in almost to the dragonhide fletching, and the red, green, black chevrons on the vanes told Conway whom he would see as soon as he lifted his eyes to the Fane vestibule.

His heart fell. If he had been asked, he would have thought that that organ had obtained very little altitude above rock bottom in his life so far, but, it seemed to have quite a long way to fall, and to smash quite sickeningly when it hit. And even though he had only seconds to anticipate the crash, when it came it was worse than anticipated.

Rosialindia stepped forth onto the top step, and beckoned gaily to him. Blundoor Kreegah was right behind her, another shaft nocked on his bowstring. Conway walked to her with all the enthusiasm of a man with hemorrhoids approaching the impaling postle. He stood there below the first step, knees a-tremble. All he could think was that her face was a little sharper and more sordlike than he remembered, but her golden hair gathered in every glint of light there in the shadowed doorway and reflected it like a benediction. She bit her ruby lips and spoke.

"How nice of you to come....er..."

"Conway."

"Of course...Comway. Do be a dear, and tell those louts, those other louts, that we are leaving now, and if they behave, not only will we not torch the Fane, we will leave the children adrift in a coracle a few flongs offshore. Tell them that we do not care to miss the tide, and that any delay will only cause needless suffering to their beloved children."

Conway could not understand the bitter emphasis she placed on 'beloved children', but he supposed it was irrelevant. He tried to think of something relevant to say. He also hoped that his voice wouldn't squeak. He hated that.

"What about Mistress Sweeneah?" He questioned. His voice did, of course, break.

Rosialindia smiled, ever so sweetly; "She is not coming with us, today. She disagreed with Blundoor and had to lie down for a while."

Conway had nothing to say to this. Mistress Sweeneah had, like Old Soopy, treated him no worse than he deserved and had occasionally spoken kindly to him or shared a sweet with him, even though he was an orphan and a spindly laughingstock. He knew that Mistress Sweeneah would be a long time arising from her little 'lie down'. Still, he had the weight of children's lives on his unworthy head.

He stumbled away and transferred the message to the cluster of Olders. They seemed to come to a realization of their peril and gaggled away from the Fane door, and perhaps by instinct, gathered around the diver, Obean. He wasn't the smartest man in the crowd, or the best respected, but he was the biggest. Suddenly, that seemed overwhelmingly important.

"We ought to rush 'em."

"Blasphemers belong in the dunking pond."

"Sit'em on the postle."

"We can't risk the children."

"Let'em go…Good riddance."

"LLord will protect his own."

Conway thought that LLord was doing a poorish job of protecting his own, but carefully kept that thought behind his lips. The babble of opinions around Obean just made his foot itch and his head hurt. It was a common set of sensations to him, and so he did what he always did when his feet itched and his head hurt. He drifted away. Nobody noticed him go, but nobody ever noticed him anyway. He let his itchy feet lead him in a big circle around a mill and the Town Pond, and up an alley and without ever quite planning it, he wound up at the Fanedock.

Naturally, every major building possessed it's own dock, and naturally Fanedock was one of the largest on East Angst. It was even thatched, to protect the Primate on his rainy season visits. At the moment the thatch served to screen a possession of a dozen small figures, one smallish figure, and one brute.

The brute bore a bow and quiver and a steel broad sword, that until recently had the status of Holy Relic. It was the Blade of Harld, Quez-talbane, and had been mounted before the very Altar, as a relic of that

Harld the Excrescant, that had led The Angsts to their day of glory, centuries before.

The small figures were bent double beneath bundles of Fane Goblets and Plate. There was little metal on Munge and it all tended to wind up in the hands of the various churches. All that wasn't used for weapons or tools, that is. East Angst's ration was being looted and carried to the Last Church's Barge of Ceremony on the backs of the Faneschool's students. The other slim figure was Rosialindia. All she bore was the Sacred Altar Cloth of Pure Woven Gold. She wore it as a shawl and stroked it with one hand, as she urged the children to greater speed.

Conway was bemused. While the Olders and the village heads debated on the correct course of action, Rosialindia and Kreegah were decamping with the loot. He debated racing back to the green and sounding the alarm, but decided after a second that any rash action, any panic, would only endanger the children more. And although he had no particular affection for children, they were just more people who hated him, these children were young enough to have never wounded him. Yet. He decided to remain invisible, and let events take their course.

By the time he noticed that the pair of villains had taken no extra coracle, to free their captives in, it was too late. The Fane Barge's sail was filling and the ornate vessel was under way. Conway was still standing there, lost in thought, when the crowd finally came to investigate. And then they were so busy entertaining themselves with blame and recriminations that they quite failed to notice the fire that Rosialindia had set in the Fane until it burned through the thatch. Then they became frenzied enough, but it was too late to do more than splash water on the flames, until the walls collapsed and the Faneknell came crashing down with a final resounding clang.

The children were gone, the villains were gone, the Fane was a small heap of embers between four scorched walls, the hierarchy was decimated and all their treasures were stolen. Even the Great Book was ash.

The populace was so shocked and depressed that it took them until Sundy evening to blame Conway for the whole fiasco. Of course it was none of his doing, but as Badmash said; "What do you expect them to do, blame themselves? You're the obvious one to blame, as you're the most defenseless. It's got to be all your fault, because you're a dweeb, and furthermore they haven't had a good dunking for moonths."

As mentioned before, Conway didn't have much of a brain, but he had real good ears.

His ears heard Badmash telling him to leave East Angst with all due dispatch. His head could find no reason to dispute his ears. He had a perfectly good boat at his disposal, and no reason to stay except inertia. Destiny beckoned. So did his heart's desire. Survival pushed. His ninety-lubb body was too puny to resist. If he had had any maturity and good sense....Well, forget that. This is not a fantasy.

Bilbeau gave him a half dozen firkins of ale, and a demijohn of perry, and some assorted hard rations. Badmash gave him a bale of wyvvern hides, and a battered compass, and a chart of the Pancreatic Sea, and a spare scraping knife, and his blessings. The village gave him nothing, but with their usual indifference to his actions, didn't miss him until he was half a day and three hundred flongs down the nor'west wind and well into the Sluys, headed for Ainsworth. Ainsworth was the nearest place he knew nothing about.

And it was due down wind. When one has no plan and no hopes, a good tail wind is sufficient. It's almost an adage. The sky was green and the sea was greener and the skippers were springing into the air from his bow wave; it was a beautiful day to run away from home. He supposed that he would try for Smith eventually, as Badmash said they played 'real music' there. He had no idea what constituted 'real music' but he knew he needed it. But even if he had no plan, he had a coracle and a wind and a good knife and some fish hooks. He would survive nature, he had no doubts. It was only the rest of humanity that he had any worries about. He was beginning to catch on to the nature of reality.

CHAPTER 2

▼

Ainsworth crept over Conway's horizon, and disappointed him with its normality. From a dozen flongs out it was the same as East Angst, the parched pink withe trees interspersed with the feathery silver stands of bamb and the dark olearth green of the palms. There were the same thatched roofs, bleached with time and sun to near white, and then shadowed with the maroon mosses of age. The only differences apparent were that the Ains left their wind mill sails the natural browns of unbleached dragonhide, without the hex signs of the Last Church, and their Fane steeples were capped with a gilded sun ball rather than the Sacred Double-cross # of the Last Church. The plain mill sails looked unfinished to Conway, and the sun sign on the Fane evoked no emotion in his breast. He was still slightly amazed that LLord had not smote Rosialindia and Kreegah for their blasphemy. More than this, he was ashamed of himself for harboring such a childish feeling.

The first Ains he saw were two young retiariae, spearing skates a few flongs offshore. They paid him the compliment of ignoring him. Conway coasted for a few tens of flongs southward and soon came to a river delta and it's dependent mud flats, complete with draken herders. The dactyls stalked the flats, dipping their long snouts into the rich maroon mud, and then raising their warty heads to crunch crustaceans between their broad teeth. The herders were naked except for ornate woven reed sombreros and net bags slung over their shoulders. Conway waved from a distance and the herders waved back with their shovel-ended goads. Conway was curious, as the rocky shores of the Angsts forbade any large-scale exploitation of the fifty lubb, wingless draken. He wanted to investigate, but had a seaman's aversion to sailing where dactyls were walking. He contented himself with a hail.

"Ahoy there, good herdsmen. Which way to town?"

"Ahoy yourself, sailor. Griffin's thataway…Up river." The herder gestured with his goad again. "Thataway…Up the Skeane."

"Thanks…Good luck."

"Luck's not what made us drakenherds…"

Conway forbear further comment, and devoted his attention to tacking up the River Skeane. As the tide was at full ebb, and the river was barely distinguishable from the mud flats, this took his full concentration. He therefore failed to notice the head tapping gesture that the one drakenherd made to his mate. It wouldn't have made much difference, anyway, except that he might have wondered how they caught on so fast to the prevailing opinion of him.

It was a slow process tacking up the sluggish Skeane, and he was disconsolately considering dropping sail and sculling up river, when the tide changed. Cat's paws proclaimed the sea breeze picking up, and he was able to sail up stream and around a bend or two to where the town of Griffin stood on, or rather, not quite slid off, a moderate headland.

The Fane occupied the highest ground, and a few thatched roofs, maroon with age, clustered around it. There were a few coracles and canoes beached at the mouth of a smaller stream and Conway was able to sail almost to the shore. He was quite proud of himself for not having to paddle more than a few yards, but no one else seemed to care enough to even stare in his direction. The no one else in this case, consisted of three gaffers and a Goodwife mending nets. Actually, the Goodwife was mending the nets and the three gaffers were supervising, and re braiding their topknots. Conway, of course, saw nothing amiss in this division of labor.

The Ain style topknot was apparently a polychrome died band of woven bamb strips holding a branch of blue coral. One of the gaffers, the youngest, did rise to help him drag the coracle safely up on the shore, and Conway offered him and his companions a draught of Bilbeau's finest in payment.

"Thankee, sir man." Quoth the eldest; "Good, B'LLord, ale. Sez'I. B'LLord." The old man passed the firkin to his mates and fixed Conway with his glittering eye. Actually one was all he had; the other was a scar so old that it had faded to a white rope of flesh. "You're not from around here, B'LLord, are you, boy?"

"Nosir….From Angst."

"B'LLord, there's not a many leave there…Think it's LLord's footstool, B'LLord. Damme, if they don't, B'LLord, sez'I." The gaffer nodded defiantly, his undone white topknot down around his ears.

"Well…" Conway couldn't think of anything forceful enough to say to stem this torrent of ejaculation, so he leapt to the nub of his quest. As we have hoped to imply, our hero's social skills were on the flimsy side. "Do they have music here, on Ainsworth?"

"B'LLord if they don't! You just walk on up to the Devout Sailback, and you'll find all the B'LLord skittering and skeedling a man could stand, B'LLord. Damme if they're ain't nany." The old man gestured with the firkin that somehow had gravitated back into his hands, and indicated a vicinity slightly to the left of the Fanespire. Conway gathered that there would be a longish wait for his own turn on the firkin and so simply turned to his coracle and laced down the oiled dragonhide over the outrigger's hatch. He hoped that would be enough discouragement to keep the old gaffer away from the remaining ale, but there was little he could do about that in any event, except sail away. The only thing of real value he possessed, besides the coracle itself, was his knife, and it was both sheathed in his spoan at his waist, and secured with a lanyard around his shoulder. He wondered what a 'Devout Sailback' might be, but he supposed that all would become self evident, uphill and to the left of the Fane. He thanked the gaffers, whose eyes were fixed on the firkin, and set off, up hill to meet his destiny.

Any person in all the human galaxy would have recognized The Devout Sailback for what it was…except for our hero, of course…it really wasn't his fault that East Angst possessed no establishments providing spirits and entertainment for the thirsty traveler. The reasons were obvious and simple enough. An inn requires three elements for its existence. These are; alcoholic beverages, music, and travelers. Of this trinity, the Angsts possessed only the first. There was no proscription against travelers on the Angsts; it just was that there was no great influx of persons in search of sanctimony and boredom. Those commodities were about all that the Angsts had to offer, except firkins. And it was a lot more profitable to transfer the firkins, fine as they were, to the Pancreatic Market on the Isle of Cashamash, than to wait for hordes of firkin deprived drinkers to brave the disdainful stares of the Olders of the Last Church.

There was not much government on Munge, and very little of what there was, was interested in abstract imposition of ethical norms on outslanders.

The Devout Sailback was a pretty normal institution of its grade, which was low. It huddled comfortably under its thatch and boasted geometric patterns woven into its wattle walls. It was getting on toward dusk, and a fat, warty man was lighting aqua and amber glass lamps against the gathering grayness. The man wore his wrappa, his kirtle, low, and in addition had an apron and an embroidered vest. Three garments were two more than were common across the Pancreatic Sea. It seemed that all these leathers could have covered the man's belly, but they failed.

Outside of his weight, he was commonplace enough. His tattoos were modest and his topknot was gray. Even his bone jewelry was worn and simple; only a necklace of draken teeth and a bracelet of moonshells. Conway nobly tried not to stare at the man, without success. Overweight persons were unknown on Angst, where everyone worked except the Olders, and they fasted five days out of the eight to maintain their purity. In fact, Conway had come to associate the Olders' acrid breath with the phrase "the Odor of Sanctity." He was innocent enough to not realize that he was not the first person to mistake malnutrition with holiness.

His amazement was snatched away by a sudden drift of...sound?...Noise?...Dacltysong?...Song! He followed his ears into the inn, below the sign of the be-spectacled, mortarboarded, amphibian, and into the darkly aromatic interior of the inn. It took him a moment to arrange his perceptions, to order his observations in his mind. Under the great oak beams that held up the ancient thatch, the room was divided into three areas, common to bars all over the universe, and totally alien to young Conway. He thought it resembled a Fane, and he was not all that wrong.

To his left was a counter, cluttered with all manner of jacks, firkins, baskets, and jars, each holding some delicacy or condiment. He did recognize sea tripe, pickled psallie toes, curried sausage, hard brot, kelp sticks and forglish, among others. In back of the counter were the smokes and steams and gleams of a more or less normal kitchen. To his right was a largish room filled with large and small tables and a clutter of benches, almost all unoccupied.

Directly in front of the young man was a platform, raised a foot or two above the dirt floor, and there...there were three men and a woman who teased oddly pleasant noises out of various objects they held in their arms, or pressed to their lips. Try as he might, Conway could not resolve these objects into his brain.

They seemed to not be constructed along normal principles, even though their materials were common enough, even mundane. That was surely unglazed clay, like a vase or pot, but why was it filled with holes and why were they placed so oddly? That was obviously a velvetwood box, albeit oddly shaped, but why did it have wires all over its face? And that was a ptortise shell, but why did it have such a long handle onto it like a hand net? And those were moby vertebrae, but why hollow them out, and cover the ends with skate leather, stretched almost to transparency?

Conway found a bench, by the painful process of barking his shins on it, and had just barely enough wit to sit down. He occasionally recovered enough composure to close his mouth and swallow his drool, but that was all the intellectual capacity he had to spare from his observations.

The four before him seemed no more than idlers, ne'er-do-wells, engaged in little more than time wastage and frippery. One would stroke a string and then twist a knob and then make a wry comment to a mate. Another would gently tap the membrane stretched over the moby bone, and then gaze pensively off into the thatch or space, whichever was further away.

The woman, whose red hair had almost totally flashed to white, would breathe into her globular clay pot and twiddle her fingers. Then she would frown and remove a portion of this clay pipe and examine it closely and then wind or unwind thread from the joint area. Then she would reassemble her pipe and breathe into it and frown again. She was slender and dressed in a casual wrappa of heather dyed hide and was the most beautiful woman Conway had ever seen. Although she was older than his mother had been when she died, he suspected that she had never been anyone's mother. He decided that she was slenderer and more graceful even than fair Rosialindia, and that she possessed a far more fearsome scowl. He decided that he was more afraid of her than he was of Kreegah. He supposed that the noises they were making were music. He couldn't decide if he liked it.

The noises would veer toward his comprehension, and then just as abruptly skitter away. The only music he had ever heard was his mother's one ballad, and Fanesong, and this was neither. He sat there, full of wonderment and questions, and as he sat, something happened. Something that he couldn't define even as he watched it happen. All the fiddling and adjustment tapered into contentment and the random tootlings and raspings congealed into....Into something for which Conway had no name. It was like a flight of ptigions, that would instantly turn from a mob to a flock in a wingbeat, where a cloud of random individuals receives direction from some invisible influence; a wind or a scent or the shadow of a wyvvern on the ground below. All of an instant, there was no doubt, Conway was hearing music. Real music. And there was no doubt but that he liked it. It lasted only a moment, and then at some imperceptible signal, it ceased. Conway discovered that he had closed his eyes. When he opened them, he was staring right into the sea gray eyes of the woman piper. She nodded, as if at a confirmed suspicion, and rose to her feet. She swept the barroom with a smile and curtseyed to the scattered folk that had gathered behind Conway. She spoke softly, but her voice carried to the murky corners of the room.

"Thank you, for tolerating our tuning up. We will refresh ourselves, and return to entertain you in less than a glass. We are Gully and the Foils, and we are honored to play for you here in the premier venue of all Ainsworth. Thank you. Enjoy yourselves and patronize the delectables and libations of our host Meinher the Bold."

She and her Foils gathered themselves and adjourned through a woven curtain at the rear of the platform, leaving their instruments behind. Conway slowly came to his feet. He wanted to step up on the platforms and to examine those wondrous objects, but was as afraid of them as a child might be of a wizard's alembic. He couldn't bring himself to approach, and couldn't bear to leave, and so hung there, stretched on tenterhooks, until a brassy voice struck his ear and he jumped back to reality.

"Lookee here, kid, are you going to buy something?....The amberjack is at it's prime and Cookie has a chouder of eels and napples near done..." It was the fat man, the host, Meinher the Bold. Close up, even his eyelids were warty.

"B-B-Buy?"

"It is customary to purchase food and beverages at inns." Meinher drawled. "Customary, my boy...necessary indeed."

"With what?"

"Money is nice…Makes the world go round." The fat man examined Conway closely. "You're not from around here, are you?"

"What's money?"

"From Angst, I see….Money is….Well look, kid, I'm an Innkeeper, not a schoolteacher." Meinher sighed and looked around his room. There were a grand total of no paying customers in sight. He sighed again and decided that half a bird in the hand was worth two loaves in the bush. "Do you want a drink?"

"I want to listen to the music."

This was progress of a sort, but Meinher was implacable.

"Let me explain music to you, kid. I pay Gully to play music. She makes people happy and they buy more drinks. Sometimes she makes people sad and they buy even more drinks. I make money selling drinks, and so I have money to pay Gully. Do you catch my drift?"

"I have quaff to drink in my coracle. I could bring it here and drink it."

"What are you trying to do, starve me to death? Have you no mercy on a poor business man?" Conway thought that Meinher's starvation was a long ways off, but realized that Meinher had a point. The Angsts had business; they just had no need of money. Maybe barter….

"How about I bring you my quaff, and you sell it and let me watch the music? It's not like I'm going to cost you anything. You're going to have to pay Gully anyway." Conway had a hard time pronouncing Gully's name; it seemed like she deserved more than a mere two syllables for a title. He had another thought.

"It's the very best East Angst quaff. My Nuncle brewed it. It's in finest quality firkins. We do a good trade in firkins…they must be worth something…" He tried to press an advantage he wasn't sure he had. "Angstian firkins are famous all over Munge."

"Yeah, yeah, yeah. Next thing you will be wanting me to feed you. I'm just near the Fane, not part of it."

"What's wrong with food? A person's got to eat." Conway tried to look firm. He didn't know it, but he just looked hungry and slightly demented. Meinher decided that perhaps this lost soul might provide some amusement, if only as butt. Plus there was the fact that his last pot boy had succumbed to the twin occupational disease of infected hands and headaches. The hands were from scouring the chouder cauldron with sand and rushes and the headaches were from swilling the dregs of customer's tankards…and so…

"Tell you what, kid. I don't need your bitter outsland quaff, we brew the best on all of Munge right here, but I might could use a firkin or two. You show me what you got, and I'll maybe let you watch the show, if you're quiet." He tried to look stern. Even Conway was not naive enough to believe that.

"I'll be quiet like beetles, Mariner Meinher. I'll run down to my coracle and see what I can spare you."

"You do that, boy. Gully and them usually spend a good half a glass tanking up before a show. If you hurry, you might make…." His speech trailed off, as he discovered that he was talking to himself. He shook his head and went to stir the chouder. Work, work, work. Worry, worry, worry. An innkeep's life was no bed of bracken floss.

Conway made it down to the beach in record time, fearing that his suddenly precious firkins had been looted, and expecting nothing but a pile of sodden gaffers in place of his ale. But much to his surprise, not only was everything as he left it, but the gaffers had neatly placed his empty firkin on the tiny fore deck of his boat. He gathered up two more firkins, and scuttled back up the hill toward the Devout Sailback. He thought of pouring out the quaff, but suspected that Meinher had been a little too ready to decry the quality if Angst's Finest. He could always drink it himself. Or, happy thought! He could offer the quaff to Gully and her band. Meinher said she was fond of drink.

Idea!

He screeched to a halt, pivoted on his bare heel and scampered down the hill again. Nuncle Bilbeau had gifted him with a demijohn of perry, which he had taken in trade at Cashamash Market a few years ago. It came from the far north, thousands and thousands of flongs away, from the northernmost Vancian Mountains of Hazlen's Land where, stories told, the very water turned solid and fell from the sky like drake feathers.

There, tales related, the Hazlens brewed a wine from the fruit of a tree, like unto a napple, but yellow. Then, in rainy season, when it got real cold, they let the pear wine freeze and poured off the residue. The Olders had forbade Bilbeau from using the perry for anything but medicine, holding that it bred Laxity and Irreligion. Bilbeau, an easy-going man, had stored the two demijohns in his thatch, until Conway's departure had given him the opportunity to dispose of one. Conway had tasted perry, once, and after coming to, had decided that in this one instance the Olders were right. But….

He unlaced the tarpaulin from the outrigger and filled the empty firkin half full, replaced the stopper in the jug and lashed the cover back on the outrigger. Then he raced back up to The Devout Sailback, and was able to corner Meinher, and strike a deal. He was too inspired to notice that there were still very few other patrons in evidence.

"Mariner Meinher…I have these two firkins of nuncle Bilbeau's finest. Would you take these in trade for…"

"I told you I don't need any bitter outsland quaff….Well, just as a favor to you, I'll taste it. Perhaps I could sell it cheap to the poor sots who can't afford better." He unlashed the firkin lid and sipped, dubiously. He swashed the brew around his mouth and tried to grimace disdainfully. "Mmmm, not real bad…actually."

"And the firkins of Angst are Munge famous. A thousand flongs in two days and they leaked not a drop."

"Well…."

"All I want is to listen to the music, and a bowl of chouder or two. I don't drink much quaff, myself. It gives me the squitters."

"Well, here's my best offer. I'll give you a bowl of chouder and all the chai you can drink and two coppers, for the firkins. If you stay and help me sweep up tonight, I'll pay you two more coppers and feed you breakfast. Where are you going to sleep tonight?"

"I hadn't given it any thought…I suppose I'll sleep in my boat. I've got a blanket. And a hammock." Conway thought a moment. "Are these 'coppers' moneys?"

"That they are, son. That they are. A copper is a good day's wages for a good man. I wouldn't pay so well but I like you, Yes, I do I like you. Remind me of myself….When I was young….Do we have a deal?"

"I suppose. Mariner, could you make that two bowls of chouder, please? I've had a long sail, and raw fish only makes me hungrier."

"Kid, you're going to eat me out of house and home. Yeah, two bowls of chouder, but only cause I like you. If you want to sleep in the loft, I'll let you. No charge…If you help me clean up tonight."

"I probably will. I'm not afraid of work." Conway had a feeling he was committing himself to more than he bargained for, but, then again, he had no other offers. "I do want to hear the music, though. It's important to me."

Meinher was a little taken aback to be spoken to as an equal by one so young and spindly and top-knot-less, but like Conway, he was getting very few other offers. And the boy did remind him of himself when he was young. He had been a pain in the behind also. So…

"Make yourself comfortable, son. I won't wait on you, I'll be busy enough, and an Innkeep doesn't wait on his workers, but if you want anything just ask Cookie. Here's your two coppers." He dug two broad coins from his apron and handed them to the boy, who examined them curiously. They were as broad as two fingers, and bore a hole pierced through the middle. Each bore the likeness of a flamboy on one side and a complex shield on the obverse, with the legend "Commonweal of the Ains, One Centum." Meinher spoke again.

"What about the other firkin?"

"Oh…this." Conway examined the leather cask as if it was as alien as the coin. "This is a present for Gully. Would you introduce me, please?"

"Don't stand on ceremony, boy. She's only a common trull, and traveling musician. Common as dirt. Just wait until they finish a song, and speak your piece. Introductions are for quality, boy, not for musicians. Common as dirt."

Conway looked over his new employer's shoulder and saw the band filing back on stage. He decided to make his move before he lost his nerve, and approached the stage and stood humbly before the piper. Then a difficulty of etiquette tangled his tongue. He didn't know how to address her. She wasn't a Goodwife, or a Miss. Surely. Some few female sailors were called Mariner just like men, but she wasn't obviously a seafarer. He had called his teacher Mistress Sweeneah, and he hoped Gully would become his teacher. He had just about gathered his wits about him, when the piper took pity on him and addressed him.

"Could I help you with something, young man?" It was the first time any person had referred to him as any kind of a man, and his face flushed, and his knees got weak. He blurted out a sentence and offered the firkin.

"I brought you a present."

"How nice of you. What is it?" She took the leather cask and shook it, as if she had gotten dubious gifts before.

"It's called perry. It's from…" She finished the sentence for him.

"Hazlen's Land. And so am I."

"Really?"

"Really. All pipers are from Hazlen's…At least they say they are." She unlaced the lid and sipped. "A taste of the peat and the bough. A kiss from the Old Soil."

"I'm glad you like it. Ummm."

"Yes?"

"Could you, I mean….Could I learn to play music?"

"Are you lonely?"

"Ummm….Yes…"

"Sexually frustrated?"

"Ummm…"

"A miserable, scorned, outcast?"

"All my life."

"Manually dexterous?"

"Yessum."

"Well....I don't teach, and I don't rescue, and I don't adopt, but you could watch us for tonight, and then if you want to learn, I could give you some advice."

"I would treasure it."

"Advice is free, and worth every penny of the price." She smiled like clouds breaking, and touched his arm. "At my age, giving advice is the most trouble I can cause. Stick around, young man, and I'll speak to you after the show."

"Meinher offered me a job, cleaning up."

"Meinher is less avaricious than most innkeepers, but he spends each copper three times. Be careful."

"I will. Thank you, Mistress Gully."

"Just Gully."

"Thank you, Gully."

"Thank you for the perry, young man." She smiled again, and his knees got weaker. "Later, then."

"Later."

And that was the way Conway began his new life. He found a bench and sat and began to learn to make music. The first thing he learned was to learn to listen. He found his eyes closing to help him listen. This thing called music did not bear him away or overwhelm him.

In fact, at first he found himself almost disappointed in that he wasn't dragged away, kicking and screaming to some far fantasy land beyond imagining. All these years of dreaming and he was expecting to be assaulted and overwhelmed. Instead it teased him, whispered to him, suggested things to him.

Even on first hearing he could feel his brain analyzing and dissecting this thing called music, even as it was moving him. He would be seduced into a mood, and then he could observe himself observing the process of his seduction. He had always been an outsider, and observer, and this new process was simply one more layer of distance, one more remove from the world. But, paradoxically enough, this remove seemed to bring him closer to the nub of life, to himself. Whoever he might be.

The band seated itself, and without preamble began a merrydown, a rollicking dance tune from the Isle of Deborsia to the north. Conway knew nothing of this, of course, but felt his blood began to gently effervesce, from the tickling melody that burbled from Gully's clay pipe. Around him toes began to tap, and smiles creased the faces of the few customers, but Conway sat rapt, trying to decipher the way the plangancies of the ptortise shell lute mediated between the rhythmic scuttle of the drums and the icy pointillism of the cymballista. Actually it took months and many, many wearisome questions before he even knew the names of even such simple instruments as the tweedle, the roane, and the tavesty. But, and it was an enormous but, he could hear the structure of the arrangements from his very first exposure to music. He did have good ears, after all.

Occasionally, his eyes would snap open and he could see that this stroke of a pterigrine quill would produce that burst of joy, and that that roll of the ivory mallets would bring this trill of melancholy from the cymballista. And half way through what became a very rowdy Tressdy night at the Devout Sailback he asked himself the question that led him down a very long strange trail indeed.

"How," He wondered. "Could someone know how to turn simple bones and leather and clay and wire into devices that could produce such subtle and powerful sounds? How can dactyl body parts be wrought into tools to shape human emotions?" He was foolish, perhaps, but he was no fool. He had gotten here in a coracle he had crafted with his own hands, eating fish he had caught with tools he had made himself.

He had a good grasp of every process and technique that was necessary to wrest a decent living from the land or from the sea in his home islands. He could sail a boat, weave a net, cook a meal, tan a hide, throw a pot, sew a seam, or thatch a roof. He knew that there was no magic in the world of Munge, no mystery under the sun, But this was different, this was something that was totally beyond his ken.

He decided that this knowledge was worth learning, that here was his calling. Making music was a wonder beyond his imagination, but crafting the instruments to make such wonderful sounds was far, far, beyond even that wonder. He was so awestruck, that for a matter of hours, he didn't even think about the point of all this exertion and travel…He forgot all about romance. He was totally hooked. He had found his Grail. Gully and the Foils opened vistas unknown to him and he reveled in them, but still held on to his analytical insight. Hazlenes followed merrydowns and reels preceded hamsters as the music rollicked on. The patrons of the Devout Sailback were not your abstract music appreciators, or indeed, noticeably bowed down with the weight of their intellects. They were there to dance and to drink and Gully obliged them. She was a professional and good at her vocation. She spoke not between tunes and wasted none of her breath trying to explain herself to her audience. Instead, she flogged tune after tune out of her globular clay pipe and her aptly named Foils were hard pressed to keep up with her coruscations of melody. The drummer, a stocky youngster little older than Conway, soon shed his vest, and the two string players' topknots were soon running sweat. What with the moby oil lamps and the flickering candlefish and the exudations of the crowd, the humid air of the inn soon became little better than an atmosphere.

The thud of bare feet on the dirt floor and the mad howls of the Ains threatened to overcome the music, but no matter what, the pure rotund notes from Gully's tubby pipe overrode the din.

She herself never sweated, or even glanced at the audience. She seemed rapt in her work as any Goodwife at the wheel, and as emotionally distant. Occasionally, when the bedlam reached a crescendo, she would tap a slender foot in time.

Actually, Conway noticed, she would tap alternate feet, in half time to the melody. He noted it, and knew it was significant, but he didn't know why. He did decide that any woman who could remain self possessed in the midst of all this chaos, was definitely not a person to be taken lightly. The revelation might have broken his heart, but instead it was just one more dollop of knowledge in the torrent that was flooding his brain. He had never thought so hard or so fast in his life. It was a new sensation. He decided he liked it.

He didn't know it, but he was becoming addicted to the most dangerous drug in the universe. He was learning how to think. He thought he had been an outcast before, when he was just a fool. He had no idea how much people would come to hate him when he finally learned to think. It's a good thing for all of us, that we remain ignorant of the future. Some suspect that this is the strongest proof that there is in fact a god…or gods. Others of course hold that this self-same fact proves exactly the opposite.

So there he sat; oblivious to everything except the music and his internal reactions to it, while all around him the Ains and assorted other Mungians pranced and preened and cavorted. Romances were begun and marriages ended, feuds started and revowed and businesses were consummated. A half dozen children were conceived in the shadows behind the Sailback that night, and two duels fought in the lamplight before it.

All in all it was a night that the Ains of Griffin were never to forget, and that even Gully and her Foils considered a pleasantly profitable night's work. When pleased beyond restraint, the Goodfolk of the Ains were wont to shower musicians with handfuls of the tiny pink and white shells called ginae, that served as change for the coppers. There were roughly one hundred ginae, so called from their pink interiors, to the copper, and long before first glass of the morning the stage was littered and heaped with the elliptical brown speckled shells. There were more than a few coppers strewn there also. The band knew its business and stopped between tunes only long enough to pass Conway's firkin around. A quick sip, wipe a hand across wet lips and then....One...two...and....

And all the while Conway studied the band, a pair of intense blue eyes set under black bangs studied him with covetous frustration. Occasionally, a pudgy hand would push back those black bangs and continue back over sleek hair and pause to caress the sharkskin wrapped haft of a very business like katana slung over a black clad shoulder. The hand would linger there, as if for reassurance, while all around the Devout Sailback rioted to the mandellas and hornswoggles of Gully and her Foils.

And much later, when the band was paid off, and Conway was earning his keep evicting the few last drink-wounded Ains, Gully looked up from her trencher of chouder and called to Conway.

"When you're done with that drunk, come back stage, young man."

Conway dropped the man where he stood, and turned to the piper. "He'll keep, Mi...Gully. Between the quaff and Meinher's cosh, he's out for the night." His heart skipped an iambic foot or two. "I'm at your service."

"You're too sweet, and I'm too old for all that. I have a present for you." She gestured to one of her henchmen, who vanished behind the curtain, and soon returned with one of those gracefully misshapen objects of Conway's desires.

"This is a fleashopper, young man, what some call a lukette, or a madoinia. It's about as simple as an instrument can get, but you can get real music out of it, if you've got it in you." The structure of that sentence escaped Conway, but her meaning was clear. It was quite late, after all. The lukette had four strings, and a long handle, and was constructed of a cut down sagitary skull, with skin stretched over the bottom where the mandible had been ground away.

She rippled her thumb across the four strings of the lukette, twisted one of the knobs slightly and cast an arch glance at Conway to see if he was paying attention.

"The lukette is tuned thus." She strummed the strings again, and sang a fragment of melody for him. "Listen; *'My sorde has lice'.*"

He heard what she meant. Each string was tuned to one note of the tune fragment. *"My sorde has lice."* Dum, dum, Dee, dum.

She strummed with one hand and manipulated the strings on the handle with the other, and a gay, sprightly tune emerged. Conway was charmed. She ceased her song and handed the lukette to Conway.

"Here. A present for a present."

"I…."

"The perry was very well aged."

"I…."

"As am I."

"Well…"

"We leave tomorrow, on the weekly raft to the Hastings. Here, take this. Almost anybody can show you how to play it."

"I…"

"It is customary to kiss old women who give you presents." She rose and presented her cheek to him, like a chalice to a supplicant in Fanemass.

"I…Yes'm."

He dutifully brushed her finely textured cheek with his dry lips.

"I thank you, Mistress Gully, for your present."

"Say goodbye, young man."

"Goodbye."

Gully bustled out, followed by her band. Conway set down his precious fleashopper and set back to work, dragging out the unconscious and the over indulged. It paid to keep both eyes on the job, as some of the celebrants had a nasty habit of regaining consciousness with a hand on their dirks and dags. Still it was a living. And all in all life was definitely looking up. Perhaps soon, a woman might kiss him! Worth hoping for, any way.

CHAPTER 3

▼

And so Conway eased into his new life, and only his ignorance of the lowliness of his position saved him from total humiliation. Still, even after he learned that scut boy at a dive like the Devout Sailback ranked lower even than drakenherd, he figured that it rated a lot better than village butt back in Angst. It was, as a matter of fact, his very origin in Angst that saved him from much grief and aggravation from the rowdies at the inn. "Just in from Angst" carried much the same connotation to the Ains as the phrase "fell off the guano barge" did to the rest of Munge. They didn't expect much from our hero, and he made little effort to disappoint their minimal expectations. Anyway, he was busy. Busy thinking. If the denizens of the Sailback thought him slow, he never noticed.

He spent every available moment with his lukette, often just examining its construction. The spoonbill of the sagitary formed the handle, or as some called it, the neck, of the instrument, with carven wooden pegs mounted in tapered holes bored through the horny yellow beak to hold the four gut strings. The upper palate and the bottom of the skull had been ground away to open the brain cavity and a piece of sorde wing skin had been split and scraped to transparency, and stretched over this opening and laced to drum tightness. Conway had always used that metaphor, without ever actually seeing a drum. The lacings also supported a few dozen ginae shells that rasped and rattled and provided a gentle percussive effect when played vigorously. The back of the lukette, the top of the skull, had been varnished a lovely green and the decorated with a yellow pollen and cone beetle lacquer paint into a semblance of islandic tattoos. If he hadn't been so ignorant, Conway might have recognized the typical patterns of far Gormley.

All this was straightforward enough. Conway could have built one in a few hours. The part that required study, the magical part was the fret board. A thin splint of hard red wood had been shaped to fit up into the concavity of the unfortunate dactyl's palate, and been secured with some tarry substance. Upon this board, and around the neck/beak had been tied twists of sinew, probably from the sagitary's wing. These twists had been glued and stiffened with the familiar resin of the cone beetle.

These twists, or frets, provided stops to the string that produced the actual notes of a scale. The trick, he discovered was in the spacing. There was an irregularity to these intervals, and there were just eight of these frets up the neck of the lukette.

He had owned it for quite two weeks, a whole sixteen days, before he noticed that the seventh fret was exactly half the distance from the top of the neck to the carved bone bridge that rested on the taunt skin head and transmitted the vibrations of the strings to the head and made them audible. Once he had made this discovery, he rapidly progressed to the discovery that the fourth note was half the remaining distance and that all seven of the notes had precise mathematical relationships to each other and to the length of the string as a whole. He also soon discovered the relationships of string thickness and tension to the pitch. He was so engrossed that he actually took no pride in these discoveries. He was too absorbed for emotion. He was pleased that he had the answer and left it at that.

Actually this was no small feat for a boy with only the slightest knowledge of numbers and mathematics. He rewarded himself with the joy of discovery, and was content with that. Millennia before, religions had been founded on the identical discovery, by people with similar cultures and a lot less humility.

Occasionally some gaffer or other lay-a-bout could be inveigled into teaching him a pass or position on the lukette, and Conway retained all he was shown. His quiet application was soon rewarded, and he could scratch out the themes to a few of the more hackneyed songs current on the island.

He first learned "Shroudlines to the Starways", and soon afterwards had a handle on "Free Dactyl Free" and "Sorde on the Run" It was a very simple instrument, and yielded cheerfully to his experimentations. The one-eyed old gaffer who had welcomed Conway to Ainsworth proved to be a fixture about the Town Green, and could be easily bribed into tickling a tune from the lukette.

He had learned "The slight of it, B'LLord, nary nurn better, B'LLord, in me courtin' days, demme if naught, B'LLord." He answered to the name of Peetie, or Old Peet, and responded to liquid bribes. There were one hundred ginae to a copper, and a jack of quaff could be obtained for as little as fourteen ginae.

So Conway had the wherewithal for more of Peetie's company than he could actually stand. But they got along well enough, bound as they were by mutual greed and symbiotic hunger of the first degree. Peetie was a treasury of scurrilous verse, and taught Conway many of the words to the long rafter's chanty, "Aboard the Saint Sallsiphy."

"We was aboard the Saint Sallsiphy,
A fool, a drunk, a slut, and I.
I remember when, but I don't remember why.
Aboard the Good Saint Sallsiphy."

Otherwise, Conway had little enough to spend his coppers on, all his animal needs were provided for by Meinher, and he found a cozy spot to beach his coracle under a lingon tree upstream from the harbor. Meinher was used to turning a profit on his scutboys, but Conway drank so little that he was able to save not only his coppers but also most of the ginae he swept up from the dirt floor, mornings.

He had his dreams, however. Every now and again, he would drift down to the Chandler's and gaze moistly at the small selection of musical instruments that hung in the most secure corner of the vast warehouse. Like most Pancreatic structures, Jomestrom's chandlery merged into the landscape, rather than defined itself from it. Theft was not unknown on Munge, but it was rare, and most of the chandler's stock was less than portable; great coils of cordage and bales of hempen sail cloth under roof, but otherwise unsecured. Heavy stuff like the massive stone anchors and stocks of woods for shipbuilding were left out doors.

But, supplying everything for maritime trade as it did, there were valuables, and Jomestrom's stock gradually graded towards the secure. Foodstuffs were behind latticework, and tools and metal stock were behind log walls. Farther in were stone walls and solid plank doors. Here were navigational instruments, charts, books, and luxuries for travelers. And here, in a space rendolent of fine leather clothing and rare spices were the prime goods for the wealthy passenger, and the Master Mariners who transported them.

And far in, next to Jomestrom's office and cubby, hung the instruments that had begun to haunt Conway's dreams. They seemed to be endowed with enough sentience to know their rightful possessors and to even judge his fitness to own them. The bassos and crumhorns gleamed at him there and the mighty portative organ intimidated him, but he found himself drawn to the strings mostly.

They were all big brothers and sisters of his humble lukette and he found himself so fascinated with their very shapes and resonances, that he could barely imagine owning one. Not that they were all that dear. The ptortise shell lutes were only twenty coppers, and the skin headed clangos but little more. He purchased every broadside and method that Jomestrom stocked and devoured them, even when he couldn't grasp their subtleties, and stole moments of quiet to strum or plunk on this lute, or that mandolette.

But there was one instrument there, a copy of an Olearth chuitar, that almost made him tremble. It was, so Jomestrom swore, made to a pattern more than ten thousand years old, a pattern that dated back to before the time when people could traverse space. Conway found the very concept disturbing and infinitely attractive.

Most of the other strings had the general shape of a something on a stick, depending on what shell or skull or carapace they used for a sound box, but the chuitar had it's own unique shape. Although the chuitar's body suggested a female torso to Conway's fevered imagination, he soon realized that it followed an acoustic logic that only incidentally made a pleasing visual statement. The chuitar was made all from the finest, rarest woods, with only touches of metals in critical places. Even after Jomestrom patiently explained the names of the woods; redbone from Gormley, and balth from South Ainsworth, and pure White Mountain larch from North Gebbon, Conway was ignorant as before. He never could get up the nerve to even touch an object that was priced at a full six Silvers, and indeed could barely imagine that any portable object could be worth two year's pay.

Jomestrom explained, even more patiently, that the chuitar had been ordered by the second son of the First Commoner of the Ains, and it was a genuine work of the Munge renowned Frerisson family of Smith and only the unfortunate demise of the young nobleman in a duel had left such an expensive item to molder in Jomestrom's Chandlery. But there was a good chance that it would, in time, sell.

Music was a common diversion for the young bloods who made the Grand Tour on the great pelagic rafts that slowly traversed the seas of Munge. Many a young man had won his future bride with a well tuned clango or tavesty, and so some sort of musical instrument was considered almost as much of a necessity as a dinner vest on a long ocean voyage. Therefore, a well-stocked ship's chandler carried a few instruments as a matter of course.

Jomestrom wisely allowed Conway to moon to his heart's content, knowing that eventually the young man would spend a few ginae on a string or a jaw harp or some lute polish or a copy of Belimay's "Fun with the Lukette."

Every merchant worth his salt knows that the annoying adolescent browser of today is the adult customer of tomorrow. And in fact, Conway was amiable enough, if distant, and could be induced to help load a carrack or turn a sluys or help count pickles for a modest bribe. Conway was truthful, work didn't bother him. He was usually so abstracted that mere reality barely impinged on his perceptions. And, after a month or two, when the music started to make sense to him, mere work, or minor physical discomfort, was as unnoticed as the evening showers.

Nobody worked that hard on the isles of the Pancreatic Sea, anyway. When one could obtain a meal by climbing a coconut tree, or paddling around on a sand bar for an hour, or simply baiting the ubiquitous beetles, there was little incentive for long sweaty hours of any kind of toil.

Conway would arise at noon, when the sun's heat became unbearable even under the lingon trees, and would amble about, looking for someone with too much lunch. After helping the fortunate provider reduce the surplus, Conway would practice his lukette for a glass or two, and then help Jomestrom or Meinher long enough to be invited to dinner. Then there were usually a few glasses of helping set up the Sailback for the night's festivities. Conway might have some jacks to rinse or a pot to scrub or some quaff to strain, and so went the evening.

Once the band started, Conway was glued to his bench, right up next to the stage, and then it would be time to drag out the drunks and sweep up and grab a nibble before bed. Ninety nine point nine nine nine percent of the human race, on all the planets, around all the suns, in all the habitats of Homo Galactica would have considered it an idyllic existence, but Conway never noticed. He was too busy to examine his life, or to grade it. He was learning music. Infinite endeavors tend to be very absorbing, and Conway was absorbed to the extent that his shins were constantly black and blue from walking into solid objects. He didn't care much about that either. Or even notice.

Most of the denizens of the Devout Sailback came to regard Conway as a species of mascot, and some few delighted in teasing or tormenting the boy. It was all one to him, and he repaid good and evil with the same dreamy, vacant smile and abstracted mumbles. He did manage to acknowledge the existence of a few of the Ains; Old Peetie, Cookie, Goodwife Besterson, who lived near the lingon grove, a few others.

He did notice others, but paid them no mind. He noticed, for example, the small, black clad person with the blue eyes, but they never spoke. He, or she, seemed to always be in the Sailback, always in a seat near to him, but that was about all. The small warrior was intent on his own business, and the Ains were content to leave him to it. The warrior was obviously an outslander, and probably a Northslander, from his trews and jerkin, all of black cotton.

Woven stuffs were rare this far south, as was much clothing. Men and women both wore a basic wrappa, a leather skirt or kilt, long or short to taste. Men, especially older or more established men, added an ornate vest, mostly for the sake of pockets. Women wore shawls, revealing or concealing their breasts as age, inclination, and temperature might dictate. Naturally there were a thousand varieties of shawls and code upon convention of colors, wrap, fringe, and degree of transparency, depending on the occasion. Often the shawls were imported woven stuff, and other times they were knotted or netted from leather thong or strung together from seashells or even drake or flamboy feathers.

Both sexes indulged in jewelry and tattoo for fun and status enhancement. The dark warrior wore none, adding to a pronounced foreign air. But warriors were not uncommon.

There was always a war somewhere on Munge, and it rarely amounted to much. All the lands had been settled a few generations after Landing, and the climate was so easy and constant over most of Munge that there was little want and no famine. Munge was in an interglacial period, and its sun was markedly constant. The sun was officially Luica's Star, or SecGalCat 8674536 (b), but the Mungians just called it "the sun". You try asking your wife; "Is old SecGalCat 8674536 (b) hot today?" a few times, and see what you wind up calling it.

Life was soft. Wars were fought for pride, and politics, and succession and were limited mostly by the warmonger's knowledge that if things got too out of hand, the population would sail elsewhere. The Flyers were a constant threat, but they seemed to be more of a constant these days, than a threat. The range of their quetzals was long but limited, and five hundred flongs from the Main, a good day's sail, provided enough buffer for normal times.

All this meant that people on Munge knew a warrior when they saw one, and were content to leave them be. Warriors were handy things when needed, but mildly unsettling to have around. This one spoke rarely, and drank sparingly, and paid cash. That was sufficient.

So the days came and went, and the bands, likewise. The rainy season set in, and people tended to stay inside and drink, which suited Meinher. This was the season he minted money, and generally it only rained evenings. LLord was good.

Fanzeels' Peripatetic Expiationeers played for the week after Gully sailed off and Conway learned to hear the traditional music of the isles of the Scatter Straights, beyond Cashamash Market. The Scattungs played a wild, exhilarating music on ensembles of vithels, bowed instruments that came in five sizes and three varieties. Many of these had resonating strings strung below the fingerboards and produced rasping drones that eventually slithered into one's bloodstream and induced excess.

Conway was already defining this new music in terms of the brilliant sweet-sad piping of Hazlen's Land and he found this skirling, as it was called, music of the Scattungs too repetitive for his taste. One experience and he was becoming a critic. Conway was no better than a human, in most regards.

But still, all in all, he admired the fine wood carving of the vithels, similar in some respects to the design of the chuitar of his dreams. Talking to Fanzeel, he learned that the Scattungs considered their music to be a direct descendant of the music of Olearth and unparalleled in its purity and grace. Pure it may have been, but it was also abrasive, and the Expiationeers did only half as well as Gully and her Foils. Still, Conway's back often hurt, mornings, from dragging out the sodden satisfied. South Ainsworth was a nexus for raft lines, where the Gormley Blue Pennant Line met and transhipped with the Hazlen-Smith Axis. The great rafts, some more than four flongs long, never came into port, of course, but they would anchor in the roads and the passengers would come ashore to revel and Meinher would profit thereby.

After the Scattungs, came a more modern group direct from Smith. They were called the Wharfingers, and were younger and rawer than the run of the mill working bands on the circuit. One or two of the five were younger even than Conway was, and they played a music they called Froust. It involved a lot of screaming and wearing of ragged clothes. Even though most of the band members were past the age of manhood, they maintained their shocks of coarse hair, eschewing the manly topknots to which they were entitled. Conway was rather intrigued, especially with the lyrics, but Meinher grumbled, for most of the audience was quite young, themselves, and they hadn't the quaff capacity of their parents. These self-same parents, of course, also disapproved.

Conway was especially taken with the band's ironic version of Fair Elsinor and the Elf Punk. In his mother's version, The Elf Punk had been a malevolent figure, and Fair Elsinor his dupe, but the Froust version had the Elf Punk the hero and Elsinor's husband the villain. All this was accomplished without changing a word, only by the inflections of Pabst, the singer. The last verse;

"*Lord Fleicx slew Fair Elsinor with a forehand blow,*
And with a backhand slew her lover,

And cast them both into the Brown River run, run, run,
And they rolled down to the Sea together,
Rolled down to the Sea together."

Now the ballad suggested total betrayal and tragedy, instead of miscreants receiving their just deserts, and all with just a lifted eyebrow and a bitter chord from the tavesty's triple bells. Most of the adults were less charmed and mutterings were heard in the merry Devout Sailback.

But the next band, the Rowdydows, reestablished Meinher's equilibrium. They were from the southernmost peninsula of Hazlen's Land, Goldendale, and were renowned over all the Pancreatic Sea.

Padergrad, the piper, was quite as good as Gully, and much more demonstrative. He danced as he played, and kicked up his heels, and flirted with the women in the audience, and generally incited to riot. His backing band was of only two pieces, a vithel player, who doubled Padergrad's melodies, and, much to Conway's delight, a chuitar player.

The chuitarist was a dour, stocky man who never smiled, or even glanced at the audience, but sturdily pumped out solid runs and graces from the seven strings of his iron wood box. Conway was entranced even beyond his usual wont, and made it a point to be below the loft where the band slept, first thing next afternoon.

Padergrad was the first to stumble down the ladder from the loft and once he had both feet on the floor, he rubbed his blue eyes and glared at Conway.

"Ask me if I'm a pie." He demanded.

"I...I...beg...."

Padergrad brushed back his topknot, and glared even more fiercely at our hapless hero. "I said, 'Ask me if I'm a pie'!"

"Gulp...A...Are you a pie?"

"Do I look like a pie?" This was delivered in a voice of sweet reason and genial tolerance, as if Conway was suspected of being slightly bereft and congenially slow of wit.

"N-n-n-n-no sir."

The piper gave a satisfied nod, and strode off towards the barroom, leaving Conway befuddled even more than normal. He watched Padergrad strut away, jaw slack and was brought back to himself by a noise somewhere between a snort and a chuckle from the next man down the ladder. It was the chuitar player. Conway was almost afraid to greet him, but he gathered his few wits, and spoke.

"Good morning, sir." This seemed to be inadequate, so Conway continued; "Would you like me to ask you if you're a pie too? Sir?"

"A cup of chai bettersome like. Would." The chuitarist was less imposing in the morning light, and his topknot was salted with gray. Conway felt a little more able to cope.

"Poorlattice, Gray, or Dunsenay?"

"Hot. Sugarsome."

"If you will take a seat in the barroom…or on the terrace?"

"Terrace? Terrace what is"

"Well…under the grape arbor…."

"Pleasantgood sounds."

"Will the others join you?"

"Companion found Slotne and elsewhere sleeps."

Conway waited for more, but the chuitarist ambled out into the dappled courtyard, and Conway scurried off to the kitchen. There he found old Cookie worshipfully pouring Padergrad another jack of Tusqueg's and so Conway contented himself with appropriating a pot of chai and a plate of bimbleberry scones. He hurried back to the wicker table beneath the grapevine. This vine was almost a local celebrity in it's own right, purported to have been planted by Carlete Ainsworth herself, one of the original Olearth Landers. The vine was trimmed back every year, of course, but it's gnarled stock was thicker than Meinher's waist where it curled up out of the red soil of the courtyard.

"Thankysome, lad. Scones too."

"Bimbleberry."

"Not having grownsome in Gormley. Scorgeberry, us."

"Gormley's a long ways...Is that where you're from?"

"South of there, many." The chuitarist dipped his scone in the chai and supped. "Macelhenney us." It dawned on Conway that the chuitarist's reticence was not inherent, or due to disdain, but was in fact a by-product of his dialect. He had a thick, rasping manner of speech, and Conway had to listen hard to get his meanings. Munge had been settled by a heterogeneous association of adventurers from one of the original Olearthean habitats, but seven thousand years is a long time and dialectical drift was setting in.

"Have you been with Padergrad long?"

"Norso, from Gormley, Black Star Line recent most come."

"I'm sorry, I didn't introduce myself. My name is Conway...I'm trying to learn music. Would you like more scones or perhaps some brotcake?"

"Thankysome, lad. No for mem. Plentyfull."

He emitted a polite belch, and then fanned the air in front of his mouth."Sayso belch good worth thousand scripture page. Namen Heoj mem." He held out his palm and Conway solemnly touched it, although the gesture was rare among Angstmen. Heoj studied the young man for a long moment, and nodded, perhaps to himself. Then he spoke again.

"Playyoum chittern muchtime long?"

"Actually, no." Conway tried to look abashed, but only looked eager. "I've just been fooling around with a lukette."

"Lukette....That mabyso hopfleaer." Heoj gestured with his hands and Conway nodded affirmation. "Not forsome music is. Forsome kidders child."

Conway had to agree. "I wonder, Mariner Heoj, if you would be so kind as to show me how you play your style...perhaps you would allow me to watch while you practice. I'll be quiet like beetles."

"Is no problems. You bring more chai. I chittern fetchsome. Rightback."

And he was as good as his word.

Conway took a moment and fetched his lukette from the kitchen corner. It seemed a disgrace to his hand, it's sagitary skull and blood-wood fingerboard seemed a child's toy indeed. But it was all he had.

Heoj was seated on the wicker bench under the arbor, chuitar on his knee, pumping out those rock solid runs that earned him his daily bee-tles and quaff. Conway seated himself on the cobbles at Heoj's feet, and tried to soak up the older man's technique by sheer osmosis.

And he could. He could see and hear the subtle hesitations and accelerations that would help propel the lead line. He immediately noticed that Heoj was a most economical player, implying many more notes than he actually played. Compared to a vithel or the pipe, the chuitar was a ponderous instrument, but Heoj's style was designed to turn its weaknesses into virtues. And as Conway watched, all unaware, his fingers danced on his lukette's rudimentary fingerboard.

He might not have noticed, but Heoj did.

And so, when Heoj took a break and a glass of chai, he urged Con-way to hold the chuitar for him. Conway was overwhelmed with joy and covetousness. The sleek curves of the body cast strange perspec-tives and induced obscure shadings of color into the lustrous dark gray of the ironwood. Where the lukette's fingerboard was integral with it's neck, the chuitar had a separate slab of badouk set with polished silver frets and inlaid with elegantly simple pattern of leaves and ferns cut from some iridescent shell or bone. Instead of the whittled bone pegs of the lukette, the chuitar boasted fine crafted brazen gears to tighten the strings to tune. It was about the third most beautiful object Con-way had ever seen.

"This is a lovely instrument. How is it tuned?"

"Callsome Vestipole tuning. Olearth waybe. Tunehim Da, Sha, Da, Sha, Da, Ma, Sha. Makesome Da Chord. Playsome easy."

"I see." Said the boy, and amazingly he did. That meant the melody notes were the same in any key, and all one had to do was to move up or down the frets to play any song. The lukette played only one key, and had to be retuned for different songs. This instrument, simple and ponderous as it was could play any song, anytime. The revelation almost made him faint with joy. To cover his emotion, he asked a simple question that opened even wider vistas inside his brain. "This is a lovely instrument. Where did you get it?"

"Nicesome box, her. Heoj maken mem." His eyes, as dark gray as the ironwood, gleamed with honest pride.

"You made this? How…how did you get the wood so thin, so resonant?" Conway's thumb gently thumped the larch top, and the whole chuitar 'thunked' in response. The idea that a real, present person could work such a wonder. And then to be so matter of fact about it!

"Mem, yar. Makem downthin planes with, scrappem longtime, many."

"It's a lovely job, it's almost as pretty as that Frerisson at Jomestrom's." Conway was so involved in noticing how perfectly the neck of the chuitar fit his hand, how honestly the waist of the body sat on his knee, on the sheer sensual feel of the chuitar that he didn't notice the impact his words was having on Heoj. Conway was in love. Again. It was becoming a habit.

"Whatyoucall, whereis?"

"Where what is?"

"Chitternbox Frerisson. Takeyou mem?" Comprehension dawned in Conway's thick skull.

"It's down at Jomestrom's Chandlery." He pointed. "Down in the harbor."

"Wegosome. Now many!" Heoj grabbed Conway's hand and tugged him to his feet. Conway had only one dissent.

"It costs six silvers…."

"Worryno….Manymem….Lookyoum." Like most Mungians, Heoj belted his wrappa with ornate leather, and carried any valuables in a dependent pouch, what some called a spoan. He opened his and pulled out a thong that was heavy with moneys. Conway counted at least ten silvers, a lubb of coppers, and a tiny, but undeniable, gold.

He had just enough time to marvel, before Heoj restored his cash to his spoan. And as they stood, and turned to go, Conway found himself looking full into the blue eyes of the small warrior in black. He had a feeling that the warrior had been spying on them for quite a while, unseen. He wanted to stop and determine a few facts, but Heoj was as unstoppable as a rutting sailback and literally dragged Conway out the archway, past the warrior and out the inn, to the street, where he impatiently awaited directions. He also, it appeared, had a Grail.

Conway pointed toward the harbor and was immediately sucked along behind the chuitarist's progress, toward the Chandler's. Once there, Conway had only time to point, once more, to the music corner, before Heoj bulled his way toward the Frerisson. Heoj's impetuous progress slowed as soon as he caught sight of the chuitar, and took on some of the pace of an approach to the altar of his LLord, whoever that might be.

It was with an almost reverent touch that Heoj lifted the Frerisson from its hook and examined it closely, back and belly. Then he turned to Conway and said; "Frerisson, truesome. Happynow, mem."

He immediately sat on the nearest solid object, which happened to be a drum of herring in wine, and began to tune the Frerisson. There was a polite cough from behind them and Conway was unsurprised to see Jomestrom standing there, attentively. Conway was reluctant to disturb Heoj, but felt it best to reassure the chandler.

"This is Heoj. He's a professional musician from south of Gormley. He's playing at Meinher's this week, and is interested in the Frerisson."

He needn't have worried; Jomestrom was a professional too.

All he said was; "That instrument has been waiting for the right musician for a long time now. It is an honor to serve Mariner Heoj." He went back towards his office corner.

"Would you like a glass of chai, Conway, Heoj?" Conway nodded assent; Heoj never heard a word. His ears were otherwise employed.

He grimaced at the state of the strings, but persevered. Soon he had the chuitar tuned to his satisfaction and stroked a full chord. Conway was expecting an exulting display of his usual runs, but all Heoj did was to stroke a full seven-string chord and let it ring. Then he moved up the neck, and stroked out the same chord in a different position, and again let it decay to silence. It seemed, even to Conway, to resound for an exceptionally long time. And then another and another.

Then Heoj rested for a moment, his face carefully blank, and suddenly his hands blurred into motion, as his left hand sounded every position on the fretboard in a brilliant flurry of notes. Then he struck a single chord again, let it die and only then rose to face Jomestrom, who was approaching, three glasses of chai in his hands. Heoj reached into his spoan, and pulled out his thong.

"Takesome silvers five, mem?"

"Ah…Yes." The two men's faces were studies in noncommittal blankness.

"Strings extra you give?"

"Take what you want. Within reason. There is a case too."

"Deal. Mem." Heoj untied the toggle on his cash string and counted out five broad silvers. Jomestrom took them without comment, but winked to Conway, in a manner that seemed to promise a generous gratuity. The two men placed their cash back in their spoans and shook hands. Then the chandler scurried off into the piles of stock and returned with a black, coffin-shaped wooden case, and a round splint box of sets of strings. He was as effusive as Conway had ever seen him, and he had good reason. Five silvers was a goodly chunk of money, even for one of the largest businesses on West Ainsworth. He tried to press chai on Heoj, but the offslander was eager to be alone with his new instrument. He was polite, but it was a struggle. Conway was struggling too, but his struggle was with a wild idea that bubbled beneath his breastbone, like fermenting quaff.

They were almost back to the Sailback when Conway got enough nerve up to ask for his heart's desire.

"Heoj, would you take half a silver, fifty coppers for your old chuitar? I'm pretty sure I have that much." He stopped, tongue-tied with his own boldness and desire. "I could get a small loan from Jomestrom or Meinher...I suppose."

"Worryno, youm. Chuitarbox, mem, give youm....Good boy, youm....Mem youngwhen...mind mem, youm."

"I don't know how to thank you, Heoj. I will treasure your chuitar."

"Sokay, back in Macelhenney, manysome...Need Frerisson pattern-for...Looklong, many. Home gosoon. Better box make, mem. Dream-long, many." Heoj touched Conway's shoulder with the hand that didn't hold his precious case. "Muchplay, earsgood, youm. Thank-some, mem."

All of a sudden, Conway found an obstruction in his throat. Hurriedly he tried to change the subject. "Thanks again, Heoj. Listen, you watch out for that warrior in black. He was most interested in your cash string..."

Heoj erupted in laughter and slapped Conway on the shoulder hard enough to make the young man stagger a step. "Noshe cashtake, mem. She look youm...watchout, youmself, own."

Conway was completely baffled with this comment, as baffled as he had been by Padergrad's insistence of being called a pie....It's hard to feel the munge shift beneath your feet like that twice in one day. He felt that the safest thing was to remain silent. Heoj chuckled all the way back to the inn. Then he gave Conway the padded bag that held his ironwood box, and vanished up into the loft.

Conway, after reflection, slowly walked back to the lingon tree grove and his boat, to try and make some sense out of his new life. He was so overwhelmed with Heoj's generosity, that he didn't even take the chuitar out of its bag, as if afraid that it might vanish entirely. For the eight glasses until time for work, he just sat and pondered. There were not even words to his wondering, just a play and flow of inchoate emotions, that he could not even name.

Eventually, his emotions inflicted him with a pain in his stomach and an aching head. He wondered if he was suffering from homesickness for a place that he now realized that he hated, or if he was losing his alleged mind. Finally, it dawned on him that he hadn't eaten all day. So he stowed the chuitar, and walked down to the Sailback and helped Cookie peel spurdads. He also helped himself to the free lunch on the bar and quite a few of the choicest spurdads, working on the time-honored principle of "One for the company, one for me."

And soon it was time for the show, but there was only a duo tonight. Heoj had caught the dory out to the southbound raft and was gone back to Gormley. This vicissitude seemed to bother Padergrad not a bit. Indeed it inspired him to greater cavortage and flirtation. He was inspired and sweaty by the second tune and soon the stage was awash with ginae and coppers. Conway deduced that sudden changes in band personnel were pretty standard in the piper's universe.

Conway was irritated by the lack of rhythm in the band and found himself irritated further, feeling the little warrior's gaze on his back all night. As soon as he decently could, as soon as the last drunk was deposited on the Green, he snuck back to the grove in the light of the spangled moon, and crawled into his hammock. He fell asleep like a sick child, and knew no more until morning. The poor lukette sat forlorn on the terrace, and only the thick foliage of the grapevine saved it from total destruction in the evening rain.

Conway was quite ashamed, the next morning, when Cookie berated him for his carelessness. After all, it had been a gift from Gully. He made a special trip back to his camp, where he wrapped it securely in oiled leather and stored it in the outrigger of his coracle, right next to the demijohn of perry. To people as poor as Angstmen, 'Waste not, Want not' was more like a genetic instruction than a mere proverb.

But when he got back to the inn, he got news that made his heart leap like a skipper. Gully and her Foils were coming back to play the very next moonth! He hoped that she would be as glad about his great acquisition as he was. It hurt his feelings to find that Cookie, and Peetie, and Meinher, of course, were indifferent to his great good fortune. Well, time would tell. He did go down to the chandler's and try to purchase every book and lesson available for the chuitar. Jomestrom, however, refused his moneys. He knew that he would have to work harder than a diver before he got even the rudiments of his instrument. But he did have the time....Or so he thought.

And he did make some progress, even though it didn't seem like it. He transferred his few songs from lukette to chuitar, and stumbled towards finding it's own voice. But more often he would become trans-fixed with the play of light on the gray on charcoal grain of the iron-wood ribs of Heoj's chuitar, and lose whole glasses of time. Perhaps he would try to deduce the exact method that Heoj had used to carve the rosettes over the three sound holes, by close examination of the tool marks and emerge from his study to discover that it was time to clean the Sailback, when he was sure it was barely noon. How could one bend hard wood like wax, or taper the moby bone so fairly, so smoothly. He mused and studied and became a complete, if quiet monomaniac, as if anybody cared. And so his life eddied on, days pass-ing almost unnoticed. Later he was to think it the most enjoyable time of his life.

CHAPTER 4

▼

In the event, Gully was delayed a day, and more, and barely made it to the stage, on Twasdy eve. Schedules were not an imperative on Munge, and nothing was said, but Conway lost his chance to corner Gully and bore her with his great good fortune, and a tedious recital of this moonth's study and sore fingers. The band didn't even have time for a flagon of ale before the show, and practically ran from the dory to the inn. Once on stage they tuned quickly, heads together to hear above the buzz of the crowd.

Two of the great rafts had already been anchored in Ains road before the "Black Star" from Hazlen's came in, bearing Gully and her band, and The Devout Sailback was packed with hearty revelers, scarcely two of whom wore their topknots in the same style. Certainly the coral sprigs and braided bamb cords of the Ains were far in the minority.

Meinher called Conway over; "Tonight, boy, tonight, I want you to keep a weather eye open for trouble, and try not to get lost in the band, like you usually do." He nodded for emphasis, and set a cascade of chins jiggling. "Tonight there might be some…excitement."

This was the first time than Meinher had ever put conditions on his enjoyment, and Conway sensed that this was more than an intuition.

"Is there a problem, Meinher?"

"Not here there ain't." Meinher tried to look resolute. "And they better not be or I'll be the one to cause trouble. There's a war brewing between Ravelli and Bluestem, and the 'Knoorson' and the 'Singwall Passion' are full of young fools off to win glory in the wars. The 'Black Star'll be full of more of the same, mark my word."

"So what is that to us?"

"Nothing and everything, nothing and everything, my boy. It's just that people who want to fight, are liable to fight for fun, even before they get a snootfull of real war." He nodded again as if for reassurance. "More's the pity, my boy. There's a plenty who will wish they stood at home in a moonth or two, but until then…"

"We keep our eyes open and coshes ready to hand." Conway resolved to creep off and stash his chuitar in his camp, first thing. He did so, and returned to find the band in full thresh, and the quaff flowing and spilling at a record rate. Meinher had hired three girls to help out, and a few village stalwarts were noticeable, stationed about the lattice walls.

Conway even noticed Meinher slip money into the hand of the Warrior in Black, which implied that our host was coppering his bets. If trouble broke out, he obviously wanted one sword in his employ. And there were a good many swords in evidence, as well as a goodly selection of maces, axes, clubs, and those other wooden and stone weapons commonly favored by novice warriors and those of limited means.

But all went well, and indeed many of the offslanders seemed subdued, and thoughtful, and even a touch homesick. Certainly, Gully was getting requests, which was unusual for so early in the evening, and the songs requested were homey airs and ballads that evoked distant homelands. More than one called out for "The Banks of the Twee," a song from Goldendale, to the north, and almost as many called for "The Farlorn", a misty lament of the Hastings. Gully obliged every request and sensing the mood, let a wistful, bittersweet mood tinge her music, even though damping down the enthusiasms of her audience might well shrink her purse. But things went well enough, and after most of a glass, she rose from her stool and faced her audience.

"Thank you, Gentles and Mariners. We are Gully and Her Foils, and we plan to refresh ourselves for a moment or two and will return…"

Her words were cut off by a great bray of voice.

"Play "The Blues Advance!"

Gully was polite, but Conway got that headachy, foot itchy feeling he had not had since the Angst Fane burned down.

"Gentle Mariner, I fear we have not the slight of it. Is it a new tune, perhap?"

"It's the brave march of the invincible Bluestem Forces of Freedom!" The last person…no….actually, the next to last person, Conway ever wanted to see again pushed his way to the stage. The last person he ever wanted to see again in his life followed Blundoor. Rosialindia still wore the gold Altar cloth as a shawl and Blundoor still carried Harld's sword, Queztalbane, naked in his hand.

The crowd melted away from in front of them. Gully made a motion, as if to oppose them, but the cymballista player grabbed her arm and swept her offstage and through the curtain, to the green room. He was so emphatic that he left his instrument on the stool behind him. Blundoor gained the stage and turned to address the crowd, the great hand and a half sword raised over his head for attention.

"Hear me!…Hear me!" The assembled warriors and adventurers had little choice. His voice was a match for the rest of him. Big and ugly.

"Hear me! I am Tetrarch Blundoor Kreegah, provisional leader of the Bluestem Forces of Freedom. I am overjoyed to announce that you are all enlisted in our…" He paused and Rosialindia leaned up on tiptoe to whisper a prompt in his callused ear. "In our Noble Cause. Every man will receive a silver, Enlistment Bounty, and will drink the health of our Brave Army, at our expense."

A cheer rose from the crowd. They had been paying little attention, but they got the free drink part. Conway sidled toward the wall, without conscious decision. Something brushed his own shoulder. It was the small warrior. He became of an unwarriorlike scent, most like…well he didn't know, but it was…nice.

"Call the watch. I'll take care of fatso." The voice seemed to be awfully treble for a warrior, but the advice was good. Unfortunately, the nearest way out was through Mariner Kreegah, and out the stage door. Kreegah continued to speak, cued by his Mistress, and the press of the crowd toward the stage prevented Conway from forcing even his slight body through the mass. Perforce, he was an unwilling witness to all that transpired. The small warrior had no scruples, and little fear. Using his sheathed katana he forced a path to the edge of the stage and confronted the massive Blundoor and his inamorata.

"You will have to leave, or else sit down and behave. This," and the Katana sheath described an arc, "Is not a recruiting hall." It would have been more impressive, if the warrior's voice had not broken on the word 'recruiting'.

Blundoor needed no prompting to reply to this opposition. "And who's going to make me?"

"I'm not God. I don't make buffoons. All I do is teach them manners."

The great sword flashed down, to split this impertinent mote, and cast it into the gutters, but, wonder of wonders, it missed. When Queztalbane fell, suddenly its target had slipped aside and the huge blade struck only dirt. The small warrior moved faster than the eye could follow. Conway had always though that a metaphor, before this.

The crowd showed its instinctive grasp of the first military principle, and backed up, rapidly. Conway had only time to wonder whom this God person might be, when there was a 'wheep' and the katana was free and glittering in the lamplight. The crowd got a lot more enthusiastic about backing up, and Blundoor leaped from the stage and swung a roundhouse hack that might have slain dozens…if it had hit anything. Blundoor swung himself half around, with the hurricane force of his own miss and there came a 'splat!' as the flat of the katana found the seat of his wrappa.

There was a burst of laughter from the audience and Blundoor's face reddened. The crowd backed up another step. Rosialindia backed up too, back up against the stage curtain, incidentally cutting off Conway's own retreat. He had an idea, and oozed toward her, trying to appear motionless, thinking about, but not daring to reach for, the cosh hanging from the back of his belt. All eyes were on the fight, except his. His were on the back of Rosialindia's golden head. His intentions were not corrupted with chivalry. The black warrior was none of his concern, but Rosialindia and her stooge had killed two thirds of all the Angsters who had tolerated him after his mother died. He knew that Blundoor would be a simple matter to dispose of once his mentor was face down. The very idea gave him a warm feeling. Too bad his knees were trembling so violently he could barely walk.

The sword battle had settled into wary circling. The black warrior's katana was held in both hands at high guard, and Kreegah was doing a lot of feints and impressive brandishings. Everybody in the room had seen enough violence to know that only harmless fights were fast and loud. This was deadly serious, and therefore was slow and silent. Likely there would be an instant opening, a flurry of blades, and a death. Neither duelist was in a hurry to die. Blundoor was a bully and a dolt, but he was good at just one thing. This was it. He snorted and stamped and glowered, but was ever so careful not to leave the small warrior any opening.

Just as Conway was beginning to think he had a chance to sneak behind Rosialindia, she caught sight of him out of the corner of her eye. Instantly she crouched and whipped a stiletto of watered steel from under her golden shawl. Her stance was so feral that Conway slowed, but continued to slide his back along the wall, in an attempt to at least turn her attention from her man. He also still hoped to reach the stage curtain and call the watch. The two combatants continued their painfully slow circle dance to the silence of the entire crowd.

Suddenly, before he could make Rosialindia turn her head, she whirled, and whipped a dart into the small warrior's back, and then scurried away from Conway to take up a position past the wounded swordsman, covering Blundoor's back. The small figure's katana sagged to the dirt, and Blundoor grunted in triumph and whirled the huge broadsword over his head to obliterate his foe.

He had neglected to consider his surroundings, however, and the massive sword chonked into the age blackened roof beam over his head. Rosialindia shifted her stiletto to her right hand, and darted toward the small crumpled figure on the floor.

Fortunately Conway didn't try to think, he just did. He snatched up the cymballista from the stool and overhanded it at Rosialindia's sleek head. It crashed right on target, aided by the fact that the blonde's attention was totally on her intended victim. It did only minor damage, one of the steel tuning pegs opening an eyebrow, but the impact and noise gave the dark warrior enough time to scuttle away before Blundoor could free his blade.

The little person made a beeline toward Conway and had just reached him, when Meinher stepped from the crowd, hand upraised for attention. Perhaps he was intending to restore order, or even offer a round of drinks to calm the house.

Unfortunately, he drew Blundoor's attention, just as that worthy freed his blade. One constant regret about having a weapon to hand is a general lack of targets. Blundoor had, as we have intimated, a pronounced lack of computational abilities, and a noticeable shortage of foresight. Meinher had both of these qualities in abundance, but sometimes brute force and ignorance will triumph over age and wisdom and right.

The blade flashed down, ruddy in the lamplight, and demonstrated Meinher's hard head softer than the beams of his establishment. Brains and blood fountained, Meinher staggered a few grotesque steps and fell, Blundoor beamed with childlike delight, and all Pancreatic hell broke loose.

Meinher's townie bouncers, showing more indignation than sense, started whaling away indiscriminately with their cudgels, while the outslanders instinctively fought back. As nobody had time to pick sides, and as some people had previous scores to settle, and as even the most seasoned traveler has an innate aversion to being belabored with sticks and clubs, it took all of three heartbeats before the melee became general.

Conway was still not thinking, and fortunately kept doing. He grabbed the small warrior under the arm and picked up the fallen katana, and finally made it to his goal, out.

Once outside in the cool of the night, he stared at the spangled full moon until he realized that he now had no employer, no job, and mostly no reason at all to stay around this locality at all. This return to thinking was almost an irritation. But thinking, he continued to think, and decided to find some attention for his companion. The Fane probably had a Healer, or at least an experienced Older, but he decided to go see if Goodwife Besterson might leech the wound. It was but a few moments walk down slope to Goody's house, and as usual, she was to be found enjoying the night air, and polluting it with her pipe, on her verandah.

Goody Besterson was the center of the community around the lingon grove, and maintained a covey of fellow gossips with joints of chai, and a table of sweetmeats. Tonight there were only two more women blueing the air and sipping chai from joints of bamb, when Conway staggered up with his burden. He was growing afraid, worried by the growing slackness of his charge, but simultaneously reassured with the increasing strength of the mutterings issuing from the bundle of blackness under his arm.

"What passes...why it's young Conway....Conway, what's all the hubbub up at the green? Is the band that good?"

"The band's not playing, Goody. There's a riot...or a fight...whatever you want to call it." This information was met with that peculiar silence caused by listener's non-comprehension of familiar words in unfamiliar order. Conway realized that he was totally out of breath, and that he also had to void a bladder, immediately. "Meinher's been killed, and there is some kind of a war breaking out, and this warrior's been hurt and needs some looking at."

Conway slid the slack body into a wicker chair, and muttered an excuse and stepped off into the dark to reduce his imperatives by one. He didn't realize that he was still clutching the katana until he went to open his wrappa. Behind him he heard clucking noises and saw lamps being lit.

Pancreatic houses were more matters of definition, rather than strictly walled off entities. Rather there were graduations of indoorsness; a sanctuary from the strongest winds and rains that graded into the outdoors by way of a series of porches, patios, verandahs, gazebos, awnings, walled gardens, and courtyards that gradually accumulated over the centuries. The Besterson residence was scarcely better than average, not that anyone cared much for that sort of competition. There really wasn't much point when building materials were free, and the size of one's manse depended on how much labor one was willing to expend on upkeep and construction.

Conway wondered if other people suffered from irrelevant thoughts while easing themselves and reluctantly wandered back to the verandah to see how his champion was faring. The black warrior was stretched out on a settee, face down, shirtless, and Goody Besterson and her sister Ruth were laving the wound with sponges soaked in the astringent juice of the sibyl bush. The warrior's skin appeared strangely white and soft to Conway, and a suspicion changed to a certainty when Ruth eased the warrior upright for bandaging. The small warrior was actually a decent sized young woman, sturdy of build, and equipped with the standard number of breasts. Conway was beyond shock. Women Mariners were one thing, but he had never even considered a female swordsman. But he had never considered hitting Rosialindia in the eye with a species of zither, either. Live and learn. Die and forget.

Just as he was desperately trying readjust his mind to at least six impossible things, and reconcile them with the peace and normality of the Besterson verandah, there was a flare of light and noise back up the hill. Every eye was drawn to the Fane steeple, suddenly illuminated as the flames burst through the thatch of the Devout Sailback.

He went over to the nearest lamp and extinguished it with a wetted thumb. He had snuffed two more before Goody Besterson opened her mouth to protest.

She closed it and opened it twice more, soundlessly, before she gathered up her basins and sponges and ointments and helped lead the semi coherent warrior deep inside her house. Conway went out to the garden, and found the katana leaning against a wall planter. He located the sheath and the black shirt near the wicker settee and bore them all into the house. Nobody spoke a word, but it did seem that a sword was a useful thing to keep track of. He did not replace the sword in its sheath. Nobody slept until morning....Except the warrior woman.

The croaking of the psallies announced dawn, right on schedule, rather early in the morning. Goody Besterson was still sitting with the sleeping swordswoman, and her sister Ruth was still brewing increasingly stronger pans of chai, and Conway's tongue tasted like the dirt floor of the Sailback, and he felt that possible danger was much less tolerable than remaining in ignorance. He thought, blearily about taking a weapon, but the katana was firmly grasped in its owner's hands, and Conway was aware enough to realize that a weapon would only slow down his flight. One should always be aware of who they are, and Conway was neither a lover, nor a fighter. He decided that his best tactic was to sneak.

So, he snuck. There was little need, in the event. All of the mobile combatants had fled back to their long rafts, and the Ainsmen had done all they could in containing the fire, and drubbing the offslanders, and had retired to hammock. There was still many a person left to cluster about, exchange gloomy views, and predict further disaster. Prominent among these, of course, was old Peetie, and from him Conway discovered that actual casualties were limited to Meinher and two offslanders with cracked pates. Blundoor and Rosialindia had faded away, and it seemed that the most of Peetie's mourning was concerned with the evaporated quaff in Meinher's cellars. Conway decided that there was little good to accomplish here, and outside of hunting up Cookie and waking her up from her slumbers to get the real story, he could best serve the forces of good by going back to his coracle and sleeping until it got too hot.

He decided to stop back and see if Ruth had perhaps fried up a beetle or else a clutch of psallie eggs. All three women were at the big table near the fountain and had been joined with a dozen more. The conversation was so many sided and dense, that his arrival was almost unnoticed except by Ruth, who laid another trencher and spoon at on the ealden table, and filled it with netbrot and hominy. There were in fact beetles in plum sauce and a stone griddle full of eggs. Ruth never said much, but her instincts were good.

Conway tucked in, and found that he was ravenous. The more he ate, the more he wanted, and Ruth had to make two more shuttles to the big soapstone griddle, before he was able to pay much attention to the conversation around the great waxed table. He was a little miffed that nobody asked him about his observations at the scene, but soon realized that there was little to report besides a pile of ashes and Peetie. The women had much better sources of information than he did, and he soon gathered that the Ain's agenda was whether to construct a new inn, which the men of the island considered the first priority, or to let the Fane have the land it had long coveted, which the Goodies tended to support.

Conway decided that all of this had little to do with him, and that his time on South Ainsworth was nearly at an end. He had nearly fifty moneys, and a genuine chuitar, and a perfectly good coracle, and what he really wanted to do, was to sail-up, and seek out a good teacher, and learn to play music. He had half an idea to find Gully, but realized that he had, in fact, destroyed one of her band's instruments, and that might lead to embarrassing questions. It was near the end of rainy season, but the wind was still out of the north-west, and Smith and all it's fabled wonders was a mere thousand flongs away.

It was northeast away, but that was no insurmountable obstacle. He knew how to tack. He rose to his feet, and thanked Ruth, who winked a most unmatronly wink at him. This wink should have given him ideas, if he had had any sense at all, but as we have seen, he didn't. Heroes, even apprentice heroes, generally find brains a liability in their pursuits. And obviously, any snippet of sense will immediately disqualify one from heroism.

So he rose, and walked out of the dining yard, and past the summer room, and through the kitchen garden, to the front gate, with nothing more on his mind than a short nap, followed by another meal and another nap before bedtime. His progress was interrupted by a sound, or combination of sounds, that quite halted him in his tracks. There was the sound of a stone on steel, and the sound of someone unsuccessfully trying to stifle tears. Sort of a whetting and a weeping, as it were.

Conway did his best without thinking, as always, and so, without thinking, he wandered over to his left into the outer garden and peered around a spaulted mango, and there was the warrior, sharpening her katana, and gently crying. He knew he best continue on, but some deeply buried, fatuous, male part of his genetic heritage, made him stop and fumble for a handkerchief he didn't have, and ask; "Is there something wrong?"

"No, dammit. Everything is just peachy."

"Then why are you crying?"

"I'm not crying!" Swimming blue eyes gave the lie to her words, even as they shot sparks at young Conway. "Warriors don't cry. You must be mistaken."

"Warriors don't toy with dangerous opponents, either." He was stung by her illogic into a un-Conwayish bluntness of speech. He was tired, after all.

"What do you mean!" More sparks evaporated the last of the tears.

"You spanked Blundoor with your blade. If you had cut him in half right then and there, Meinher would still be alive, I'd still have a job, and Griffin would still have an inn, and I wouldn't be planning to sail away tomorrow!"

This outburst was the most forceful statement Conway had ever made in his life, but there was something about the tiny black clad figure that irritated him in a way precisely unlike all the other irritations he had ever suffered in his short life.

"Why wait until tomorrow?" She spoke sweetly; "The wind is blowing today....Why don't you emulate it?"

"Huh?"

"Blow," she smiled. "Away."

This idiom was lost on Conway. "You talk funny." He tried to soften this observation, but didn't know why he should bother. "When the tide turns, there will be an offshore breeze...I'll leave then." He reconsidered his gentleness. "With your kind permission, of course."

She made a semicircular gesture with the hand that held the whetstone. It might have meant anything. He interpreted it as dismissal, and turned to leave. She half rose from her seat on the rustic bench, setting down the stone, but retaining her hold on the sword. It wasn't a threatening gesture. It just was that she never left her sword out of touch.

"Wait." She swallowed some obstruction in the throat. Perhaps it was her pride. "I suppose I should thank you."

"For what?" He was honestly baffled.

"For saving my life!" She bit off an unfamiliar word, perhaps a characterization of him.

"Oh....That." He thought for a long moment. "It was nothing."

"Are you saying my life is nothing?"

"Ahhh...No. Not exactly."

"Then what?"

"I was just being modest."

"And you do have so much to be modest about, don't you?"

"Look here, Mistress. I don't have to stay here and be insulted. I could go home for that."

"I'm sure they know best."

"......" Conway just politely turned and walked away. This conversation was much less desirable than a nap. He thought that his feet should be itching, and his head hurting, but they weren't. Oddly enough, he felt rather splendid, except for a bubbling below his sternum...."Ate too much." He thought. And thought very little more until after noon.

On awakening, he took counsel with himself, his being the wisest head available, and thought to find a meal, and then to visit the chandlery. There was a chance of a job, perhaps and if not, there was the need to lay in a few supplies for the sail to Smith. Some preserves would be nice, and some sourweed sauce and limes for the fish he would catch, and definitely an oilskin bag for his precious chuitar. There would be a very few good-byes to make and then a good night's sleep. And then away. Perhaps some jerky. And a straw hat for the sun. And just maybe it was time to visit the barbers. He slid from his hammock and hung his lone blanket over its usual limb and turned to face the black warrior. He said nothing. He had nothing to say, and was afraid of uttering any pleasantry. So he kept his lips closed. He was learning.

There was a longish silence. Finally she spoke.

"I suppose I should apologize."

"For what?" He was honestly innocent.

"For being rude to you, you dolt."

"Oh. That."

"You did save my life, and the women all said you're really a nice boy."

Conway decided definitely to visit the barber. And the jewelers. And maybe the tattooist. He thought for a while more, and couldn't seem to find a sensible thing to reply to this.

"Well?"

"Well what?"

"Cat got your tongue?"

"What's a cat, and what's it got to do with my tongue?"

"I mean," And sparks danced in her blue eyes again, "What have you got to say for yourself?"

"I'm hungry, and I need to do some things before I leave and everything I say to you gets bitten off."

"Poor baby…Where are you going?"

"Why do you want to know?"

"I'm going with you."

"You think so?"

"You can bank on it."

"What's a bank? A river bank?"

She suddenly shut her mouth and smiled and took his hand and led him over to his coracle. She tested the tight shrunk hide of the fore deck with her other hand and sat down on it. Then immediately rose again, and smiled again. He felt the ground shift beneath him again. She spoke in a softer voice.

"May I sit on your boat?"

"Sure. It's dragonhide. It's strong."

"Would you sit next to me?"

"What do you want?"

"I want to leave here."

"Take a raft."

"I don't know who my enemies are."

"Blundoor Kreegah for one."

"You know him?"

"We're from the same island."

"Did he follow you here?" There was a small note of panic in her voice.

"Like a draken follows a sea slug."

"Huh?"

"It's a proverb."

"What does it mean?"

"It means no." She accepted that, and then changed subjects with baffling rapidity. At least to Conway, who had less knowledge of women than he had of the rest of humanity. Even less, we should say.

"I could have beaten him, you know." Her eye was steady, her lip was firm.

"Him, who?" Conway got it a beat later. "Oh, him....If you say so."

"I do so say. He's slow and stupid and looses his temper. Easy meat." She settled back on the deck and clasped her knees, and became distant. Conway thought of things to say. They all seemed stupid and inappropriate. Or worse. Young. Then he had an inspiration, and asked what he wanted to know.

"Where do you want to go?"

She drifted back from somewhere. Actually she was reviewing the duel in her mind; she could have taken him. She had to say something and settled for an old standby.

"When?"

"When, what?"

"When do I want to go where?"

"Tomorrow. With me." Conway tried to be firm. "You said that you were going with me. I'm going to Smith." He paused and continued. "To study music. The have records of Olearth music there. I want to hear them. And I want to see how Frerisson makes chuitars."

"No....that's out. There are no wars on Smith. I want to go to Bluestem and see the war...that's why I'm here."

Conway refrained from saying that the only contact he wanted to have with Rosialindia or the redoubtable Kreegah was dancing horn-swoggles on their graves and instead politely pointed out that it was his boat. He was foolish, but not foolish enough to be rude to a warrior. She was amazed.

"Don't you want to be a hero? To have adventures?"

"I'm having an adventure. I'm trying to stay alive."

"You're as boring as the rest of this world. I thought it would be different. But it's just as boring as...." Conway thought there was something odd about the phrasing of this sentence, but was more interested in getting away from this crazy person. Conway, at heart wanted to be a very conventional person. It was just that the other conventional persons all thought him odd. This is a common problem for odd persons. Normal people can always tell.

She shrugged, or rather started to shrug, and then felt the tightness of her wounded shoulder, and thought better of it. She settled for a smile, trying to win Conway. It was a very nice smile. Conway never noticed. She, similarly, never noticed that he never noticed. She tried another tack.

"Look here..." She paused and he looked. All he saw was a small dangerous person who talked funny. He was not impressed. She began again.

"Maybe I could help you get your heart's desire. You don't know who I really am. I could...what do you really want?"

He considered. "I want to learn all about music. I want to play and I want to learn to make chuitars. It's not much, but it's harmless. I could make a living...maybe." He didn't mention his motive for all this unmungian ambition. He had no inclination to share his secret desire to taste romance with this...this warrior. He would sooner unburden his soul to Old Peetie. He could see she was unimpressed with his expression, as it was.

"Don't you want riches and power?" She nodded as if to herself and tried to look confident. He thought she merely looked smug and dangerous. "I could help you. We could find a small island and take over. You could have anything you wanted. You could be king."

"What's a king? If it's like First Commoner or Alphate, I'm not interested. I told you what I'm going to do. You're not part of my plans. I just saved you, because..." He didn't want to examine his own motives closely. Or at all. "I hate Rosialindia, and Blundoor. They hurt people. Every time I get comfortable, they come and mess it up. And they never even notice me! They just....Ruin things." His voice had peaked, but soon fell back to it's wonted monotone.

She appeared to understand. "The enemy of my enemy is my friend."

"I guess." He had never heard such an equation before. "Look, if you need moneys, I could pay your fare to Bluestem. Maybe."

"That's not the problem. Warriors would have no problem getting to the war."

"So go."

"I want to go with you."

"Why me."

"Don't you know?"

"No."

"Then that's for me to know and for you to find out."

"I'm going to Smith."

She thought for a moment, small face set into a pattern of will. "Don't you want revenge on what's-her-face and Fatboy?"

"I never want to see them again." He was a firm as only a rootless person can be. "I'm going to Smith."

She considered for a moment more. "Will you give me a lift?"

"A what? Do you want me to pick you up? Do you want to climb a tree?" He was honestly puzzled. A lot of the words she used seemed to have hidden meanings. Heoj had been easier to follow.

"No, no trees. I want to know if you will please take me with you when you go. To Smith or where ever." She bit her lip and tried not to smile, or to beg.

"Please take me with you. I'll pay my way. I have money. Please."

"I don't even know your name."

"My name is Attilina. And you're Conway. The women told me. They like you."

"Hum…Hurumph." He thought. What he thought was that he would rather do anything rather than continue this conversation. Also there was the fact that she was a warrior and he wasn't. He was on dangerous ground here. Even a person as unworldly as Conway knew that one should not needlessly offend people who bore swords. Perhaps he could use deceit.

"Well. I just don't...Why don't you...why don't you give me time to think. I have to lay in some supplies for the voyage. I could go to Jomestrom's, and you could meet me here in...Oh say, three glasses, and then we could talk some more."

"I'll go with you to the chandler's. I'll pay for all you need."

There didn't seem to be much escape from her, no matter what. He couldn't imagine her motives, but knew for certain that he could do nothing to dissuade her. All he could think was that he was in trouble and he didn't know why. As there were no cats on Munge, he had no model for cooperating with the inevitable, barely or otherwise. He was left to his own intuitions, and so cooperated in a surly manner. But then again....

"If you want to go to Smith, I can't stop you. If you want to come with me, it will cost you."

"How much?"

"One silver." He expected her to blench, but she just nodded again. She stood and waited. "Let's go."

"Well...all right." He plucked his blanket from its bough, and folded it and set it on the fore deck. Then he went and began to untie his hammock from between two of the lingons, carefully unclipping the beetle shields and rolling them inside the netting. These homely chores were interrupted by a stifled noise of displeasure from Attilina. He turned to face her, his face carefully innocent, hers beginning to storm.

"I thought were going somewhere?"

"To Smith."

"Then why are you fussing with your bedding?"

"If you prefer to walk to Smith, you won't need me or my coracle."

"What are you talking about?"

"South Ainsworth is an island."

"Yes it is." The esses hissed only slightly.

"So is Smith."

"And?" No esses in that word, but it hissed anyway.

"There is water in between."

"Go on."

"I don't walk well on water."

"I thought we were going to the chandlery."

"Why carry supplies back uphill?"

"Aren't we leaving in the morning?"

"No need. I can sleep on the coracle."

"And I?"

"Haven't you sailed before?"

"No. Not like this."

"Well, I suppose you will have to learn." He tried to not look like a person searching for a way out of a dilemma. She looked like a person who was being led astray by lack of opposition. He finished stowing his bedding and picked up one end of the coracle to swing it around to the creek's edge. She continued to stand, face carefully blank. He noted her confusion and secretly gloried in it. He set down the bow and walked around toward the rounded stern, and placed both hands on the dragonhide covering. The sturdy material flexed only slightly between the withes of its framework. A logical conclusion came to him.

"You're not from Ains...did you come here on a longraft? Are they nice? Like riding on a whole village, isn't it?"

"Ah...no. I'm not an Ains."

"Well," He looked at her over his shoulder. "Are you going to help me?"

"What?" She was honestly baffled.

He spoke as if to a child. "To help me push my coracle into the water. Boats work better in the water."

"Oh." Her voice was neutral. It sounded scared, but what Mungian was afraid of a simple coracle? She did come forward and placed her hands along side his. He gave the word and they pushed the frail seeming craft into the creek and Conway scrambled in, and grabbed his steering paddle. She waited a second and then followed over the gunwale, ungracefully. It was the first clumsy move Conway had ever seen her make, but he had little eyes for that. The coracle was almost as long as the creek was wide and he had to back and fill to keep it from running aground. Attilina surveyed the coracle with a pinched look on her face as realization set in.

"We're going to use this little thing to row out to the real boat, right?"

"No, we're going to Smith. This is all the boat I have. It's called a coracle. A long coracle. I made it." These statements did not reassure the warrior. She surveyed the craft with blue eyes that seemed rather larger than usual. There was little to see and nothing out of the ordinary. A withe and dragonskin hull three feet wide, and not quite thirty long, a mast, and an outrigger perhaps two-thirds the size of the main hull. Continents have been discovered in smaller craft.

"Is it safe?"

"It's not as far from here to Smith as it is from Angst to Ains, and rainy season is almost over. It might take a while longer, we will sail cross the wind, but we'll probably get there."

"Probably?"

"Probably." He finally noticed her discomfort. "If you're scared, you could always take the longraft. I'll drop you off at the chandlers. The dorys dock there."

"I'm not scared!" She snapped, as if to convince herself. "It's just...."

"Yes?"

"Where's the bathroom?"

"Do you want to take a bath?"

"Something like that."

"We will be on the Pancreatic Sea. It's made out of water. One takes baths in water. You tie a rope around your waist and you jump in." He looked at her as if he had never seen such a sight in his life. Actually he never had, but he didn't realize that yet." It's easy, you'll figure it out."

Hearing himself, he could barely believe he was speaking like this to an armed and dangerous warrior of unknown antecedents.

"What about fish?"

"They rarely bathe. They can't afford the soap."

She started to snap at him, and then realized that she had asked to be where she was now, and desisted. They remained in this uncompanionable silence all the way to Jomestrom's Chandlery.

Once there, she was as good as her word, and had to be restrained from buying more than the coracle could hold. Conway made no comment when she bought two tourist grade life jackets, that came complete with little pockets full of survival rations, whistles, and skate repellents. All completely useless, of course. No fisherman on all the Pancreatic Sea would be seen dead floating in such a device. They had too much pride in their seamanship. But Conway demurred, and made sure he had his sourweed sauce and his dried beetle egg clusters and not one, but two, oilskin bags for his chuitar. He had been practicing it obsessively for a month, but felt he had little to show for it except sore fingers. The little lukette had strings twisted of psallie gut, but the larger instrument boasted wire strings that wore deep grooves in his fingertips. He had asked Jomestrom, and found that the making of these strings was a craft practiced on only a few of the larger islands. So he bought a few sets, glad to let her pay the three coppers a set.

She paid with a gold, and Jomestrom had to scrounge through drawers and chests back in his quarters to make change. He laid the money on the ealden counter while he hunted and Conway inspected it curiously. He had never seen a coin so large and finely struck, or one that was without a central hole. He peered closely and managed to make out the legend on one side. He turned to her in innocent curiosity.

"Where's the African archipelago?" She didn't speak, but he plunged on. "And what's a kruggerand?"

"African Archipelago?"

"Well, it says Union of South Africa. It doesn't say what it's united with, but I figure it's like South Ainsworth, or East Angst…you know, a bunch of islands."

She bit her lip, but her eyes danced. "It's a long way away, and very old. Kruggerand was a man's name." She handed him a single silver, and he carefully spoaned it.

"Alpharch or something?"

"Something like that." Just then Jomestrom came bustling back, hands full of moneys, including some golds. "Here, now. This should do. I'll give you another spoan or a money belt if you want. This is quite a load to carry."

"Thanks. I'll manage." She crammed the moneys into a strange black pouch she wore as a belt, and then gathered up a grass basket containing her smaller purchases. The larger stuff had been carried to the coracle already. Conway gave one more try to escape, even though he felt shamed at his duplicity. He reached for the basket.

"Here, I'll take that. It will take me a while to stow all these supplies, so you might as well get the rest of your stuff from where ever you were staying, and meet me at the coracle in half a glass or so." Give him half a glass and a good wind and he would be almost out of sight. But it was not to be. She held on to the basket and turned to go.

"Everything I had was in my duffel, behind the bar in the Sailback. All I have left is Beauty," She tapped the katana hilt over her shoulder. "C'mon, let's go to Smith."

CHAPTER 5

▼

And so they set out on their great adventure. Or perhaps it was only an adventure for one of them. It was hard to tell who was having an adventure and who was just having a difficult time in unfamiliar surroundings. There is a difference, or at least people suppose there should be a difference. Perhaps an adventure is only someone else having a difficult time, a long way away. Be that as it may be, it is important not only to know if one is involved in an adventure, but also to know exactly whose adventure one is involved in. Regardless of the implications of romance, adventure is always personal; there is never a generic adventure.

It all depends on attitude. An adventurer, a true adventurer, can find an adventure on a deserted sidewalk in the most boring city in the universe. Contrariwise, a prosaic person can be surrounded with elves, dragons and unicorns and find only irritation and discomfort. It might be argued that war is a generic adventure, and that any occupation that can get one killed is, de facto, an adventure. The silliness of this assertion is obvious to the discerning person, and requires no elucidation.

All that aside, it was becoming obvious, even to one as unworldly as Conway, that his passenger was a very different type of person from the run of the muck in the Pancreatic Ocean. Certain conversations he had had with Badmash lingered in his mind, just below his consciousness. It wasn't that she was so unusual, one expected that from a female warrior, but she was so unusual in such unusual ways.

For example, she demanded privacy for the exercise of her bodily functions. When she washed or otherwise exposed her person, Conway was obliged to sit in the bow of his own craft, eyes averted. This struck him as peculiar, coming as he did from a culture that lacked walls to their houses. During dry season Pancreats lived in groves and gardens, and clothing was minimal or less. Also, both sexes, in the tropics, were perforce semi aquatic. The idea of an item of dress specific to bathing would have struck Conway as ridiculous as, say, soap for fishes. Conway had all the knowledge of normal body functions, male and female, as any person might desire. He wasn't ignorant. He just couldn't tell the difference between romance and sex.

The gentle reader might mock him, or pity him, but in fact he was not the only person out of the quadrillion or so in the galaxy to have this problem. There was another in the same boat with him. It's not that uncommon a phenomenon. It just always feels like it must be to the poor nebbishes involved. A person can be so poisoned by their own loneliness that they are incapable of recognizing the only medicine that might cure them.

In spite of all their shopping, Conway discovered that he had forgotten limes for the fish. Sourweed sauce was fine, but it cloyed. What with fish and skippers and the smaller varieties of skates literally leaping into the coracle, food was no problem, but he had forgotten limes to wash the raw fish with. Attilina discovered that there is no way to cook on a boat as small as Conway's, and sulkily subsisted on the survival hardbrot in the floatation vests, and the psallie jerky Conway had brought to have something to chew.

This exercise at least kept her mouth occupied with something outside of finding fault with Conway's boat. At least it did most of the time. She seemed to have quite definite ideas how things should be, and Conway had little hope of satisfying these preconceptions. For example;

"What's the name of this boat?"

"It's not a boat, it's a coracle. Boats are made of wood."

"It still needs a name."

"I know which coracle it is, it's mine."

"It still needs a name."

He chewed on this concept for a while, as if to flavor the ribbon of blue kelp he was varying his diet with. "Well, I could name it after my mother."

"That would be nice. What was her name?"

"I'm not sure. I just used to call her Mamma." This information seemed to turn Attilina's attention inward to that unfathomable gulf that exists just inside all of us. For his own reasons, Conway was just as glad for the silence. He had never learned the art of conversation, and his speech was limited to things he cared about, and so, was hard pressed to cope with the constant presence of a stranger, a very strange stranger indeed, in his coracle and in his life so blatantly. They had only been sailing for five glasses and twilight was creeping up the sky in the east.

It seemed like it had been much longer to Conway. If he had been able to experience the monumental queasiness that filled Attilina's stomach, he would have realized that had seemed much, much longer to the girl. The breeze was very mild and from the west-northwest, and the coracle ambled along at little better than a walk. However it was faster and a lot drier than swimming, and so Conway was content. Before them, in the east, the moon rose into the declining day, a spangled pale gold ghost in the dusky aquamarine sky. Luica's Star, the sun, was yellower than the star that human eyes had evolved to under, and they saw Munge's sky and seas as definitely green. But it was not something than anyone but poets and other idle fools noticed. Surely Conway didn't; just as he never noticed the moon, unless he needed its light for something. So he was completely baffled when Attilina named it with a word he had never heard before.

"Abaraxis." He looked at her and realized that she hadn't meant to speak aloud. Another beat and he realized what she was talking about, and then he knew who she was….Or at least he knew where she was from.

"Why did you leave there?" She was as baffled as he had been.

"Leave where?"

He pointed with the droopy strand of blue kelp. "There. Abawhatsis. What you said." Her head snapped around and those blue eyes, black in this light, blazed into his, bright with fear and sudden respect.

"You're smarter than I thought. Most lumpen would never imagine that a Spacer would come to ground. Especially not in a place like this." She grimaced in a fashion that Conway found incomprehensibly unflattering.

"Is that what you call us . . . lumpen?"

"Well…what do you call us?"

"We rarely even think about you. I knew a man who wanted to space out once. He called you Outers."

"That's typical."

"What is?"

"For you lumpen to ignore the universe off this mud ball."

"Hey! That's not fair. We're busy. We have lives to live. And what did the universe ever do for us?"

"Allowed you to rusticate here in your little idyll, for one."

"I thought that us primitive preserves were established for your benefit, not ours." He had missed the exact meaning of several of her words, but her tone was hard to mistake. "Anyway, you didn't answer my question. If you're so superior, why did you come down here to lord over us poor…lumpen."

"Well, it seemed like a good idea at the time. I'm…I was the greatest swordsman in my whole sector and when I heard about a world with real dragons and real vampire demons to fight, I had to come. And now I'm stuck here on this mud ball and it's bo-o-o-ring." She deflated her chest, and peered uneasily over her shoulder. "And the sky is so big and intimidating."

"So climb in your space ship and go home to daddy."

"I can't! This is a Preserve! You can come, or you can go, but you can't round trip. And anyway I don't have a ship. It's not allowed. I surfed down here." Her voice rose to a near shriek. "And leave my father out of it!" Unaccustomed as he was to interpersonal relationships, he knew he had offended. Actually he was used to offending all unawares. He backed his sails quickly.

"How do you surf from the moon? I thought there was no air, much less water."

"I'm not here to rectify the deficiencies of your education!" She snapped and then relented. "I didn't surf from the moon, it's too far for any survival mod. We were at Leo for an Anthro sim and I surfed from there. It was really fun. When the mod hits the atmosphere and the silica foam starts to ablate it's a wild ride. I didn't have much cross range and was lucky to para right onto Ainsworth. The para is biodegradable so there was no evidence after the first rain. But I didn't realize what a bore this lump was until it was too late. And now I have to spend my life here!" Conway missed a lot more words in this tirade, but got the important point.

"Well, you're going to have to make the best of it." He felt an urge, a need to reach out and comfort her, but dared not. A warrior was one thing, and female warrior was another, but this person was almost incomprehensible to him. He could have been boat mates with a Flyer and his quetzal easier. After all, he had seen a Flyer....Once. It had been years ago, and the poor creature, far from seeming a demon, had seemed only a tattered rag as it writhed and mewed around the impaling postle. He generally kept that memory buried.

Above them the moon brightened, mostly full, and the spangles brightened to multicolored glory on the darkened limb. The sight prodded Conway to a child's question. Every child asked this question, but on Angst, they only asked it once.

"If you don't mind....What are the spangles? On Angst we were told they were furnaces for the damned sinners." He hesitated; brow furrowed, and then plunged on. "I always wondered."

She failed to grasp his meaning. "Spangles? What are spangles?"

He pointed up at the gold moon, set with gems like a brooch on Night's Gown. "The lights," He said. "The lights on the moon."

"Oh, those." Nothing could be more commonplace to a spacer girl. "Cities."

"Cities." The idea took a while to settle to the bottom of his mind. "Cities are full of people." It wasn't exactly a question.

"The population of Abaraxis is seven or eight times that of Munge."

"Indeed." It was easier to believe in cities on the old familiar moon than to believe he was having this conversation. "And which one is the one you lived in?"

She allowed a snap into her voice. He was so ignorant! "I keep telling you, I don't come from Abaraxis. It's a backwater. We...my father and I...travel. He's a very important Savant, a Disseminator. I've been all across this system and two more. Space is full of people. Institutions evolve to keep humanity unified..."

He interrupted, struck with the novelty of his place in the Universe; "Like us, like the Preserves!"

"Well...you are like the least part of the system. You're like a safety net, a backup. The Disseminators, the Spacer's Guild, the Institute of Humanity, the Surveyors, The Artistic Enterprises Confederacy are all much more important." She paused, wondering how much it was safe to tell this bumpkin. "Even the disneys are more important than the Preserves."

"What's a disney?"

"It's a park, a theme park, full of sims and history. It's fun but it keeps us human with the power of myth. We lived in a disney called Mesosaur, around Ponder." She could see, even in the moonlight, his bafflement. "Don't you have parks, or resorts, where people go to have fun?"

He considered the concept. "Fun?"

"Yeah, fun. People dress up in historical costumes and play games and dance and duel and stuff."

Conway had never considered the idea that people had dressed differently in past times. It seemed unlikely. Clothes were clothes, and varied only with latitude and station in life. "They have fairs sometimes. And then there's the regional markets like at Cashamash. I hear they gamble there."

"Can we go there? There might be something to do, somebody to fight, some action." She bit her lip, and tried not to plead. "Please?"

"Well..." Then an unsettling thought came to Conway. "You must be a lot older than I thought...I mean...to have traveled so much. Stars are far apart. Ponder is..."

"Ponder is a planet in this system. It's two out, a gas giant, just past Meniscus, the water world." She was ready to snap, but reminded herself that it was a very small boat and she needed him. "You don't know the half of it about stars being far apart. Even at...the speeds we travel at. Well...." She was desperately trying to explain interstellar concepts to a person who thought a steel knife was a really wonderful invention. "Look, Conway, do you know what year this is?"

"I'm not ignorant. It's 12987. I was born in 12971. That's Olearth years. We keep Fanetime in Olearth years. It's year 7784 Mungian. There's thirteen years Mungian for every decade Olearth. And two days for Penance."

She ignored the theology. She definitely didn't want to go there. "I was born in 12573."

"You are..." His voice trailed off, as he tried to figure the age of this...creature inhabiting his boat. For the first time he was deathly afraid of this strange person, or demon, or...he lacked words. She saw his panic and tried to reassure him.

"Don't bother trying to figure it out. I'm not quite sixteen years old. I just finished secondary school. I'm younger than you."

"How could that be? Were you enchanted or..." Half forgotten stories, whispered in the dark came back to him.

"There's no such thing as magic! Don't be an idiot, even if you are a primitive. Do you know that nothing can travel faster than the speed of light?"

"In Faneschool…"

"Do you know that the closer you go to C the slower time goes?"

"How could time slow down? Time is time?"

She could see that she was taking on too large a contract. And anyway, she had specified that she was not here on Munge to rectify the deficiencies in his education. "Just take it on faith that I'm your age…All right?"

He wanted to pursue this matter of time slowing down. It made his mind itch. He kind of liked it. But he obviously had to placate and humor this creature. Perhaps she was mad. That was the simplest explanation, after all. And actually, she was as she was and as soon as possible, he was going to be elsewhere. Given half a chance, she would be somebody else's problem, and he would be an apprentice chuitar maker someplace far away from spacers, war, and people with swords and incomprehensible motives. His plan was clear. His mind was made up.

"I don't understand, but I suppose…"

"Trust me."

He just nodded, and forego mentioning that Badmash had explicitly and repeatedly warned him against trusting anybody who asked to be trusted. It was always a bad sign. There was a flurry of foam as a moby breached and spouted, too common a sight to attract much of his attention, and so he covered his confusion with her words by pulling in the line to the plankton net. It had been several hours since the last examination and he was mildly pleased with the half cuppa transparent pink-green jelly caught at the toe of the fine mesh net. Once again he wished he hadn't forgotten the limes.

He dug in his spoan and found his chitin spoon and scooped out a dollop of the plankton, a few portions of which still writhed feebly.

Spoon half to lips, he offered the net to Attilina before he slurped down the first mouthful.

"Want some?" He swallowed and dipped out another spoonful.

"Don't you have any cheese or bread on this planet?"

"Brot's in the cubby...What's cheese?"

"It's a food. It's made from cow's milk. It's good."

"And a cow is an animal?" He felt a little queasy at the very idea. Milk, human milk was for babies. It seemed obscene to eat the natal fluid of another animal.

"Don't you have any other mammals on Munge?"

"I don't think so....They have goats up in Hazlen's Land."

"Uck...goat's cheese stinks."

"I suppose it's important to you...In Faneschool they said the Landers tried to keep the ecology of the planet as native as possible...except for some food plants....Napples and coconuts and limes and corn and such. People and goats are the only Olearth animals on Munge...except for the beetles, of course, and they're an accident."

"Those beetles never came from Earth! They're all so weird! All those colors and shapes....I'm not sure I've ever seen two the same!"

He tried to placate her. It was becoming a reflex. "Well, that's what they said in Faneschool. They came in by accident and just exploded. That's why there's mostly just dactyls and beetles on Munge. They'll eat anything that's dead, and some things that don't move. Especially eggs."

She thought for a long moment. "How odd. In only seven thousand years...It must be the Gould gene. Funny they never stressed it in Eco class. It would be a textbook..."

He voice trailed off, and he finished eating the plankton and, inverting the net, replaced it into the water. And then he rinsed off his molded chitin spoon, slipped it back into his pouch and said. "Beetles aren't all bad. They taste pretty good and their shells are easily shaped in boiling water. Handy little critters, and some are quite attractive."

"How you could eat something that lives off of human wastes...Bugs!"

And that seemed to be the last word on that subject.

He tried to think of a neutral topic. He was getting tired of placations and put-downs." What's a gold gene?"

"Gould Gene...It's the mechanism behind Punctuated Equilibrium. You know."

"Sure I do....Punctuated what?

"Look it up in the Aludium!"

"Sure. What's an Aludium."

She started to snap again, but bit off her spite and swallowed it. It wasn't his fault he was ignorant crude savage.

"I'll have to explain a little. With no faster than light speed drive, the stars are decades apart, of course it seems like a lot less at one G, but still there can't be any real government. Do you follow?" It sounded like a regurgitated lesson, even to Conway, and of course he didn't follow her, but at least she wasn't being actively insulting, so he just smiled and nodded. He had had a lot of practice back on Angst, of just smiling and nodding. Sometimes he wondered what would happen if he frowned and shook his head for a change. He did get the part about no government. That sounded like Munge.

"So," She continued, "Private and charitable organizations have evolved to fill some of government's more necessary functions. One in particular, the Institute of Humanity, has established libraries, Aludiums, on every habitat that contain humans. Supposedly they contain all human knowledge. Even Preserves have at least one. They are supposedly free and open to all comers and they are constantly upgraded by a radio link in every solar system. It's slow, but it works."

"What do you mean, 'supposedly free'?"

"Knowledge is power. Some governments feel the need to control all power."

"So there is a device?"

"A building."

"Somewhere on Munge?"

"That contains all the knowledge of all of humanity. Yes." She brushed back her bangs, and looked slightly less fierce in the waning sunset light. "It's in New Ahven, of course."

He came more alive somewhere deep in his heart. "And do they have music?"

"All knowledge...Subject to the limitations of relativity of course."

He really had no idea what the last half of that sentence meant, but still...All the music of all mankind.

"Well, I'll have to go and see it, this Aludium. It sounds interesting."

"That's putting it mildly. We will check it out. I need to look up something myself."

Strange how that little word 'we' kept creeping into her speech. He would have to see about that. He couldn't see himself ever attracting a romantic partner with this....Warrior hanging around. She was definitely an obstacle to his plans of learning the chuitar and attracting a girl. Somebody like Gully, but younger, or Rosialindia, but sweeter. Slender. Yeah, slender. And with long blonde hair. Maybe long red hair. Maybe she would let him brush it for her. His reverie was interrupted by the harsh tones of his passenger.

"Are we going to sail all night?" Her voice grated on him, her accent foreign and cold to his sensitive ear.

"Sure, why not? There's nothing to run into."

"Oh yeah?" She pointed into the gloom. "Then what's that light right over there?"

He strained to see. Not for the first time he suspected that his eyesight was less than adequate. Yes, there was a light. It seemed to be steady, and was neither green nor red, as a ship's light should be. Her voice broke in.

"I can see palm fronds in the light. It's an island."

Now he could hear the soft sound of lazy surf in the night, at no great distance. He already was committed to humoring her, so he traded places with her in the narrow hull, and unlashed the tiller. He couldn't hear the sharp sounds of waves on rock, just the gentle surf, and in fact, the islands to the south and east of the Pancreatic Sea were lower and less mountainous than the Angsts. The three-quarters moon would help, too. He strained into the darkness and could barely discern the froth of waves breaking against the dark mass of a forested island. He thought he could ease into land, and who knows, maybe he could find a lime tree.

"You're right. We'll land and stretch our legs. I'll sleep in the coracle, and you can use the hammock." He put the steering oar over and headed along the line of surf, as much as the breeze allowed. The sea was as gentle as the wind and the angles were pretty much in his favor. There might be some weather making up behind them, but that was then and this was now.

He was looking for the break in the surf that would indicate an inlet or river mouth. If nothing else he would try to round the point of the island and land on the lee shore. If that failed, there would be lots of time to find a soft spot in the beach and just crash on in. There was no haste, no matter how itchy Attilina grew. But...

"Tell me about your life in space...do you play music?"

"What kind of....Oh, you mean on instruments." He was hurt by the indifference in her voice, and was glad that he face was hidden in the night. "I'm into hisports. Musicians are in arts. Different curricula. We never meet. There is so much recorded stuff that only people who want to play, do play. Nerds and such. Normal people never listen to that stuff, anyway. We're too busy. Just set the netset to random and let it go. It learns what you like after you blip the delete button enough times."

He had no idea what she was talking about, but gathered that the answer was no. But he still wanted her talking about anything but his and his planet's inadequacies. He was willing to take her word that Munge was not much on the galactic scale, but it was, B'LLord, his world and he liked it. Sort of. He tried again. "But what do you do? What are your friends like?"

Her voice remained silent for so long, he feared he had offended her. Then she spoke. "I really can't explain it to you...so you could understand. What with the netsets and the holos and the prosthos and the surgies and the eets and the mutes and all, you couldn't see most of my friends as human. Some aren't, of course."

"Aren't what?"

"Human."

"What else is there?"

"Well, some are ayes, of course." She realized that she would have to speak baby talk to him. "Ayes are Aye Eye's, artificial intelligences, computers, and some are recordings of real people and some are eets, Ee Tee's, extra terrestrials. It gets confusing if you try to categorize, so we just take people as the come, on their own terms."

He wondered why she couldn't take him on his own terms, but realized that that was likely to be a fruitless line of speculation. She continued, unheeding.

"Let's just say that anything is possible, and all at once and you do the best that you can. We just...I'm still in school...was still in school, that is, and so my choices were limited. We just hung out and shopped and surfed the net and did sports and studied and had sex and....well you know, just hacked around. Childhood is such a bore, don't you know?"

"I wouldn't know...I never had one."

"What did you do?"

"What ever they told me to do."

That comment opened up even deeper gulfs of incomprehension and anyway, the surf was angling closer. He decided to take his chances and laid the helm hard over.

"Hold on!"

"To what?" He ignored her. She'd figure out something.

She gripped the gunwale, and he suspected her knuckles were white in the dark but most of his mind was concentrating on sucking in all the sensory information he could get. The slap of the waves against the resonant dragon hide of the coracle, the gleams of the spangled moon off of the creamy froth of the surf, the sigh of the breeze in the palm fronds on the beach, the faintly lit white of the beach, all brought their quotas of information to his senses, and that wondrous computer inside his skull came up with a time and an angle and a precise amount of force to push a paddle and an exact time to drop the sail and then they were safe on land, the prow grating coarse sand aside. This welcome sound was drowned out by a gust of breath from Attilina.

"Whew!"

"What's the matter, don't you trust my piloting?"

"I guess….I've never been out on so much water before." There was a tentative note, almost, could he believe it, a fear in her voice. He had begun to fear her, to credit her with an almost superhuman competency. After all, she was a Spacer, and an Outer.

"Huh?"

Her voice regained its normal scorn. "In the Dysons, water is kept in its place."

"And that is?"

"In glasses. With ice and flavors and alcohol."

"Don't Spacers swim?"

"Ahh…No, we don't."

How could it be? A primitive possessed skills that an Outer lacked? She seemed to detect his thoughts.

"After all," She said firmly, "This is the first actual planet I've ever been on."

"Oh." This concept had little reference to him, but it opened up whole vistas of questions. He bravely swallowed them. "Well, we're safe now. Let's beach the coracle and sack out. It's not all that long to dawn."

"Suits me."

Their simple plans were disrupted by a hail from the dark forest inland.

"Ahoy....What craft is that?"

"It's mine."

"And who are you, if I may be so bold as to inquire?"

"My name is Conway...I'm a...I'm going to Smith."

"Hrumph!"

"And this is Attilina....She is a warrior."

"And how are you classed?"

"Excuse me?"

The voice from the dark was light, supercilious. Conway felt his hackles rise Something about all that politeness from some one who wasn't civil enough to display themselves....

"We may excuse you, or, not. Depending on your classifications."

Attilina broke in; "And what precisely are our choices?"

"You can be guests, or you can be prey."

"I see," the girl replied. Conway didn't know, but this was familiar ground to her. Her primary recreation in the disneys, or on the net, was gaming. Riddles were standard opening gambits.

The pale glows of the moon revealed a pudgy figure at the edge of the woods that backed the white beach. It, or he, was very erect, as if straining for stature. He seemed to be wearing a headdress and the multicolored moonlight sparked highlights on a metal blade carried bare in his right hand. There was a 'wheep' as Attilina freed her blade. Conway hastened to head off trouble, although he really had no reason to, outside of his native diffidence.

"And how do I qualify as a guest?"

"You bring us a gift."

"All I have is some food, and some perry. It's supposed to be quite well aged."

"And how much do you have?"

"Perhaps half a demijohn, or more."

"Perhaps me no perhapses. I rule here. I am Mighty Wizard, and am quick to anger. You trifle with powers unknown. But that should suffice."

The figure stepped from darker to lighter shadow and was revealed as a pudgy light skinned young man, rather more than a lad. He wore an ornate, pagoda headdress that reflected the moon sparkles, and a cape woven all of feathers that was worth a Panarch's ransom.

"In fact, we are pleased. It has been moonths since we have indulged our subjects in a revel. Fetch your perry, and," The youth gestured with his long wavy blade, "Bid your retainer to sheath her sword. It would avail her little against our forces." He gestured again and the bushes rattled as perhaps a dozen lads stepped out into the moonlight. Most had prods, or regular crossbows, and the rest were equipped with slings and darts.

Obviously, Conway's mild tone had saved them all from sudden death. Attilina turned and sheathed her katana over her shoulder, and cast a hooded glance at Conway. He felt a significance, but was unable to decipher her intent. He dragged his coracle further up the beach, past the tide wrack, and fumbled out the perry with fingers that seemed stiff and stupidly unresponsive.

He set down the demijohn, relashed the hatch and carried his tribute toward the imposing figure. The thought struck him that their captor, or whatever, would probably would probably be subject to placation, and so Conway halted a few paces away, and genuflected, as he presented the perry. By his right side, Attilina stifled a sound. It was not a respectful sound.

The long sword gestured and two of the dark clad lackeys scurried forward and conveyed the large withe wrapped jug to their lord and master. Conway noticed that each had a symbol painted in white on their breasts. Oddly enough, it was a symbol he recognized, a symbol that increased his unease. This was going to be tricky. If only he had remembered the limes back on Ainsworth…

The leader thrust his sword into the sand, and allowed another brace of his subjects to pour him a sup of the pear liquor. He tasted it, and all motion ceased, as the company awaited his judgment. The moment stretched out like taffy.

"Welcome to the Island of the Flies, Honored Guests." He handed the cup back to his retainer with a sweeping gesture. Soon they would realize that all his gestures ranged between the sweeping and the grandiose.

"I am the Wizard Hignore the Mighty, Panarch of this Island, and Mage, and these..." He plucked the long sword from the sand and indicated the dark figures around him; "Are my loyal Flies."

Conway smiled and nodded, and muttered something innocuous. It worked well enough. Conway immediately classified Hignore the Mighty with the vast majority of people Conway had ever met; a threat, subject to simple placation.

"Lord Panarch?"

"Yes, Ah...Comroy?"

"May we be about our journey now?"

"My boy, I won't hear of it. You are Our Honored Guests, and you must revel with us. Otherwise would be rude, and We are never less than gracious. Perhaps in the morning." The Panarch paused, waiting. Conway took his cue.

"Your hospitality is proverbial."

"We are pleased. Follow to our Manse." He waved imperiously at his minions, who all seemed on the small side. "Codi, Wylox, bring up the rear. MARCH!"

Without further parley, Hignore strode off into the dark, and Attilina and Conway followed. They had little choice, for the dozen or so "Flies" pressed close around them, and urged them on. Conway had an ugly feeling that the two of them were to provide farther amusement for Hignore before the evening was over.

They passed through a screen of bushes, and found the forest, the wood, to be quite open and free of encumbrances to travel. The island was flat and sandy, and of no great extent, but as they progressed toward the center, they began to step over shelves and steps of limestone or cochina. Gradually, over a few flongs, less than a dozen, the trees grew larger and the steps became higher and the land rose to some small immanence. They also became aware of some faint, ruddy glows above them, which refused to resolve into a structure, no matter how close they approached. Finally, they were traveling through and underneath clusters of these flesh colored blotches of light, still without understanding their nature. They appeared to be angular, and flat, and flexibly supported, but Conway was still mystified. Attilina steamed alongside him, and sounded as frustrated as he felt, but none of her mutterings were quite resolvable either.

Conway had just decided that the glows were colored most like sunset through windmill sails when Hignore halted himself and his men and called out for a light. Immediately a glow above them appeared to crack open and a slit of more brilliant lamplight opened into a window of lamplight. A head popped out and then a knotty bundle unrolled itself down from the window to ground level. Hignore slung his wavy blade in a baldric and scrambled up what proved to be a perfectly common rope ladder. Things were starting to make sense to Conway now, and so he ushered Attilina toward the bottom of the ladder. She balked until he showed he how to climb, with one foot on each side of one of the rope uprights, so that the ladder didn't twist away from her. She scrambled up agilely enough, and he followed, musing on the deficiencies in education suffered by a person of such godlike powers.

Once at the top, they were in a small passage, or long skinny room, constructed of dragonskin stretched over ropes and odd lengths of wood. This slap dash construction was casually attached to the trunks and branches of trees. The dragonskins were randomly decorated in bright discontinuous colors, and Conway took a few moments to realize that he was inside a building, a species of treehouse, constructed of salvaged sails, stiffened with copious amounts of cone-beetle varnish.

The nature of his captors immediately became clear, and the chances of continuing their voyage changed from "maybe tomorrow" to "never".

They padded down this flexible hall to a larger, irregular room fitted with a motley assortment of cushions and chests, and lit with several mismatched fish oil lamps. The self-styled wizard, Hignore, beckoned them to seats and appointed a guard and slid off down the branching hall way without a word. He seemed less affable, now that they were in his "Manse", as if he no longer had to pretend amiability, but then on the other hand, he hadn't taken Attilina's katana, so there was some semblance of freedom left them. Conway sank to a pile of dingy cushions and let his back sag against the hide wall. Here it was decorated with a vile purple sorde with a worm in its beak. He supposed they could slice their way to freedom and jump an unknown distance to the ground and flee into the night, but that seemed a little on the futile side, so he just sat and tried to think, without thinking too much. Attilina had no inclination of letting him rest.

"What did he mean, Island of the Flyers? They're as human as you or me."

"He said 'Flies'."

"What's the difference?"

"The difference is that we're in trouble."

"Oh goody!" Her hand slicked back her black hair, and continued back to caress her sword hilt. "Maybe I'll get to kill a few of them. What's a fly?"

"It's a mythological beast, like a beetle, sort of, it flies around and lives on carrion. I never understood why they fly, carrion can't escape, but that's the story." Conway sighed his very best sigh. She cared not, nor noticed.

"So?" The syllable dripped sarcasm and disdain.

"So flies are the companions of Him."

"Him, who?"

"Capital Aich Him. LLord's adversary."

"The Devil?"

"We never say that name on Angst."

"We're not on Angst."

He actually had to smile a very thin smile at that. "Well, even so, Him. People who use the name of His minions are up to no good in general, and mean us no good in particular."

She shrugged and sat on another pile of cushions, beneath a large eye inscribed on the wall in baby blue. "Are you sure?"

"You saw the symbol on their chests?"

"I thought it was two leaves and a berry maybe."

"No such luck." Conway looked across the room at the guard, who appeared to be half-asleep and totally oblivious. "Flies for sure. And looking at this room, I think they're wreckers." He shuddered involuntarily.

"You mean they lure ships onto this island and..."

"Kill everybody and loot the valuables....Probably. One thing for sure, there's been a lot of sails cut up to make this...this manse."

"So they will kill us as soon as they find it amusing." She smiled a very cold smile.

"Perhaps. Perhaps we're young enough to join the Flies...who knows." He turned words over in his mind and couldn't find any right ones. "I didn't see any other women...maybe they keep a harem. Maybe they don't like girls. Maybe they will let us go...in the morning."

"Maybe I'll get to kill somebody." She nodded with dour satisfaction.

"How many people have you killed, so far?"

"Well, it's not allowed, actually. But the sims are most realistic."

"What's a sim?"

"It's an orc or a demon or a stiff, some kind of enemy being. All the disneys have them. I've killed thousands." She shrugged and searched his face. "Don't worry. That's why I came down here to this lump."

"Oh, I'm not worried. Impending doom always makes me calm."

"Are you mocking me?"

"Perish forbid."

She leaned tensely toward him and bit off a sentence. "Listen up, lump, I didn't spend my whole life exercising under a gravity and a quarter, to truckle under to any bunch of lightweights like these."

"Huh...what?"

"You lumps are all light in the loafers. I could go through this whole planet like a knife through butter."

"If I knew what you were talking about, I might share your confidence. What's butter?"

"I told you...I'm into Hisports...Historical Sports. I'm the greatest swordsman in this whole Solar System." Her voice hissed with emotion. "Your wimpy little mud ball is less than two thirds of an Earth, what you call olearth, gravity. I've trained in a centrifuge at a full gravity plus a quarter." She snapped a finger at his shoulder. It felt like he had been pecked with a psallie's beak. "I may look like a little girl, but I'm probably the strongest person on this whole dirtball planet."

He couldn't think of anything to say...except. "Well, in that case, I'll follow your lead."

Satisfied, she sank back into the cushion. At least he began to suspect that his eyes had not been playing tricks on him back at the Sailback. She could move faster than the eye could see. He wasn't as reassured as he might have been.

They were left alone for only a half a glass or so, until Hignore bustled back in; the room swaying beneath his tread. In the lamp light his feathered cape and sequined headdress appeared dingy and befouled, and his person was revealed as pudgy and unclean. The two made no mention of these flaws in grooming; feeling that forbearance was a virtue in these circumstances. Hignore was affable again and complimented them on the quality of their guest gift. He led them along a maze of runways in the trees, all made of madly decorated sails, a kaleidoscope of heraldry, each room and hall packed and cluttered with rich, tattered, furnishings and loot of all descriptions. Some rooms were more or less devoted to weapons or preserves or clothing, for example, but the more usual plan was hodge podge interleaved with higildy pigildy. The complex was by no means on a level, and corridors and rooms debouched into one another without plan or by-you-leave.

Eventually they reached a larger room, or perhaps it was a node of intersections of rooms entering at all angles and levels until there was a space perhaps half the size of the lamented Sailback, back on Ainsworth.

Quite a bit of the area was draped with hammocks and walkways and rope ladders so that it had a resemblance to a cobweb or to the muzzy interior of a fanchion nut. Apparently all the Flies were assembled here, totaling a dozen or two. It was hard to be sure, for they were in constant motion and constant conversation. Conway wondered what a few dozen boys all permanently living together could have to talk about so vivaciously. He hadn't learned that for many people, the less there is to talk about, the more there is to say.

There was a hogshead of quaff broached about halfway down one side, with a cluster of Flies in attendance. Hignore ushered them over to a lower level, where there was an arrangement of Fane furniture and furnishings. There three Flies, slightly older and more ornately dressed than the rest, were heating some mixture in a brazen vessel obviously looted from some altar somewhere. Hignore viewed the proceedings with a supervisory eye, and muttered cryptic questions to the three acolytes. They had a collection of leaves, powders, and beetle parts around them, and would judiciously taste the brew and add a pinch of this or that unrecognizable ingredient, and stir vigorously.

Finally, the brew reached a sufficient viscosity or color and a spoonful was offered to Hignore for his approval. He supped judiciously, smacked his fat lips and nodded approval. Suddenly Conway noticed that the room was still and all eyes were on the chieftain of this motley band. It seemed that the shank of the evening was at hand. Hignore turned to the expectant crowd, raised the carven bone ladle over his head and gestured grandly.

"Faithful Flies...Honored Guests...the Soam is of proper piquancy...all is well...I, your Wizard and Panarch, declare this Revel must commence."

He waved the ladle once more and the Flies lined up, as well they might, along the walkways, and up the shroudlines to receive their Soam. Each took a ladle full and Hignore improved the occasion by taking nips off of his subject's doses. Each Fly shuddered and spat at the taste, but none refused his ration. Conway decided to try and miss his allotment and tried to convey this decision to Attilina, but she seemed excited at the prospect of a party, and would not catch his eye. He was left to conclude that she was as grown as she was liable to get, all things considered, and he had no control over anybody's actions except his own. Or was that "hopefully" his own?

In the event, he managed to only wet his lips with the Soam. That was enough to make them tingle and burn. Hignore was intent only on taking his sup of each ladle full, and maintained his grip on the ceremonial spoon, the better to control each Fly's dose. Every one's except Attilina's, of course.

She swaggered up, regardless of the floor's swaying beneath her feet, and stared solidly into Hignore's eyes until he actually handed her the ladle. She drained the first dose, and dished herself out another before handing it back to the Head Fly. She showed no effects from the draft, did not shudder, and only wiped her mouth with the back of her left hand. She nodded once, eyes still locked with Hignore and walked off to examine the clutter of loot stacked against the dragonhide walls of the strange nest in the trees. She had been the last in line and Hignore scraped the bottom for one more slosh, as his minions separated into groups.

Most gravitated down the ladders to the quaff barrel, but Conway noticed a few slide over to an anteroom and select musical instruments from a clutter in a corner.

Naturally he had to investigate, even if it meant he had to turn his back to the majority of the Flies. To his blinkered vision it was worth it. He had little actual choice, anyway. He had become a fanatic, without ever noticing, slightly after he learned his first song on the lukette. The Flies had accumulated a motley assortment of instruments, most much the worst for wear.

Each of the Flies scooped up the first instrument that came to hand, and immediately began to blow into the tavesty and beat on the frame drums and tunangle without delay or, apparently talent. Conway had located a decent enough chuitar, lacking only a single string. He tried to tune up to the others, but soon discovered that they weren't in tune and had no intention of getting there. They just made such noises as their instruments provided and were happy.

Conway was less so. He huddled into the corner and tried to become invisible behind his instrument. It seemed to be as good a place as any. He had about half an idea to wait until the party got rolling good and sneak off. One always requires a plan, no matter how futile. A few more of the wreckers drifted over and began to scrape and hack at various tweedles and scorns.

They wore such expressions of bliss that Conway could only conclude that they were making exactly the sounds that they desired. His bafflement only increased when some more Flies began to spasm and twitch, more or less in unison, in a fashion that Conway eventually realized was supposed to resemble dancing. He was further shocked to see Attilina among the dancers. Her eyes were closed, her head thrown back, and she showed every sign of being in ecstasy. Although her motions were slower, she resembled the Suppliants of the Last Church back on Angst during the Lustral Fetes. Conway was already as scared as he had been since the Devout Sailback burned…was it only last night? He wished he could believe in something enough to pray to it.

He did notice that each Fly maintained the traditional topknot style of his home island, here the three jet beads of Isinggore, there the ruby feather of Biggard. He deduced from this that it was possible for males at least to join this merry band and become full-fledged Flies. He wondered if it was worth it. Simple escape seemed a better alternative.

Especially if he could also escape Attilina. Some how he knew this desire to be unworthy, but it was heartfelt. Without her he would be cuddled up in his coracle's tiny cabin, with nothing to worry about but getting broached by a moby. Ahhh…paradise.

In the center of the space, in a web of cordage, was a species of pulpit, decorated with the Flies' symbol and some of the choicer bits of loot. Hignore clambered up to this lectern, suspended like Mamet's Tomb, and used the carven ladle to strike a great spun bronze gong that hung behind his head. The reverberations caused most of the Flies to devote a portion of their attention to their leader. He swayed a little in his roost, whether from the effects of the Soam, or from the general flexion of the entire mad structure around him, Conway could not tell.

In fact, it seemed that the manse was swaying noticeably more than before and that certain creakings and groanings from outside might mean that the wind was up.

He resolved to keep an ear on the weather. A storm, not unusual at this time of the year, might help cover his escape, if escape was possible. He had hoped that the Flies would become drowsy from their imbibments, but instead they appeared to be more intense and active than before. He wondered what effects were likely from the Soam, but had no way of knowing. His thoughts were interrupted as Hignore began to speak.

"Welcome all, all our brothers and residents! I, Hignore, your beloved Wizard, welcome you to this, our Revel and Fete." He blinked nighternishly, belched, and tried to gather his thoughts about himself. "Decades ago, our Forebrothers liberated themselves from the chains and the oppresses of Smith, from the toils of the Archarch himself and came to this blessed isle to live and to prosper in the manner which Almighty Him has ordained. We weave not, nor do we spin, but Him Provides."

Hignore gave a mighty nod at the righteousness of this noble sentiment, the violence of which nearly dislodged him from his perch. He fluttered about until his equilibrium was restored, a series of flailings that gave him even more of a resemblance to a chubby, befuddled night tern in its nest. Conway was not reassured by the wizard's air of fuddlement. He had seen an equally ineffectual Older back on Angst sentence a child to a dunking for crying in Fane. The Wizard of the Flies smoothed his feathers, grasped his train of thought in both hands and continued.

"Our Forebrothers, as I have stated, fled the oppressions and entitlements of the Despot of Smith and came to this blessed isle, here to establish the freest, most egalitarian society that has ever graced the Fair Seas of beautiful Munge…Or indeed that shall ever so grace these rolling billows."

This sentiment brought a ragged cheer from those Flies still coherent enough to react to even the most obvious cues.

Immediately in front of Conway, the alleged musicians continued their alleged music, and the dancers spasmed as before. At least they now were facing their leader. Fortunately for them, Conway supposed, they noble leader was even more oblivious than they were. He continued with his oration, and Conway felt in his spoan for his knife. Outside, the wind increased another level, and the creakings and groanings of the mad manse increased.

Hignore raised his voice to match the tumult outside and the Flies picked up the tempo of their raspings and bleatings. Almost all the Flies had abandoned the quaff barrel and were variously clustered below Hignore, or gathered in front of the musician's alcove, moving spasmodically to the noises of their fellow Flies.

Out of the corner of his eye, Conway noticed that Attilina was right there the thick of the press, twitching and jerking with the best of them. Conway decided to ease down the lowest level of this maze and to cut a peephole in the hide floor and to see what might be seen. It was still eight glasses to dawn, and the quicker he was in his coracle the better. No one seemed to be able to see much past his own eyelashes, and as the sages spoke, there was "No time as precious as the eternal now".

He rose, still clutching the chuitar as protective coloration, and gently wound his way through the crowd of dancers. He couldn't think of another word for what they were doing, but really couldn't consider their jerking as dancing. His mind kept veering off on tangents, as if it was unwilling to face the seriousness of his current actions. He had always considered himself a timid, even fearful person and felt no need to redefine his personality. Actually he was indifferent to danger as such; he just, like most overly bright people, tended to think too much and act too little.

He sidled from the cluster of dancers to the clot of Flies that were apparently spellbound by Hignore's speech. Now, the wizard was expounding on the beauties of the Flies' social contract, and the phrase "from each according to his strength, to each according to his appetites" brought another ragged cheer from the minions. To Conway's sensitive ear, there seemed to be a mocking note to the applause, but he was ill inclined to point this insight out to the assembled revelers. He tried to stiffen his gait and glaze his eyes to match that of the others in that nest and determined that he would try for the quaff barrel as an alibi for his movements.

He obtained his goal after a few more cheers from the Flies and was greeted by the crowd of serious quaffers still around the convivial butt.

"Hola, Stranger...Welcome to the Manse....Great revel, no?"

This Fly was perhaps a little older than most, stouter and redder of face than his companions. He filled a jack and thrust it into Conway's feeble grasp and refilled his own goblet for good measure. "Welcome, drink up. I'm Sykx, and this is Codi and that's Jarvic." He slapped Conway on the shoulder, making him slosh a gout of quaff from his jack, and guffawed jovially. His red face and well rounded belly left little doubt as to his major interest in life, just as the copper ring in his hair, similar to Badmash's back on Angst, left little doubt but that he was a native of Smith, perhaps even from the Caliabu Peninsula.

Conway wasn't sure if the alcohol in the quaff counteracted the drugs in the Soam, or if these veteran quaff-faces had taken only a token of the communal bowl. It was obvious that this bunch was a lot more coherent and observant than their fellows at the upper levels of the mazy room were. Sykx drained his jack with a mighty swig and mightier eructation. He dipped his jack in the barrel, regardless of the husks and chaff floating on the surface, and swilled again, and then indicated his leader with and expansive sweep of his jack.

"Goes on, don't he though…Tell a man every thing but what he needs to know."

Conway took the bait; "And what do I need to know?"

"Well," Sykx wiped his loose lips and considered a moment. "Well, he's going to invite you in to our merry band. You're definitely Fly material….It's a great life…all the quaff you can drink and Soam once a moonth…the loot is good, and now and then we get some."

"Some what?"

Sykx winked and dug an elbow into Conway's ribs. "You know. Some."

"Oh…Some.'

"You get it. It sure is fun…sometimes they last for weeks." He turned and questioned Codi; "How long that bint from the Knowles last? A moonth?"

"Little less…course she didn't move much after the first two weeks." Codi was a scrawny rascal with a squint eye. "I like that better when they fight."

"Yeah, Brother!" Sykx turned back to Conway and winked again.

"Sometimes Old Stepe will send us a ship load of bints from Smith, but they ain't as much fun, as the ones we capture fair and square."

Codi cut in, confidentially, with the air of a man sharing secrets. "Old Stepe buys stuff from us. Sometimes he pays with moneys, some-times with quaff, some times with bint. We don't have too much use for moneys."

"Got nothing to buy with moneys for true. Him provides." Sykx made the Sacred sign of Him, left thumb to right nostril, fingers spread. His bother Flies responded in kind. Conway followed suite after a second's hesitation. He had more to worry about than simple blasphemy.

"That one come with you looks like she would last a good while." Jarvic put in. "She's nothing to you, is she?"

"No….she just hired my coracle."

"She's an odd one," said Jarvic, dubiously.

"It don't matter, how odd," stated Sykx, confidently. "Once we blanket her, you'll see she's just like all the rest."

Conway was tempted to ask the obvious question, but another Fly spared him the effort. What ever else the Soam did, it certainly released inhibitions. "What we do, is put the lights out, sudden like, and every brother has a blanket, and we wrap'em up in the blankets."

"Wrap up the top end, any way." Sykx, and laughed coarsely. Conway got the picture. He felt some emotion, but whether it was fear or disgust or even pity for Attilina couldn't determine just at the moment. Whatever, he wanted no part of this evening's program. However the party resolved, he decided to flee as soon as the lights went out. He felt a lot more secure in the Spacer girl's competence with her sword, than in his ability to partake of the Flies' plans. His only real loyalty was to his personal corpus. Outside, the storm continued, the Manse's supporting trees creaked and swayed in time to the rising wind. Splatters of heavy rain, or perhaps hail occasionally beat at the dragonskin roofs and walls. Nobody seemed to notice.

"Yes, Conway, we need a man like you. You could lead the orchestra. Isn't it unique?"

"That's exactly the word I would have chosen." Conway held the jack to his lips, but drank not. It couldn't be much longer until the blanket party started. He wanted to warn Attilina, but didn't want to get into trouble. More trouble. He decided to go back up and join the musicians and await eventualities. He pretended to refill his jack and nodded to the Flies and climbed back up to the musician's loft. There he kept his head down and pretended to contribute to the festivities. He practiced runs and scales, it really didn't matter. One note went as well as another with the cacophony the Flies produced. The dancers still danced, the players played, and the quaffers quaffed.

Above the fray, Hignore still orated. Occasionally the audience cheered his efforts. None of these activities seemed to relate to each other, and Conway wondered if he was losing his mind by trying to make sense of all this madness. It seemed that he must be the maddest of them all, for he was certainly the only one who worried about the incongruity around him. The creaking and groaning of the mad structure increased and the dancers were forced to incorporate the building's movements into their spastic choreography. It didn't seem to bother them, but Conway had just about had enough of the whole affair. He set down his chuitar, and quietly tipped his jack of quaff into the cushions of a wicker settee nearby. He needed an excuse to visit the quaff barrel. Perhaps he could inquire the way to the jakes. On the surface of Munge, people deposited their by-products casually, leaving the beetles to dispose of the residue, but such was clearly not the custom up in this tree dwelling. Conway supposed that there were actual facilities for waste, such as were provided for in crowded structures, such as inns, or areas with some pretensions of gentility, like Fanes. The beetles got everything anyway, but some people insisted on proprieties.

Anyway, he decided that there was no sense in waiting. Things could only get worse. He caught a glimpse of Attilina's face through the cluster of dancers, and the ecstatic, vacant smile on her face convinced him that she was of in some land of her own and was unreachable by mere mortals. He had never seen her smile before, unless she was talking about killing something, and so...

He rose and wended his way through the dancers, and just as he passed behind her, there was a sudden cessation of movement and wind noise. All human sound stopped, as if every Fly held his breath simultaneously. Each looked around him with wide eyes, as if their instincts were shouting incomprehensible messages into their inner ears. Conway grabbed Attilina's left hand, without thought, and fled through the crowd, with only one direction in mind.

He wanted to be on solid Munge. He didn't want to be there soon, he wanted to be there already. He wanted to have been there for hours.

Attilina snapped a look into his face, and perhaps saw something there that froze the glazed smile on her lips. Whatever she saw, she didn't resist his tug, but followed behind like a lost child. Conway tried to slip through the throng, without touching any of the Flies, without provoking their chase reflex. They all stood motionless, waiting for instruction, perhaps, and Conway slithered down the slanted floor and into the first convenient opening.

This hallway also trended down, although it was cluttered with all manner of furnishing and loot, great piles of bales and crates and drums of unknown import. Conway grouped out his knife and slashed at a wall beneath a lamp as he ghosted past. He had barely enough wit to slash along the aktins, the integral stiffeners of the dragonhide, and not against them. The tension of the fabric immediately tugged open a gash in the wall, and Conway glimpsed the ground in the moonlight, uncomfortably far below. Behind him, in the assembly room, there was a babble of pursuit that was cut short by a great resonant crack, and a lurch of the whole structure. The two scrambled to maintain their footing and were forced to fend off from the wall as the hallway they were running down twisted at an acute angle to the ground. Lamps spilled behind them, and tongues of flaming fish oil spread down the acutely slanted walls. They rounded a corner and slid into a junction of three more pathways, just as the floor dropped beneath their feet. Conway chose the steepest downwardly slanting hallway.

The building lurched again and a tumble of boxes and buckets cascaded down the hallway to their left. Conway scampered amongst the rampaging clutter, swerving to avoid a leathern trunk that shed silks as it rolled into his path. He realized that the hallway was collapsing before them and started taking long lunging strides, almost floating off the resilient floors and walls. Perforce he released Attilina's hand, but she was finally aware of her surroundings and scampered and bounded behind him. Their mode of progress became a dreamlike series of ricochets from wall to floor to corner to alcove, as the angle of the collapsing Manse increased. Here they would swing on a lamp bracket to check their speed, only to drop madly down a room that was rapidly becoming a shaft.

Where ever possible they would slide and stride down inclines, mostly on their feet, but frequently on their rumps. It was a nightmare progression and seemed as if it would never end. But it had to, they weren't that high off the ground, and end it did in a crumple of cloth and leather and broken branches, at the end of a long slide across a large room that was crumpling around them like a house of cards. Attilina landed hard, but sprung to her feet, katana in hand, and cast only one look over her shoulder at the avalanche of furniture that was following them down the slide, before she slashed mightily at the dragon hide wall that imprisoned them.

The sword rebounded from the wall, and she looked at it dumbly as the wave of loot bore down on them. Conway had not sheathed his hand long blade, and it was as sharp as only a sailor keeps a knife, and he slashed smoothly at the wall along the direction of the reinforcing aktins. The wall obediently slit open and Conway and Attilina darted on through, just before the pile of smoldering wreckage descended on the spot they had vacated.

Conway waited not, but scampered away from the collapsing Manse as fast as he could scamper. It was just pre-dawn and there was barely enough light to find a clear path through the incredible maze that was falling around them. There were snaps and splitting noises as the ropes and anchors that had held the manse in place pulled away from the tree limbs that supported them.

Lines snapped through the air like whips and pieces of debris and small limbs and leaves whirled around them as they fled. There was one ultimate crash behind them and all was still. It sounded final, but they didn't stop their flight until they were sure they were clear of all danger.

Finally they found a clear spot and turned to see what might eventuate now. Now in the gray light, they could see that the Manse of the Flies had been built around one magnificent eldar tree, with runnels and extensions attached to other lesser forest giants. The snap they had heard had been breaking of the main trunk of the great eldar, and as it fell, it pulled all the extensions of the Manse out of the surrounding trees and flung them to the rocky ground. Only the immense strength of the dragonhide lashings had slowed the collapse long enough to allow them to reach the ground safely. A few tendrils of smoke rose from the wreckage, before being whipped away by the wind, and Conway could see no organization that would prevent the inevitable fire from roasting any trapped Flies.

Watching, Conway discovered that his legs were trembling so violently that he could barely stand. He stumbled over to a nearby eldar, and grabbed a convenient branch, and held on to it until he felt he could go on. The collapse had finally stopped and all was silent except for the diminishing wind.

Attilina spoke; "Whipping party. I liked the music. It was like home." She smoothed back her hair and sheathed her blade. "What shall we do for excitement now?"

"Let's get in my coracle and go away."

"That's not very heroic of you."

"You stay and fight then."

She whipped her head around and glared at him. "I might just."

"Have fun. I'm going to Smith."

"Says you."

He was just about to snap a reply when they became aware of a chittering behind them. They turned to look, and saw a solid wave of something dark flowing toward them across the forest floor.

Conway was trying to imagine what kind of liquid the Flies might have stored in their Manse to produce such a wave, when Attilina said; "Urrugh! Bugs. Millions of bugs!" And the wave resolved into a solid carpet of scavenger beetles fleeing from the wreckage of the Flies' headquarters. Apparently the giant eldar that had supported the tree house had been hollow and filled with beetles. Normally they were harmless, but they would eat almost anything, and the two humans were in no mood for entomological research. Especially not from the inside of a myriad of beetle bellies. Attilina turned and fled, and Conway was right behind her. When in doubt…run.

CHAPTER 6

▼

They ran, more or less blindly, until they reached the shore. They had no idea where their coracle might be, except that it was on the beach some place. Conway thought for a moment and decided that their best bet was the north lee shore. The sky was overcast with the tail of the storm, but they could tell that the sun was lifting from the Pancreatic Sea directly before them….So, that meant that they were on the east coast of Fly Island. That made it easy. Turn left and go north. It was a small island, and hopefully any surviving Flies would have more to worry about than two escaping "guests". As they walked up the line of sea wrack, they thought to see a flicker of red light through the woods, and they hoped it was flames consuming the ruins of the Manse.

A few flongs later, it was full day, a gray day to be sure, but the sun was beginning to creep out from the cloud cover. It might have been the last storm of the rainy season. Conway chose to regard this as a good omen, even though he didn't believe in omens. Psigils regarded it as just another day and went single-mindedly about their business of plunging into the surf for their sustenance. Inland, assorted dactyls chattered among the bushes and flying snakes whopped from tree to tree, as was their wont. The business of nature assured Conway that they were unobserved. He allowed himself an iota of hope,

They crept into the woods a little deeper, as the very possibility of escape made them more cautious. Finally, Conway saw the prow of his coracle peeking out from a bimbleberry copse. He sighed a great gust of relief, but it had barely passed his lips when there came a whistle behind them and Hignore and five of his henchmen stepped out from a screen of bamb. Conway heard the 'wheep' of a blade leaving its scabbard behind him. There was no need to turn, and two of Hignore's boys had cocked crossbows in hand. Conway really couldn't think of anything helpful to say, and Hignore was likewise reticent. Perhaps he had missed breakfast. Some people let the slightest disturbance of their daily routine turn them all surly. Certainly he looked surly. Surly, disheveled, and singed around the edges. He had lost his ornate headdress and feathered cloak and was mostly clothed in soot and char. He had retained his sword, however.

He used it to encourage his lackeys, who quickly tripped Conway, and threw him to the yellow sand. Three of the Flies surrounded Attilina, who raised her hands over her head and backed toward a large tree, casual like. Two more of the Flies produced a raw drake hide and soaked it in the sea. Every body seemed to know what was expected of them; Conway expected to die, slowly.

The two Flies dragged back the hide from the surf and spread it flat on the sand. Two more dragged Conway over and plopped him down on the slimy leather. They forced his hands down to his sides and deftly wrapped him up in the stretchy wet hide, pulling it as tight as possible and smoothing it down over his body. The slimy cold hide adhered to itself, and the Flies neatly tucked in the loose ends. He had a sinking feeling in his gut as he realized what they were about to do to him. He wondered that he could be so calm. After all, they were killing him. He supposed that it didn't really matter, in the larger scheme of things, but felt a massive disappointment that he would never, in fact, learn to play the chuitar, after all. It all seemed so futile...All because he forgot to bring limes. It didn't seem worthwhile to protest, much less scream. Who was there to help?

Hignore stood over the roll and tried to strike one of his poses, but the effort was a bit too much for his hungover state. He opened his mouth, winced and then just nodded and directed his minions to roll

Conway out into the sunlight. There was no real need for words. They both knew what would happen as the leather dried and shrank. Conway would slowly find it impossible to expand his ribs enough to breathe and would therefore expire. The clouds were burning off and the day promised to be a fine one. Conway supposed that he should be grateful, but all in all, he would just as well that it would rain.

He was hopelessly swathed in the wet leather, with only his head protruding.

Hignore cast him a significant glance and spat full in his face, and then turned his attention to Attilina. Conway craned his neck and could see that tableau as before; Attilina backed up against a sagamore tree's rough bark, with her hands over her head, under the threat of three crossbows. Hignore sidled around the tree trunk and slipped her blade from its sheath. He was ever so careful to not expose himself to any possible danger. He examined her blade, sneered and cast it into the bimbleberries. Then he brutally kicked her out away from the sagamore, and the rest of his Flies pounced on her with blankets and lengths of rope. In a few moments she was a shapeless bundle with only her legs protruding. Hignore ripped the black cloth pantaloons from around her legs and jerked her to her feet. Conway thought he had never seen legs quite so white, ever before.

One of the other Flies, perhaps his name was Wylox, asked, "Why stand her up, we just gotta push her down again?"

Hignore spoke his first words of the ambush. "Take her to the catacombs. This sun makes my head hurt. I want to nap after we get some."

"Some?" whooped Wylox. "We're gonna get it all!"

This rather feeble joke produced a chorus of guffaws from all the Flies except their leader. Conway hoped his head really hurt. He turned his own head so that he would not have to watch them walk away in triumph. Although it really wouldn't hurt them any, or help out his cause in the least. But it was about all he could do at the present. Or for the foreseeable future. The scuff of their feet submerged under the curl of the surf and the usual squirreling dactyl noises that one never heard until one listened, and Conway was left alone to his fate.

The sun was fully out now, and he lay there, considering his options. There didn't seem to be many. If he struggled, it would just draw the rawhide tighter and dry it out all the faster. He was trying to think, but it seemed such a futile exercise, that he amazed himself by falling asleep. It had been a long couple of nights, after all.

He couldn't have been out for more than a few moments, but when he woke, he had an idea. Thanks to Badmash's tutorial, he was more than familiar with all the properties of leather and dragonhide. In particular, the property that was going to stop his breath in a few glasses. Wet leather stretches, dry leather shrinks…Therefore….Very slowly and carefully, keeping his body as relaxed as possible, Conway rolled himself into the surf. The tide was coming in, fortunately enough, and the beach was quite flat. It was actually rather easy. All he had to do was to not panic or struggle. Easy.

He humped himself like a beetle larvae, and started his roll down to the water's edge. By flexing his body, he was able to angle his rolling just enough to keep his head out of the waves some of the time. It wasn't at all pleasant, but it was doable. Fortunately, he, like all Pancreats, was as at home in the ocean as on the land, and soon enough his body was floating in the gentle surf. He did manage to roll his ear onto a crenulated spinabugger and would have a swollen, itchy ear for most of a week, but that was contingent on gaining another week in which to itch.

All in all, it was a fair trade. Almost as soon as he got into the water the hide began to loosen and unroll. A few pins or a knot in the wrapping, and escape would have been impossible, but the Flies were used to shocked, shipwrecked victims and even their tortures were slack in the extreme.

It took almost to noon, and quite a bit of slow, careful rolling, and more than a few snootfuls of seawater, but finally he was free. He staggered up on the shore, leaving the rawhide for the amusement of the fishes, and went immediately and rooted around in the bimbleberry thorns until he found Attilina's sword. He really didn't know how to use it, but he really felt better with it in his hand. He felt even better still with a few mouthfuls of the nearly ripe, puce, berries in his belly. Now to escape.

He had pushed his craft almost into the surf, when some thing, some obstinate crevice or convolution in his brain made him stop his pushing and to look at the katana rebuking him from the cockpit. He cursed it, he sneered at it, and he tried to reason with it. But all it said was one word: "Coward."

"Of course I'm a coward....It's healthy to be scared. It's good for you. Makes the blood flow. Makes it flow in your veins and not out on the ground. I like being a coward. My whole family is composed of ptigions."

But it was no use. He knew it even as he tasted the words in his mouth. So he splashed around to the prow of the coracle and began to push it back on shore. Then he heard a familiar voice say; "Don't you want to leave? I thought you wanted to go to Smith."

"Attilina"

"Yeah…so what?"

"What happened to the Flies? Why aren't you…"

"After the first few had their fun, and God, were they ever inept, I convinced them that they would have a lot more fun with my cooperation."

"And?"

"And…So they took the blankets off, and we had fun together until they all felt it was time for a nap, and then I took a sword and killed them all."

"Just like that."

"Just like that. There were only eight of them. I woke Hignore up before I killed him. He deserved it."

Conway thought for something to say. "Are all women as ruthless as you?"

"I don't really know. I'm not all women. Seen my trou?"

"Over under that sagamore tree."

"Thanks. They have lots of goodies in that catacombs." She indicated a wyvvern skin bag in her left hand." I took some…If you want, we could go back and pillage some more."

"Did you see any food?"

"No. Not really."

"Let's go to Smith. I'm hungry."

"Plan." She nodded agreement. "Me too."

Together they pushed the coracle into the water. This time Attilina showed no hesitation about clambering over the gunwale, and settled herself in the stern sheets with the air of a person who has spent the morning in worthwhile labor. Conway thought she looked little the worse for wear, considering. He set the sail, and lashed the tiller, and dropped the plankton net over board, and all was as it was before they landed on the island of the Flies. Externally, at least.

"May I ask you a question?"

"I have one for you too."

"You first."

"OK. I'll bite." She furrowed her brow and searched for words. "Were you…You were pushing the coracle back on shore. Why?"

"I was coming to look for you."

"Why?"

"I don't really know." He hesitated, waiting for words to well up into his mouth. "I just felt it was the right thing to do, I guess."

"What would you have done?"

"Snuck up and tried to get you lose from them, I suppose."

"Do you like me that much?"

The answer leapt into his mouth so fast; he had to bite back the words. "No. I mean, I don't know. You're all right."

"For a girl?"

"For a…for being something I never met before."

"I guess that's honest enough." She said. He knew it wasn't honest at all, but stampeding axebeaks wouldn't have gotten any more out of him. She cut into his thoughts, letting him off the hook.

"What did you want to ask me?"

"When you killed those boys…did it bother you?"

"Did what bother me?" She was honestly puzzled.

"Killing eight people." Conway tried to keep his voice even.

"Oh that." He voice was flat, uninterested." Well…they smelled worse than the sims.…It was messy. They thrashed around more than I expected. Not an aesthetic experience. It was OK."

"Do these sims bleed, then?"

"Sure." She considered his face, as if plumbing the mysteries behind it. "What did you think?"

"I guess I thought they were just like…you know, animated dolls."

"No, that's not it at all. They're more or less human. Humanoid bodies, with a link to the computer brain. They aren't beings. They have no minds." She considered her words and amplified. "Beings…people, are defined by having minds…intelligences. Bodies don't count. Many beings don't have bodies at all; or else change bodies…only the mind counts. That's been law since the beginnings of Homo Galactica. See?"

"I guess not. How can a person exist without a body? Are they ghosts?"

"We know of no immaterial life forms. A computer program can become a person. A person can be recorded into another medium. Brains, minds can be transferred from body to body, cyborgs and such." She looked him right in the eyes. "Bodies don't count. Trust me."

"They do down here. They're all we have." He decided to try and change the subject. "What's a computer?"

"It's an artificial brain. It runs on electronics or else biotech."

"I'm so ignorant. I don't know what half the words are you use. What's an 'lectronic?

"Electronics is the science of using electrons in circuits and things to make useful devices; computers, recorders, casters, just about everything." Before she could ask, she elucidated. "Electrons are the smallest quanta, little bits of...of lightning."

"Oh." This explanation left him less ignorant and more baffled. "Lightning."

"It's really simple, but it's not my field. Nobody studies stuff like that, anyway. Technology matured thousands of years ago. It's all applications now."

"Really?"

"Oh yeah. The action is in apps. Everything else is drudgery." She stared off into the green. "Computers design computers; have for millennia. People just live. Game or vid or art or sport or whatever...Real life...Apps...You know. They say that we live so long that we don't crave novelty anymore."

"Oh." Silence fell on the coracle, the profound silence of mutual incomprehension. Conway was content to listen to the slap of the waves, the luff of the sail and the occasional cry and splash of the feeding dactyls. As a matter of fact...It had been a long couple of nights. He checked his sheets and lines scanned the horizon and then crawled into the cubby with a muttered; "Wake me, please if you see something big enough to hit. I've had enough excitement for one day."

The last thoughts he had were that she was more of a monster than Blundoor and Rosialindia put together. She was either totally heartless, or so alien that her motivations were incomprehensible to him. Either way, he decided, she was poison...he would sooner mate with a sting skate...it would be safer.

She stared without sight at a flock of diving, feeding, purple mottled dactyls, and could only think that he had been coming back to rescue her. He could have escaped, but he had been coming back for her. For her! He cared about her. And the fact that he had an almost uncanny resemblance to the webstar Lance Resiste didn't hurt any either. All it would take was time, she was sure. His shyness made him even more attractive, in a way. He was so sweet. Not like the spacer boys who used her as an appliance. All it would take was time....

He woke just at sunfall, and watched a lemon yellow sun sink through blazing crimson orange clouds to a olearth green ocean, wishing he had more words for the colors he saw. Sometimes he felt such a fool to be so ignorant of the world's beauties. But, his stomach growled, and the plankton net was full and there was still some sourweed sauce in the cubby. He attacked the sea jelly with a will and his chitin spoon. Attilina could spare him only a single sneer, before she crawled into the cubby for her sleep. He watched her settle onto the pad with a mild, but total, lack of emotion. He wondered that he could have gotten so used to someone so strange in such a short time, but mostly wanted some limejuice and some time to practice his chuitar. He supposed he could dig out the lukette, but somehow it seemed it might cheapen his memories of the island of the Flies.

There were a few tiny crabs captured in the plankton, and he used these to bait a gang hook that he trolled hopefully behind the coracle. Probably get something to eat. Fish bit good at dusk. It couldn't be too much farther to Smith. One could hardly miss an island that size, even if it took a day of coasting to reach New Ahven. They herded axebeaks on Smith. He had had a skewer of axebeak meat once. He could remember it as one of the highlights of his childhood. He had money in his spoan and a hunger in his belly. How convenient. Now all he needed was some land and some people. Perhaps they had inns on Smith. But for the moment, he was as content as he ever got. He never had had much acquaintance with joy, usually a simple lack of pain was sufficient to satisfy him, and at the moment, he was satisfied.

And later, around midnight, when he saw the first lights of Smith come over the horizon, he was in serious danger of being pleased with himself.

But then he was faced with one of those mariner's decisions, that can range from mildly aggravating, to life and death, and the poor sailor is never sure which it is going to be until it is too late. If he anchored, or lay offshore, he stood a good chance of getting run down by a larger vessel. If he lay into land, he faced all the dangers of an unknown shore, and unknown people, in the dark. He dithered for another glass and then the hunger in his belly and the lights of shore made his decisions for him. He had never seen so many lights. The clear yellows of the fish oil lamps of the well-to-do offset the smoky reds of the poor's candlefish. There were many, many colored lights, also, russet and amber and even blues and greens and purples, from expensive glass globes. He couldn't think of any other reason for so many lights so late at night, except that they indicated taverns or inns.

His mouth was watering so badly he almost retched, and his ears hummed with the lack of music. Now that he thought of it…perhaps there was a suggestion of a tune, a wisp of timbre on the evening breeze. He couldn't resist. He called out to Attilina, and she rustled awake in the cubby. He needed her eyes. He came about and slanted down the wind for the thickest cluster of lanterns. He was sure he could hear music now, even over the spacer girl's mutterings. He felt like he was going home, and that was odd, because he knew quite well that he had no home. No home in this world no more. And, he reflected, neither did his passenger. It was the first time he had thought that he and she might have anything in common.

In the event, he had no decisions to make: a few flongs from land he was accosted by a hail from the dark and a beam of light from a dark lantern.

"What ship? Where faring?"

"It's just me and my coracle…from Ainsworth…" The words sounded incredibly stupid even as they left his lips and he wished he could recall them and stuff them back down his ignorant gullet. But the voice made no comment on his callowness, and remained professional, even bored.

"Do you have a name?"

"M-M-M-M-y name is Conway…I'm from East Angst. I have a passenger, named Attilina. "There was a long pause that ached for expiation. "We're looking for New Ahven. We're hungry."

There was a chuckle from the other craft that managed to be scornful and genial and bored all at once. "You sound harmless, and your navigation isn't too bad. This is the Ahvener Littoral Patrol. Heave to and accept a tow."

"Yes…thank you."

"You're welcome. The correct address is Patroller."

"Thank you…Patroller….Sir."

The dark lantern creaked shut and a masthead light was shuttered open. Their accoster was revealed as a twenty-man galley, all in black, with a single mast and a furled sail of no great expanse. Conway was very glad he had at least kept a civil, if ignorant, tongue in his mouth. There was a trio of indistinct figures on the poop; one setting a hailing trumpet in its rack, while another other shouted orders and the third started cadence on a deep toned wood block. As the galley neared, Conway noted with respect a torsion crossbow on the fore deck. It wasn't exceptionally large as such machines went, but it had a crew of three and looked able to shoot a bone shaft as long and probably half as heavy as he was. He tried to look harmless and even simpler than they already thought he was. He loosened the halyards and bundled his sail along the gunwhale.

As the galley neared, ram creaming the dark water, one of the catapult crew expertly cast a coiled line. Attilina was in the bow, and she clumsily caught it. He came forward and secured the line and then went midships to secure the sail. Attilina had the wit to seat herself and remain silent under the searching gazes of the six men standing on the decks of the galley. They were much of a muchness, all healthy, if overweight, young men in dark wrappas and vests. They seemed to have a goodly amount of metal about their persons, insignia and jewelry. Their hair shone, even in the faint lantern light, with pomades, and the copper bands of their topknots gleamed with polish. Their fine appearance was offset with the reek of sweat and bilges from the rowers on the benches, and Conway, innocent as he was, suspected that the penalties for not appearing innocent to the scrutiny of the Littorals could involve some strenuous exercise under less than optimum conditions. He bent his mouth to Attilina's ear.

"Better don't give these gentlemen any ill mouth."

She snapped her head around and glared at him, as if it was all his fault, but she did remain silent.

He continued, quietly. "You want to be a galley slave?"

She gave her head the barest shake. No.

"Well, be nice. And be ready to pay out some moneys."

"A bribe?"

"Probably they will call it a towing fee, or harborage, or something. Just smile and be nice."

"Grrr…" She growled, but obeyed. She might come from a culture that could destroy whole worlds, but that bolt in the crossbow wouldn't even slow down after passing through both of their bodies, and she had the wit to realize it. She relaxed and then he relaxed also.

There was not much else to the night. The Littorals efficiently brought Conway to a berth in the shabbiest part of the big harbor and accepted a surprisingly small gratuity and were on their way. The Sarnt in charge of the catapult was kind enough to direct them to a tavern; he called it a pub, which would serve food this late at night. Conway gifted him a copper for himself, and they set off up the road to the "Misericord Pub". Conway had to stop and examine the roadbed as soon as his feet left the timbers of the dock. It was covered with smooth stones! He had heard of such things, they were called paving, but he never….

Attilina tugged at his arm. "What's the hold up?"

"Oh, nothing. Stepped on something."

"C'mon…Hurry…I'm hungry…I wonder if they have cheese or steak."

"They have axebeak and sailback most likely."

"What are those, pray tell." Her voice was acid, expecting the worse, no doubt.

"Axebeak is a big, flightless dactyl. They're very good. Sailback are bigger and dumber and have four legs. Remember…sailback…The Devout Sailback?"

"I thought that was a joke. They're ugly."

"They eat good."

"Are you going to stand here all night? I'm hungry."

CHAPTER 7

▼

The sign of "The Misericord" was a peculiarly thin dagger or represen-
tation thereof, hanging from a beam in the gable over the wide, low
front door. In contrast to The Ains and the Angsts, buildings in New
Ahven had stout walls of cemented limestone, set in lime mortar. The
walls and their constituent stones were black with age and maroon
with mosses and lichen. The nocturnal beetles of the city appeared particularly robust and complacent, and Conway had to step around the
larger specimens, some of which must have scaled more than a lubb.
Attilina shied away from even the smallest of these scavengers, of
course. Odd that a person who could kill people so easily, could be so
skittish around these gentle insects. Conway spoke to this end.

"You don't have to be afraid of the beetles, you know. They mostly
only eat dead things."

"You know that and I know that, but do they know that?"

"Why do you let them bother you so much?"

She stopped in the russet light from the fan light over the pub's door
and regarded him as if he was some species of insect himself. Then she
relaxed visibly and answered; "That's not a smart butt remark?"

"No, it's not."

"Well, an honest question gets an honest answer. In the habs…in
space…everything that moves is either intelligent or controlled by
intelligence. We have no pets, no subclasses. There are robots, servos,
but they are likely to be remotes for some intelligence somewhere. I

don't like the idea of uncontrolled…creatures wandering around with no programming, no control."

"Is that why you didn't know what flies were?"

"There are no vermin in space. Only on planets. If I had realized how filthy…"

He had sense enough to hold his tongue at this. He tried to change subjects. "What's a robot?"

"It's a machine that acts or looks like a human."

"A machine?"

"Well, they call them machines…actually most are biotech. Machines haven't had moving parts since the space age began. The names stay the same even if the tech changes."

"Oh."

"Let's eat. I'm starved." She pushed her way into the crowded pub and Conway followed. He had taken only the first step when his nose was uplifted by the aroma of sizzling meat and quaff. The air was also thick with profanity and baccer smoke. Nobody smoked on Angst, it was forbidden, and only the Goodies smoked on the Ains, but here it seemed that every person had a stumpy clay pipe clenched in their teeth. The food bay was over to the left and they immediately bellied up to the moab wood counter, and tried to get the cook's attention. As they waited they perforce had to listen in to the many quaff fueled conversations that bathed them

"Arr. Times are out of joint, not when I was a tad…big storm a week after rainy season and the smeltling ain't running.…Man can't make a copper no matter what, and now hear there's a ship up to Murka Ahven that runs on steam…"

"Steam?" The questioner was younger, and wore the braided top-knot of Ravelli. "How could that be?"

"LLord only knows, but mark my words, it will lead to trouble. Always does."

"Everything leads to trouble…it's nature."

"What are you, some kind of philosopher?"

"Drink up and don't worry about it…Who's round is it this time?"

"Yours, I hope. If the smeltling don't run soon, I'll be rowing below decks for the Littorals."

"I'd rather go off to the Bluestem war, or ship off mobying,"

"All right for you young bucks, but what's an old man to do?"

"Drink up, and worry about it in the morning."

"Arr."

The cook, a sallow woman with warts, who was approximately the same size in every dimension, slapped two bowls of psallie stew on the counter, and turned to them. She didn't try to speak above the crowd noise, just waited impatiently for their pleasure. Conway spoke for them both.

"Do you have axebeak?"

"Hot, cold or limed?" Cookie had gold metal inlaid into her front teeth. Conway was so amazed that he had no inclination to question her about the food choices. What did it matter anyway?

"One of each, please."

"Sixty ginae." Conway handed her a copper, just as the distant stage erupted into familiar music. Cookie turned away, her hands flew, and she turned back with three arm long skewers in one hand and four slips of paper in the other. Conway was mystified, but in no mood to argue. He jammed the papers in his spoan and took the skewers of meat and fruit. One was glazed with red, one with green, and one was normal food colors, meat red and napple white, interspersed with translucent onions. His mouth was watering so badly that he couldn't have spoken anyway. So he sidled into and through the crowd, letting his ears drag him toward the stage. Attilina followed, still fuming.

Surprisingly, to a person of Conway's fanaticism, the only space in the big room was next to the stage. There was even a vacant table, and they seated themselves, and Attilina snatched one of the skewers from his hands, sneered at it, and chomped down. She had grabbed the red glazed one and immediately opened her mouth, stood up and slammed the meat down on the greasy table. She scurried off toward the bar, katana slapping at her shoulders. Burly men were thrust aside by her passage, took one look, and left well enough alone. Conway, curiously, picked up the discarded skewer and gingerly bit down. Hmmm. The glaze was a tasty mix of sourweed and chilies, probably crippens. Not bad.

He nipped at the other two, experimentally. The "cold" had only a taste of sourweed sauce and brine, and the "limed" was just that; lime and syrup glaze. He had just decided to offer Attilina her choice first, when she returned with two tankards of quaff. She sat and drained one, and belched like a sailor. She indicated the red skewer.

"That must be the hot?"

"Yes…the green is sweet and sour, and the cold has very little spice."

"I'll take that one." She picked up the plain skewer and began to gnaw on it, head turned sideways like a sorde with a bone. Conway picked up the red one and reached for the other tankard, but Attilina's hand cut him off.

"I didn't get you one. I was in pain."

"That's all right. I don't drink much." He said. He noticed that she didn't offer to get up and get him a drink, and he decided to not volunteer either. He just ate on his axebeak, and watched the band. He had thought it was his acquaintances from The Devout Sailback, The Wharfingers, but it was another Froust group, similar in instrumentation; two drummers, tavesty, cymballum, bass tamboura and sphrinx, but this band had in addition a chuitarist. He, no actually she, was as scruffy and as shock headed as the other six musicians. She was a slight, intense, girl, with nondescript hair and all Conway could see of her face was a slant of cheek bone and a purse of lip, and she played with her head cradled in the waist of her instrument, but there was something about her that dragged at his attention.

Her playing was not as rock steady as Heoj's, but it was most adequate. Actually, as he listened it was more than that, there were little hesitations and graces that piqued his ear and urged the band's music on into slight eddies or byways that added an gleeful charm to the typical overseriousness of the Froust style. Conway finished the hot axe-beak and glanced at his companion for permission to eat the second, but she was rising to her feet.

"That was good, but not enough. Do you want another, too?"

"No thanks…but wait, ask if they have a plate of spurdads or some kind of fries, please."

"Sure…I'll buy this round."

"Thanks, Attilina. I'll just sit here and watch the band."

"That's fine. Right back."

Naturally he became so lost in the Frousted melodies that she had to slam his bowl of napple fries on the table to get his attention. He came to for the length of time it took his hand to establish a bowl to mouth circuit, and was gone again. The accents of the chuitarist were being accentuated, almost mocked by the frame drummer, and….

Attilina finished her skewer of cold and her third tankard of quaff, and started looking around for excitement. Most of the better-dressed men in the Misericord wore long curved blades depending down their backs from hooked epaulettes on their shoulders. The grips of these engraved swords were ornate and jeweled to an extent that actually had forced the swordsmith to extend the decorations a full span past the crescent cross hilts. Attilina was envious and contemptuous in equal measures. She decided that she needed a rack on the wall of her room to store a few of the more magnificent trophies that might come her way in her adventures. She didn't let her present lack of even a room disturb her musings. Actually she had quite a nice bag of lootage and Hignore's sword back in Conway's boat….Ahh, coracle. Now all she needed was a room, even a house of her own. Smith was reputed to be one of the larger islands on this benighted lump, perhaps….She turned to ask Conway a question, and noted he was fixated on the band. More exactly, he was fixated on one member of the band. Hurumph!

"Conway!" She punched his arm. "Where are we going to sleep tonight?"

"You slept all day." He pointed out, reasonably enough, it might seem.

"I want a place of my own, to sleep in to night. I hate sleeping in boats. I want a bath and I want to sleep without my clothes on for once."

"Oh. Is that important?" He had never slept in his clothes, except once when drunk. He peered around, very like a night dactyl in lamplight. He considered. He spoke.

"We're in an inn. Ask the landlord. They generally rent rooms. You have money. I'm going back to the coracle." He rose to his feet, and bowed politely.

"I'm tired and am going back to my coracle. I'll put your bag and stuff near the bow. Good Night."

"Wait!"

"For what?"

She thought quickly, all the while submerging her real desires. After all, he had spoken only truth and sense and logic. She hated him. "I'll walk you back and get my stuff. I don't want to tempt any thieves. It's late."

"Good thinking. I think I'll get another skewer of axebeak and a skin of limejuice for breakfast. Tomorrow, I want you to help me find the Aludium, and I'll help you find somewhere to stay."

"That would be nice. I'll meet you at the door." They left, with only minor diversions to various places of easement. Attilina cornered the landlord of the Misericord, who happened to be a woman, one Tchage Browling, and arranged for a room. She offered to pay for a room for Conway, but he felt like a hermit crab bereft of his shell, if he was too far away from his coracle. He felt that she would never understand, but whole families supported themselves from boats no larger than his coracle. It was, after all, all he had.

There was an ungraceful moment at the dock, with the east just beginning to yellow, but her pride and his ignorance managed to ease then through any rough spot. They made plans to meet at the Misericord for lunch, and went to their several reposes. Conway had one last thought that he should paddle out and catch the dawn tide, and away, but he was just too tired, and anyway, here he was, on Smith, right where he wanted to be. "Weren't plans wonderful things?"

He tumbled asleep, and all the shouts and bustle of the morning fishing fleets awakening, and the creaking and squeaking of their cordage and the flocks of blue tailed sagitaries setting out on their daily forage, disturbed his slumbers not a tittle.

In the nooning, he dragged himself out of the cabin, and rescued his chuitar from its double wrappings, even before breakfast. All was well with his precious ironwood box, and he allowed himself almost a glass and a half trying to capture the piquancies he had heard in the young woman's playing of the night before. Try as he might, the exact timing escaped him, and this frustrated him enough that he remained oblivious of the real progress he was actually making.

Finally he packed up his chuitar in a single bag and slung it over his shoulder, and set off to try and find Attilina, and/or some breakfast. Or lunch. He felt easy as to definitions, as long as the quantity was sufficient. She was, in fact holding down a table in the Misericord, but that establishment had no one on duty to cook them any repast, at this hour. They were directed to the Greeble Inn, just down the street, and there Conway was pleased to find the young Frousthead of the night before, and most of her band, engaged in a major refueling stop, instruments leaned up against their legs and scattered around nearby tables. The food was cheap and plentiful, if light on meat. Conway ordered spurdad soup and brot pudding.

Conway was trying to gather enough nerve to actually talk to the band, when the tavestist noticed his chuitar bag and invited them over for breakfast. There was a flurry of introduction, out of which Conway only retained the name of the female chuitarist, which was Cynchie. He was so pleased with this information, so easily obtained, that he was quite oblivious of the pure hate that sparked in Attilina's eye. Cynchie bore the light of day with ease, and was, indeed a decent looking young woman, of the type that will remain much the same regardless of years or children until she suddenly is revealed a quite an old woman, bony and sharp-eyed as any dactyl, and people realize that her whole life was just a preparation for old womanhood.

But that unveiling was decades in the future, and this morning, she was the life of the table, intense, vivacious and witty. She didn't actually eat a meal, but seemed to be content with tidbits filched from everyone else's plates. Conway was smitten, and was a long time realizing that almost every other male that Cynchie ever met was equally mad about her. Attilina hated her on first, second and all subsequent sights. Cynchie apparently never noticed.

Of course she apparently never noticed the effect she had on men and boys either. But then again, she never had to carry moneys about her tiny person. Some one, some male one, was always there to provide a plate of spurdads, or a tankard of fripperies, to her taste. She was quite a girl, and was quite aware of it. Only her passion for music above all else saved her from being the center of dozens of duels. Any man who made himself too obvious a fool for Cynchie found himself gently left in the lurch, while she managed to recruit a half dozen other boys to help her play some serious tunes.

Tunes were the order of conversation this morn; tunes and gossip, proving that musicians were at heart, persons, and Conway sucked up this elixir through both earholes as if it was the fabled Blam of Glad itself. Attilina, less interested in who had just traded his girlfriend in on a new trebuchet horn, perforce had to examine the interior of the tavern for amusement. The design motif involved many representations of peculiar creatures; small, squat, hairy beings apparently equipped only with large pleading eyes and furry feet. These creatures were depicted painted on boards, or constructed, perhaps stuffed, in three dimensions. They looked imaginary to Attilina, but one never knew. She wished, not for the first time that she had paid a little more attention in her Planetary Studies classes back up on Abaraxis.

Finally there was a pause in the flow of conversation, and Attilina seized the moment. "These creatures." She waved a hand at the depictions." Are these real?"

"Real whats, darling?" The speaker was a tall ungainly lout, otherwise occupied in drawing cartoons on the table top with spilled swill.

"Animals, of course." Attilina had the serious adolescent's aversion to being mocked. Especially by her inferiors. The tall youth wore no sword, so he was by definition, inferior.

"Oh...these." His gesture was the very essence of languid indifference. "These, dear," He drawled. "These are genuine Greebles, the larval form of musicians. I," He indicated himself. "Was a Greeble. These," Another sweep of his arm. "Were all Greebles, once." When Attilina bristled, he affected not to notice.

He expounded. "If you doubt my word, just ask anyone."

His companions were quick to uphold his veracity. "Oh, yeah. I'm a Greeble."

"Sure, me too."

"Yup, yup, yup."

"Unhuh, Greebles...that's us."

"N-n-n-n-no bout a doubt it, we're all Greebles, yup, yup yup."

Conway, realizing that they had fallen into a very old joke collapsed onto the table, laughing as he had never laughed since his mother had died, if then. He couldn't help himself; it was as if something had broken inside him. He glanced up at Attilina, to share his joy, and the sight of her stern, rigid face set him off, even deeper into pyroxems of totally ridiculous glee. His convulsions served to turn the chorus of synthetic agreement around the table into genuine hilarity and soon several of the musicians were slapping each other on the back in efforts to regain their breath. Attilina's chair scraped back as she stood. She spoke not a word, but stalked out, clutching a few tatters of her dignity around her. The table erupted into the final stages of terminal silliness and then the lanky boy capped the event by falling backwards out of his chair. It took several pitchers of quaff to even begin to restore order, but eventually, some semblance of decorum was imposed, without having to call the Wards.

Conway bought the first pitcher, and thereby cemented his status as a worthwhile musician, and hail-fellow well met with the forward-looking younger set in the city of New Ahven, Smith.

Cynchie laid a gentle hand on his shoulder, and asked him if he thought he should go placate his woman, and bring her back for a drink or two.

"She's not my woman, not at all. She just hired me to bring her here in my coracle. She's just a…" His lips closed, while he pondered exactly what she was, and to whom. "She's just a traveling companion."

"Oh, I see. Are you not married?"

"Not at all. I'm just a lad. I'm out seeing a bit of Munge. I think I want to learn to make chuitars, and play them. I'm from Angst."

This admission meant little to the musicians. One asked if Angst was not west. Conway confirmed his mungiological correctness and the conversation veered off from theory to immediate matters, such as who was playing tonight. It seemed there was a bit of a problem. Cynchie had a constitutional inability to say no to a gig, and so, she was double booked for tonight. Her face lit up, and she lay one of those expressive hands on Conway's arm, again.

"You could take my place at the hex tonight, you could. It pays good and all you have to do is pump out the rhythm. You could do it!"

"Well, I…"

"Good! Then it's settled. Woody will be here at the fifth glass to pick me up, I'll meet you here and introduce you. It's easy. Woody always plays in La, so all you do is…"

"Just pump out the rhythm. Right." She had placed her other hand on his biceps as she pled, and Conway was incapable of negative speech. Or coherent thought, to tell the truth.

She was diverted by the sight of Conway's swollen ear.

"What ever did you do to your ear, dear?"

"A spinabugger."

"Most people step on them."

"Except for Cynchie, who sits on them…" Interjected the long tavestist. Cynchie slapped him, without ever losing her look of concern for Conway's ear.

"It's one of those long stories. I'm all right, really."

"Then it's all settled! My hero!" She kissed him on the cheek, most chastely, but it melted Conway's heart like moby blubber on a grill, and he was helpless. Unbeknownst to the happy pair, Attilina had chosen that moment to return and try to rescue Conway from the clutches of the musicians. She was familiar with the species, as she saw it. The habs were full of artist types, who chattered exactly like that table full of fools in the Greeble. Not at all like the worthwhile, measured conversations she and her hisports friends held in their wassails. The sight of slight little Cynchie's dry lips pecking at Conway's blushing cheek, did things to her entrails that she did not enjoy in the slightest. She went back outside, before she killed somebody. It wasn't that she didn't want to kill people, it just was that the Wards were in the tavern, tanking up for the afternoon shift. They were almost sure to disapprove of blood shed so early in the day. Spoilsports. She left them there, leather vested louts, with their massive flails of office leaned against the bar, and went off to sulk and plan revenge.

There was an edgesmith's a few paces down the road, and she managed to find a spot where she could observe the smith at his work, while keeping an eye on the front door of the Greeble. Surely that dolt Conway couldn't spend the whole aftermorning swilling quaff with his newfound friends. Surely he would remember her…And in the meantime she became fascinated with the play of light and sound from the smith's anvil.

He was folding and welding an ingot of white hot metal, and she found herself admiring the play of light on the flex of his muscles, the flicker of sparks against his sweaty hide. His wares were displayed in a rack near the door, ornate blades, rippled with damascene, and waved into fantastic shapes, but admirably deadly for all that. She had found Hignore's blade a crowbar, barely serviceable, but some of these blades cried out for her touch. They lacked hilts, that was the province of another artesian, but these blades seemed to whisper to her. "Me, I am the one. Take me, I will kill for you." It was all a fantasy, but it must serve until he left his newfound circle of friends.

And sooner or later he did leave, but it must be admitted, not with her in mind. Indeed, the sight of her glowering face gave him quite a start, and it took all his resources of self-possession to stroll toward her and say;

"Ah, Attilina, there you are. Ready to show me the Aludium now?"

She just turned and led the way, quite coldly. He followed all unaware. Fanatics are like that. Actually, she had no idea where the Aludium might be, but had not the slightest intention of letting him know that fact. She managed to ask directions after a crossing or two, without his noticing. She clutched this small victory to her side like a wolf cub, but he was all agog at the sights of the city of New Ahven and heedless of her moods.

The humblest buildings here in the center of the town were much larger than the Fane of East Angst. And the paved (paved!) streets intersected in spacious plazas and squares, many with public fountains or statues memorial to heroes of Smith's long history. Attilina was much less impressed. She was used to the planned, spotless ways of the habs, and this city struck her as messy and untidy. Even the sims in the historical disneys were neater than this, and they all were equipped with modern sanitary facilities. Had she only realized that Munge lacked plumbing, she would have stayed at Leo.

However, eventually they wound their way to the eastern side of the town, where the Prime Fane and the Palace of the Smithmost were set among acres of olearth green. They walked past the towering elms and rowans, following a winding path whimsically set in ocher flags, and eventually came to the focus of the park. It was a small open pavilion, cast apparently of some gently sparkling pink stone. It was round and perhaps twenty paces in diameter, and the arches of the walls flowed into a domed roof without trace of joint.

"Here we are." Conway looked around for the Aludium, until Attilina took his arm and led him inside. Inside there was little to see, except a circle of some dozen waist high columns, all devoid of ornamentation except for some obscure buttons and markings on the slanted tops of the truncated pillars.

"Is this it?"

"What were you expecting?"

"Oh…I don't know what to expect. Something more impressive, I guess."

"This is it, trust me."

"All of human knowledge, in here?"

"All of human knowledge fits into a cube about this big." Her hands described a cube smaller than her head. "I told you, machines have been perfect for thousands of years."

"I guess I don't understand perfection."

Her voice took on a pedantic note. "A perfect machine shall have no moving parts, should last forever, and should not look like a machine."

"I guess I don't know what a machine looks like. The tannery was full of machines. They ran off a windmill."

"This is a long way from that. In the habs, the only way you can tell a machine is by the controls."

"So how do we control these?"

"Like this…" She walked toward the nearest column and thumbed a depression set in its top. A voice, neutral, and vastly reassuring uttered a single word.

"Ready."

"We want to know about…." She stopped and turned to him. "What do you want to know? Just speak in a normal tone. If it doesn't understand you, it will tell you."

"Really?"

"Oh, sure. It's a lot smarter than you are."

"That's reassuring." He diffidently approached the column, clutching his chuitar bag a little tighter, as if for security. He cleared his throat and said; "If you don't mind, I'd like to hear some music....Ole-arth music."

"Ready."

He turned to Attilina. "Now what?"

"Say; 'Proceed'."

"Proceed."

"We have thirty petrabytes of data on Old Earth Music. Where would you like to start?"

"With the oldest....Please."

Suddenly there was a quavering pipe tune, or near tune, in the air. It was so realistic that Conway could hear the breaths of the piper and the almost subliminal pads of her fingers on the holes. It played a simple phrase and fell silent. Conway was unimpressed. Gully was much better.

"What was that?"

"That was a recreation of a Neolithic elk bone fife, over forty thousand years old. Of course there is no record of the actual tunes played, but that demonstrates the dynamic and tonal range of the instrument."

"Oh." Conway thought for a moment. "How about something more recent?"

A cacophonous blare of jagged chords practically flattened him to the pink floor. A vastly amplified voice raged about something incomprehensible. Conway could not decide whether the voice was male or female, and after a moment's pain, could care less. "Stop!"

"That was a piece called "Pullistic Revenge", by a group called Gorgasm. It dates from the late Twenty First Century, just before the Great Cleansing."

"The what?"

"The Great Cleansing was the event that caused the near depopulation of Earth, and the Diaspora into space. I can inform you about those events, if you chose. There are several hundred petrabytes of data available."

"Excuse me?" He waited, while Attilina stifled a snicker at the idea of being polite to a machine, especially such a simple machine as the Aludium. The Aludium remained silent, having been given no orders, and Conway eventually plunged on. "Excuse me, but how much is a petrabytes, exactly?"

"A petrabyte is defined as one billion megabytes."

"And a megabyte?"

"A megabyte is approximately one book, or one small piece of music, or ten pictures in color."

"Oh." It was a very small 'Oh'." Conway ciphered rapidly. So you mean that you have…Thirty million olearth songs on record?"

"There is text and pictures, but perhaps one third of that data is expressed in actual sound recordings, yes."

Conway stood silent. "And how long would it take to hear all that music, please?"

"Less than seven hundred of your years."

"And the average life expectancy on the planet Munge?"

"Is approximate thirty one earth years, less for males."

"I think I better come back later."

"Ready." Conway tried to hear a mocking tone in the Aludium's voice, but it was a calm and a reassuring as before. It didn't help. He felt mocked. Perhaps by his own ignorance. Twenty odd lifetimes, just to hear all of the music that existed before mankind left its cradle planet. And he had been daunted by the prospect of making sense out of the music only on Munge. At least that little project had a human scale to it. As for what must be going on out in space…That conjecture led to a question. He turned to his companion, as they left the pavilion.

"How do you listen to all the music?"

"Oh, nobody cares all that much. It's like I said before; you just keep punching 'delete' on your netset, and eventually it learns what you like."

Questions always lead to more questions. "What is a netset, exactly?"

"It's a little thing, with a few buttons on it, it's usually worn as a piece of jewelry, if it's not implanted, surgically implanted, you know. It connects you to the web; it's a communication device. Everybody's got one. It's like a baby toy that grows up with you. You get one before you learn to talk. It's really simple."

"And it connects to something like the Aludium?"

"Sort of. The Aludium is really retarded, you know. The netset is like everything. It's interactive."

"Sure." He decided to just shut up and be suspected a fool, rather than ask any more questions, and confirm her suspicions. He also decided to sneak off and quiz the Aludium, without her help, someday. It probably would tell him how to use it, if he asked the right questions. But now it was lunchtime, and then he might find a music shop and browse until the fifth glass, when he was supposed to find out about his first music job. The idea, he supposed, should fill him with joy, but all he felt now was a weak, shaky feeling in his knees, and a grumbling in his gut. Maybe he was hungry…Yeah, that's it, just hungry.

When they finally made it back to the Greeble, it was just past the fifth glass, noted by a contrivance, of which Conway had been ignorant, called a clock. This mechanism was ensconced in a large tower of its own in on the Skerzag, the main square of the town. It was some what similar to a mill, and it ran on water, and ground not grain nor pounded hides, but measured time, and proclaimed it's menses with strokes on a brazen gong. Conway had asked a passerby about the periodic notes that resounded through all of New Ahven, and was so informed. He was so amazed with the implications of a standard time, a time that applied to all persons, whatever, that he stared so long at the single hand of this clock device, trying to see it actually move, that he was late for his appointment.

Attilina was, of course, amusedly scornful of his innocence, but forbear audible comment. Conway noticed her mood and decided to not inquire how spacers managed their affairs temporally. He was sure it was perfect, and had no moving parts. He was finding it hard to address even the simplest sentence to her. He felt too childish and ignorant, and grew ever more ashamed of his backward world. He was learning a lot, and it was painful.

He did learn, another thing, however....That musicians were always late. There was no sign of Cynchie, but the long young man of the morning's joke welcomed them to a table, and offered them a draft. Conway requested limeade, but Attilina wanted a jack of quaff and the youth, whose name proved to be Hwoldt, offered to buy. He was the tavesty player of Cynchie's band, and seemed quite amused with the idea of a female warrior. It appeared that most things amused Hwoldt, the son of an axebeak herder, who had traveled from the far inlands of Smith to do as little as possible here in New Ahven.

Hwoldt was expounding on exactly how amusing he could be; "Yes, indeed, all the ladies love a tavestist, it must be something about the wind control, one supposes, but actually it's the drummers that seem to pluck, as it were, the tenderest blossoms....I say, do you know how to tell if the stage is level?"

Conway bit; "No, how?"

"When the drummer drools out of both sides of his mouth...then the stage is...Oh, there she is, now." He rose to his feet and mocked a courtly bow. "Right on time, only half a glass late."

Cynchie was unapologetic, and had an older man in tow. He had a wry face and a sandy topknot bound with carnelian beads in a style unfamiliar to Conway. He also had a coffin shaped case dangling from one ropy hand and a lack of social graces. He nodded to Hwoldt, ignored Attilina, and examined Conway closely.

"Play chuitar, ay?"

"I'm learning."

"As are we all, ay?"

"Yessir."

"Well, maybe you'll do. If you don't, I won't pay. Fair?"

"Yessir."

"Well, c'mon." He turned to go, but turned back to address Cynchie. "I'd rather it was you, but...."

Cynchie planted a smoochie kiss on Woodie's cheek, and slapped Conway on the shoulder. "He'll do fine. You just prompt him, and don't worry."

"We'll see, ay?"

Attilina was torn between asking for permission to tag along, or just seeking her own amusement for the evening. The only alternative was the company of the despicable Cynchie. She decided to just take permission for granted, and scowl at anyone who denied her. She was tired of being intimidated and ignored by these lumpen. Damn them, but they were so arrogant in their competence. They really had no idea how ignorant and backward they were down here. Ah, well, she might as well go to the dance. Sometimes they got drunk and had fights at dances. Yeah, maybe she could kill something. Or somebody.

Cheered by this plan, she followed in the vitheler's wake. They traveled away from the center of New Ahven, back toward the docks, and passed three or four of the plazas that defined neighborhoods in this city. Soon they came to a roofed pavilion, with wattle and daub walls that had been painted blue for thousands of years, but never twice in precisely the same color. The plaster had chipped and spalled, and been painted over, and the process had continued for so many generations that the whole building below its thatch was a riot of blues, of every pastel imaginable, that might have ever been even considered as being blue.

Conway was captivated and wanted to just spend the sunset hour drinking in the blues of that incredible wall. But his companions were immune to such diversions. Woodie had seen it all before, and Attilina was still sulking.

They entered into the building, under a sign that logically enough, proclaimed it the "Blue Barn" and set up on the raised platform at one end of the dance floor. The dance floor was already full, and the bar was open. Conway's nose twitched at the aroma of unfamiliar spices from the kitchen area.

The caller, a woman named Bettser, was already at her lectern, and the third band member, a cymballist from Ains called Schwar, was engaged in tuning his unwieldy instrument. This was only to be expected. Cymballums had at least seventy strings, and were always being tuned. Or else needed tuning.

As soon as Woodie's foot touched the stage, he seemed to gain stature; his step firmed and his shoulders rose back. He squatted, rather than stooped, and placed his case on the stage. Conway noticed that it boasted metal catches instead of the almost universal thongs. He took the hint, and unwrapped his instrument and approached the cymballist and asked for a La. He was not far out of tune, and wasted little time twisting knobs. He had an idea that wasting Woodie's time would decrease his pay. The vithelist politely waited for his inferiors to finish, and then nodded to Schwar, who tapped a single string with one of his ivory mallets. Woodie touched a peg or two, and then rosined up his bow. He turned to face the caller and nodded his head, curtly.

The cymballum sparkled off a complicated phrase, the vithel screeched out an answer to that run, and Conway realized that he was in the music business. He listened for a half a chorus and remembered that "Woodie always plays in La". Therefore…He grabbed a handful of the music, as it rolled by, and swung aboard. He used his thumb gently until he discovered that there were to be no surprises, and then dug in, playing one note to every eight of the vithel and the cymballum. On the next round the caller started her chant, in some dialect incomprehensible to Conway. He really could not spare any brain cells to try and understand the words: he was concentrating so hard on the music that he was pouring sweat by the third round.

Long before the first drop hit the polished boards of the stage, the dancers were in motion, solemnly shuffling around in sets of six. They would form larger circles, make one round of the hall and then break back into hexes, and perform evolutions, around each set. No dancer produced the slightest attempt at a smile, and the men seemed to never look directly at the women, and the women held their eyes strictly on the floor. Conway had never seen dancing before, except for some impromptu cavorting at the Devout Sailback back in Ainsworth, and so was not impressed with the stolidity of these revels.

He really hadn't known what to expect, but had supposed that there would be more fun being had. It had been a day of disappointments and misapprehensions, but right now, he had to concentrate. There was a little hesitation in the beat of this song, and it occurred only once a round and he felt like a dolt every time he missed it and had to sluff a beat back to the tempo. Finally, he became able to anticipate this hesitation, and just as he was ready to snap the beat nicely, the song ended. He was left hanging, in mid air, and felt more of a fool than ever.

He felt his face grow red, and then even redder as Woodie turned and cast him a hooded glance. Conway braced himself for a harsh word, or even an immediate dismissal, but the vithelist only nodded, and said, apparently to the cymballist; "A little faster, Ay? 'Wilton's Surcease', if you please."

Another nod, a ripple of the ivories, and off they went, Conway just beginning to experience the exaltation of being able to move a whole room full of people with pulses of this thumb. And after another tune or two, he began to relax and sense the subtleties of this event. The rasping of the vithel's sympathetic strings, the brilliant pointillism of the cymballum, and his own steady pulses seemed to lift the feet of the dancers, and their shuffle became a living thing, a breath, a natural force, that enhanced the natural processes of nearly a hundred people and eased their heartbeats and breaths into one whole.

The steady chants of the caller began to fall into words and patterns in Conway's ear, and he actually began to enjoy himself. He began to anticipate the hesitations and slurs of this music, and to accent the off beats, almost in the style of Heoj back on Ains. There came a point in each song where the music lifted the dancer's shuffling feet to an airish grace, a perceptible rise in the music that reminded Conway of the exact moment when a sailing coracle takes the wind, trimmed just right, and seems to fly over the water, rather than cleaving through it.

At one of these lifts, during the song "Blue Tipped Sorde", Woodie lifted his chin from the vithel, reared back his head and called out;

"It's whether the weather will wither the withes,
It's whether the wither the wanderer goes."

Bettser and all the women in the hall lifted their chins likewise and ululated a single wild note, contrasting so poignantly with the solidity of the men, that Conway felt the hairs rise right up on the back of his neck. He felt that he was where he belonged, doing what he was made to do. It was a new experience. He liked it. And then the music swept the moment away, and he was back to listening and playing and working harder than he had ever before in his life.

After a dozen or so songs, the caller left her booth, and the dancers variously headed for the quaff, or sat on the benches that ringed the floor and eased their sandals. Conway noticed for the first time that he was the only barefoot person to be seen in New Ahven. Then Bettser returned and the revels continued.

He noticed that while the stolid dancers kept their eyes fixed into neutral space, hands touched and waists were caressed and shoulders nudged. He also observed that every man eventually danced with every woman, and some lips touched some ears, and some whispers were exchanged. He developed a suspicion that certain arrangements were being made and broken, and gained his first insight to the actual function of music. These Blues, with their mobcaps and starched ruffled vests were far from uninterested in each other, and he felt as if he was an integral part of their community. This was such a revelation that he dropped his time and earned another smoking glance from the vithe-list. But he recovered, nicely, he thought, and ended the song with a flourish.

Woodie turned to Conway and spoke; "I'd rather have Cynchie, but you'll do...Ay? Have a drink, and we'll hit it again in a few. I'm off for a smoke."

Schwar crossed his ivories on the strings of his cymballum and came over to clasp Conway's shoulder. "You done good, but you shouldn't be so fancy. That may be the style off wherever you hail from, but these vithelists don't like anybody encroaching in their air. If you keep it simple, you won't lack for work."

"Oh, really. I didn't realize."

"Sure thing. You listen, and notice that I never slop over Woodie's lines. I just stay well below his melody and he's happy. You stay below me, and all will be well."

"Thanks for the advice...I'll try to restrain myself." He felt a vast relief that he was judged as overqualified for this exercise. It should be easy to play less.

Schwar slapped his shoulder again; "You'll do. These Bluestemmers are a thickheaded lot, but they pay well. And Woodie is far from the worse vithelist on Smith...You take 'Old Pegs', Pegs Josperrin. There's a man that will make a chuitarist toe the line. And if you don't he'll spit right on your feet to get your attention. He's from the old school, is Old Pegs!"

"I'll try to behave."

"You'll do."

Conway turned, thinking to get a drink, and there was Woodie, not a yard away, taking in all this advice with a wry smile on his thin lips. He allowed no change of expression to cross his face, but he did give a curt nod, and squatted again to pick up his instrument. Bettser huffed up the stair, and took up her position behind her lectern. She waited until the dancers regrouped, and then said, over her shoulder; "I forgot to tell you, the war is getting worse, so what ever you do, don't play

'The Blues Advance' or any thing from Ravelli. Play no hornswoggles tonight!"

Woodie spoke not, he just glanced at his band, as if to see that they were attentive, and then put bow to string and scratched out 'Golly-wogs Countdown', a tune so common that even Conway had learned it back on Ainsworth. The rest of the evening went in a blur, with Con-way mostly focused on listening, and playing simply, and watching his sweat drops soak into the hand planed boards of the stage. He did notice Attilina try to join the dance, only to be ignored by the boy she had approached. He supposed he could worry, but was to busy. She had been in a rotten mood all day and this rebuff could scarcely help. He hoped that she would leave in a cloud of indignation, but all she did was to fetch another jack of quaff, and retire to a corner. Oh well, he thought, I'll pay for this later, but right now, I need to keep Woodie happy.

Remarkably soon, the dance wore to a close, and the Blues, instead of applauding the band, filed up and each pressed a coin in Bettser's hand, nodded, and went home. Bettser, in turn, silently passed a stack of moneys to Woodie, and thanked him, and departed. The cymballist followed her out the door.

Woodie was more effusive, almost up to laconic. He pressed a hand-ful of coppers into Conway's grasp, and spoke almost a whole para-graph. "You did well, Ay, you did. I'll hire you anytime Cynchie's busy. Let's go to a place I know, and we'll eat."

"Thank you very much, Mariner Woodie. I learned a lot tonight."

"Let's go. Playing makes me hungry, Ay?"

"If you don't mind…"

"Mind? You're in my band, Ay?" Woodie halted for a moment, and considered. Then he spoke again. "This place, the Belly? They have the best food in New Ahven…."

"But?"

"But watch your step. There's Somebodies there, and they're touchy sometimes."

"I'll be careful." Conway had no idea who these Somebodies were, but he was always careful. Fearful even. He looked around to see if Attilina had heeded this warning, but she was across the room, wiping the foam from one last quaff from her lips with the back of her hand. He resolved to speak to her, later.

Woodie slung his case over his shoulder and set off, Conway right behind. They traveled only one square along the seaside, but in that short space they passed from a seaman's district to one that was mostly residential, and much richer. Here the homes had the unmungian attribute of walled gardens, complete with barred gates. Incredibly, some of these gates even had metal clasps and latches. Obviously this was a most affluent neighborhood indeed. Conway was wondering exactly who lived in this quarter when they rounded a walled corner and entered into a wash of light and noise that obviously marked their goal.

There was a swinging sign above the open door; a cutout of a grossly fat man, whose vast abdomen was highlighted in gilt. This manne-quin's feet rested on a sign that announced 'The Belly' in open work letters. The music and clamor was almost unbearable, even out here on the street. Conway had a moment of trepidation, but pressed on in Woodie's wake. Attilina, still silent, followed right behind.

The interior was a stew of smoke and hubbub, and was broken by tables and shoulder high walls of live plants. Conway wondered how anything could survive in the cacophony. The lights were low and the clientele was of a different class from the other folk Conway had observed in New Ahven The band was all horns and drums and played a violent loud music that every one ignored. Conversation was impossi-ble, but that didn't stop everyone from bellowing in each other's faces at the closest possible range. Every table had a game board inlaid into it's top, and Conway could only identify checks and draughts and chizni. Play was as violent as the music; especially one game where the opponents brandished tiles high over their heads and then slapped them down on the board with slams that were occasionally audible above the rest of the racket.

The players communicated by means of extravagant gestures that seemed to approach the flexibility of a language. Waiters scurried between the tables, slapping down vast bowls of wonderfully aromatic stews and soups. Conway noted that each dish was paid for as served and that each gaming table bore stacks of moneys taller than the gaming pieces. He followed Woodie to an obscure table, far from the band, near the wall, and secured seats for himself and Attilina.

A waiter was instantly there, and Woodie gestured briefly, and the waiter vanished, to appear moments later with a tray laden with sliced brot, spurdad flowers, and three tankards of quaff. There was also a triplex bowl of sauces to dip the food into. Attilina immediately grabbed a quaff, and Woodie went for the brot. Conway discovered that he was starved and tried the fried flowers, each as large as his hand, and crispy with brodding. Woodie spared a hand and dug into his spoan to drop a handful of coppers onto the table. The waiter selected a seemingly extravagant number of the moneys and paused for an impatient moment. Woodie leaned to Conway's ear.

"What soup you want?"

Conway decided that it was all edible, so…"I'll take chouder, please."

Woodie repeated his request into Attilina's ear, listened to her, and rapidly gestured to the waiter, who vanished like smoke. Actually he vanished faster than the smoke, for the smoke went nowhere.

He was back in just moments, bringing two bowls of soup, which went in front of the two men, and two more quaffs, which he placed in front of the woman. Conway realized that this might possibly be a bad sign, but his hunger over rode everything else. The flowers were sweet and crunchy and delectable, and the three sauces were each an experience beyond anything he had known before in his life. He hadn't known that music could be such hard work, and armed with this revelation, he dove for the bottom of his bowl with a will.

When he emerged, partially satiated, the room was much as before, and the waiter was back. He indicated the empty plate of spurdad flowers and his favorite of the three sauces. He dug for a handful of coins, and the waiter was back almost before he had the money on the table. His table companions were still deep in their dishes, and he took a moment to survey the crowd around them.

He began to grasp who the "Somebodies" might be. Most of the crowd was composed of the common ruck of Ahveners; seamen, tradesmen, frousters, goodwives, gaffers. But there were quite a few of a different style, similar to the epauletted bravos in the Misericord, but more extreme in their clothing and gestures. They tended to be young, and whip thin and dressed in swatches of very rich fabrics; even gold mesh and feather cloth. All in all, they bore a disturbing resemblance to the Flies of recent incident, especially in the long swords that depended down their backs. And each and every one of them bore livid scars across their faces and shoulders.

As he studied them, he supposed that the Flies had taken these, these Somebodies, as their models, and he further realized that he would just as soon be resting in his coracle, listening to water slap the hide of it's sides.

He looked over at his "Traveling Companion," And discerned a certain looseness of lip and slouchiness in posture that boded ill for a restful evening. Woodie was mopping up the bottom of his bowl of soup, and Conway rose to thank him for the employment and the dinner. Just then, a chair from an adjoining table flew backwards and toppled onto his bare toes. He jumped back, and instinctively looked for an exit. One of the bravos had cast his chair back unheeding as he leapt to confrontation with another of his kind. The two Somebodies drew their wavy swords as one, and then paused, and pressing the hilts to their lips, bowed simultaneously to each other. The crowd formed a circle around the two, and the cacophony in the room subsided to a roar. Moneys exchanged hands around the circle and the two nobles crossed swords ceremoniously, while another of their type ostentatiously flourished a kerchief over his head.

And then Attilina removed the tankard from her face, sat up and began to take notice. Her eyes lit up and she rose to her feet. Conway's feet began to itch so bad he couldn't even feel his stinging toes.

It was time to go. He looked left and right and found every avenue blocked by eager spectators. He cursed this big city passion for putting walls on buildings and thought it most unfair and unwise. He clutched his chuitar to his side, and watched Woodie single-mindedly pursue the last drop of gravy in his bowl.

His heart fell as Attilina pushed her unsteady way into the circle of bettors and confronted the two duelists. Her mouth moved, but he couldn't hear her words.

But then, he didn't have to. He knew exactly what she was saying. And he knew that...

One of the bravos that formed the circle placed a hand on Attilina's shoulder. At least that was his intention, but suddenly he found himself staring in horror at the bloody stump that terminated his arm. He grasped himself and fled, and Conway yearned to follow, but it was too late for anything but backing up against the too stout wall, and watching in horror.

Attilina's katana was a blur, cleaving the smoky air on its way to unprotected throats and bellies. The two duelists were the first targets, and barely had time to turn, and no time to realize what was eventuating. The female warrior had been drinking all night, but it didn't seem to slow her blade any, and the first pair of Somebodies hit the floor before anybody else even got their blade out. She made an incredible leap to the ceiling and managed to swipe the head from a richly clad pair of shoulders before she touched down.

Conway got a splatter of blade slung blood across his eyes, and bent down to hide behind a table, only to come face to face with Woodie, who was unashamedly trying to burrow into the terrazzo floor. Just about then, the band trailed to a discordant stop, but the raving of the crowd easily replaced the noise.

Woodie cast one of his significant glances at Conway, and asked; "Friend of yours?" Conway couldn't think of anything to say that could comprehend the rain of body parts and blood around them, and so contented himself with trying to get all of his body and his precious chuitar under the table with the vithelist.

A caroming body removed the table from over them and Woodie scrambled to his feet and scurried towards the door. Conway knew a good move when he saw one and followed close behind, slipping and sliding in the slurry of gore and game pieces and spilled food. He got past the cluster of combatants and got to the entryway just as the Wards came in. He didn't exchange words with them, and they had eyes only for the duelists. He did look back long enough to see their heavy wooden flails in action, and decided to not give them any opportunity to lay one of these wrist thick staves against any portion of his anatomy. He followed Woodie out of the lamplight at the entrance and stopped to blow.

Woodie was saying words that Conway had never heard before, but he had no doubt as to their meanings. "Herusalem Tabernac....Slug spittle, but that was a little more groasping excitement that I care to enjoy on a regular basis. Young man, you're welcome to play anytime, but..."

"I know...don't bring her."

"Flalung Ay!"

"I'm not responsible...I just can't get rid of her."

"You might have to convince the dactylcak Wards of that."

"For winning a duel?"

"She killed them."

"Isn't that the point of a duel?"

"Unless you're a spoiled brat of a Somebody. Those bravos stand...stood to inherit a good portion of this city. They only duel to get those pretty little scars so to attract the lower class girls. Nobody has died in a duel in the Belly for….Their fathers will not be amused. Therefore the watch will not be amused. Therefore….”

“I'm not amused.”

“Ay.”

“I may have to go for a small cruise.”

“If you need some moneys…”

“I have a coracle.”

“Good lad.”

“I'll leave you now, Mariner Woodie. I should catch the morning tide.” Conway paused searching for words. “It was an honor to play with you. I learned a lot. Perhaps. Some time.”

“Aye, you're a good lad, remind me of myself…you do. Be careful, and look for a…a more restful woman.”

“Good advice. Thanks again.”

“Cashamash is a good place to find work, playing.”

“Thanks…maybe later on….”

“Ay.”

They parted, without touch or gesture. Behind them the noise in the Belly reached a new height, and the spatter of fleeing diners became a spate. Conway's feet still itched, and he knew which way to go to get back to his coracle. He thought for a moment of going to the Misericord to say good bye to Cynchie, but it was only a thought. He shouldered his bag and set a fast but hopefully unobtrusive pace toward the fishing harbor. He was tired, and heavy with coppers, and it was way past his bedtime. He wondered if he would see his nuncle Bilbeau on Cashamash.

CHAPTER 8

▼

He clambered down into the coracle, relishing the fishy quiet of the docks. All the good little fisherfolk were long asleep, and even the rookeries were silent except for the rustle of leather wings. He dropped into the cockpit, bringing the rope end with him, and prepared to paddle out to sea. The moon was rising, and he hoped he could achieve the open roads, without alerting the Littorals. He supposed that they would have no reason to detain him, but they were paid to be suspicious.

As he slipped the paddle into the black water, he wished them well at it. He silently backed water and then dug in, stirring the faintest of phosphorescence, to swing the prow towards the ocean. He had little water, and only the hardest of rations, but the time was as ripe as a fruit, as they said. Time for a new adventure. He supposed that he could return to quiz the Aludium, and visit Frerisson's, and perhaps see Cynchie again, but as for now he was free from Attilina, and therefore content. He wished that he knew the meanings of some of those words Woodie had used. It would take words like that to express himself adequately. It was later than he had realized, and there was the faintest touch of gray over his shoulder. Perhaps it would be best to rest here, barely out in the harbor, until the sun and wind came up, and then ease out to sea, concealed in the flock of fishing boats. He decided to do so, and if the Littorals came up, to plead insomnia, as his excuse for early rising. It would be no more than a half a glass, before the harbor stirred to life, and he might as well relax for a moment.

He stored the paddle, and gratefully sagged back into the cubby. His back ached for the softness of his bedding. But his back touched softness of quite another order.

"What!"

Cold steel touched his throat, and he felt warm, quaff fouled breath on his ear.

"Hush! The Wards are looking for me."

"How did you get here?"

"I fled."

"Good move."

"Why were you sailing away."

"Because of you."

"Don't you like me?" There was a sob in her voice that contrasted with the steel at his neck.

"You kill people."

"What's wrong with that?"

"It causes adverse comment."

"If I didn't need...I could kill you too."

He had to agree. He swallowed hard, hoping that the lump in his throat wouldn't press hard enough against the edge to empty his veins. "I can't stop you."

"If I ever see you kissing another woman, I'll do it."

"She kissed me." His nervous system couldn't take much more stress. His only recourse was the truth.

"Don't care. You heard me. I'm not made of iron." He voice sounded like she was swallowing something. He couldn't imagine what. Then the sword clattered to the floorboards, and she bunched her body and Conway found himself lying next to the blade. He shrunk away from the razor edged steel. Just enough light filtered into the cubby for him to see that she was sobbing into her hands.

He was totally at a loss. He felt very young and very dumb and very male and very helpless. He paused for a moment, torn between comforting her and possibly gently tipping her overboard. It was a real dilemma. He hung there, dumb as a stump, until he heard the heavy wing beats of the morning's flight of sagitaries out to their feeding grounds. Regardless of emotional upset, it was time to set sail. He was worthless in this cubby with this mad woman, so he fled to his area of competence.

He exited the cubby and tugged up the sail. As he did he saw the stern of the Littoral's galley sweep around a point of land to starboard. The sight reminded him that he was primarily a fugitive. It was a role he was beginning to hate. But, whatever he felt about his fate, the morning breeze was about its business, and it behooved him to be about his. By the time the sail was set, and the harbor cleared, the sun was fully up and he was ready to seriously seek easement.

He looked into the cubby and saw that his passenger had succumbed to inebriation, and was not an immediate trouble. So he set out a line of hooks and settled himself into a semi-comfortable position against a thwart. His toes grasped the tiller, and he soon managed to achieve a state approximating slumber. As he drifted off, the thought came to him that he really should be disturbed by yesterday's events, but his dreams, such as the were, were untroubled.

He awoke before noon, and was cleaning and devouring fingerlings from his line when Attilina awoke. She was obviously in pain and seemingly uncertain about the exact sequence of events of last night. She crawled to the stern and rinsed out her mouth with seawater and splashed more on her face. Then she managed to affix something resembling a smile to her face and rake back her hair with her fingers. The whole process looked painful. She gathered her wits and addressed her captain.

"It there anything to drink?" She thought hard for a second, and added one word. "Please?"

He was tempted to have mercy, but only for a moment. He sliced the head off the largest fingerling and squeezed its entrails over the side. He rinsed it as carefully as he would for himself and held it out to her.

"This is all there is. Chew it slowly and it will quench your thirst." Her head was back over the stern, and her body was convulsing with, dry heaves in an instant. He thought how easy it would be to grab her ankles and tip her into the water, and was disgusted with himself for sparing her. He really couldn't think of a reason, barring his own ineffectualness.

The thought didn't cheer him. Finally, he unlashed the tarp over the outrigger storage, and dug out the last firkin of Angst quaff. He bore it to her, and tapped her on the shoulder. He had an instant mental picture of the last hand that had touched her there, and how it had tumbled over and over in the lamplight, before it hit the tile floor. Fortunately her katana was still in the cabin. He had checked.

He had to clear his throat to speak. "Here," He said. "Drink this."

She looked daggers at him for a long moment before her eyes focused on the firkin.

"Oh God!" It was a prayer. She dived into the firkin, and came back up after a considerable interval. Conway felt large and manly as he stood over her, there in the stern sheets. The feeling couldn't last long, but he savored it.

Attilina emerged after a while, belched like a soldier, wiped her lips with the back of her hand, and said; "Thanks, Conway, you're a lifesaver."

"And you're a life taker. You can wave your sword around all you want, threaten me, do whatever you want, I can't stop you." The words bubbling out of his mouth made his knees tremble, but he had no control over them. He had never spoken to another person, especially a warrior, in such a manner in all his life, but he had lost all his censors, and had to ride his mouth like a herder might straddle a wild axebeak. His words continued, and he tried to hold on for the ride. "You can kill me, for all the good it will do you. You can't sail, and you can't swim, and you can't eat raw fish. So if you want to die slowly in this sea, get your sword and use it. One way or another, this is your last ride in my coracle."

"What have I done to you?"

"Twice I've managed to find a home, and twice you have managed to destroy it with your bloody sword. I had a job, and a band and a place in this world, and you chopped it all to pieces." He paused for breath. "You threatened me last night, and now you expect me to save you. I'm sorry, but you make my life too exciting."

"But what am I to do?"

"I'm taking you to Cashamash, it's the market for all of the Pancreatic Ocean. You can hire out as a mercenary, or join some army, or murder fat merchants for all I care. You're a warrior, and I'm a musician. You go your way and most likely I'll go mine."

"But...But I love you."

"What is that supposed to mean?"

"It means I like you and want to be with you. "She wiped at an eye, and blinked furiously. He supposed that he was supposed to reassure her, but he looked inside himself, and found a great seethe. All the loneliness and pain of his childhood on Angst rose up inside him, and every disappointment since came up in a great raging sad wave. And opposed to this were the snivels of a pug nosed little person who thought she had some claim on him.

He tried to think of some way to express himself to her, for oddly, he felt no real need to hurt her, but nothing came out. In fact, he had to squelch faint stirrings of a peculiarly predatory protectiveness. It felt a particularly unworthy emotion.

He opened his mouth and closed it a few times. And then he turned away. He worked his way up to the bow and busied himself with the plankton net. There was always some needful chore on a sea faring craft. He examined his emotions as he worked. It was a thing he rarely did, out of fear of pain, but now all he felt was hunger. Hunger and impatience to get to Cashamash. He could let her off on one of the

Knowles, he supposed. He would stop at one or more for water, and food, but he supposed, he would be a fool of his word, and take her to Cashamash. He couldn't imagine anyplace on Munge where she would fit in, but the great Pancreatic market was the meeting place for half the world. She would have as much of a chance there as anywhere. And he could work or play for a few moons and then drift back to Smith. Surely the watch would not have that long a memory. He, after all, hadn't killed anyone. Perhaps a few difficult questions, but he could work on being unobtrusive. He had had any amount of practice back on Angst, but it seemed to be more difficult out here in the world.

Things would heal themselves given time, and Cashamash was only seven hundred flongs away. He used the last of the fingerlings to bait his biggest hook, and trolled it over the side. He looked aft and saw that she had apparently taken herself and her quaff back into the cubby. Good. The Knowles should be in sight long before dusk. He would be good and hungry by then. Meanwhile the sea was green-blue and the sky was blue-green and the dactyls were on the wing. It would be a long tack to Cashamash, but he would get there. He hoped.

The Knowles were unexciting, for which Conway gave thanks. The people there were particularly lean and tall, with light hair, and strong features. Their fingers and toes were exceptionally long, which tended to give their gestures a sinister aspect, but they treated the voyagers with indifferent ease. Conway and Attilina feasted at the Blue Bottle Inn, a hostelry built out over the bay on a thousand eccentric pilings. Much to Attilina's joy, they had not only cheese, but also goat milk in several forms, in soup, and as a species of pudding. The very idea of imbibing the natal fluid of another animal, made Conway as queasy as raw fish made the space girl, but he managed to remain at the same table.

He indulged in more axebeak, and tried a goat stew, but found it gamey. He purchased some hard rations, and filled a demijohn with water and this time he didn't forget the limes. The Blue Bottle Inn was also a chandlers and provided him with several of those trinkets and semi useful devices few mariners can do without.

He stowed the goods and they were off again just at sunset, and only after they were under way, and Attilina had taken possession of the cubby again, did he realize that they had not exchanged a word since his little speech that morning.

Oddly, he was piqued for a few moments, but shrugged and decided that he was just as well off. It would make their parting all the easier. He sailed out well away from land, and hoisted a lantern, reefed the lateen sail and composed himself to sleep out on the deck. Attilina had purchased several firkins of fortified quaff at the inn and he expected little from her until morning. However, about midnight, she came out and went to the stern. There were various splashes and tinkles and then she crept forward to where he lay in the light of the moon. It was nearly new and the spangles shown brightly. The many lights weren't as bright as the full moon, but it seemed as if they should be. She sank to a seat near him, but made no mood to disturb him. He was already awake, however. A sailor at sea is awakened by any change in the status of his ship, and the smaller it is, the more sensitive he must be.

He could smell the drink on her breath, but she appeared relatively sober. He took a chance.

"I still can't believe they're really cities."

"What?" She was taken aback, her thoughts had been far from Abaraxis. "Oh, the moon. Some are mines or ports or factories, but yes, most are cities."

"What are they like?"

"I can't explain...you're too..."

"Ignorant?"

"Well...it's that you don't know the words mean. It's like a dream..."

"How...what is?"

"My civilization. Things change. Things move while you watch. The walls are all alive, every surface is displaying vids."

"What's a vid?"

"See?" She sighed, audibly. "A vid is a moving picture, but just saying that gives you no idea what it's like. You have no idea what we can do…What happens all the time. We are so powerful, we might as well be gods."

"You're no goddess."

"Too right. My people created this world, and now I can't even get home."

"What!"

"Sure. It's called terraforming. This one was easy. We moved Abaraxis to give Munge decent tides, for example. Before that the seas were mats of algae and scum. That's why the fauna is so limited. It hasn't evolved to all the niches yet. The Gould gene works fast but not that fast. We were the equivalent of an extermination." She pondered for a moment, brow furrowed, as she tried to find baby talk words for this lumpen before her. "You probably weren't taught about evolution?"

He nodded…mind elsewhere. She plunged on, unheeding. Mutual incomprehension defined their relationship.

"Some people think there is a plan, a direction to life, but we know it's just a random series of spasms. Something kills off most of the life on a planet, and then there is a burst of new life forms…" He cut her off with a burst of words.

"You moved the moon." He was too shocked to make it a question.

"It used to be around Ponder. Orbit Ponder I mean."

"I know what an orbit is."

"Do you?"

"It means to go around in a circle."

"Ellipse."

"Whatever." He tried to marshal his thoughts. "How do you move something that big? What do you push it with?"

"If I told you they either use a fusion torch or mass drivers or dirigible planet flybys, would you have a clue?"

He was silent for long moments, watching the moon change from a coin, just out of reach, to a vast sphere looming dangerously close above his head. He felt he should flinch. Then some known words in her last sentence joined into a new concept in his head. Then he really wanted to flinch, but he couldn't figure out in which direction.

"Dirigible planets? Does that mean…" The concept was so immense that he wasn't sure his head could hold it. "Does that mean that your people move planets around like…like sailboats?"

"Of course we do. When you travel between systems, you either go fast enough to dilate time, or else you bring your whole world." She softened her voice, perhaps out of pity. "We don't move really big planets…normally."

There didn't seem to be much to say after that. He thought of reclaiming his bunk for the rest of the night, but he had an aversion to lying where she had lain, smelling her smell. So, he just lay back, with his head on the gunwale, until he drifted off. And in the morning, she was as uncommunicative as…well, as he was.

And soon after that, they came into the traffic that thronged around Cashamash and he became too busy to converse. There were vessels of all shapes and sizes there, chubby sluys from Monica, and rakish hoons from Glenco and even father north. There were coracles and canoes and boats by the score and dozens of slow barges and bateaux from all over the Pancreatic Sea.

The Cashamash Navy was particularly in evidence. While they were nowhere near as smartly turned out as the Ahvener Littorals, their running gear was taunt, and their catapults and onagers were well greased and their massive bolts were ready nocked and gleaming sharp. The Cashans were the richest people of all the Pancreats, and they weren't adverse to spending moneys on their navy.

Some of the heads on the catapult bolts were even of polished steel, a fantastic expense, but one deemed worthy by the Council of Magnates that ruled, or at least regulated, the markets of Cashamash. It was said that everything was for sale by these merchants, including the virtues of their daughters, but they were quite ruthless when protecting their profits.

Nobody ever accused them of foolishness, and all the pirates of the all the seas of Munge had spent many a fruitless glass trying to figure out a way to loot the riches of the Cashamash Magnates.

Cashamash refused to resolve itself in his eyes. They were within a few flongs of the shore before it became more than a clutter of bright faded colors. Most of the pavilions had that sad aspect that comes from temporary structures that have out lasted their lease on life. Each building, tent, pavilion or lean-to was an entity unto itself and if any two touching shelters were of the same style or color, it was a miracle due entirely to the workings of chance.

What the buildings lacked in permanence they compensated for in gaudiness, festooned with pennants and banners, bunting and gonfalons. Every surface that would accept paint had been painted the wildest possible colors. Strings of banners of varicolored leathers, some woven with drake feathers, were slung from peak to peak and every point of every tent pole was improved with dyed streamers of translucent dactyl intestine. Every prospect was designed to enchant the eye and befuddle the brain, and Conway felt a little ashamed that he could see through their expensive illusions. He wondered how he had managed to get so old without ever being young and happy. Or even, just happy.

Cashamash was built around a large sandy bay, and as the coracle rounded the point, Conway had his choice of moorings, docks and slips. He knew, from nuncle Bilbeau's tales, that these facilities were not free, and so he sailed down past the convenient landings to a muddy strip of beach, near the swamp that served as the sump for the city, and found a relatively solid place to beach his coracle. They were at an inconvenient distance from the center of the market, but the price was right. And also, if Bilbeau came to sell his firkins, he would come here. Conway scanned the nearby craft, but saw no sign of his nuncle's barge.

That exhausted his store of plans, both concrete and tentative. Except for one.

He turned to his passenger, and said; "I won't say it's not been memorable."

"But you wish you'd never met me…right?"

"Well…" He didn't want to lie to her, but he also didn't want to hurt her feelings. "I won't forget you. At least…"

"Don't bother!" She snapped. She grabbed up her swords and her bag of loot and stalked off. He tried not to watch her go. He suspected that he would never meet another person like her for the rest of his life, and supposed it was just as well.

He pulled the coracle a little further up on the mud bank, and made the painter fast to a snag. There were a few other vessels beached near him, but there were no other persons in evidence. He thought of this and that, and considered the list of nautical chores he might well be doing. This contemplation fatigued him to the point of yawning.

Conway stifled the yawn and then let its successor escape. His considerations produced no other results and so he stumbled into the cubby, and had only enough energy to shake her smell out of the blanket. That was all he knew for quite a while. When he awoke, the sun was lower in the east than it had been when he fell asleep. It took long moments of squinchy eyed blinking before he managed to realize that he had slept the day and the night away. He had no memory of any dreams, and decided that it was just as well.

He thought he might practice for an hour, just to settle himself, but on reflection, he thought he'd rather play than practice. Perhaps someone might buy him lunch or teach him a song or something. So he slung his chuitar over his shoulder and set out to trust his fate…again. It was getting to be a way of life.

He was learning about being a musician. To everyone else, the adventure is being able to play music, to create, to control the emotions of others. To a musician, the adventure is staying alive without being forced to resort to honest work. Romance is in the eye of the beholder.

It was immediately apparent that there was no plan to the market, only the permutations of applied greed. The most desirable locations were in the center of the market and were correspondingly more expensive. The fringes, especially down near the sump, the swamp, were lower rent, trailing off to establishments so marginal that it was hard to imagine any profit ever being made under any conditions. Here were scrawny people, old women mostly; whose booths were ragged blankets spread on the mud, and whose entire stock consisted of a few tethered beetles, or dubious psallie eggs. Conway wondered why the women didn't devour their total inventory and set out for home, as their only faint chance of survival, but here they were, crying their wares in cracked voices.

A few paces on were vendors of hot water, whose stock was a brazier, a pot and a single bowl. A customer would bring a pinch of chai or an egg, and the proprietor would cook it for them and allow them the use of their precious cup for only the length of time it took to consume their morsel. Conway was almost totally ignorant of the ways of industry, but it seemed a little thin, even to him.

A few steps more and the establishments boasted awnings and low tables, behind which the merchants squatted monotonously hawking their wares, each with her own song or chant. The cacophony began to creep into Conway's blood stream and his step quickened to a new heartbeat of commerce. And beneath it all, he felt, rather than heard, a subterranean pulse, a subliminal beat that began the minute that he entered the area of covered vendors and never left him for all the time he spent on Cashamash.

He was not to become aware of this beat for a while yet, but he did perceive it as a current under the chorus of hawker's songs and dactyl cries that filled the crowded air of Cashamash.

"Hey dey hey dey hey, psallie's eggs I pray. Psallie's eggs she lay, Hey dey hey de hey".

"Red hots, get your red hots, twudseyfrudsey, I scream, get your red hots."

"Squarik!"

"Finest finest axebeak, limed slimed, and mimed, only a copper."

"Right here, right now, right here right now."

"Bersaglies, Bersaglies, finest quality Brown Bersaglies!"

Copperfounders beat on gongs and edgesmiths clashed blade on steel, while dactyl herders mimicked the cries of their charges. The sights and sounds and the smells of a thousand of different items assaulted Conway's provincial brain, until he felt faint. All around him the clamor rose as fast as the peaks and spires and pendants of the market until he began to think he might as well return to the fringes and purchase a few eggs and break his fast back at the coracle. And then before him was the oddest sight so far; it was a tavern, one of the few structures that deserved the name of building, and instead of a name it had only a signboard, painted black and relieved with a sketch of a knowing grin. The rest of the tavern was unpainted bamb and cochina, and from inside came only the sour smell of aged quaff and the scrape of a burnish on a stone grill.

Conway peered in. Yep, a tavern. There was the bar, and there the kitchen, and there the stage. Home. He shifted the bag on his shoulder and walked in, as if he owned the place. He might as well, he thought. Places like this were where he was liable to spend the rest of his life. The thought gave him pause, but then an image of West Angst flashed in his brain and settled his qualms. There were worse places than this. And he was beginning to savor that desperate freedom that arises when all else is lost. At least it was cool and shady inside. And quiet. He could fix the last, however. In he went.

CHAPTER 9

▼

The first thing that caught his eye was a carved plaque, pegged to a beam. It read; "Things are not as bad as they seem, they're worse." The one next to it said; "They told me to cheer up, things could be worse. So I did, and sure enough, They got worse."

That seemed to be the sum total of the interior decoration, wooden plaques variously crude or polished, with ever more cynical mottoes burned, carved, painted, or even gilded thereon. Over the stage was the largest of these slabs of wood, a burl of pricey maddack, purple and brown and yellow-white, with the legend "The Mocking Void Welcomes You." Conway pondered this statement for a while, and could only suppose that this was the name of the establishment. There was no one else visible, and so after reading a few more slogans, he cleared his throat, and called out.

There was a bustle behind him and he turned to overlook a diminutive slattern, complete with broom. This apparition stood her ground, arms akimbo, with the broom jutting up from one fist like the tail of an enraged draken. She was as wrinkled as a draken, also, and her eye was blacker and brighter. She cocked her head and regarded him so intently that he felt he should throw her a fish. Throw it from a safe distance. She looked like she might snap at him, and take a finger.

"Well?" Her voice was a salty rasp like that of a sea dactyl, too.

He tried to regain his voice. "Well, what?"

"Well, do you want something, or did you come all the way from South Wherever just to gawk at an honest business woman?"

"Is this your...place?"

"Indeed it is. The Listen to the Mocking Void Tavern, Goody Maceyrose, proprietor, at your service." Somehow he got the distinct impression that this statement was to be taken as a traditional greeting, with the real level of welcome to be determined later.

"I would like something to eat....And some advice."

"Food is cheap and necessary and good. Advice may be none of these."

She cocked her head over to her other shoulder, and returned the broom to the floor.

"We're not open for business until noon, but if you can pay, I can cook." She conceded.

He thought that she might not value mere words, so he pulled his cash string part way out of his spoan. She nodded, and turned to the kitchen without another word. He decided that he might as well find another to dispense advice, so contented himself with detaching two coppers and ringing them on the kitchen bar. He was rewarded with another flash of those black, black eyes and soon a plate of cold dactyl, a dice of beetles and hard boiled psallie egg, and a plate of hot fried brot was slipped in front of him. The two coins were whisked away, and when he asked for only a jack of limewater to drink, a scant handful of ginae was returned to him. He set to his meal and the old woman returned to her cleaning. He ate in silence, accentuated, rather than broken, by the whisk of her broom on the blue tile floor.

He finished his meal standing, chuitar bag resting against his leg, and considered his options. Apparently, the market was at low ebb. Perhaps after noon, or nearer dusk, there might be some action, or then again, he hadn't seen any of the great rafts offshore. He might as well go back to his coracle, and indulge in a nap, or else find a shady spot and practice for an hour. Or both.

The broom ceased its surrusation. He looked over his shoulder to catch one of those black eyes.

"Do you hire musicians?"

"Aye, but…"

"But?"

"The Ravelli Ravishers play every night except Twasdy."

"And then?"

"Twasdy eve we have a singthing….Anybody can play, what wants to."

"I may want to."

"You'll be welcome." She closed her mouth with a snap and turned to resume her duties.

"Excuse me…when is that."

She snapped around, obviously not one to chew her brot twice. "I told ye, Twasdy."

"No. I mean what day is it now?" He flustered a moment. "I lost track of the day, I'm sorry."

"Who better to know." She relented. "It's Sundy….All day." She bit off another snap of civility. "Half gone now."

"Thank you, so much." Could it have been only six days since the Sailback burned? LLord! He thanked her again and gathered up his bag and set off into the sunbright noon of Cashamash. There must be other Inns and taverns, other places to play. All it would take was time…

He felt the weight of his spoan and decided he had enough moneys for survival and even a little excess. He couldn't think of anything he needed to buy, but he supposed that someone on the island sold musical instruments, and so…He meandered about for a while, trying to find any plan to the market, but without any success. There was no apparent center to Cashamash, no Principal Square, or nexus of concentration, except for the Magnary and the public pillory. He was impressed with the pillory, which were the more humane foot stocks, in this case. A person had a chance of survival here, at least if he had a friend to bring him food.

Indeed, there was no obvious government at all, no police or watch, no officious busy bodies paid to investigate other person's activities, what so ever. He had grown up under the constant eye of the Olders of Angst, and the very idea of a society free of such surveillance made him happily oblivious of the fact that somebody had to pay for and maintain the Cashamash Navy. It really wasn't his fault; he just didn't know any better. The road to hell is paved with the behinds of people who don't know any better.

He found himself back at grassy common opposite the Mocking Void, which was distinguished only with some immense feather palms, and the shabby pillory, unoccupied at the moment

So, serene in his ignorance, Conway found a shady, quiet corner under a moab tree and unlaced his bag and brought out his chuitar and commenced to play, to the total indifference of all passersby-by. He tried to maintain a pleasant smile on his face, but it really wasn't a well-practiced attribute, and soon his smile slipped off, and he became absorbed in his music. There were a few more people on the street, but they all were intent on their own business, and paid the hopeful busker little heed. Conway barely noticed, as he was intent on enunciating a semi-quaver on the third string, while arppegiating the other six strings evenly. He eventually was dragged from his reverie by a shadow that fell across him, blocking the setting sun and chilling him enough to attract his attention.

He looked up and saw a bulky person, of indeterminate sex, wearing a garish wrappa so long it touched the ground, and a swathe of vests, shawls, and feather boas. This gathered his attention, especially when he noticed that this person had, apparently, three hats on its head, each crownless, with his extravagant topknot poking through all. Conway unashamedly stared upward, and was quite unprepared when the person said, apparently to itself, "Well….If that isn't the silliest thing I've ever seen in all my days!"

He was irritated at being dragged from his concentration, and had been feeling a little battered by fate recently, and so spoke a little more harshly than he would normally have.

"I'm not a mirror."

"If I was, I'd be reflecting a dummy." The oddly dressed person apparently had painted its face a dead white and touched up its eyebrows a sickly blue. Conway thought he might be in the presence of a mad person, and so temporized his tone.

"And if I am, what is that to you?"

"I might be the Aesthetic Committee, and offended by your aspect."

"And then?"

"Steps may be taken to beautify this vicinity."

"Am I being mocked by an idiot or by a mad man?"

"I am neither, I am a Fool....An Official Fool. You have been warned." The words were stern, but the tone was one of squeaky mockery. Conway became surer that he was in the presence of dangerous madness and bent over to stow his instrument in its bag. It was time to evaporate, although his feet, for some reason, didn't itch.

The mad man spurned Conway's precious chuitar with one oversize sandal and Conway's sight went red. He was, with one part of his mind, amazed at this reaction. He was Conway the orphan, the unwanted, he never had been brave enough to be mad at anyone or anything...Not him.

But, another part of his mind was carefully picking out the exact spot on the Fool's face that he was going to try to hit. And hit hard, given half a chance.

And then, as he straightened, he became vaguely aware of another bizarre figure behind the self announced Fool. This one had a totally shaven head, black lips twisted into a scowl of concentration, and a length of dragonhide wrapped bamb in one hand. Almost before Conway could register this image, the figure, the man, whipped the length of bamb down on the Fool's nape, just below his hat brims. .

There was a crisp, if hollow crack, and the Fool folded up and then folded down to become a pile on the paves. Conway went into full emergency mode, and pulled the sack up around the neck of his chuitar and made to flee back toward his coracle. But the other man grabbed at Conway's shoulder and dragged him off in the opposite direction. Conway's most urgent need was to flee, and one direction was as good as another was. Or so it seemed at the moment.

They galumphed around several corners, actually Conway did all the galumphing, his companion was silent as a sea breeze, and slid into a narrow alley behind a rank of privies. The black lipped man placed a knotted finger on Conway's lips and listened intently for a long moment. He removed his hand from the boy's face, formed a loose fist, and gently punched his shoulder. Conway noticed that most of the man's fingers were twisted or shortened. One ear was a clot of tissue.

"Well, we lost the Fools. Close."

"Am I missing something?" Conway was still a touch irate. "Why am I afraid of a painted idiot?" The sense of the last utterance penetrated his brain. "Are there more than one of those idiots?"

"That wasn't an idiot, me lad. That's a Fool." The voice that came from the black lips was as soft as the man's footsteps. "Was a Fool." This close, Conway could see that the mucosae around the man's eyes were black too. Then, the color was no cosmetic….Hmmm.

"And what's the difference?"

"The difference's that Fools have the 'thority to lock you in pillory until you be a leather sack of bones." The black lips twisted in a grimace that might have resembled a smile, if it had possessed any humor. "You new here. Fools are the Wards of Cashamash. The powers that be, be unwilling to drive off payin' customers, but they willing to mock them. Unlicensed vendors, illegal buskers, 'nother matter."

"You mean that you assaulted what passes for a law officer on Cashamash?"

"You mean we…Killed him, if I know my business."

"Why!"

"I like you, lad, remind me of 'self when I young and foolish. Plus I been waiting for a chance to stiff one of those dactylcak busybodies. Cramp my style." The man looked about in what seemed a habitual manner. "Least it wasn't the 'sthetic Committee."

"He said something about the Aesthetic Committee beautifying the area."

"Means kill you."

"What did I ever do?"

"Be'd poor in Cashamash. Only crime they got. Let's squit." Then he turned around and thrust out a battered hand. Conway blinked at it and tried not to flinch when he grasped his shoulder. The feel of the twisted digits was repugnant on his skin, but he stood firm. He didn't seem to have much choice. The man smiled, horribly with his black lips, and Conway noticed that the tissue under his nails was black too. The outlaw spoke again.

"I'm Rogue." He waited again, as if Conway was supposed to recognize him, and then continued. "I'm a Labionecroe. Banned from Cashamash. That's why I'm down on the Fools."

"Oh, I quite understand. What's a Labio…what you said."

"You'll find out. Com'n?" He turned to go and Conway followed. He wished he had another choice. Any other choice.

They crept, rather than walked, from one wall to another, always around corners and up innumerable alleys. Even if Conway had known the city, he would have been instantly lost. The faces of all the stalls and kiosks might have been gay with paint, but their backs were decorated only with squalor and refuse.

Eventually they reached a lean to, a barnacle of palm fronds and discarded hoarding that clung to the blind side of a psallie butchery. The alley stank with the offal that the beetles hadn't gotten to yet, although every surface was domed with the hand sized insects. The clucks and chattering of the psallies filled his ears and the sizzle of the grill on the other side of the cochina corral wall provided a counterpoint to the rich, rank tapestry of other aromas. Rogue ducked into the waist high hole that served as doorway to his home and beckoned Conway inside.

The interior of the lean to was decorated in perfect accordance with its owner's personality. It contained a water skin, a net hanging from a rafter with a few crusts of brot in it, and an oil skin roll that looked to contain swords. A spear leaned against the wall. There were two hammocks.

"Aren't you afraid some one will steal your weapons?"

"Nobody steals from Labionecroes." He reached into his plain leather spoan and pulled out a twist of black leaf. He bit off a morsel and his hand crept back to the spoan. The sequence of actions was so habitual, that Conway was sure it was some kind of a stimulant. Rogue noticed Conway's interest and pulled the plug back out.

"Want some?" A peculiar smile touched his black lips. "Finest lavada, from the Contoax Peninsula."

"No thanks, I just ate…Wait a minute! Contoax is on the Main…"

"An'?" Definite mocking note to the smile now.

"Isn't that dangerous?"

"So is fire. Don't stop cookin'."

"True." Conway didn't like being dependent and ignorant all at the same time. "So what do we do now?"

"Depends on who 'we' might be."

"I don't think I grasp the difference."

"I…me type we…We here to rip and run." Rip and run was pronounced as one word and Conway inferred that this phrase was Rogue's method of existence.

"So where do I come in?"

"Might could use 'nother pair of hands and legs."

"And if not?"

"Big ocean out there."

"The thought has crossed my mind." Conway felt very lonely and somewhat adult. "If you don't mind, I'll wait here until dark."

"Welcome….The Fools will be upset."

"I imagine."

"You have a boat?"

"A coracle."

"Need passage."

"To?" The laconicness of the labionecro's speech was infecting Conway.

"Don't care....Away."

"That's exactly where I'm bound."

"Two days...If you help."

"Rip and run?"

"Ripanrun!"

CHAPTER 10

▼

As if that cryptic comment settled everything, Rogue settled into one of the hammocks and composed himself for sleep. Conway eased into the other, and tried to relax. He would be unable to sleep, he was sure. The light that filtered through the fronds was sufficient for him to catalog the injuries to Rogue's wiry frame. Every limb seemed to bear its quota of injuries and scars. The left hand, where it dangled out of the hammock, bore only two fingers and part of the thumb, and the rest of the man's components were in equally bad shape. But Conway decided that there was quite enough of him left to be dangerous. He decided to play along and to make an exit at the first safe opportunity....Perhaps sooner.

As he mused, the life of Cashamash began to stir, to bustle, to evening life. Beyond the wall certain truncated chitterings and augmented sizzles declared the conversion of several more psallies from dactyl to delicacy. Conway's nostrils were trying to convince his belly that he was hungry again, and his belly was trying to convince his feet to lead him astray, when his eyes noticed Rouge's hand slipping closer to the dirt floor of the shelter. The dangling limb attracted the attention of a particularly large yellow spotted beetle, which trundled over to investigate. Conway made no interference, knowing that beetles only eat offal. Hammocks and beetle shields were only to prevent annoyance from the constantly inquisitive scavengers.

Much to his surprise, however, the beetle lifted itself up on its four rear legs and attacked Rogue's finger. The Labionecroe slept on, oblivious to the rasping of the beetle's jaws. Conway slipped from his hammock and touched Rogue's shoulder. Instantly, before his eyes could even detect movement, he found himself flat on his back with Rogue's blade at his throat.

"What? What you want?"

Conway was sure that Rogue didn't even open his eyes until the third word.

"It's me…Conway." Conway was infinitely relieved to see recognition in the warrior's eyes.

"Oh…the boy." He sheathed his knife and drew back a step. "Don't you know better than to touch a labio?"

"I do now." Conway eased to his feet. "There was a beetle gnawing on your finger."

Rogue examined the digit, and gestured apologetically. "Sorry I hit you. The lavada. It make hands immune to pain, so we always covered with little nicks. They get high. The beetles like us, even if nobody else does."

"That's all right." Conway swallowed some words, and then continued. "Do you think it would be safe getting some food from next door?"

"Just don't let any Fools see you…Best leave your music box here."

Conway wondered if there was another reason for the request, but could think of no good way to demur. "Sure. Want anything?" But the black lipped man was already back in his hammock, his twist of leaf at his mouth.

The butchery was in full swing, and nobody took more than commercial notice of the newly christened desperado. There were plaited mats and straw cushions scattered around for the comfort of the diners, and most were occupied. So, Conway, after purchasing a brace of skewers and a jack of quaff, found himself standing about between two mats, the one occupied with matrons, and the other with warriors.

One of the women, perhaps a little younger than the others, patted the mat at her side in invitation.

"Here you go…good meat, ar?"

"Thankee Mam. Yes…sure is…I like the red, don't you?"

"Oh sure….We're from Crippen….Can't get to hot for us…makes the blood flow." She considered the young man and then said. "Are you new come to Cashamash?"

"I'm from Angst, we sell firkins."

"Oh, you must have come with Bilbeau."

"He's my nuncle." Conway was afraid that they would be close friends with Bilbeau, but he was unused to evasion, and took refuge in the truth. But they seemed to be only concerned with classifying him as harmless and the conversation veered off in a thousand directions, and soon became simple gossip. On Munge, however, gossip was the major glue holding society together, and was scarcely distinguishable from an art form. The only other media were equally handmade and so…Conway kept an ear tuned and the conversations washed over him like water washing over a mossy rock. There was no urgency to the talk, and no emergency. The assault on the Fool wasn't mentioned, although no other detail of Cashamash commerce went unnoticed.

Most of the talk was of prices and supplies, suppliers and debtors, but the war on Bluestem had led to an unusual influx of would-be warriors, all gathered here for the next long liner to the area. There was even skeptical comment on the Magnates' decision to purchase a steam-powered ram from the Northerners of Murka Ahven.

"Well, to think I would live to see the day…"

"Thusila, just because you don't understand a thing, don't mean it don't work."

"It's just like steam lifting the lid of a chai pot, is what they tell me."

"I had the loveliest copper chai pot one time, all enameled with drakes and draken. Red it was, and blue."

"Surely they're not going to build a copper pot big enough to drive a ram boat!" The woman shook her head and clasped her apron to her belly. "Taxes are high enough now."

"My Viltem says it's made all of glass and clay."

"And how could that be! Men are such fools."

"Just little boys, it's so. Never do grow up."

"What Viltem says, they spin glass into a thread and wind the boiler, the pot, up all tight like a rounders ball."

"Well I never...."

"Me neither, but my Viltem is a real smart boy and knows all of that 'losophy stuff. He says that those Murkans are making cloth out of that glass thread, and it's all lovely and shiny, like silk."

"Now, Bhethna. How can a body make cloth out of glass? It'd break and cut a body to ribbons. T'ain't natural."

"Well, you'd think so, but my Viltem knows all about those 'losophy things and he says it's so."

"Your Viltem, he's a good boy."

"Yes he is. He ain't too proud to talk to his mother. Not like some."

"Like most."

"More's a pity."

Conway decided on a another jack of quaff to settle his food, and rose to fetch it, as he passed the cluster of warriors, he heard a familiar voice at his very elbow.

"Anytime, anywhere, you think women can't use a sword..."

"All I said was..."

"How about right here, right now?"

Conway increased his pace, as unobtrusively as his fear would let him. The last time he had heard that tone, his dinner had been ruined by a rain of body parts. It was her, and she was drunk as usual, and looking for a fight, as always. He slipped around the corner of the wall and slid into the doubled gloom of the lean to. He crawled into his hammock, at least, the other hammock, and had time for only a few worries before falling fast asleep.

An unknown time later, he was awakened, by that same, hatefully familiar voice, now in an urgent whisper.

"What's the matter, don't you like me?"

"You fine, you just wastin' time. Labios can't feel nothin'."

"Oh yeah?" There was a rustle in the dark, a shifting of hammock strings.

"How about that?"

"Ohhhh…LLord! What you do, girl?"

"Want me to do it again?"

"Oh LLord."

"Does that mean yes?"

"Please!"

"My pleasure."

"Ohhh."

Having no other choice, Conway fell right back asleep again. It seemed like the only safe thing to do. And in the morning he woke to a council of war.

There were strange voices that woke him, mingling with Rogue's. He stumbled out of the hammock and shambled out to the jakes and then to the nearest chai vendor's. Repeated libations brought him to the edge of humanity, and gave him the strength to stick his head in the local municipal fountain. Refreshed, he went back into the lean to continue his new career as a desperado.

Rogue's visitors were a couple, if a very assorted one. The woman was dark of skin and sharp of feature, and her face was inlaid with spirals of silver and gold, seemingly cut into the skin. The slack of her wrappa was slung behind her and coved over her shaven head. Her most blatant oddity of ornament, however, was a dragonskin sash slung from shoulder to hip, bearing a graduated series of knives, perhaps a dozen in all, from a finger long eating knife, over one flat breast, down to an arm long slashing sword at her hip. Several of the blades in the middle appeared to be designed for throwing, and all were worn and polished with long use.

The man was pale and rotund and also shaven of head. His hooded robe was of a green so dark as to be black, and innocent of ornament. He bore no weapon, except perhaps the shiny steel chain that bound his garment. It was in fact heavier than it might have been, and the ornaments at the ends were perhaps a little spikier than necessary, but still, it was nothing overtly offensive.

The man himself could not have appeared more benign. His cheeks were shiny, his teeth sparkling and his smile ready. His voice flowed like happy waters and he more than made up for the taciturnity of his companions.

He hopped to his feet as Conway entered, and bowing, introduced each to another. "Ah, you must be the noble Conway. We've heard so much of you. Welcome, welcome, welcome. Fair Gwinnis Herself will smile on our meetings. Welcome. This lovely woman, this jewel of the west is known as Zharrissa, and her beauty outshines the glory of her very name. You know the redoubtable Rogue, of course and I, my humble self, labor under the cognomen of Mention. I am of the Pice, but have been led by my fate to become a citizen of the whole of this beautiful world. I call myself only a Pancreat. And now seat yourself, young man, and refresh yourself with this fine vintage and allow us elucidation upon this marvelous opportunity to grasp riches beyond the dreams of lesser persons. Sir, I promise you, that this is not only a caper to infame the fi...four of us, but to make our very names shine sacred down through-out all the ages of great Munge, yet unrolled."

Mention didn't stop for breath, his flow of words seemed not to require air at all, but he was instantly silenced with a curt gesture from Zharrissa. He sank to his haunches and Conway availed himself of the hammock, and Rogue and Zharrissa, each more cryptic than the other, set out a plan to loot the Magnates' gold, and more important, escape with their lives.

"It is thus:" She said, "We wit well that the Magnates, skankards all, deem it sooth to purchase this ram of steam from the wrights of Ahven in Murka."

"An' they Murkans give no credit. Metal clinks, dactylcak stinks."

"And also is it known that these Magnates converse privily through the very firma beneath our fundaments." She patted the packed earth of the floor with one bejeweled hand.

"And all we need to know is where...and when."

"And we strike...thus." And suddenly there was a blade blurring from Zharrissa's fingers and an innocent beetle was pinned to the wall across the length of the lean to.

Mention chimed in. "So you see, my boy, this is why we need you. Nobody has ever been able to decipher, to understand, the language of the underdrums. But we hear that you have a talent for music, for understanding dialects of foreigners, and so all you have to do, is to listen to the underdrums and let us know when the moneys will be handed over to the Murkan wrights. Then we will help our selves, to liberate, as it was these same moneys and you will receive a share sufficient to satisfy your very heart's desire. What an opportunity for a young man! I know you will help us." Here the older spread his hands unctuously and smiled a smile so innocent and warming that Conway was almost won over in spite of his cold knowledge of three facts.

One was that, nobody on Cashamash could have told of his musical gifts except for a certain lethal Outer, two, that nobody was about to invite a callow stripling like himself on any desperate venture unless they were prepared to eliminate him as soon as his usefulness was over, and three, that Attilina must have set up his meeting with Rogue that lead to the cold murder of a civic functionary. So all and all, he knew that he was as expendable as that poor beetle, thrashing its legs around Zharrissa's throwing knife. He had only one card to play, and it was obviously futile to mention that his sole desire was to be left alone to play his music.

"Oh, of course. I want riches as much as anybody else and I don't owe the Magnates a ginae." He tried to firm his jaw, and look stern, to little avail. "You can count me in." He paused, trying to radiate resolution. "Now what are you talking about...these under drums?"

"The slight of it is plain, even so." Zharrissa gestured downwards. "Each of the Magnates hath a privy closet, most secluded, and therin a leathern membrane stretched upon an great earthen pot, set level with the floorage"

"An' they beat out secrets, and plots."

"And all that is well known, but none wot the slight of the cryption thereof."

"Wait a minute…" Conway was grasping the point of all this assorted verbiage. "The Magnates talk through the earth?"

"Verily."

"And all you need is for me to decipher a language that nobody else on all of Munge knows and tell you what you want to know?"

"Exactly, young fellow, and you will share and share alike, a band of brothers…" The older's lips smacked together, and he continued….."And sisters too…of course….Ahh…sister, I mean."

"Well…all I can do is to listen. Actually I have been vaguely hearing something, but I wasn't…" Conway lay down, and pressed his ear to the ground. The other three fell silent. He thought he could hear a percussive rumble, like a wagon at some little distance, but it was unclear. He crawled over to the wall hoping to hear more at the base of the angle, but it was less distinct.

Then he pressed his ear to one of the posts that held up the thatch and was rewarded with a doubling of the deep sounds. They were patterned, and to come alternatively from different directions, as if a conversation. They were right, it did seem to contain meaning, but it was muffled, and overlaid with random noises, footfalls and the sounds of work, such as hammering and what might be the rasp of a pit saw. He needed to get closer, or to find a quieter vantage or…

"I've got an idea." He rose and grabbed his chuitar from its bag. Touching it made him realize he was wasting time, if not his life. He was a musician, not some adventurer. He had important things to do, and the whole world conspired to thwart him. He gently placed the chuitar's back to the ground and laid his ear over one of the sound holes. Instantly, the muffled drumming became clear and began to resolve itself in his ears. Still bunched over the hole, he waved his free hand at the others.

"Go away somewhere...I need silence." He didn't even notice that he, mild Conway was ordering three assassins about. "You come back later...I have to concentrate."

Obediently, almost sheepishly, they obeyed and filed out into the burly of a Cashamash morning. Conway set his ear back to the hole. Perhaps he could scratch a hole and set the chuitar down deeper, or maybe he could even find a hide and make a drum. Was there anything on the coracle? Maybe if he turned a coracle over and lay under it...He listened to the beats under him and concentrated. He was having fun.

He could hear the patterns but there was no...He became lost in his listening, and sat hunched in that cramped position for hours, until various pressures and voids in his internal organs forced a break. He visited the jakes and then the psallie butchers and on his way back to the lean to, he came on Rouge hunkered patiently on his haunches.

"How it goin'?"

"I can't hear good enough. Either I need a drum like they have, or else I need to block off outside noises."

"I don't want to kill any magnates just yet. They get ideas. Nervous."

Conway was horrified. Apparently Rouge had only one tactic with which to cope with all the world's troubles.

"Murder won't be necessary just yet." He temporized. "If you could find me a big pot, and a thin skin, I could make a drum, and if I had a small coracle, a dinghy, or a heavy blanket, like a tent to crawl under..."

Rouge's forehead creased. Conway had the amazing thought that perhaps the labio wasn't very intelligent. It was perhaps his first thought that anybody else on all of Munge might be his inferior. But come to think of it, Hignore had made a lot of stupid moves. Maybe, just maybe, outlaws were people who couldn't make an honest living, and relied on scaring regular folk to compensate. Hmmm. He tried again.

"Here's what you do, if you want this to work. Get me the biggest, the widest clay pot you can carry, and a split rawhide, and a couple of blankets and a thick hide bigger than a man, and a few fathoms of thong, and a water bottle." He paused, searching the outlaw's face for comprehension. It took a while but it came.

"Right, a tent, and a drum. What do you want the water bottle for?"

"To drink water out of. I don't want to go to the fountain every hour."

"Good thinkin'. You not so dumb. I'll bring you some food too."

"Thanks...And a chamber pot, if the budget will bear it."

"Easy to steal, but hurts my pride."

"We'll rub the sore spots with moneys."

"Hehehehehehe. You all right, boy. I be back."

"I'll be working."

Conway listened to the beats growling out of his chuitar until full dark, when he had to exchange body fluids again, and eat. A little while later Zharrissa and Mention showed up, the latter stumbling under the biggest crock Conway had ever seen. It was cracked and dirty, and reeked of rotten fish, but it should do the trick.

Zharrissa had two hides and a hank of thong, and, proving that she, at least, had a few brains, a shovel. Conway was impressed, and resolved to watch out for her in the future. The three of them spent a few glasses sinking the crock into the earth, setting it with only a hand's breadth of the rim sticking out. In the mean time, the thinner of the hides had been soaking in water in the chamber pot. Conway wrung it out, and they stretched it as tight as they could, while thong-ing it tightly to the edge.

Then there was nothing to do but to wait, and to affix the larger hide to the wall and ground, making a smaller lean-to inside the old one. They banked the excavated dirt around the bottom of this internal tent, to block as much sound as possible.

Conway had been thinking of a way to dry and tighten the drumhead, and towards dawn crept out to the butchery, and stole a chamber pot of hot ashes from under their grate. He spread the hot ashes on the drumhead and accepted the admiration of his companions. And then there was nothing to do, but visit the jakes again, fill his water bottle, and try and sleep until the head dried.

In the morning, actually in the nooning, he brushed off the ashes and was rewarded with the underdrum messages, loud and clear. He spent some of his listening time whittling wedges and tightening the drumhead even more. After that, the beats were so loud that he could even practice chuitar while listening, and he was almost content, as content as he could be while embarked on such a dangerous venture. He spent several days improvising tunes to the rhythms of the underdrums, and trying to learn their secrets. The other three, awed by his mastery of simple acoustics, brought him sweetmeats and odd delicacies to help him wile the hours away.

He soon became aware that the beats, the rhythms were not a code, where a certain pattern of beats symbolized a letter or a word, quite soon. It seemed that the drummers used sticks of different weights and produced several different sounds with each stick. One stick was obviously padded, and the other was not, so that there was simultaneously a brisk rapping sound and a deeper, thudding, booming noise. He made a couple of sticks and painstakingly tried to duplicate the sounds that resonated out of the earth, tapping on the back of the ubiquitous chamber pot. The rapping stick rattled on much faster that he could duplicate, until he held his stick in the middle and let it bounce back and forth between his fingers. This doubled the beats and allowed him to alter the tones, depending on the distance the pivot was from the drumhead. This simple discovery filled him with as much joy as anything ever had since Heoj gave him the chuitar.

There was also some method of changing pitch, and Conway spent a lot of Time pondering on the method. They could have some control, perhaps a pedal to tighten and loosen the head, or else they could have a system of patches of lesser of greater thickness, here and there, so that striking one spot or another would give a varied tone. He loosened and re-tightened the head on his drum in segments and managed to get almost an octave of notes around the rim. He padded his drum with a blanket, so that his practicing would not be audible to the Magnates.

But still he speculated about the correct manner of changing pitch on the underdrums. It didn't really matter, but such thoughts were of much more interest to Conway, than any amount of illicit money.

Not that he hated money, or held it in disdain. It was great stuff. With sufficient money, one could practice all day and get good enough to play all night. He never realized that he was barely distinguishable from all the other fanatics around him. He just had different goals. But, after all, it was his trying to play along that finally gave him the insight he needed to decipher the language of the underdrums. There was never any single eureka moment, but eventually, gradually, he began to realize that there was no code, no cipher. The underdrums were just talking; the drummers were just vocalizing, as it were, actual words and phrases of the common tongue of Munge. This common language was so universal that it didn't even have a name, other than ling, as fish have no name for water. The Aludium could have told him that it was mostly ancient Ang with more than a trace of equally ancient Espanol, but what ever it was, Conway could understand it. It was not much harder than understanding the far southern accent of Heoj. It seemed so easy, but then not many had the ears that Conway possessed. It was like trying to understand a person with a speech defect and a foreign accent, but it could be done.

He was becoming wily, if not wise, in the ways of the world, and made no outcry at his discovery. He allowed only minor progress to his coconspirators, giving them just enough encouragement so that they continued to ply him with kind words and delicacies. If he couldn't play out in public, then unlimited practice time was a close second. And indeed, he began to try and phrase his chuitar phrases in the cadences of language. It sounded good to him to mock the words of the people around him in intervals and chords, and he had great hopes of making his instrument actually sing.

He also tapped along with the chatter of the magnates. They talked constantly, but on such a limited range of topics that he was soon able to understand almost every "word". It was amazing how much commerce and emotion could be transmitted with only a few hundred words of language.

The outlaws were seemingly content to idle around, robbing enough to survive and he soon came to realize that this was their normal mode of existence. To rob a little and to constantly dream of a score so big that they would…actually, they had no clue what they might do if they became rich. The outlaw life was all they knew, and their only joy was the actual breaking of the various laws of Munge. It couldn't last forever and finally it a conference was called. Unsurprisingly, it was Attilina who provoked the crisis. Conway knew about it before Rogue and the others did. She had gotten into a dispute with an axebeak dealer, and had been slightly injured by the lead axebeak. Each herd was led by old female axebeaks, experienced leaders called queens. These matriarchs were the closest things to native intelligence that Munge had produced, and were in any case acute enough to sense the spacer girl's difference. Perhaps it was her smell, or her attitude, but one had snapped at the female warrior, and she had tried to decapitate it.

Attilina had not known that dactyls kick forwards, like earth birds, and not backwards like people or quadrupeds. The queen's retaliation had stretched the spacer in the dirt of the corral, and the olsters had made the usually fatal mistake of laughing at her. When the dust settled, Attilina had been trussed with a deftly thrown bola, the olsters were still laughing, and the Fools clapped the spacer girl in the pillory in the square outside of the Mocking Void, until she expiated the value of a watchsorde who had been crippled by a foot in the scuffle. There was no proof as to the actual owner of the foot, but Attilina was the outsider. She had immediately offered to pay cash for the dactyl, but her attitude had induced the Ajudicor to place her in pillory, "For the Good of the Market", anyway.

Conway was informed of all this by the underdrums, and then a few hours later by his partners in crime. It was less than a satisfactory conference, as they couldn't mention Attilina by name, and he couldn't let on that he knew what they knew.

Mention, that master of obfuscation, opened the conference. "My lad, we can't rush, we understand, an artist, and we all understand that you are indeed an artist, but time presses. The tide waits for no man, nor woman either, and we must move with that tide." He beamed reassuringly at Conway, and only the fact that his eyes were cold and dactyllian gave the lie to his smile. "We must act quickly, the Murkans are expected any day and the Magnates have amassed the cash and gifts for them. We must, we must, I say, know when to strike."

"Sooth," Hissed Zharrissa. "There are bolts of silk and the finest leathers, coifs of pearls, and broideries of the best Hazlen wool displayed for all to gawk at right at the Magnary. The time must be nigh."

"An' a music box from New Ahven that cost a full gold…they say." Rogue chimed in.

Conway was interested in spite of himself. Could it be? "Is it a Frerisson?"

"An' if it be?"

"Then it's all I want for my share of the loot." Conway plunged on. "Could we go look?"

"Hast the sleight of the underdrums yet?" Zharrissa had never looked more dangerous, with the pure light of greed in her flat black eyes. "Hast?"

"I've almost got it. I understand most words, I think."

"Think? How will you be sure?"

"Well…." He temporized. "If I knew for sure what one message meant, if I could be sure that one beat referred to one specific event, then all I've learned so far would all make sense. I think…think, that I know what's going on, but I'm not sure enough to risk your lives on it."

"Our lives, my boy, our lives."

"Of course."

"What you want to do, kill somebody?" Rogue had only one tactic for survival.

Conway thought quickly. There was a limit to the blood he was willing to shed, especially his own. "We could start a fire or a riot or loose some dactyls or something. Something that would get every drum on the island talking at once."

"Well..."

"Makes sense to me...out of the mouths of babes, as the Olders say."

"Done, then." The warrior woman rose to her feet in one sinuous motion. "Hasten." Conway's fear of her increased. He wanted many things, but mostly he wanted to be far away, preferably alone. He desperately wondered if his coracle was still beached down in the sump. He couldn't think of a reason to go and check, as of yet, but making up reasons was what LLord had given men brains for. Something would turn up. If it didn't, he'd just have to run for it. Attilina was the greatest danger, because she knew him well enough to predict his actions, but she was conveniently out of the way. It might be time to take action on his own. If it wasn't already too late.

The formed up, a most motley array, and set off, and always Conway was surrounded by the other three. He didn't think it was any accident. The outlaws might not have been too bright, but they were survivors, and not at all trusting.

The night was falling, and Cashamash market was in full blossom. Torches flared, incense smoked, vendors hawked and buyers gawked. All the produce of half a planet lay about them in heaps and careful displays, and folk from the whole of Munge bustled and dickered with all their might. And the outlaws moved through the crowds like sordes through gaggles of psallies.

They passed the Mocking Void and the pillories, and Conway successfully tried to not appear to notice the pathetic black clad figure they restrained. In his attempt to ignore the obvious, he focused in on an even more pathetic sight. One of the emaciated women from the outskirts of the market, had brought her ragged blanket and few tethered beetles up from the sump, and had attempted to set up shop in a corner of the Common. She had attracted the attentions of the Fools, and three of them were mocking her, while another crushed her beetles under foot. The woman cowered away, and Conway noticed a whip thin woman with close-cropped red hair watching this drama from the shadows. Rogue touched his arm and jerked his head in the direction of the lurking woman.

"See th' red head? That's the 'sthetic committee."

"Just one woman?"

"One's plenty. She can kill a man with one fingernail."

"Strong?"

"Poison."

They crossed the common and came up to the verandah of the Magnary. The building itself was distinguished only with that complacent shabbiness that true success bestows on its possessors, but the riches heaped there were enough to capture any eye. Zharrissa had understated. There were enough luxury goods there to stock a mansion and not a shabby mansion either. Just at a guess the value of the merchandise displayed there was eight times greater than that of all of the Angsts, East, West and Angston Corners included

There were precious ingots of steel and whole suits of armor, gleaming helmets and casks of spices and liquors. And right in the center was the most opulent chuitar that Conway had ever dreamt of, much less seen. It was of variegated bloodwood and golden teak, and the headstock and sound holes were lined and encrusted with pearls of all colors. The keys were golden, of course, and the fingerboard was a single priceless sheet of black opal.

Rogue nudged Conway with a scarred elbow, and whispered. "Pretty, ain't it." He leered like a man telling a dirty joke, and said. "You can have it in your hands anytime. You say when."

And Conway's desire for the beautiful instrument died somewhere in the curl of the assassins black lip. Conway knew that Heoj's battered chuitar was all he needed, and he knew that the music was in his, Conway's hands, and he knew that he had just grown up. All the way up, and it was time to leave and live his own life. Or die trying.

He nudged Rogue back, and jerked his head back toward their hideout. They all filed back, and now, he noticed, they made no effort to surround him. They thought him properly hooked, a true member of their conspiracy. He knew that they could never understand the concept of having enough. Like honesty, it was as alien to them as breathing water through gills. He also knew what he was going to do, and how to sell them on it.

Once back in the lean to, he spoke first, telling their expectant eyes and ears what they wanted to hear. It was easy, just like music.

"I'm all the way in, and you know why. What I think you should do, is to go tonight, right now, and start a diversion, perhaps start a fire in an oil store….Or…you could set fire to that tavern near the commons, maybe free the prisoners in the pillory…Make as much noise as possible. I'll listen in to the underdrums and with what I know already, we will be ready to strike. All I really need to know is when the Murkans are due in, even what Longliner they're riding, and then the moneys are as good as ours."

"Right. An' Mention can torch the tavern, 'haps smash a keg of perry and poof! Zharrissa can free Att…Any prisoners and I'll kill a couple Fools and nip out with your music box. It's gone work."

"With outlaws like you three, how can it fail?"

"There's a nursery on the common too. It'll burn good."

"Good thinking."

They stood up, jaws steeled with resolve and filed out. Conway thought of a final touch, and whispered in the labio's ear.

"Do me a favor?"

"Ugh?"

"Don't forget the case."

Rogue just winked. Conway gave them about a thousand heartbeats, even though his hands were sweating and his knees trembling with eagerness to be gone and then he sat down at the underdrum and tapped out the beats that shaped the words "Alarm! Alert! Danger! Thieves!" He had never heard the word for arson before, so he pounded out "Fire! Fire! Fire! Danger! The Magnary! Danger!" As loud as he could. And then he picked up his chuitar bag and slipped into the night. He didn't blow out the lantern, or even take the chamber pot, of which he had become quite fond. He thought about taking it, but he really couldn't. It wasn't his, after all.

All the way to the sump, he fought the urge, the necessity of looking back over his shoulder. There were so many things that might be pursuing him. Fools, outlaws, the serried ranks of the Magnates in all their glory, a wave front of flames, a stampede of queen axebeaks, unknown dangers beyond even his wildest fears. But outside of his mind, none of them eventuated, and when he wound his way down the swampy bottom toward the sump, all he heard was the croaks and rustles of the omnipresent dactyls and beetles of the island. And when he finally touched the bow of his coracle, his knees were so weak that he could barely budge it from its bed of mud. The tide was out, and his precious coracle was almost its own length from the water, but he had no options left. He dug his toes into the cold black mud and heaved with all his might, the hide shell bent, but didn't move more than a hand's breadth. He was beginning to despair, and desperately think of where to get help, when another shoulder thudded next to his and the mud relinquished its clutch on the keel.

Once it was loose, it slid away so fast that Conway measured his length in the black slime of the sump. But he scrambled up and clambered aboard, and the paddle seemed to leap into his hand of it's own accord. His benefactor splashed alongside, so Conway grabbed the scruff of his neck and slid him over the gunwale, his sword hilt thumping on the bottom of the floorboards as he tumbled aboard...Her sword....All the fear he had suppressed during the long walk to the sump washed over him and he prepared to do something rash.

"Tired of Cashamash already?" He reversed his grip on the paddle and raised it in the dark, until the tone of Attilina's voice penetrated his fear. She sounded more amused than accusing.

He answered her question with another.

"What are you doing here?"

"My time in the pillory was up, and they let me go at sunset." The spacer had settled to her accustomed seat forward, and seemed totally at ease. "They even gave me my katana back.

"Why are you at my coracle, I meant?"

"I was staying here while you were helping Rogue. Everybody has to be someplace." She scraped a handful of mud from her breeches and cast it overboard. "I didn't think you would mind...Do you?"

"No...Well...No" He wanted to say more, a lot more, but he had the sense to stifle himself. He tried to think of something innocent to say, and couldn't think of much that wouldn't get him into trouble.

Attilina had no apparent suspicions. She asked; "Are you not going to help them loot the Magnates?"

"I want to play music."

"I want to see a war."

"Well..."

"Where are you going now?"

"Which ever way the wind blows." He thought that was a little cold and said. "We're fairly close to Hazlen, I might go study pipe tunes."

"Could you drop me off on Ravelli?"

"I'll drop you off at my first port. I need water and food, so I can't sail very far, without an ahven."

"You really don't like me, do you?"

He was silent for a long moment, and then decided it would be simpler to just tell the truth. "Not really."

"Would you like to do it anyway?"

"Do what?"

"You know…"

"With you?"

"Yes…Who else."

That seemed to be a question better left unanswered. "No, thank you."

"Do you not like women?" She inquired, indifferently. "Not that there is anything wrong with that?"

"Not all women, no…"

Warrior or not, she was woman enough to pursue the matter well past his comfort point. "Did you want to do that little girl on Smith?"

"Cynchie?"

"Yeah, her."

"Well…" He couldn't actually say, yes, I dream of her most nights, and some days, but Attilina must have detected his interest.

"That little sorde…A lot of good she would be in a scuffle."

"Maybe some people don't want to spend all their days in battle." He said, stung by her tone. "Some people have other goals in life, than killing as many other people as possible."

She dismissed the possibility as trivial. "Life is a struggle. Only the strong survive. That's the way the world is."

"Your world, maybe. I thought Spacers were more advanced than us primitive mud suckers. We try to cooperate down here."

"Like the Flies and the Somebodies and the Labionecroes."

"They're….Not typical. Most people get along with each other. It's called society. It's like…like being in a band. You have to help each other."

She was not deflected from her path. "That red head from Hazlen. Did you like her? Is that why you want to go there?"

"She is older than my mother was. Are you jealous of every woman I ever talked to on Munge? Are you jealous of Zharrissa?"

"Zharrissa?" The spacer sounded shocked, there in the night. "Did you want her?"

"As much as I wanted Rogue." The venom in his voice amazed even himself. "You're the one that wants every thing and every body. All I want is to play chuitar…"

"And get rid of me."

"As you say." His voice was like the slam of a chest lid.

She sighed loudly, but said nothing else.

CHAPTER 11

▼

She remained silent for the rest of that night, although she occupied his bed in the cubby as if it was her right. For his own cowardly reasons, he did not protest, although he did manage enough bravery to be silently resentful. So all night he ran straight down the wind to the nor'east, sliding down the slot of Skatter Strait, hoping to avoid the dozens of Skatterlungs, dark islands in the dark night. He didn't wake Attilina to tell her, but he was avoiding the war between Ravelli and Bluestem as much as possible. Dawn, when it came, was almost as dark as the night, and there was not a flying or swimming dactyl to be seen. Conway figured that he was half way down the Slot, and he began to look for an ahven. The clouds grew lower and blacker, and the wind began to gust against itself, violent squalls bursting out of the east against the steady dry season trades. He took a few battens up in the sail and unlashed the tiller, so as to steer manually. It was tiring, but he felt that he needed to maintain control of an increasingly deteriorating situation.

Actually, he thought, the more apt word was closer to influence, than control. A gust of contrary wind slapped the sail back against the trellis of the mast, and lurched the coracle so far aback that the outrigger came out of the sea for a desperate moment. He scrambled for the sheets and loosed them with one motion. The battened sail collapsed on the gunwales in a loose bundle and he struggled to lash it down along the length of his suddenly tiny craft.

There were muffled protests from the cubby, but he had no time for conversation, or placation. His options were few; he could rig a bow-sprit and a sea anchor and flee down wind, back up the strait, flying blind. Or else he could work a miracle and find an island, and land on it, in some approximation of one piece. He couldn't do either until the squall settled into some kind of steady blow, and from the looks of the sky, it would be an ill wind indeed. Attilina had disentangled herself from the bedding and was now on deck, clutching a shroud, and using unfamiliar words. He ignored her, and scuttled like a beetle to the prow, where he lashed a spare bamb batten to the angle of the bow and affixed a tiny yard and a rag of dragonhide for a bowsprit. He rigged stays and sheets back to the tiller and then rummaged in the cubby for the makings of a sea anchor. Attilina must have grasped the severity of the situation, for she subsided into a huddle midships. Conway got half a blanket lashed to a cross of bamb and into the water on a line, and still had time to secure his chuitar into its doubled bag and was lashing it to the overhead of the cubby when the storm hit.

It struck like a black wave, more water than wind, and it came from the northeast, as he had expected. He took his place at the tiller and motioned Attilina back into the cubby. She didn't argue. Then there was little to do but hold on and try and see any obstacle in the whip-ping dark.

It took most of a glass of white knuckled tension for the storm to reach its full strength, and when it had, Conway was unable to see even the bow of his coracle. There was a faint white wash from the wind whipped foam, but soon all was the same, sea, sky, and foam, lashed to an indescribable lack of color, an almost totally black whiteness that was indistinguishable from blindness. The only sensory imputs were the howl of the wind, like a thousand sordes in pain and the pounding of the seas over the stern. The wind drift, the foam, was so thick that breathing was more a matter of straining air out of almost solid water, than any process normal to mungely creatures. Time vanished, replaced by duration, a constant howling now, that just was, was without past or future, a constant, like gravity, like wind, like the ocean.

Conway knew he was dead, hung between death and life, and he began to think of himself as a money, flipping through air, without any chance of determining whether he was to land; heads or tails. Those three words became his mantra, heads or tails, heads or tails, as hypnotic as an irradicable song, so loud in his brain that it seemed his ears would ring with the very intensity of his obsession. He was so enwrapped with the struggle and the constant beat of his mantra, that it wasn't until a grizzled sailor actually came up and touched his shoulder, that he realized that he was safe, and beached on the heaving deck of a longliner.

At first all he could do was to blink into the storm, and try to resolve the blurred figure before him into reality, to some semblance of humanity.

"Wha...?" His best vocalization was a stammered interrogative.

The figure leaned into him, and shouted into his ear. "Cap'n wants, requests you clear this wreckage from her decks, and come to quaff...sir."

"Err...."

"I'll help you," The sailor bellowed into his ear, and Conway pried his hands from the tiller, and fumbled the bowsprit sheets. The loose sheets snapped away in the howl and Conway tried to rise to his feet. He succeeded only in tumbling into the sloshing seawater that nearly filled the coracle, but the sailor more or less gently raised him to his feet. Conway realized that he had been fighting the storm for more than a day, perhaps, and all his body was one great cramp. He staggered down the wind to the cubby and immediately stumbled over a huddle of black that had to be Attilina. She twitched from the impact, and raised her head. He gestured and shouted something into the wind, that the sailor never the less understood. The sailor scooped up the girl and half carried her away. Conway's knife was still at his belt and his moneys were still in his spoan and so he drew that knife and slashed away the lashings that held Heoj's chuitar to the roof beam of the cubby. He was regaining enough wit to notice that the cubby had collapsed to half it's normal height, and was vibrating like a live thing. Only the fact that bamb bends, rather than breaks, had saved any semblance of structure. Once the bag was in his hands, he staggered and stumbled out into the shin deep water that rolled over the deck of the great Longliner. The sailor, and two of his fellows, were there and he thrust the precious bag into their hands. Then, still clutching his knife, he crawled back upwind toward the stern of his coracle. The outrigger and mast were entirely missing, and there were only lashing ends of the rigging left.

The keel of his coracle was most surely snapped and as he crawled back, the sheets of hide that were the walls of the cubby flapped off and vanished in the white howl of the storm. He grouped his way to the stern thwart of his coracle, and his hand found the bar tight strain of the line to his sea anchor.

It was probably fouled on one of the great logs of the longliner. One slash of the knife and his coracle, his pride and joy, his life, was shot forward, down the submerged deck and vanished from his ken into the blazing dark forever. He had no time for any emotion, even if he had had the stamina. All he had mental capacity for was a beetle like scuttle across the wind toward a dark loom that might have been, and in fact was, the stern cabin of the longliner.

Horny hands helped him up two steps inside and led him to a pile of cushions. Softer hands handed him a towel and when he had dashed the salt from his eyes, were there with a horn of quaff that was the best thing he had ever tasted in his entire life. He drained the draught, nearly slashing his own cheek with the knife he still clutched in his hand, and then settled down into the softness and tried to take stock of his miraculous new existence. It was obvious what had happened, of course.

Hulled ships are almost unknown on Munge in any sizes much larger than a barge, or a galley. The great longliners were great rafts of valcewood, logs larger than two men could span. These great logs were lashed together, a hand span apart, into huge rafts, flongs long and wide, and equipped with hardwood centerboards and trellis masts and cabins of the ubiquitous bamb. They more closely resembled villages under sail, than any thing that might be correctly called a ship, but they were the backbone of Mungian commerce.

They had no freeboard, and needed none. They were unsinkable and any possible wave would simply wash through the spaces between their great logs. If the cargo wasn't actually washed away, then all that happened was that things got wet. As aquatic as Pancreatic culture was, this was little more than an inconvenience for everybody involved. The longliner had been doing as he had been, riding downwind on a sea anchor to survive the storm. Being larger and lower, it had been per-force slower, and he had simply overtaken it and washed up on deck like any other flotsam.

One of the diversions for crews on the longliners was collecting the fish and other edibles that came on board of their own volition, usually during the nights. Canny sailors left lamps burning on clear nights to attract such free delicacies. It helped if one was prepared to regard any thing that swam or floated in the ocean as edible, but Mungians were not dietary quibblers. Conway was just more flotsam.

Conway drained the last dregs of the quaff, burped respectfully and tried to inventory his surroundings. He was in a mat walled room, raised a few feet above the deck on short pilings. All the walls were racked with weapons and navigation gear. The decor was utilitarian at best, but the silver maroon of the rushes and the brown yellow of the bamb had their own beauty. These were especially beautiful to eyes that were capable of vision, and not, for example, ten flongs under the raging sea. He sheathed his knife and looked around again.

The only furniture was a low table or desk, in front of the pile of cushions that seemed to be Captain's station, and a sideboard lashed to the Starboard wall, next to the ladder up to the quarter-deck. There was a shuttered alcove to port, which might be Captain's berth. The ceiling sloped toward the stern, where two brawny men wrestled the great steering oar shaft, thick as a big man's thigh. The wind and spray and rain blasted in around this shaft, soaking the steersmen, glistening their naked skins.

They were of the Miaiai, a separate ethnic group that crewed the great liners. Their skins and hair and eyes were all the same russet brown, and they wore no topknots, braiding their locks into long plaits, that were never cut for their entire lives. A person could read their histories of promotion in their hair, as each raise in grade was recorded in a decreasing number of braids. So in this way, an apprentice would have dozens of braids, and a seaman would have eight, and a mate two or three. Joikor had five braids. Only Captain had loose hair. When installed in command of a vessel his hair was ceremonially shorn, and then allowed to grow out, for the duration of his command...Or in this case, her command. Captain, here, was fetching Conway another horn of drink with her own hands. She was a blocky woman, whose waist length locks were thoroughly shot with gray. Her face was a mass of weather wrinkles and her eyes wide set and brilliant. Conway unconsciously raised himself from his slouch when he felt her eyes upon him.

"Hola, Mariner. Welcome to the Longliner Grimshaw Evaunt. Where bound?"

"I'm not a mariner, Captain. I'm just a chuitar plunker from the Angsts...and...and I'm not bound anywhere in particular, just looking for work."

"Any soul that survived that storm for a day and a half is a mariner in my log, younker. Do you have a name?"

"Conway, Captain." He thought it was too small a name for such a grand location, the captain's cabin of a longliner, but he held his piece. "I'm very grateful for your rescue."

"You made your own rescue, younker, I mean Conway. The bottom of the sea is paved with the bones of sailors less skillful than you." She paused and cast an official eye across the cabin to where two sailors fussed over the sodden bundle of black that was the star girl. "Is your paramour from the Angsts also?"

"She's…We are not espoused, she was my passenger, and I think it would be better for you to ask her yourself. She is quite capable of speech."

Captain seemed to get more out of this statement that Conway wanted to put into it, and gestured with her chin to her two sailors. They half carried the star girl over and helped her sit on the brocaded cushions.

"And your name?" Captain was less polite to a non-sailor than she had been to Conway. Perhaps her attitude has something to do with the blade that Attilina still clutched in her hand.

"Attilina." A flat statement with no salutation. Conway was almost shocked; Longliner Captains were the most absolute monarchs on all of Munge, perforce answerable to no one. It was part of their total power that they had no names, except to other Captains. Each was simply Captain of his or her longliner. It was possible that Attilina was simply ignorant, or that she didn't care about any other woman, no matter the circumstances. Conway was most glad that he had disowned the star woman, and implicitly absolved himself of any responsibility for her actions.

Captain did not acknowledge the slight. "And your destination?"

"The war." The two women had locked gazes and held for a long beat. Attilina broke the lock first. "I'm the greatest swordsman on all of Munge."

"That doesn't salt my smeltlings…girl." Captain pondered another beat. "We're for Bluestem. Ravelli first. Fare is two silvers to Ravelli, two more to Bluestem. In advance."

"All I have is my katana, and you can't have that." Attilina's lip twisted slightly. "Your sailors let my treasure wash away. Don't you have a distressed seafarers tradition?"

"I don't need instruction from a clawfoot about my traditions. All I need from you is two silvers. You're not any seafarer." Conway could have told Attilina that the liners, the Miaiai, were loyal only to them-selves, referring to all island based Mungians as clawfeet, or mudfeet, or grubbers. The only things that the sea didn't provide the liners were the giant valcewood logs themselves. Attilina was too proud to beg from Conway, but he reached into his spoan without being asked.

He counted and calculated. He would have a little money left…"Four silvers, or eight?"

Captain held up one battered hand to forestall him. "I need a musi-cian in the second class lounge. Cabin and found and tips, and a small bonus at the end of the run. Accept?"

"Yes, very…I mean, thank you, Captain."

"Done. Welcome aboard, younker." She jerked her chin again toward the gnarled sailor that had rescued them. "In a glass or two, when the wind abates, Joikor will show you to your berthing."

She took a breath, as if this was a long speech for her. "Now as for you…girl. There are three classes of people on a longliner. Four. There are Miaiai, crew and passengers."

"What four?" Interrupted Attilina.

"The fourth, and most important, is Captain. I'm her." She paused to let this sink in to the spacer's mind. "Everybody does what I say, or…"

Attilina was still defiant. "Or what?"

"Or you walk to land. It's only ten flongs." Captain pointed with her thumb, straight down. Attilina got the message, especially when her peripheral vision located the sailor Joikor lounging next to a rack of crossbows on the starboard wall.

"You're the boss."

"No. I'm the Captain." Something that might have approached a smile creased her lips. "You can't be a liner, unless you find one of us to marry you." She looked quizzically at Joikor, who pursed his lips and shook his head, no.

"Passengers have moneys, and you don't."

Conway said; "I could pay."

"Crew doesn't speak to Captain without permission."

"Permission to speak, Captain?"

"Denied."

Attilina spoke up. "All right….I will do what you say."

"Captain."

"I will do what you say, Captain."

"Apparently you can use a blade." It wasn't a question. "Report to steerage gallery, see the steward, Chuinlisa."

"And?"

"Now!"

"But…Yes, Captain." Attilina, still clutching her sword, scurried out the door and three legged it to the next cabin forward through the waning storm. Joikor secured the door behind her, and then squatted down, awaiting his next orders.

"Your duties….Conway, are to report to the bandleader, Yhe, in the second class deckhouse and do whatever he says. If he finds you competent, well and good, if not, you will report to one of the mates or to Joikor, here."

"Captain."

"Then you will either have to pay passage, or work as crew."

"Captain."

"I have no doubt that you will suffice. That was a nice bit of sailsmanship, to survive that storm. Who built your coracle?"

"I did, Captain."

"Hmmm." She placed wrinkled finger to wrinkled chin, and surveyed him until he blushed. "Where did you get the dragonhide?"

"I worked for a tanner on Angst, Mariner."

"Hmmm." She pondered again, thoughts sailing seas unknown. "And your chuitar?"

"I did a favor for a man, a player from Gormley, and he gifted it to me."

"Quite a favor."

"It wasn't all that much of...I was just in the right place at the right time."

"We say, right place, right time, right man." She changed the subject with speed that left him dizzy. "Where are you bound, what are your plans?"

"I...don't know, Captain. I want to make music and learn to make chuitars. I guess the first thing I need is another coracle. I don't particularly want to go to the war."

"That's a smart boy." She nodded approval. "Do you mind if I sit next to you?"

"I beg your pardon?"

"May I sit? Next to you?"

"Ahhh...It's your cabin, Captain". He could not imagine a Captain of Longliners asking his permission for anything, but she just sank next to him on the pile of cushions.

"The best way for you to get another coracle is to come with us to Bluestem. All these fools that are so eager to see the war, leave their boats and ships at Lissa or in Blue Ahven. More in Blue Ahven, they seem to be recruiting more...The harbor is cluttered with empty shipping. It's a pathetic sight." She sighed, a most unmarinerly sigh. "All that commerce, all that shipping, just gone to waste. I hate wars."

"Really? I would think it good business."

"It is for a while, but every man killed is a loss to their home islands, that won't be filled for a generation."

"I never thought of it that way. I just hate war cause I don't want to be hurt."

"At least you're sensible."

"All heroes are dead."

"So true. Would you believe that even some of my Miaiai are planning to desert and seek their fortunes?"

"Really?"

"In fact, even knowing that if they touch land, they can never come back, except as crew."

"You have a good life here, on these liners."

"Indeed we do, younker. But we have one big problem." Her russet eyes searched his face. This close, he could see that her hair had a tight wave to it. He wondered how it would feel in his hands and then wondered why he would wonder such a thing.

"Yes?"

"Our numbers decrease, Miaiai are too inbred, every liner that gets his feet muddy is an injury to us all. We breed too many girls. We try to marry out, but most clawfeet don't find us attractive, too harsh." She placed a horny hand on his thigh, just below the wrappa's fringes, and then she lifted it to stroke the thin worn hide that covered his waist. "Do you find me harsh, Conway?"

"You have been most kind, Captain." He swallowed, making his prominent Adams apple do a little dance. His ears burned, although he couldn't see them. She could and smiled to herself. "Indeed, I owe you my life, Captain."

"She does, you don't. You saved yourself." She lifted the flap of his wrappa, and rubbed it between thumb and callused forefinger. "You need to get something dry on, younker, before you get sick."

"Perhaps I could borrow a towel, until I get dry?"

"I might have such in my close," She pointed with her chin again toward the port side. "Come with me, if you please."

"At your service, Captain."

"Tell me, younker, do you have many children on land?"

"Ahhh…I don't think so."

"Just as well, just as well. Come this way, and we will soon have you warm and dry." She spoke over her shoulder. "Joikor, tell Second, it's his watch, I need a little nap."

"Captain." He didn't giggle or smile, just obeyed. Conway didn't suppose he could have stood it if the old sailor had giggled.

CHAPTER 12

▼

Conway's official duties were as easy as his unofficial ones were arduous. And he became aware that granted wishes and realized dreams were tricky things.

All he had to do, officially, was to strum slow chords that no one listened to for lunch and dinner, in the second class dining lounge. He had been outfitted with the silver and aqua crew wrappa and a half lubb of arm jewelry, and looked well enough, he supposed. Several of the female passengers had similar opinions, and made advances that he would have found catastrophically flattering, except for his night work. He had been berthed in an unsold first class cabin, and every other night he was visited by an unwed liner woman, apparently chosen by lot.

He did his best to broaden their gene pool, but felt little attachment to them. For one thing, he knew he would never see them again, except for casual encounters on deck. For another, longliners tended to the wide and narrow and sturdy, and he had little doubt that any one of them could tie him into a monkey's fist if he was to favor another, or attempt to sneak a repeat performance. Orders were orders, and all. Third, they were so much a part of longliner culture that they had no conversation on any topic that he could respond to. The forty-nine Miaiai women and thirty-seven Miaiai men aboard had known each other since birth, and had such total knowledge of each other that they literally had no means of conversing with a mudfoot. They talked more or less standard ling, but their vocabularies and references were always eluding his grasp. They also smelled different, salty and dry, not bad, but different enough so that he could not desire them, as he desired almost every other young woman he had met. He wondered if he was flawed in some way, incapable of appreciating what he actually had, rather than what ever it was that he desired. His inexperience was such that he didn't realize the universality of these emotions.

In an odd way, he had to became closer to Attilina, just to have someone to converse with. She never ceased to twit him about his shyness, and seemed to never tire of trying to seduce him. She had no idea, that he was…servicing, a different liner women every other night, and sharing Captain's cubby all the rest of the time. She had him categorized as a helpless virgin, and he was forced to realize that he was, no matter how many red-brown Miaiai he serviced. At least he ate well, as each liner woman felt it her duty to fatten him up a little, and brought him trays of sea fruit and other delicacies, in lieu of conversation.

He made it a habit to meet Attilina in the lee of the second class lounge every forenoon after she finished preparing the vegetables for the day and before he had to play for the luncheon. One morning, a few days after they had passed Cashamash again, they sat in the shade of the third mizzen and watched the upper class cavort about a follyball net, that was swung 'midships over the Second Class Pool. The pool was made by omitting a few logs for a quarter flong or so. It was bottomed with netting to exclude sting skates and the more voracious varieties of moby, but was otherwise open to the ocean.

As usual, he brought her the leftovers from his midnight tray and strummed chuitar idly as she sorted through the unfamiliar morsels.

"Do I want to know what this is?" She demanded, holding up a stick of pressed willie skin braided with seaweed.

"How do I know what you want to know? I have enough trouble deciding what I want to do."

"You're getting quite a mouth on you, for a leek."

"A leek?" That's a new insult." He said with half his mind, while trying to invert a La eleven chord, so as to free the fifth string for the melody.

"A leek is a light gravity freek."

"And?"

"A freek is a person who lives in micro gravity. They live in free fall."

"How interesting…what does that all mean?" Let's see: the third of la was sha, and with a flatted ra on the fourth…no…A chi…

"There are two basic divisions of humanity; those who live in some gravity field, and those who live in free fall, who don't live on planets or in gravhabs."

"Free fall? Do they just float around in space?" He considered this idea for a long moment. "I thought there was no air in space."

"Well, at least you know something…." He ignored this slur, as he ignored most of her comments. Even though he knew she could and would chop him to gobbets, at whim, his night work made her slurs amusing, rather than irritating. Although he wasn't having the kind of relationships he dreamed of, the sheer animal enjoyment of the act itself was enlarging to his spirit. She continued, unaware. "Freeks either modify themselves to cope with vacuum, or else create habs without gravity. Some live all their lives in…Well, suits, gives you the wrong idea, but they make themselves into creatures that can live in raw space…."

"What is that like?"

"The Freeks tend to the long and thin and fragile."

"No I mean, what is it like to live in space, itself?"

"Well, I don't know how to explain it to somebody who is so ignorant."

She had the grace to look a trifle embarrassed, or at least uncomfortable.

"They erect great…you don't have the words…they use fabrics, to hold gasses, to focus sunlight, to generate power, to distill chemicals, to sail space. They can't tolerate accelerations, of course, so they sail about ring systems, powdering bergs and sieving dust clouds. They tend to live very long, mostly solitary lives, and evolve into individuals who are so solitary, they can't communicate even with each other." She stopped and searched his face for a moment, there in the shade of the thatched roof. He wondered what she might be thinking. She went on. "And they have trouble breeding, of course."

"And why would that be?"

"They are so fragile, that the act itself is dangerous, much less actually bearing a child." She tried to look concerned, with a moderate lack of success.

"So how am I like that?"

"The lower the gravity, the slacker the person." There it was, like a law of nature in her mind. "Leeks are less forceful than full geers, and we are wimps compared to people who travel highboost, or live in deep wells."

"Wells?" Abstractedly trying to make his little finger reach right…There.

"Gravity wells…planets are mostly useless, but sometimes there are botanicals or minerals that can't grow in lighter gravity fields…You wouldn't understand."

"No…Probably not." Now, if he could hammer on the ra on the second…

"And of course if conditions are different…Harsh enough to activate the Gould gene, then anything might happen. Heavy gravity planets are usually seething with mutations."

"Really?"

"Sure. That's why it's so unusual to find human variants like the Flyers on such a small planet. And as for the beetles…"

"They really bother you?"

"Yetch!"

"Well then, don't eat the things that look like blue strings."

"Beetles?"

"Egg clusters...Miaiai think they are a delicacy....No beetles on long liners."

"Oh. You're right. I hadn't..."

Just then, an old man with an eye patch came up and sat down without invitation. "Arr, boy, you play any songs from the Crippens?"

"I might know most of Parachute's Whimsy...But I don't sing."

"Does the lass?"

"I'm a Warrior, old man."

"And what of me? Do you think me a sorde groomer for fat old goodies?"

The old man thumbed the hilts of a brace of short swords worn low on his right hip. The twin hilts were worn smooth and totally devoid of decoration. They matched the old man perfectly. He also was worn smooth; even his abundant scars were seemingly burnished into his skin. He was one of those compact men who make the best warriors and sailors. Conway chose to take the old man's comments as genial and took his right hand from his strings to indicate the wooden tray of delicacies.

"Help yourself, if you care to, Mariner. If you could sing the words, I'm sure I could find the melody."

"Sing?...arr...I used to sing, when I was a lad." His hand hovered over the tray, and then descended like a wyvvern striking. "Egg clusters...Me favorites. A squeeze of lime..."

"Yes, they are good. Where would you like to start the song?"

"Oh, just play, lad. I'm a long way from my singing days, and near my last battle, and peaceful times like this will soon be rare enough."

Attilina had been inventorying the old man, and asked, with a trace of respect in her tone." Are you bound to fight for the Blues, or Ravelli?"

"Who ever asks me first. It's all the same to me, as long as the moneys ching."

"How can you not care who you fight for?"

"They're all the same, lass, all the same. Pirates or preachers, no different." The contents of the tray were rapidly disappearing, but Conway was content. Usually he had to tip the leftovers into the sea between the great logs of the longliner so as not to hurt the feelings of his Miaiai benefactors. They would have never noticed, but Conway was becoming used to the attempt of women to fatten him up, and had no intention of cutting off any potential supply. Like many emaciated young men, he could consume a tenth his body weight in food every day, without noticeable effect. He modulated his exercise into an approximation of the Crippen song, and the old warrior paused his foraging to wink his only eye in approval.

"That's the song, lad." He paused again, swallowed and said. "Takes me back...Arr, those were the times..."

"Was that your homeland?"

"Nar, it was me first war." His unoccupied hand indicated a scar, here on his shin, and another, there on his wrist. "That was when I learned how worthless I was..."

Attilina protested. "But you must be a pretty good swordsman."

"The best on all of Munge, but like I said, worthless."

"Actually, I am."

"Arr...Are what, lassie, worthless?"

"No. I am the greatest swordsman on Munge."

"Indeed?"

"Absolutely."

"And you don't know of Old Machmeell?"

"Is that you?"

"Arr."

"Am I supposed to be scared?"

"You....You do as you please, I don't much care. All I want to know is when do we get to Lissa. I came aboard at Cashamash, two days ago."

Conway tried to go with the change of subject. "I was talking with Captain the other n...Day, and she said that the winds were too variable to sail up past the Cluts to the Pice, and so she was going to sail south of Ravelli and then take a larboard tack to the Pice. We are just past the southeastern end of Ravelli now. It should take a few days more. You can see the back swell from Ravelli now."

Attilina cut in; "You seem to talk to the captain a lot."

"Not 'the captain. Captain. It's her name." He shrugged, without lifting his fingers from the chuitar. "She likes me, what can I say?"

"Somebody must…" She turned to Machmeell. "How much do you want to bet that I can beat you?"

"I don't fence, or joust, or play with wooden swords, little girl. I'm a warrior. Take me word for it."

"I didn't ask you to play games. I asked you how much you wanted to bet."

"No need to bet. Winner gets looting rights. Arr…winner takes all. But I won't fight you."

"Scared?"

"I told you, I'm a warrior. I don't duel either."

"I think you're scared."

Then old man didn't bristle, or laugh, or even look at her in reply. He just dipped his hand into the tray again, and said. "You play well, young man, what's your name?"

"Conway, Mariner. Thank you."

"I said, I think you're scared." Attilina never gave up, like a sorde on a bone.

"Did you say you thought me deaf?"

"No, scared."

Machmeell looked her up and down, chewed, swallowed slowly, and said; "Is it important to you to be the best swordsman on Munge?"

"Yes, it is." Attilina bit the words off.

"Arr….Fine. You're the greatest swordsman on Munge…Do you want it in writing?"

"Are you mocking me?"

"I'm trying to eat, and listen to music. You are trying to pick a fight. Each to his own."

Conway tried to sidetrack the conversation again. He knew Attilina had gone most of a moonth without killing anyone, and must be totally frustrated. "So, if you are the second greatest swordsman on all of Munge, why do you call yourself worthless?"

"Because, laddy, all I can do is to kill, to destroy. The most lack-witted kitchen scull can create life, cook food, feed the hungry, raise children. The most worthwhile thing I have ever done in forty years is to over tip-barmaids, and employ edgesmiths."

"But what of all the evil men you have thwarted, all the noble causes you have upheld, al the damsels you have rescued?"

"One man is much like another, as is every cause...As for damsels...The ones that were stubborn enough to need rescuing were too stubborn to live with. I give it up as a bad bargain."

"Then why do you still fight?"

"What else do I know?"

"Is that all the choice you have?" Conway wanted to know.

"I am very old."

"Lots of men older than you."

"Not many warriors as old as me...Arr?" He looked up into the sky and back to the tray of food, now sadly diminished. "If I was an Innkeeper or a Fane Older, I would be in the prime of me life, but as a warrior?" He pointed to the sky. They looked and saw to the Northeast a few cumuli such as form around the peaks of an island and below the clouds a few specks of black, on wing.

"They know, the demons, the bastard drakes. They know. They smell me blood yet unspilled."

"Drakes ? Carrion draws them. Has there been a battle?"

"Arr...Many a battle and many more to come. They know and fly from island to island...Always searching for the blood of warriors. Some day soon they will lap me own blood, and wipe their cruel lips on their black and blood red feathers. They know, they do."

"I guess….Would you like some more food, Mariner?"

"No thank you, laddy, all I would like is some more music, if you would be so kind?"

"My pleasure."

"I still think you are scared of me." Attilina had her hand over her shoulder now, close to her sword hilt.

"Mortified, My Dear, mortified." Attilina got to her feet and turned to stalk off, just as the look out at the foremast head called out…"Galley to port…Signals for boarding and parley."

The cry was passed aft, down the line of tripod masts to where Captain strode her quarter-deck. She leaned over the rail, and spoke, and an order was passed back up the line, to where one of the mates stood near the mainmast signals locker. He bent to the halyard and balled flags mounted to the top of the mast. There they broke out into vari-colored swallowtails. The galley responded in kind, and dropped its sail and out oars. Then, a large ensign rose to the galley's masthead and Conway got a familiar itch on the soles of his feet. He turned to Machmeell.

"An azure rose on a aquamarine field is what ensign, Mariner?"

"That would be…My eyes are not what they were…Is there a gold fringe?"

"Yes…I think so…Attilina?"

"Gold fringe…Yes, there is. Why?"

"Then that flag is the personal emblem of the Tetrarch of the Blues."

"Then, Attilina, you just might get your fight."

"Who is the Tetrarch of the Blues, pray tell ?"

"Remember Fat Boy from Ainsworth ?"

"Oh…Goody." She pulled her blade from its scaffold and let it slide back down into its slot.

The old warrior also caressed the hilts of his swords. "You know the Tetrarch?"

"We've met."

Conway expounded, while thinking he might ask Captain if he could hide in her cubby. "Blundoor is from my home island. He and Attilina fought a duel before, on Ains."

"Couldn't been much of a duel, if you're both still alive."

Attilina just snarled at him, and Conway temporized once again, although he had no idea why he bothered. "Things got confused...Blundoor's girlfriend darted Attilina. There was a riot. We left."

"At least you have some sense, lad."

"I'm a musician, not a warrior."

"Then you better find a place to hide. I've heard of the Tetrarch."

"I think I'll stay behind you, Mariner."

Whatever retort Machmeell might have had was drowned out by the bustle incident to the galley coming alongside and making fast to the lee side of the "Grimshaw Evaunt." As it happened, this was less than a tenth flong from where the three sat, and so they had a front line seat for the ceremonies. The pool emptied as the passengers drifted toward the galley, putting on their wrappas as they went.

Captain came up, not hurrying, but not dawdling either. All four mates were on duty, and the galley's gangplank was deftly shipped aboard and lashed to a pair of bollards. Two tavestists appeared at the top of the gangplank, and raised their triple belled horns in an unfamiliar fanfare. Attilina was staring skyward and plucked Conway's shoulder, to say: "I didn't know you had such huge birds on Munge..." But he was more interested in his first glimpse of Rosialindia, than deciphering unknown words in spacer talk.

First down the gangplank were a brace of guards, in dragonhide greaves, breastplate, and plumed helmets, all enameled in blue, brave with pearl inlays. They bustled down the walk and rudely pushed back the welcoming mates and middies.

They surveyed the crowd of Miaiai and passengers, and once assured all was innocent, signaled to the galley with their heavy spears. The tavestists gave another blare, a bit out of tune this time, and a chubby, officious herald strutted half way down the ramp and bellowed; "Behold the Tetrarch of Bluestem, Knight Regent of the Pice, and Emperor of Free Ravelli, Kreegah the First, Magnificent, Conqueror, Regis. Look on Him you Mighty, and Despair."

It sounded even sillier to Conway than the pretensions of the late Hignore, Mage of the Isle of the Flies, but he remained standing, chuitar slung behind his back. However, many of the passengers knelt one knee to the logs of the deck, and Machmeell rose and strode toward the press at the gangplank. Attilina rose also, but she remained at Conway's side.

The herald swept down the gangplank and strode over to the guards and then likewise knelt, and Blundoor and his Queen paused magnificently at the top of the gangway to drink in the adulation of the assembled masses.

Conway thought him heavier than ever, but he still bore Queztalbane naked in his hand. Rosialindia was perhaps even thinner and more predatory than before, although her hair gleamed in the sun like spun gold, and her gown was of a richness he had never seen before. Instead of a wrappa and a vest Rosialindia was swathed in yards of cloth of gold, so embroidered and beset with pearls and iridescent shell and precious stones as to require the assistance of two adolescent girls to carry her train. Rosialindia's gown was worth more than all the Ains and all their population put together. Conway was almost nauseated with the intensity of the hate he felt for the couple. Obviously they had done well for themselves in the short moonths since he had last seen them in the Devout Sailback, back in the Ains.

Blundoor preened himself before the crowd, but his consort gestured imperiously to the herald, who produced a scroll from an inside pocket of his vest, opened it and proclaimed: "All Persons assembled, herein, rejoice! We, Blundoor Kreegah, By Grace of LLord, Tetrarch of Bluestem, Knight Regent of the Pice, Emperor of Free Ravelli, do hereby proclaim you, Our subjects, Members in good standing of the Victorious Armies of Bluestem, Triumphant. Given by our hand this

Tressdy, the...." As powerful as his voice was, it was easily over ridden by the storm-tempered tones of Captain.

"Just exactly what do you mean by that?"

Rosialindia answered for her mate. "It means that all able bodied men on this vessel are now soldiers of the Blue, except for those unfortunate Ravells, who will have a nice bath."

"Not on my liner you don't." Said Captain, evenly.

"Easily corrected." Rosialindia smiled her sweetest and placed a golden whistle to her rouged lips. She blew a single note, and the two soldiers at the foot of the gangplank grabbed Captain's shoulders without even setting their spears aside.

Surprisingly, Captain made no struggle, just raised her left hand to her lips and blew a kiss back toward the quarterdeck. Conway felt, rather than saw a flicker of motion half behind him and turned to see Joikor vanish into the Second Class lounge. He turned his attention back to the galley in time to see at least two dozen blue armored soldiers tramp down the ramp and take the mates and all the other nearby Miaiai captive. Blundoor remained posed half way up the ramp, but Rosialindia charged down to the deck of the liner to better order the chaos.

At this, Attilina tugged Conway to his feet and dragged him, protesting, to the front line of passengers, clustered around the foot of the gangplank.

Just as they reached a vantage, they saw Machmeell stride forward and touch a knee to the deck before the Blue Queen. He drew his swords and lay them on the deck before Rosialindia.

"Accept the service of the warrior Machmeell, O Great Queen."

She gestured to him and he rose to present his hilts to her touch. No sooner had she touched his hilts than another, hooded figure, knelt to the Queen in his place. Conway recognized Mention, his late partner at Cashamash, and wished for a hiding place. Things were about to get complicated. He didn't know the half of it, for even before his heart had reached bottom, Attilina bustled forward, bowling passengers out of her way, spat on the deck logs and called out in her high clear voice.

"Hey Fatso! Remember me? You owe me a duel."

Her katana was free in her hand in a second, and just as fast, Rosialindia smiled to Machmeell, and said, "For your first task, Warrior, kill me this wench."

Machmeell said not a word. He just reversed his blades in his grasp, and swung to face the star girl. She was ready, and began that slow circling movement that was the precessor to serious bloodshed. Machmeell was content to wait her movement, but all his experienced reflexes were barely fast enough to parry her attack when it came. Only his unorthodox double bladed defense saved his life from that blindingly fast flurry of cuts and thrusts. Her movements were literally too fast for normal eyes to follow, but Machmeell seemed to barely move at all.

Conway was reminded of Heoj's fingers, that were so practiced and economical, that they seemed to not move, but to have always been where the were most needed. Conway shook off the fascination that gripped all the observers of this battle and edged left to where Rosialindia stood at the aft edge of the gangway. He had no ideas, so to speak, but felt that something might turn up.

Mention followed the Queen, bowing and flattering all the way. She cut him short with a gesture, and whispered something in his ear. He nodded, bowed and scurried away past Blundoor, and aboard the galley accompanied by the Queen's two train bearers.

Just as Conway reached the edge of the 'liner, perhaps two strides behind Rosialindia, a female hand reached out of the water and tagged his ankle. Startled, he looked down, and a bundle of sharp ivory objects sprang out of the sea and landed on his toes. His startlement turned to astonishment and then to relieved comprehension, and he saw a cloud of russet hair and two sparkling russet eyes just beneath the surface of the sea. A feminine hand broke the water and gave a single wave, and Conway thought to recognize Kelsoij, his companion of last night.

Quickly, he looked up in fear, but all eyes, especially the eyes of the Queen, were fixed on the flashing blades of Attilina and Machmeell.

The duelists separated for a second, and in the instant Attilina relaxed, Machmeell's left hand sword licked out like a sagitary's beak into a wave, and the star girl's right ear detached itself and flopped to the deck. The old warrior stepped back and crossed his swords before his chest, as if he expected the girl to surrender, or concede. Instead, she gave a single shriek of black rage and launched herself into one of her impossible leaps. As she leapt, she flipped forward, so that at the top of her trajectory she was upside down and traveling backwards. Her katana swept downwards and Machmeell's bald head seemed to hop off his shoulders, nod knowingly, and then thump down to the logs of the 'liner. His body stood there ignorantly for a long second, and then his swords tumbled from his fingers and his knees folded and his body collapsed into a heap.

Even before Machmeell's swords fell from his nerveless fingers, Attilina landed, flexed her knees, and flung herself up the gangplank to land right before an astounded Blundoor. His mouth was open and his eyes were wide, but Queztalbane was on guard. He had the advantage of reach and heft and height, and was also a few feet higher on the gangway, but he was instantly on the defensive. His heavy hand and a half sword, called a bastard sword by some, was a clumsy tool to turn the vicious sidling blows that Attilina threw at him, but he was one of the great swordsmen of all this planet, and he held his own for a few moments.

Rosialindia reached over her shoulder and her hand darted into the back neckline of her ornate gown. Conway had been expecting just such a move and strode forward, one step, and then another, until he was close enough to smell her perfume. She smelled expensive, very sexy, and not overly clean. As her hand reached for the dart sheathed below her right shoulder blade, Conway simply put out his right hand and grabbed her wrist. She had no leverage, and when she tried to squirm out from under his grasp, her left foot slid off the slippery round of the valcewood log and she slithered out from under him and right under the guard rope and into the ocean. She had only time for one venomous glare at her thwarter before the weight of her golden gown dragged her under the surface.

Conway was somehow left holding her dart, and one look at its black gummy tip assured him that it was poisoned. He didn't take time to dither, but cast the dart with all his ill will at the unsuspecting Herald. The luck of the uncalculating was with him and the silver dart, as long as his hand, zipped across the deck and right into the crease below the second chin of the unfortunate functionary.

Captain, as if she had been expecting exactly such a diversion, shrugged out of the soldiers' grasp. reached behind them, and deftly smashed their helmeted heads together. Actually, one of the helmets had come off in this evolution, to the detriment of the soldier, who had slackly failed to fasten his chinstrap in the regulation manner. The second soldier had no time to congratulate himself, however, before his own spear was most unfairly jammed up under the skirt of his cuirass and into his kidney, which soon failed to function, due to stress.

The other two dozen or so soldiers turned to cope with this outrage, which left them more or less at the mercy of Joikor and the other Miaiai, who had swum up under the logs of the 'liner, and had cut the net under the pool, and swarmed up from the water, and swung down from the rigging and unexpectedly began to snipe and spike and hamstring any Blue they could reach. The Miaiai have no tradition of dueling or of warfare or of fair play.

To them, pirates and warriors and mobies and customs men and police are all one and the same; nuisances to be disposed of as expeditiously as possible. They war using such tools as are natural and available, such as nets and tridents and grappling hooks and poison spines from sting skates, such as the ones that had been dropped on Conway's toes. Each spine is about two hands long, more or less, and stabilized for flight with a length of frayed rope yarn. Conway stooped and retrieved his bundle, stripped off the leather that bound their tips together, and began to look for targets. He was up in time to see Blundoor miss a roundhouse swing at Attilina, who didn't spank her foe this time. She daintily pinked out with her sword and severed Blundoor's spinal chord right above the hips. He dropped Queztalbane and joined his lover in the depths of the Pancreatic Ocean.

Attilina pounced on the great sword to save it from sliding into the sea, and then shook herself, and looked around for someone else to kill. Conway discovered an astounding lack of targets for his darts, and was shaking his head, trying to assimilate these sudden changes of fortune, when the sky darkened and something great and golden swooped down over the deck, with a buzzing demon on its back.

Flyers! Conway looked up past the rigging to see the sky dark with the great golden Quetzals. There were hundreds in sight, most well above the mast heads, but perhaps a score were swooping down to allow their green gray riders to broadcast baskets of writhing spiny objects. There were even stranger objects higher in the noon sky, huge round objects that refused to resolve in his brain.

Another of the great feathered dactyls swooped down between the masts of the galley and the mizzens of the "Grimshaw", and Conway realized that he had a genuine weapon in his hand. He threw with all his might and ignorance, and missed the Flyer by feet. He had forgotten to lead, and indeed had never seen anything else on Munge that moved as fast as the quetzal. Out of the corner of his eye he saw Attilina sheathe her katana, and heft Kreegah's bastard sword. He expected her to be smiling the smile of a realized dreamer, but her face was grim and white and streaked with blood from her amputated ear. The Flyer banked his mount around the base of the third mizzenmast. The great wings barely had room to pass between the yard and the deck, but the Flyer's control was exquisite and back they came. As they swooped low over the deck, the Flyer dumped out the last of his basket, and clapped a blowpipe to his wrinkled lips. He was coming dead on toward Conway, and Conway couldn't miss. He didn't, but it was a wasted blow, as two Miaiai topmen dropped a bight of line around the quetzal's long neck, and that was approximately that.

Conway turned, attracted by a flash of movement at the top of the galley's gangplank. Conway bellowed a warning, and Attilina bounded down to the foot of the gangplank just as Mention and the two girls cut the lashings that bound the gangway to the galley. The galley veered off slowly, and as soon as it had clearance, Mention was at the helm, and one of the girls was pounding out a frantic rhythm on the cadence block. The rowers at least knew their business and the galley stroked away from the Grimshaw at its maximum speed.

Conway was close enough to Attilina to restrain her from charging across the cluttered, bloody deck.

"Watch where you step!" He pointed down, to where tubular warty sea creatures writhed on the deck.

"Wha?"

"Spinnabuggers." He pointed to where an unfortunate passenger lay convulsing on the logs. He had stepped on one of the poisonous echinoderms, and in falling had contacted several more, and was now turning blue and losing interest in external events.

"The Flyers dropped them to cause confusion."

"It's working..." Indeed it was, but only among the passengers. The Miaiai were not interested in anything but protecting their 'liner from all enemies. Captain was scampering up the shroudlines to the Third Mast top, the better to direct her crew. The surviving passengers were either gingerly trying for the shelter of the lounges or scavenging the corpses of the Blues for weapons. The Flyers had no apparent organization, and were equally hampered by the web of rigging above the spacious deck of the 'liner.

Conway asked Attilina; "Who do you want to kill now?"

"I want to go home."

"That seems to not be an option."

"I've been wounded."

"I've seen worse."

"That's not much help." Her voice was flat and small.

Conway was shocked at her lifeless tone. "Let's get out of the war and get something on that ear."

"My ear has been cut off." It sounded like she still couldn't believe her injury.

"The lounge..." He pointed, and then said, "Loan me that sword, would you?"

"No." She snarled. "Mine!"

He finally realized that she was in shock, or berserk or something. What every state she was in, it was not one conducive to reason. He shrugged, and picked up a light spear or javelin. It had a steel head two hands long and apparently had belonged to one of the Blue officers. Whatever. Nobody visible had a better use for it than himself, so he carefully tucked the bundle of darts into his belt and then he used the point of the spear to flick spinabuggers into the cracks between the logs of the deck. The lounge was only a few tenths of a flong away, but it seemed a long journey. They only had to brandish their weapons at a single Flyer, but Conway suffered a slash across his calf from the terminal twitch of the quetzal he had helped down. The attack seemed, in fact to be abating, when Attilina gave a gasp of amazement and pointed toward the stern, where a giant sphere of translucent dragon intestine was settling to the deck, just afore Captain's cabin. Once more, Conway's eyes were seeing something his brain could not believe. There was some species of woven basket dependent from the globe, and this basket seemed full of Flyers. Grappling hooks were thrown to snag rigging, and Flyers launched themselves over the edge and glided to the deck, brandishing their moby tooth studded wooden swords. Attilina took one look and charged aft, scampering around spinabuggers, entanglements of combatants, and bloody corpses. Conway, although he had no clear idea why, followed close behind, making vague waving motions with the javelin.

The Flyers attacked, turning each stride into a long glide, supported on the webs of skin that extended from their wrists to their knees. This close, Conway could smell their dry reptilian musk, and see that their eyes were a lighter gray than their wrinkled green-gray skins. Attilina was capable of longer leaps than the Flyers, and swept them from the air with sweeps of Quetzalbane. Conway was content to stay behind her, and take the occasional stab at the merely wounded. There had been a half score of the Flyers in the basket, and star girl dispatched them with ludicrous ease. Conway was surprised in some distant corner of his brain to see that the dread Flyers were small, almost tiny. They couldn't have weighed more that thirty-five lubbs, and were individually no more dangerous than seven year old children.

The winged devils had been bugaboos for his entire life, and to see them so feeble was twisting some deep strata of his mind. It was as if he was diminished, as if his lessened fears made him less of a person. He even wondered what kind of an idiot he was, to have such thoughts while pursuing a mad woman across a corpse littered deck, while shriveled monsters chittered and snapped and died.

Pancreats believed the Flyers incapable of speech. but the last two rasped some sounds at each other, and then separated to pin Attilina, one front and one back. But their plan was foiled when he came gasping up and clumsily, but effectively, stabbed the second through the lungs just before it could leap on the female warrior's back.

The monster's tremors transmitted up the javelin shaft, made his knees buckle, and his guts lurch but he retained his feet and panted out to Attilina; "What's all the hurry, we were almost safe."

She looked at him with eyes madder than those of the Flyers and said; "I'm getting off this damn boat, and you're coming with me."

"I like it here."

Instantly Quetzalbane's point was at his larynx. "Think I won't kill you?"

"Um…I won't help you if I'm dead."

"You want to stay and burn?" He looked behind him and saw black smoke and orange flames lick out from the gable ends of the First and

Second class cabins. A new wave of Flyers was skreeching down the length of the deck, and these were dropping flaming torches.

"I never heard of Flyers using fire…"

"What do you suppose works that balloon?"

"Ball…"

"The flying ball." She jerked her thumb back over her shoulder and he swallowed against her point. He realized that his life was over and his only choice was between demises, so he let her herd him aboard the basket.

"Hurry, before the envelope cools!" She lay the bastard sword against the wattle of the basket and began rummaging around in the cluttered jumble in the square basket.

"What are you looking for?"

"Fuel."

"What's….Oh something that burns?"

"Dork!"

"How about moby oil?" He reached across the basket, it was barely two arm spans wide, and tugged out a black sagitary skin of oil.

"Bosto!"

"I wish you would talk normal." He said, perhaps pettishly, but she paid no heed, just hefted the skin, unlashed the spout and poured a healthy gout into a complicated thin pottery bucket suspended in the mouth of the balloon's neck. Conway had no idea what she was trying to accomplish, but was committed to help her. Above them, the balloon envelope began to sag and droop. Attilina, seeing this, became even more frantic.

"Help me!" She turned and screamed right into his face. "Help me, you primitive lumpen dolt!"

He was seized with the calm that is granted to people who are beyond the comprehension of fear. "What do you want me to do?"

"Set fire to this oil, you ignorant grubber!"

"Oh." There was an oilskin pouch hanging below the edge of the pottery burner, half concealed among a tangle of tubing and pipes. He opened it, and there was a flint rock and a steel striker, and a wad of waxed moss. He had no reason to be frugal, and so scraped a shower of sparks into the moss, and when tiny glows began to form, blew them into a flame. He cast this fire into the puddle of oil in the burner and was amazed when it phooffed into instant flame. There must have been some other liquid mixed with the oil to make it more volatile.

The hot air rushed into the balloon, and they both felt the basket stir beneath them and try to lift from the deck. Attilina looked wildly about her, and screamed, "Pour more in ! We need more fire!"

Conway started to dump the rest of the skin into the flame, and then visualized himself as a crisp of black wafted through the sky like a cinder. Even though he really didn't want to fly, there seemed better ways to accomplish it than that. He looked around again, and some of the fittings to the burner came into focus. Let's see…If this spout was attached to this length of tanned intestine, and…He looked up, and sure enough, there was a line and a pulley hanging down from another line that seemed to depend from the top of the balloon, far above their heads. So he attached the spout and found a bone ring sewed to the skin and attached the hook to the ring and hauled the skin above the level of the burner. It was designed to hang well over to one side, out of the direct heat of the flame, and he knew that he was on the right track.

But the oil refused to flow, while Attilina pummeled him with unknown words, none complimentary. He examined the intestine hose more closely and found a cleverly carved bone clamp that seemed to have several racheting settings. He flicked it all the way open and was rewarded with a fresh burst of flame that settled down into steady roar. The balloon lifted more confidently, and tugged gently at its restraining ropes.

"Cut the ropes…Cut the ropes!"

Conway leaned over the side of the basket and applied his knife to the closest anchoring line. It fell away with a dull sprang, and he reached for the next. Attilina had made short work of the others, and when his rope parted the balloon leapt clumsily into the air, barely cleared the quarter deck, brushed the head of the helmsman steadfast at the binnacle, and then floated behind the "Grimshaw Evaunt". Fortunately, the liner had come about with no one to trim the sails and the gentle wind carried them away from the tangle of rigging. No sooner had the balloon cleared the after cabin, then it gently began to settle toward the water. Conway was still draped over the edge of the basket, and it was easy, actually too easy, to see the rounded backs and massive tails of a school of mid-sized mobies following the raft. They were obviously hoping for just such morsels as a basket of fugitive idiots. In a few moments, the basket was low enough that Conway could smell the rank dactyl breath of their spouts, and feel the droplets of water they blew up. Attilina was screaming again, and he turned to look.

The fire was blazing cheerfully, but somehow, it was not providing enough lift and the spacer was frantically throwing the contents of the cluttered basket overboard. Conway was almost as mystified as he was scared.

"What are you doing?"

"We got to lighten the balloon! We're sinking!"

There didn't seem to anything to say to that, so he looked around for things to throw away. There were some Flyer weapons, blowpipes and twirl spears, and over they went. The skins of oil had to stay, and when he reached for Queztalbane, she snarled at him.

"Throw away your chuitar!"

He just ignored her, and rummaged for a pile of skin or leather huddled in a corner of the basket. It seemed strangely warm and heavy, and as he persisted, it unraveled a spindly arm. Startled, he stood back, and the arm reached for a lever that protruded from the side of the basket. The arm jerked the lever. There was a gasp of indrawn air, and then the arm was joined with another, and the motion reversed. There come another great whoosh of air and the flame above them tripled in intensity. The bundle of skin unfolded further, and Conway found himself staring into the eyes of a particularly dark and misshapen Flyer. It released the lever, and gestured imperiously. Conway had a flash of insight, exclaimed; "A bellows!", and set to pumping vigorously. The flame roared, the envelope tauntened, the balloon gained altitude, and Attilina stopped cursing.

So far so good. The balloon rose gracefully, and when it was a few flongs up, Conway ceased his pumping and the flame in the basket subsided to a dull roar....The Flyer had shrunk into a huddle again and it seemed time to take stock, and make plans.

It also seemed a real good time to not look over the edge of the basket, so naturally he had to...The bottle green sea was so far below them it seemed like an abstraction, and Conway was fascinated by the patterns the light wind made on the water and by the thousand subtle colors the golden sun struck from the living sea. Attilina joined him and they could see that they had left the turmoil below them. The 'liner was few dozen flongs behind them and they could see the gentle mountains of the central spine of Ravelli downwind of them. But their attention was drawn to a closer commotion immediately to the Northeast

At first all they could see was a long thin cloud that hugged the surface of the sea, and then soon they could discern that it was a line of dark smoke that trailed back from a wake sketched on the surface of the ocean. It was so amazing to Conway to see so much, so clearly, that he quite ignored the protests of his gut and strained over the wicker edge of the basket. He noticed that the wake was arrowing southeast, and the line of smoke was being blown northeast. Not an impossible tack, but the wake looked very robust, and he wondered...Deep inside his mind, fragments of hearsay began to coalesce.

As they soared over the wake, they thought to distinguish a commotion, a flurry of activity around the vessel below. The ship was white, that much was clear, and larger than the usual galley. He strained to see the oars, but try as he might, he just couldn't make them resolve....Perhaps it was a galley on fire, but then it wouldn't leave a wake. It was obviously under way....

Next, the flurry around and above the ship became clear as a swirl of gray Flyers, mounted on their golden winged quetzals. Again and again they swooped to attack the strange ship and again and again they banked away, seemingly in frustration. As the balloon approached even closer, Conway clipped the bone clamp down on the feed line and the fire in the clay brazier subsided. As the rush of the flames quieted, he could hear the squalls of the quetzals, the rasping of their riders and a strange, breathy chatter that seemed to reach a crescendo as the attacks peaked and then lessened as the Flyers swung away downwind. Conway and Attilina were so far away that there was a noticeable lapse between the sight of an action and the arrival of its sound. A wounded quetzal, separated from its fellows, slammed violently into the green sea, and only after five long heartbeats did the splash reach their ears.

Wondering, he reached for the bone fuel feed clamp. but Attilina's hand knocked his fingers away. "Take it up!"

There was a note of panic still in her voice, and somehow this lessened he in his sight. He remonstrated.

"I want to see!"

"I'm hurt! I want to get to land and..."

"I don't care! You're not hurt that bad...I want to see what kind of ship that is. I've never seen..."

She cut him off. "It's obviously that steamship from Murka, that the Magnates bought..." She reached back over her shoulder and touched the hilt of her sword. "I won't ask again....get me to safety...Grubber!" Her voice was as cold as her eyes and Conway gave up without another quibble. Wordlessly, he released the clamp and reached for the bellows. Below him, he could see a cloud of white wash into the thickest flock of quetzals. There was a flurry of confusion and golden forms fluttered into the sea. A few seconds later came a vicious hiss, almost a shriek, as from a psigil the size of a Fanekeep.

"I think the Flyers are being slaughtered."

Attilina didn't even look over the edge of the basket. "Don't care."

"What?" Conway was as outraged as he was shocked.

"I said I don't care. All you leeks can kill each other off as fast as possible. I'm leaving."

"I thought you couldn't go back."

"If I can't, I'll figure out some way of killing enough of you off so I can be left alone. I've had it with grubbers."

"Is that fair? We never asked for you."

"Don't care. Get me to land." The blood had clotted around her wound, but enough had leaked out to stain her neck and half her shirt. She looked sick and desperate and very, very dangerous. Conway concentrated on getting enough altitude to get them safely to Ravelli. The first skin of fuel was almost gone, but he located another next to the animate bundle that was the odd Flyer...or what ever it was. It had huddled back into its corner and made no further display or sound, as if it was afraid to attract the attention of the outer girl. Conway knew how it felt.

CHAPTER 13

▼

Soon enough, they were over the purple hills of Ravelli, and Conway turned to the star girl and shrugged a question. He couldn't trust his voice. He was afraid that the hate and fear he felt for her would be audible in his tone, but he needn't have bothered. She was barely paying attention, standing hunched under the rim of the basket, one hand held near, but not touching, the place where her ear had been. He stammered something, and got her attention.

"What?"

"Where do you want to land?"

"Don't care....Away from grubbers." Her eyes blanked over again and he began to look for a soft spot. Landing seemed much more chancy than taking off, but he had little choice. Inland, the sea breeze had faded to a mere whisper and the balloon was moving at a less than a slow walk. He could try to set down somewhere, or else wait until the oil ran out and take even more chances.

Ravelli was one of the low islands, like the Ains, as opposed to the rocky, cliff-girt ones like the Angsts, but it was relatively large, perhaps twice the size of all the Ains together. Most of it was wooded with indigenous Mungian growths, and the interior appeared relatively uninhabited. At least there was little of the telltale green of olearth cultivars. One spot seemed as bad as another, and Conway could see no way of changing his course, so he simply lessened his labors at the bellows, and clipped down the fuel feed, and hoped he could land in one of the clearings that wild sailbacks grazed into the forest. He was lucky, to the extent that the sailbacks favored the gentle elevations of the Ravellian hilltops and so he was soon able to clear a last stand of purple decids and then, by shutting off the fuel, was able to thump down into a brushy meadow.

Apparently, there was none to notice but a pack of ridge runners, small wingless carnivores. They scattered, tails flirting the air, and Conway made to leap from the balloon, but his companion roughly grabbed his arm to halt him. It was the first time that the spacer had ever used her strength on him, and he was chastened by the strength in her small fingers. She really wasn't of this world at all. He wondered how he could have ever thought her a human, a mere Mungian.

"Wait until the balloon deflates, or it will take off again."

"Oh." That was all he could say, choked by the desire that the balloon, the girl and the flyer creature would all waft away from his life forever. But, fearful for his life, he waited and soon the intestine envelope sagged to the bush strewn meadow, and Attilina allowed him to scramble to the ground.

He looked around and saw no life, no green, no habitation. He shrugged and touched his chuitar for reassurance, stroking the neck where it hung beneath his right arm.

"Now what?" He asked the outer.

"Go away."

He wanted to say something along the lines of, "My pleasure", but he didn't really have the nerve. He didn't even want to turn his back on her, but he did, even though it made his shoulder blades itch with fear. He just sidled off, downhill, because he happened to be facing that way, and had almost reached the safety of the tree line when she came running after him, katana banging her back and Quetzalbane in her hand. He prepared himself for death, and his knees almost buckled when she halted a few feet away and said; "Look, Conway, I'm sorry. Don't go."

"What do you want now?"

She flushed and shifted her grip on the great sword. Her chin trembled for a moment and then she firmed her features, and simply said; "I'm hungry."

"And?"

"You're the grubb...I mean, you're the local. Find me something to eat, and we'll be even."

Something about this logic made his blood burn in his veins. "What do I owe you, pray tell?"

"I mean...I got you off that burning ship."

"It was a raft, a 'liner. I wanted to stay."

"It was burning."

"You had a sword to my throat." He looked her right in the eye. "Liners can't sink, I was safer there, than here with you."

"Look...Conway, let's not argue. I was upset."

"What are you now ?"

"Hungry."

"Well..." He could feel himself temporizing, trying to find a compromise. His hand fell to his waist and he felt the bundle of darts he still had tucked into his belt. No, that's what she would do. So...

"What did you have in mind?"

"Don't you know what plants to eat?"

"I could catch you a beetle and start a fire."

"Noooo!!!!" A wail of despair.

"Are you a choosy beggar?"

"I'm the one with the sword."

Conway wished again that he knew some of the words that Woodie had used back at Ahven. He sighed and turned back to the collapsed balloon.

"Where are you going!" She demanded.

"Back to the balloon...I'm a seaman, not a herder. The only two ways I know to get food is to get it from the water, or to get it from people."

"So?"

"Both of them are down hill from here. Let's make a pack and see if there is anything of value to salvage. You might hate grubbers, but we need at least one, right now."

She pulled a face, but followed his lead. They had taken only a few steps, when she said, "Maybe we can get something at that house over there." She pointed.

Conway couldn't think that he had overlooked any sign of life, but he raised his eyes and sure enough, there, on a little hillock was a wattle hut huddled under a couple of palm trees. He must be more exhausted than he thought, to miss that splash of green amidst all that purple-red. He didn't stop to think that palms grow only on the shore. He was busy with another thought; "Did you kill that Flyer?"

"No. It's harmless, it has no legs. It will die anyway."

Conway had no response to yet another tragedy, if a small one. He tried to put it out of his mind and to try and plan yet another escape from Attilina. But, as they pushed back through the bushes, they came upon a person who approached them, right hand out stretched in apparent greeting. He was dressed as a Ravel, but his skin was paler than anyone Conway had ever seen on all his travels. The man ignored him and walked up to offer his hand to Attilina. She just stared at him dumbly, and when he said; "Hyacinth Formyle? Your father is most concerned. You had best come with me." She dropped her sword and collapsed in tears, right there on the hillside meadow, sinking to her knees in the red grass.

Conway, numb, walked away. For lack of better direction, he went to the downed balloon, thoughtlessly thinking that he might find some salvage, or perhaps cut out enough of the envelope to make a blanket, or perhaps a bag for his chuitar. Conjectures revolved in his brain, and he wished they wouldn't. But he clung to the hope he was finally on his own. Obviously, the pale man was another outer, and obviously, Conway could not care less.

He reached the basket, and put one hand on the edge to peer over. Long spindly fingers wrapped around his wrist and his arm was jerked into the basket. He pulled back in a spasm of revulsion, and ripped his hand from the grasp of the Flyer, and when he examined his wrist, there were two long parallel scratches on it that welled red blood. He reached for the bundle of darts at his belt, pulled one free in a blind rage and brandished it over his head, while he looked for a good place to stab the mutant Flyer. After all the harassment and loss he had suffered, there was finally some one even weaker than he to take revenge on. He knew, with shame, that he was feeling an unworthy emotion, but he couldn't bring himself to care. The Flyer cowered back into its corner and crossed its sticks of arms in front of its wrinkled, hideous face. Conway could see its pleading gray eyes, and he hesitated just long enough for the male Outer to come up behind him and say; "It wasn't attacking you, you know."

Conway turned in amazement. He couldn't find a word, or even a sound to emit.

"Its just hungry. They have to live on blood. Their digestive tracts are severly atrophied."

"Good. You feed it."

"I'm sorry, but our blood is too…unnatural….Too medicated for Mungians. We would poison it."

"What are you talking about, and why should I care?"

The man smiled and put out his hand again, as if he expected Conway to do something with it. Conway just stared at him until the spacer let his hand fall to his side. He started to speak, hesitated and then started again.

"Allow me to introduce myself. My name is Feggio, Salvadore Feggio. Call me Sol." He smiled again, and again, Conway was having none of it. His shock and disgust was transmutating into pure raw anger. The man, Sol, went on, unheeding; "You don't have to hate it, you know. Its hunger is natural. It's not a demon."

Conway wondered with part of his mind what the spacer thought he was talking about. But he didn't really care. He only wanted them to go away. He responded, civilly, but didn't have his heart in it.

"I know it's not a demon, and I don't hate it. It's my enemy, and I'm going to kill it. That's natural too."

Sol hesitated, thinking so hard it was visible on his face, as a crease in his brow and a narrowing of his blue eyes.

"Do you know what a Jinn is? How about a Fairy Godmother?"

"No."

"I can grant your every wish." He hesitated and firmed his speech. "I can grant your every wish."

Conway stepped back and made the sign of the Double Cross of the Last Church, a gesture he hadn't made since he was last in Fane School. He thought he had forgotten how.

"You're Him!"

"Him who?"

"The devil, that's who."

Sol realized that he was faced with a failure to communicate. "No, no." He placated. "I'm just an anthropologist from Sinclair....That's on Abaraxis."

"Anthro......?"

"A man who studies men."

"You should ask a woman."

"Ah....Ha." He said uncertainly, and then decided it was an actual joke. "Hahahahaha." It wasn't a very convincing laugh. He tried valiantly to get back on track again. "If you keep the flyer alive for a few hours, I will do you a service, feed you, teach you, whatever you want."

"Why can't you...make blood for him, or something?"

"Exactly what I was going to do. It just takes a little while." He smiled benignly down at the Mungian.

Conway was just coming to see himself as a man, and one of the first symptoms was a distaste for being treated like a boy. He frowned and said; "So take a little while. I'm in no hurry."

"But the Flyer is. They have very fast metabolisms."

"Wasn't there any provisions in the basket?

"Dried blood, probably. But maybe not. That's why they're attacking."

"Why is that?"

"Famine…There has been an ecocrash and they have left the Main."

"What, all of them?"

"All that's left."

Conway had to stop and think. He turned and rested his elbows on the basket rim, a motion that let his right hand dangle over the edge. He became aware of this mistake only when he felt the gentle leathery touch of the Flyer on his wrist. He started to jerk away, but forced himself to relax. He contented himself with turning his head over one shoulder and saying, with irritation, "You better have some good food in your house, spacer."

Sol beamed and laid a gentle hand on the boy's shoulder. "Don't worry, Conway, everything is under control."

"Right." There was no sensation on his wrist, beyond a warm, dry kiss, and then a pleasant numbness, but the idea was repugnant to him in the extreme. In a few moments, he felt his hand released, and he turned back to Feggio.

"So now what?"

"Pick up the Flyer and follow me."

"I've got my chuitar."

"The Flyer is important to my work here on Munge."

"So…" The spacer succumbed to this logic with concealed ill grace and reached into the basket. The Flyer immediately tried to suck his blood and Sol irritably slapped its hands away.

"It wants to bite me."

"And?"

"It will get sick if it drinks my blood." The spacer looked ill at the thought, and Conway sneered as he hopped into the basket. There was little there of any use, but there was the bag that had held the flint and steel. Two slashes of his knife and it became a gag for the Flyer's mouth. The wrinkled creature was small and feeble even for a Flyer, and Conway managed to bind the Flyer's jaws and to lash its hands with a length of the thong that suspended the blanket.

"Here," He said to the anthropologist, "You take him, it's safe now." Conway was losing any awe he once might have had for the spacers, but he wasn't yet sure why. Feggio easily lifted the trussed Flyer and Conway gave one last look around the basket for useful salvage. The flint was gone but the file like steel striker was there on the floor of the basket, and he spoaned it. There was another skin of fuel, and a few empty gourds, but nothing else…Except, tucked into the wicker where the Flyer had huddled, a gleam of off-white. Conway pulled it out, and saw that it was a length of hollow bone, perhaps a human shinbone, but maybe not. It seemed lighter and thinner and might have been the leg bone of an axebeak or smaller striding dactyl. But the important thing was that the bone had been worked. It was covered with incised spirals, and was pierced with seven holes. There was a large one at the closed end, and six smaller ones in a line down the length of the tube.

Conway was reminded of the first olearth music the Aludium had played for him. He tucked the pipe into his belt, next to the bundle of darts, and said to Feggio; "I changed my mind. I'll carry him. Lead the way."

Conway clambered from the basket, settled his chuitar strap over his shoulder and took back the Flyer. He hefted him in his arms and jerked his head at the spacer.

"Do you want me to carry your instrument?"

"No."

"You don't seem very happy to be rescued."

"You might have rescued Attilina, and you might have rescued this Flyer, but all I want from you is a good meal and directions to the nearest city."

"Lissa?" Sol jerked his thumb over his shoulder. "It's that way, less than twenty clicks."

"How much is that in Mungian?"

"Oh…Less than two hundred…Er…Say one fifty flongs."

"A half days walk. Let's go. I want to get there before dark." Sol didn't protest this rudeness, just led the way towards the incongruous palm trees.

Halfway there, Conway was struck with a question. "How did you find us so easily?"

"Oh, her netset was always on. We can monitor it from orbit. Once I knew she was hurt, it was easy to fly ahead of you and wait for you to land. I just picked the highest hill downwind of your flight path and once you stopped moving, I just hopped my goship here."

Conway digested this for a few paces, the musty smell of the Flyer filling his nostrils. "That hut?" He swallowed a few more stupid remarks and composed a sentence that might not disgrace itself. "That hut is your space ship?"

"No, that hut is camouflage. The hill is my ship, and it's not really a space ship. It will barely get to the moon. It only goes to orbit. Ground to Orbit. Goship. Get it?"

He got it, but there didn't seem to be anything to say that wouldn't make him seem even more of an idiot, a grubber. So he just hefted the slight weight of the flyer, and followed Feggio up the hill, past the cold fireplace, and into the hut. It was a little more solid than was normal for it's size, boasting a mat roof and wattle walls. Inside, it was divided in to three rooms and furnished in typical Mungian style with stools, chests, and mats. Conway noticed that the several pieces didn't fit together, but it might have been the home of a seafaring bachelor. There was nothing overtly alien about the hut, but it wasn't exactly right either.

Feggio pushed past him and went to a cupboard that was slung between two posts on the back wall of the hut. He touched the carved trim in several random places, and a carved snail shell moved aside disclosing a small, round red light. The spacer pressed this light with his thumb and turned to Conway. "We do it this way so that people without netsets can get in…" A remark that totally escaped the boy. There was a chime, and a whole section of the floor matting sank down an inch or so. Sol stepped briskly onto this section, and gestured Conway to do likewise. The musician complied, and then grabbed for support that wasn't there when the mat sank beneath them, carrying them down into a blare of light and a cacophony of sound. Feggio grimaced, and the sounds abruptly changed to different, if still grating, music.

He said. "I can't stand that disney choptime stuff, but it's all the younk like Hyacinth listen to. I put on some classical olearth artraoc, just for you."

Conway was too befuddled to comment. They descended down only a few body heights, but it was like dropping into all the dreams he had ever had, all at the same time. There appeared to be starry space with huge noisy space ships fighting to one side, and a rush of brightly colored mechanical beetles to another. The floor was olearth green garden and several other walls, Conway supposed they were walls, were thriving confusions of incomprehensableness. He could see that one wall was organized into square segments, each displaying a different slice of reality. Or maybe it wasn't reality. He had no way of telling.

He had seen pictures, before, and some had been quite lifelike, but these had depth and were moving, contorting into bursts of raving action. He tried to ignore them, but they seemed to sneak his attention, to suck his eyes into their colors. He was rapidly getting a headache, and he never got headaches. The very thought was enough to give him a headache. But then he noticed that most of the squares showed purple vegetation or green sea and he began to realize that some of these pictures showed different places on Munge. His headache was joined with a sense of violation.

In the midst of all this multichrome confusion was a bed, or ornate chair, where Attilina reclined, a brown bottle in one hand, some white layered comestible in the other. The wounded side of her head was covered with a ruddily transparent jelly, and she was talking vociferously to nobody.

The music, or whatever it was, was too loud to hear what she was talking about, and Conway was not all that interested, he decided. The platform stopped descending, and he turned and spoke to Feggio, louder than he had intended; "Where do you want the Flyer?"

Feggio looked at him, as if he couldn't remember who Conway might be, and then just pointed to another of the great chair beds. Conway walked over the few steps, and dumped his burden on to the soft fabric. As the Flyer fell back until Conway could see its lower regions, and was shocked to see the obvious scars of amputations where the creature's legs had been. A horrible suspicion formed in his mind, but he said nothing. He just unsheathed his knife and freed the creature's hands and mouth.

The Flyer reached for Conway's belt, and the boy, afraid that the Flyer was reaching for the poison darts, jerked back and brandished his knife, before he shamefacedly realized that he had the crippled Flyer's only property also in his belt. He slowly replaced the knife, and handed the bone flute to the Flyer, who took it gently, almost wonderingly. Conway let his hands fall to his side, and then waited for a second, as if expecting a thank you. But the Flyer ignored him, examining the flute closely and then blowing a gentle scale in to the mouth hole. Conway thought that the Flyer had done exactly as he might have done on regaining his chuitar, and felt a certain kinship with the deformed being. He also heard that the scale of the flute was nearly the same as the skirling scale used by the Skatterlungs except for a flatted third note, like the minor of the Hazlen pipers. It was another kinship with the green gray, wrinkled Flyer, and he wasn't sure he liked that identity.

These actions reminded him that his chuitar had likewise been through a busy day, and so he unslung it, and checked it over. It seemed all right, except for some new abrasions along one bout, and a few splatters of something that he hoped weren't blood. Most importantly, all seven strings were intact, because his spares were in the bag, presumably back in his cabin aboard the "Grimshaw". Automatically, he strummed a chord, grimaced and tuned up the sadly loosened strings. There was always a moment of fear as a string comes up to tension, but all was well. He ran a passage of "A Mother's Plea", just to feel that all was really well, and was surprised to hear the Flyer join in without hesitation. The scale wasn't the same, but the Flyer had some sleight of bending notes to make them fit into the song's tonality. The bone flute had a dark, raspy tone, but Conway found it not unattractive. They played the rest of the passage and as soon a Conway let the theme fall, the Flyer restated it in it's own native mode. Conway supported it with sparse chords, it wasn't all that different from the original Hazlen lachrement. They played a few rounds, and then by unspoken consent, they stopped, with matching flourishes. Conway mocked a bow to the grotesque piper, who nodded, and touched the flute to his brow, in salute. Conway slung his instrument back over his shoulder, and turned to look for Feggio.

The spacer was ensconced in yet another chair bed, and was, like Attilina, talking to the air. Conway walked up closer, and cleared his throat. His delicacy was ignored, Feggio's unfocused eyes seemed not to even notice him. So Conway reached out and tapped the man's shoulder.

Feggio shook himself like a man awaking, and asked. "Oh, yes…"

"Conway."

"Of course……Convey. Hyacinth will get you some thing to eat." His eyes glazed over again, and Conway had to touch him again.

"Just let me out."

"Out of…my ship?" He seemed incredulous, as if he was LLord himself, and a very minor angel had asked for the day off.

"I want to get to Lissa before dark."

Feggio seemed to try and compute this data, but failed. He shrugged, and pointed to the center of the room. There was a chime from above, and the section of floor began to descend. There was a slender steel pillar that supported it, and Conway was relieved that something in this space was comprehensible. He nodded and turned to go. The spacer surprised him by asking; "Is there anything you want? Any reward for helping Hyacinth?"

"Moneys are always useful."

Feggio groped at his spoan, and then tossed Conway a purse. "I don't have much made up at the moment, but you are welcome to this." The purse was lighter than Conway expected, but he didn't protest.

"Thank you." Conway said, but Feggio's eyes were already glazed over. So he made his way to the platform. He passed within arm's length of Attilina, but she paid him no mind at all, being deep in conversation with someone who wasn't in evidence. She said something about; "Nothing but grubbs and grokes…"

Conway just nodded, and stepped on the lifting platform. A moment later he was back on the surface of Munge. He shook himself like a sorde with a bug on its crest, spoaned the purse, and set out on the rest of his life. He allowed himself to hope that it would be a little less cluttered with spacers, and walked off downhill.

By following the easiest, most obvious way, he soon came on a path that wobbled its way down by a grassy stream. In the manner of grazed fields all over the universe, the stream supported stands of taller growths, and as usual people had built their houses under the shade of these dendrons and decids. Most of the houses were empty, with all the occupants out in the fields and groves working, but after fifty flongs or so, Conway came to a local inn, complete with attendant local loafers. They, in the easily enthused manner of all such unoccupied persons wherever situate, inquired if he could, in fact, play that box.

When he replied that he could indeed, he was invited to "Take a drink and pick a tune." He did both and the afternoon waned into the evening, and eventually Conway, replete, exhausted, flattered, and full, stumbled off to a welcome hammock and retired, to await another day.

CHAPTER 14

▼

Awaking wasn't as easy as falling to sleep had been, and Conway renewed his vows to drink less quaff, but he did manage to de-hammock himself for lunch. There were fewer loafers about, but there were enough to carry on a decent conversation. Conway realized that he had been foolish to set off blind in an unsettled land, and so the first question was about the dangers of the road.

The lead loafer was a hunchbacked man with one hand, named Slaglow, and Conway already knew he was to be depended on for a constant flow of opinion and information, regardless of expertise or experience.

"Ah'ell, I hear 'e Blues have slowed their attack on No'th Cape, and 'e don't expect another push until next dry, No'th been so wet and all, ah'ell."

"So Lissa is still free ?"

"Ah'ell, free enough. if 'e can afford 'e."

"And the Flyers?"

"Ah'ell, been no telling of 'e Flyers, many a moon, Nosser."

"I was on a liner, and saw thousands of Flyers, attacking everything, just yesterday ! You best arm yourselves. They might get this far!"

"Ah'ell, yes'teddy, indeed. And 'e suppose 'e flew here, did'a theen?" The subordinate loafers nearly burst their wrappas at this sally, and Conway decided to ease on down the road, as the alternative was to either embark on a lengthy course of education for these good herders, or else be prepared for a stay in the local pillory equivalent. So he suffered the next few japes with as good grace as a person his age could be expected to muster, and made his escape, to the mutual relief of everyone concerned.

Conway soon was on the road again, to embarrass only the local breed of sailback, small and red of wattle as they might be. At least Lissa was not a battlefront at the moment, and so he bent his steps thitherward. He needed a chuitar bag, and some strings and a meal, and perhaps transportation off island. It might well be time to get back to Smith, and take up his career as Woodie's second string rhythm section. And maybe Cynchie could get him a gig...The wind was still from the southwest and should be for most of a moon. And he had no desire to see another Flyer.

The omens were good and things seemed to be at a turning point. The path became a trace and the trace became a road, and soon enough he was in the outskirts of Lissa on Offal Avenue. Lissa seemed to be larger than Griffin, on Ainsworth, and smaller than Cashamash. The streets were paved, in places and some of the buildings aspired to a second story. With his newfound worldliness, Conway classified it as a ten inn, three Fane town. Most of the outskirts were stockyards and slaughterhouses, with their dependent cooper yards, drying racks, and tanneries, and Conway hoped that he might be spared another malodorous stint with a scraper in his hand. Though there were worse occupations. No sooner had he formed this desire, than he heard his name being called.

He thought, of course, that it must be some other Conway, but there was something familiar about the voice, and indeed it was only the incongruity of the location that prevented him from recognizing his Angstian mentor, until a heavy hand slapped his back and a familiar foul odor assaulted his nostrils.

"By LLord, Badmash!" It was the old sailor in the flesh, ugly as life and twice as pungent. "Did they finally run you....I hope I didn't get you in trouble."

"Man!…Conway, boy, you don't know the half of it!" Badmash couldn't seem to unhand Conway. "Have I got a tale for you!"

"Do you?"

"Man!" Badmash finally loosed his grip on the lad, and looked at him for a moment, and then slapped his back and then stood back to look again. "You've grown," he said. "Near a man now."

"You look good yourself, Badmash. But you've got to tell me what happened back on Angst."

"Arrr, man." Badmash looked the street up and down, as if he was a stranger. "Telling tale's thirsty work. Let's get a firkin and set down."

"I need lunch, while we're at it."

"Dinner, you mean."

"I don't care as long as it has food in it."

"Man! That's my boy. Let's go to Momma Bill's." He set off down hill without another word, dragged by his thirst, and Conway was perforce drawn in his wake, like a school of skippers behind a great moby. Badmash, on closer inspection, had not changed much, if any. He might have gained a few lubbs and his wrappa might once have been more ornate than was his wont, but still and all he was the fine aged rendolent Badmash of old.

Momma Bill's was soon attained, and it proved to be yet another of the taverns that were Conway's landscape. Momma Bill, herself, had apparently gained her name from her majestic proboscis, a caudal appendage that might well have graced the granny of all sagitaries. She had carried her nasal over-endowment into a decorative motive that dominated the beams and trellises of her establishment. Every possible vantage was crowned with some variety of billed skull, and Conway was noted several variants of the skull wrought flea hopper, the lukette, that had been his first instrument.

Badmash ordered quaff, and Conway ordered sailback on toast. He was pleased to see that Momma Bill offered fried spurdad flowers as an appetizer and so he indulged himself. He still hadn't investigated the purse that Sol Feggio has tossed him, but he still had a good supply of moneys left from his previous travels.

"So how did you get here?" Both started the same sentence in unison and then sputtered into protestations of "You first, no you tell your tale, go ahead."

Badmash went first, as Conway had his mouth full. Or at least, Conway had his mouth fuller.

"Man, what a mess. It didn't take them Angsters more than a week or two to blame me for everything that had gone wrong, the Fane fire, Rosialindia and Blundoor's murders, your escape, the drop in the price of firkins FOB Cashamash, the smell of the tannery, and all."

"I was afraid of that." Said Conway, shaking his head and dipping a spurdad flower in red.

"Me too, but I was too slow and drunk to leave. So they decided to dunk me, and then, some said that I was too foul and would pollute the Town Pond, and some wanted to impale me for blasphemy, and then the decided that that would be way too noisy, and then they decided to hang me like they do in North Angst."

"Mmmmm."

"So they did. Man, they put a rope over the limb of that big old withe tree on the green, you know, and they had me up on a stack of barrels, and there I was."

"And then what happened?"

"Well, they hung me, and I died and went to heaven."

Conway almost fell for it. "And I suppose this is heaven?"

"No, this is Lissa, Ahven's on Smith." Badmash, always fond of a bad joke, had to stop and resuscitate himself with another swill of quaff. "No, man. What happened, when they Olders kicked away the barrels, I fell like a bag of...stuff, you know, and the rope broke. It was as old as the Olders, and it broke and there I was, flat on my good behavior, cursing a blue streak."

"Cursing is not allowed on Angst."

"You're right, they impale people for that." Badmash wiped foam from jowls and waved a battered hand at Momma Bill for a refill. "Old Fewmet, that was Rector after Fernster, you remember, that Blundoor killed…"

"I remember."

"Anyway, Fewmet, he came over and was trying to hush me, and I was cursing him, and he was getting all red in the face, and man!"

"What?"

"He turned all blue and died, right there on the green. And then Seamich, the Vice Rector come running up and he had a stroke and died too."

"And what did you do then?"

"I kept on cursing. I was on a roll." He paused and stole one of Conway's spurdad flowers. It would probably be most of his solid food for that day, if Conway was any judge. Badmash continued. "And just as I was warming up for my finale, old Beensteem lost what little mind he possessed and ran away right into the Town Pond, and drowned. And that was that."

Conway was lost. "What was what that?"

"There was no more Olders. They hadn't gotten around to synoding more, they was in such a hurry to hang somebody, and now they were all dead. Man, what a mess."

"What did you do then?"

"I quit cursing." Conway glared at him, until he continued the story.

"Obean, you remember him, he cut me loose and then somebody said it was a miracle, and the next thing I knew, they was all down on their knees, praying to me!"

"Uh……"

"That's what I said. And then I thought that here was my chance, you see, to get out of that tamn dannery, and so I lifted up my hand, like this, and I said, 'Bring me a drink', like that, and they did, and I figured that as long as I kept giving them no time to think, I was golden, and so I did."

"Did what ?" Conway had lost track again.

"Man? Oh. I gave then orders. I had them rebuild the Fane, and dedicate it to Sacre Conway, the Martyr, who had been borne away on the back of a White Moby, and then I proclaimed myself Chief Prophet, and made everybody dance naked on the green every Tressdy and Sundy, and started dictating a new Fanebook, and like that. It was kind of fun, until my harem started fighting among themselves and all, and so I left."

"Left."

"Yep. Stole a coracle like yours and sailed north to Ravelli, and here we are. I had a bunch of moneys, but I must have lost them or something, and now I work in a tannery again."

"Funny how that works out."

"Man." Badmash heaved a great sigh, and then vented his sorrows in a great belch. Conway waved for the next round, as Badmash finished his story.

"But the quaff is really good, and there are lots of other tanners to talk to, and no Faneiacs to bother me."

"Is Faneiac a word?"

"Ravelli was Last Church, until a few centuries ago. Then they got sense and lost their religion. Now all we have to worry about is the war. Those two pirates will never let us be, will they, Conway?"

"Yes they will. They're dead."

"Really ?"

"Really. In fact I helped kill Rosialindia."

"Do you feel bad ?"

"Not really….But, Badmash…You wouldn't believe it! I flew here! with a spacer and a Flyer! I've been in a spaceship! Yesterday!"

"- - - -" All Badmash could do was to gasp for air. Even his favorite expletive failed him. He leaped to his feet, and grabbed Conway's arm and dragged him out of the inn and down the street to a vacant area behind a deserted warehouse. Once there he backed the boy up against the wall, and then looked all about before hoarsely whispering; "You never lied to me, did you? Ever?"

"No Sir, I never."

"A spacer? Here? On Ravelli?"

"Two of them. I met the woman, the girl, on Ains. She's a sword fighter. She's seriously beetles. She kills people for fun. She got me run out of Ains and Ahven and the Isle of the Flies and Cashamash. Then we were on a 'liner, and Blundoor and Rosialindia attacked, or tried to pirate us or something. She killed Blundoor, and I...tricked Rosialindia, and she fell into the ocean and then the Flyers attacked and we escaped in a balooboo or something, and then when we got to Ravelli, up in the hills, there was this spacer, this anthro something or other, waiting for us. He walked up and greeted Attilina by name, her real name you understand, and asked me to carry the Flyer into his ship, and gave me a purse and I left."

"How could you not stay?" Badmash was incredulous.

Conway was scornful. "They're all crazy. The inside of that ship is like a nightmare, like a dozen nightmares all at once. it's so noisy, I couldn't even think. So I left."

"Don't you know about the law of access?"

"I guess not."

"The spacers have a law than any human must be given a ride into space, just by asking for it."

"So?"

"Man!" As if Conway was so stupid. "All you have to do is to find one and ask him. Don't you know? Spacers live for ever and never have to work."

"Not ever?"

"Not never." The old man sighed, a sigh of such tragedy that it ennobled his rags and stenches. "And you could have had that for the asking."

"So that's what Feggio meant by saying he could grant my every wish."

"And now he's gone."

"We don't know that. We could go back and look. It's only a few hundred flongs."

"Hmmmm…Man."

Conway grabbed the old man's arm. "Let's go back. It's worth the walk. Let me buy a few things and I'll walk back with you I'm sure I could find the hill again."

"Hill?"

"Yes, the goship is disguised as a hill with a little hut on it. And two palms. It's up at the top of this creek."

"Man." Badmash could scarcely allow himself to hope. "What if it's not there?"

"Then we walk back down hill and get drunk. Or I get you drunk. Or something."

"Conway, you are a……You are a real person. Thank you." Badmash clasped the boy's shoulder again, but there was a world of tenderness in this touch this time. "Bless you, my son."

"Don't get all silly, Badmash. Its just….Ahh, forget it, let's go."

With Badmash's guidance, Conway bought a few sets of strings, and a oilskin bag for his music box, and then they got a pair of light packs and filled them with two string hammocks and a few supplies and a water flask apiece. Actually it was one water flask and one firkin of quaff. It took only a little more than a glass and then they set off up the path again. But all these preparations were wasted, for no sooner had they left the city's outskirts behind, than they met a small sturdy figure, dressed all in black, swinging down the road, with a sword slung at her back. It was Attilina, as she ever was, with only a black rag over her wound to hide the spacer medicine.

Conway was ready to invent some new words, but as usual, he had little chance to say anything around Attilina.

"C'mon. You need to come back to the goship. That damn Flyer won't talk to anybody but you."

"Yes?" Conway was ironic, caustic and bitter. Attilina didn't notice.

"I said, it's important."

"Actually, you didn't say anything of the kind, and I suspect it's only important to you."

"I can't explain just now. But that Flyer is my ticket back to civilization, and he wants you. It's all politics."

"I don't know what a politics is and I don't know what civilization has got to do with it. Lissa is a city."

"Only to grubbers like you."

Conway was close to walking off, on the grounds that anything Attilina wanted would prove bad for him, until Badmash cleared his throat. It was a sad, resigned and hopeful sort of a sound, but Conway had good ears, and he got the message. He thought and then said; "I'll only come if my friend here is welcome too."

"Must you clutter up my ship with all the riff raff of the planet?" Then she relented and said; "C'mon," and set off up the road.

"We will have to stop and eat soon." Said Conway, just to be difficult.

"You can stuff gut on the goship." Said the girl. "It's right up behind this grove."

"What?...Oh, that's right. It flies."

"Yes, you stupid grubber, it flies. Now c'mon." And it was there, just behind the grove of jacamines, as advertised. They didn't walk together. Attilina went first, it wouldn't be correct to say she led the way, for she didn't care to temper her pace to the others. Then came Badmash, almost scampering on his old man's legs to his young man's dream, and finally, Conway came dragging tail behind, not sure he wanted to be anywhere near here, and getting increasingly bored and resentful of other people's dreams. He felt he had some perfectly good dreams himself, only his were always last on the list to be dreamt.

Feggio was waiting for them at the hut doorway, and Attilina passed him right by, so intent was she on getting back to her lounge chair. Badmash had been rehearsing speeches all the way up the hill and when he saw the anthropologist, he walked right up to him and saluted, open handed, in the style of Ahven, and said; "My name is Badmash Doming, human, and I claim Right of Access to the Community of Man."

Feggio acted as if this scenario was played out before him every day, for he just extended his right hand, and replied; "Welcome, Doming. You are welcome to Community. We will not leave until certain business is concluded, but if you have any needs, voice them and they will be met."

Conway expected the old man to immediately ask for a drink, but instead, Badmash, just clasped the spacer's hand in both of his and kissed it in joy. Feggio, tried not to wrinkle his nose at the old tanner's reek, and was partially successful. He retrieved his hand from Badmash's grip and said, "If you are to be a citizen of Community of Man, you must be fitted with a netset, and taught how to communicate with the goship. Wait here for a moment, and we will all go down together." This was Conway's cue to say; "I don't intend to go back down into that madhouse. If the flyer wants to talk to me, you can bring him up here. He doesn't weigh that much."

Feggio looked at him as if he was mad. Then his eyes glazed over with a look that Conway was beginning to recognize, and after a few seconds, the outer smiled and suggested, "If your friend, Doming, doesn't mind?"

Badmash knew a cue when he heard one; and turned to Feggio. Feggio in turn, turned and led the way to the elevator. The chimes sounded and the pair sunk out of sight. Conway dragged the nearest chest and stool out to the fireplace before the entrance to the hut and placed them comfortably near the blackened stones. Then he shucked his chuitar and pack and rooted out his new hammock. It fit nicely between one of the house posts and the nearest palm tree. Then he scrabbled up an armload of dead litter from under the jacamines and dumped it into the fireplace. It was too early for a fire, but he felt better after making these token gestures toward establishing a place for himself. The loss of his coracle, always nagging, seemed to oppress him constantly since he had left the "Grimshaw". He needed almost everything, he supposed; a place to live, something to do, some people to play music with, perhaps. His dreams of making instruments and finding a lover were more distant then ever, and oddly enough, the deaths of Rosialindia and Blundoor seemed to deprive him of the last ties to his homeland, miserable as it might have been.

Indeed, if Badmash was to be believed, East Angst had been transformed beyond comprehension, and surely he, himself, could never go back there unless he wanted to be impaled, dunked or worshipped, or perhaps all three at once. All he had left was his chuitar and a few coins, and a bundle of poison darts. He started up at the thought! He had been walking around all day, actually for two days, with a handful of deadly weapons tucked in his belt. He gingerly plucked them from his belt and then looked around for a safe disposal. There seemed to be no place safe enough for them, so he lay them on the hearth, and grubbed in his pack again. There was a compressed brick of trail food stuffed into a length of psallie gut. He transferred the lump of pressed berries and meat to his own gut, and wrapped the points up in the translucent tan membrane. One thing leads to another and he was wreaking havoc among the last crumbs of his provisions when Badmash puffed up carrying the Flyer.

"Man....Whew. I never thought I would touch a Flyer and live." He sat the Flyer down on the stool, and then handed him a floppy flask of red liquid. The Flyer took the flask, but his gaze was locked with Conway's. "They say that they want him to contact his people so they can end the war, but I don't know why he won't talk to the Outers." Badmash produced a round shiny object from his spoan. It was complexly round and seemed melted or polished to total smoothness.

"What might that be?"

"I forget what they call it, a commy thing, but if you want anything, just touch it and say something."

"What I want is something more to eat, and somebody to tell me what is going on here."

"Touch the commy thing."

"All right, I will." He reached out and found that the commy was smooth, lighter than he thought, and oddly without temperature. It was as soft as flesh, but neither warm like a body, nor cold like a stone. There was a chime, and Feggio's voice spoke out of the air above the smooth object.

"Yes? Can I help you?"

"I'm hungry, and ignorant. What do you want me to do with this Flyer?"

"Send....Um....Badmash back down, and he can bring you food. As for the other, it's complex."

"Start somewhere and tell me enough so I can ask dumb questions."

"The Flyers are doomed. Something happened on the Main, and they all fled. Most perished trying to cross the sea and many more were killed when they attacked a primitive steam boat."

"We saw that..."

"Yes, Hyacinth told me." There was a pause, in which Badmash ankled back into the hut, and the Flyer stretched out long arms and walked himself on his hands over to the hammock and swung himself into the security of the meshes. Conway noticed that the Flyer had his flute tucked into one armpit and had carried the bag of blood in his mouth, and was soon comfortably swinging in the hammock and sucking the blood out of the bag. The comm clicked back on and Feggio's voice continued. "The remaining Flyers have taken over the Partchmon peninsula on the extreme west of Ravelli. It's relatively mountainous so they can nest their quetzals. They could survive there, but they won't."

"Why not?"

"Because the Ravels will kill them all, as soon as they realize that the war is over. You and Hyacinth effectively ended the war, but no one knows until that liner you were on docks."

"Liners don't dock, they anchor off shore and are lightered off."

"Whatever." Conway could hear worlds of indifference in Sol's voice.

"The Grimshaw survived?"

"Apparently. I don't have any......eyes on board, but from orbit they look fine. They are under way, bound for Lissa, in any case."

"Good." Conway's next question required only a little thought. "So why do you care?"

"I don't, academically. If they live or die, become exterminated or conquer all of Munge is just...grist for my mill, as it were. I, personally, just study the peoples of primitive preserves as a portion of my schooling. But...."

"But what?"

"Hyacinth needs to go back."

"So take her back."

"I can't. Officially she is not here."

"So?"

"You don't understand. Everything we do, every action we take is recorded and is subject to review. Hopefully, probably, they will not monitor these conversations, or the food converter data, but they will review any passengers brought to orbit from Munge."

"So bribe the reviewers."

"You can't....They are machines. Hyacinth's father, Geoff, is a very powerful person. He has managed to obscure the fact that she stole a reentry pod and has left Leo. But there is no way that she can get from Munge back to Leo without notice. There are different domains involved. Her father is a Disseminator, they carry knowledge from system to system. I am a very minor functionary in the Institute of Humanity. We study the different races of humans, and try to preserve genetic diversity. Her father has little influence on the IOH."

"And?"

"If we bring back enough indigenous life forms to confuse the issue, we can more or less smuggle her in, in the herd, as it were. Then we can muddle Leo into thinking that she was there all along, in a blank-tank or sensepod, for example. Do you see?"

"No, but who cares? What do I have to do?"

"If the Flyers ask for Access to Community, we can take them, and all is well."

"So? Ask them."

"The Law is strict. We can't ask them, they have to ask us. And they, or rather he, won't talk to us."

"Oh."

"We want you to convince him to tell his people to emigrate to space. It's really their only chance of survival. As soon as you do that, we leave."

"All of you?"

"All of us." The voice took on a rich 'trust me' tone, that Conway immediately distrusted. "And you can claim any reward you desire, including Citizenship in Community."

"One thing bothers me. How will the Flyers live in space? How will you Outers take to a bunch of people, so violent, so blood thirsty?"

"We will make them a hab, a place where they will feel at home. It's trivial, really, just mass and energy. And don't forget, we have lots weirder people in Community already."

"If you say so…" Privately Conway thought that Attilina was one of them, but he was learning a modicum of discretion. He plunged on trying to get to the core problem. "So you don't really know why they left The Main, and you don't know how to talk to them and you don't really care, but you expect me to do your work for you."

"Was that a question?"

"Was that an answer?"

Feggio's voice took on a harsher note; "Just do your best, and you will be rewarded amply."

"I'll try." Conway wanted no part of any of this, but had a suspicion that Badmash's trip to space depended on his success. Feggio tried confident reassurance; "I'm sure that will be sufficient. If there is anything else?"

"No, thanks." There was another chime from the comm and Conway placed it down on the hearth. He looked over at his charge, who had finished the bag of blood and was studying the boy intently. Well, thought Conway, that was a start. At least he had the Flyer's attention. He dragged the stool over closer to the hammock and then went back for his chuitar. He pulled it from its bag, and tuned and nodded to the Flyer. "I'm Conway," he said, feeling like an idiot, "What's your name?" The creature ignored him, except for pulling out his flute. Conway, tried to think what to do, and came up blank. Automatically, his hands picked out a thread of a tune, and the Flyer immediately followed it on his raspy flute. Conway added a sparse chord beneath the melody, and they were off on another musical exploration. "Oh well," he thought, "Music is supposed to be communication, isn't it?"

It might have been, but music was all that the Flyer would share with Conway. In between songs, he would try dumb show, interrogation, bribes, charades and any other tactic he could think of, all to no avail. The Flyer was attentive, interested and even friendly, but also mute. He would take no sustenance but the synthetic blood, and never offered to feed from any human's veins again. Conway never heard him vocalize a single syllable and he paid no attention to any sort of diagram or sand scratched picture. Conway decided to call him Phezen, after a minor demon in the Last Church's Great Book.

As a musician, he was without equal in Conway's limited experience. He could abstract the melody from any set of chords the boy could display, and was equally apt at playing counter melodies to any lachrement, hornswoggle or gallivant in Conway's repitore. And so the days and nights passed, each eating, sleeping and playing to their hearts content, or so it appeared. And slowly Conway gained insight into the Flyer's personality. When two persons interact so intimately, as two musicians do in duet, they come to know each other's nervous systems better than lovers do. For in truth, love is a crude thing, of grasping and holding, but music is intertwining of one's very heart's breath with that of another. And it lasts longer, and perforce might well be more intense than carnal grappling.

Badmash was a rapt observer for the first day and most of the second, until he was fitted with a iridescent metal collar that was his trainee net set. And then he vanished into the bowels of the hill, the goship, for seemingly endless lessons in proper spacer deportment. Every time he answered the comm's signals he was dressed in new finery, all of which were alien to the simple wrappas and vests of Munge. He was less and less the old soak that Conway had come to know back on Angst. His diction improved, as did his accent. Conway never saw him drunk, or even drinking, again. His bearing straightened, and Conway began to notice that glazed look in the old man's eyes. Conway began to suspect that some form of communication caused that abstracted look from the other spacers, or even from the goship itself. One day Conway decided to test his theory, and so asked; "Badmash, what makes the ship fly?"

The old man's eyes glazed, and there was a pause in which Conway noticed that his friend, in fact didn't look so old as before. His hair was fuller and darker, and his skin was less wrinkled. Then his eyes cleared and he said. "The goship's primary reaction mass is atmospheric gasses compressed to nearly degenerate matter status and expelled through appropriate venturis, as needed."

"Fine. Thanks." Badmash turned to go, and Conway asked, "And what does that mean?"

Badmash started and turned back to face the boy. He thought for a moment, and said; "They take air, like, man,…air, and press it until it is a solid, until it's….really, really, compressed, and then they squirt it out a little hole, and it expands, and pushes the ship where they want it to go, like a spinabugger swimming."

"Really?" Conway was impressed. in spite of himself.

"Well, not really, but..."

"That's all a grubber could understand?"

"Man......" Badmash's voice dripped hurt. Conway was ashamed. He tried to make amends.

"Tell me how that necklace works, how you can know something, and not know it at the same time. Please?"

"The netset is linked, they call it, with...invisible...light beams to the brain of the goship, and the goship is linked to...bunches of other....things. Ahh...beings. Or...entities."

"Like the Aludium?"

"Sort of, but lots more. When I ask it a question, I hear it its voice in my head. If I don't understand, I just say so, and it tries a simpler way. In time, it will understand what I know, and tell me what I can understand the first time."

"How do you ask it? Do you just think to it?"

"No, you just talk without breathing out. If you set it to answer when you think, you can't get a word in edgeways. It's so fast...."

"Fast?"

"Man!"

"Doesn't it drive you crazy, all this stuff you don't know?"

"I asked it that..." Badmash grimaced, his heavy features creasing. "And it said that there is so much to know that nobody can understand enough to comprehend anything, and to not worry about it."

"But you know all there is to know about tanning." It was a question, the way it came out of Conway's mouth.

"Well, I might, but there is no such thing in Community."

"No leather?"

"Not really. There is stuff that looks like leather, but it's all made by nanos. Every thing is made by nanos."

One question led to a million more. "What's a nano?"

"It's a bunch of little critters, too small to see, that make things. They can make anything."

"Anything?"

"Sure, they can even make you young."

"I don't need to get any younger. Is that why your hair is growing back in?"

"Is it?" Badmash beamed, and ran his hand through his reappearing locks. "Man!"

The glow on his face told Conway all he needed to know. And more. He shifted his chuitar on his knee and turned back to Phezen. He was swinging in his hammock, and he had such a look on his face, that Conway was almost sure that the creature understood every detail of the last conversation. But it was so hard to read emotions on a face that was mostly composed of wrinkles and fangs. So, having no better plan, Conway strummed out the first few chords of the old Ains half-step, The Drakens Murmur. As usual, the Flyer was instantly with him, following the implied melody as if he had been playing it all his life. Conway used this thumb to pluck out the melody and Phezen slid down the scale to a counter melody in the bottom register of the simple flute. He was a master of under and overblowing his instrument, and could play in an incredible five octaves on his simple flute. But Conway realized, he never harmonized with the tune. The Flyer could play the melody, or against the melody, but never played with the melody.

Conway tried. He started the simplest harmony in thirds, and the Flyer immediately veered off to play in unison, as a shared counter melody. Conway knew it meant something, but he sure didn't know what. Puzzled, he let the melody drift away and contented himself with easing out the chords while Phezen wove brilliant flurries of notes above him. The human sank deeper and deeper into his thoughts, until finally he spoke, all unaware; "I wonder why they cut off his legs?"

"No. I." It was long moments before he realized that the Flyer had actually spoken. Conway started and almost burst out into a flurry of questions, but once more, his ears saved him. The melody the flute played was suddenly a march, an inversion of "The Blues Advance". It was sad and brave and desperately lonely. It modulated into a scurry of notes that were nearly a typical hornswoggle, like sailors all over Munge danced wild jigs to, but....

But, he realized. if he just listened, he could hear the bustle of normal village life, but at a distance, as if through a wall. Then he could hear a wailing lullaby, and he intuited that this was the memory of the Flyer's mother, much as the melody of "Fair Elsinor and The Elf Punk" was his memory of his own mother. The thought was a good as the deed and his hands shaped his loss into that aged ballad, and the Flyer followed instantly. Their two losses became one, and Conway discovered a unity with this strange misshapen creature, that was so intense, that for a second his eyes scalded with tears, and he was playing blind.

But his ears were unclouded and he heard the flute tell a tale of loss and separation, followed by the hard rasping tones of scorn and derision. These were also familiar to the young man, and he began to deduce the outlines of the Phezen's story. These deductions obviously indicated a method of communication, which he immediately implemented.

"You. Bone. Flute?"

"I."

And that was the start, and slowly, slowly, the two evolved a language, and exchanged histories. The Flyer, who had no name, was equally innocent of verbs. Among themselves the Flyers relied on scent, body language and verbalized sounds that were less than words for what little communication they needed. They were socially little above a herd of axebeaks or a pack of hunting sordes. Their brains, like their digestive systems were severely atrophied to allow the weight reductions needed for flight, even in Munge's light gravity. But they had retained the ability to mimic the cries of their great golden mounts, and amazingly, they had retained some ability to make music. It was the music that served for what little language they absolutely needed. They might be no bigger and were probably less intelligent than a five year old human child, but they were functional adults in charge of their own lives. And they had no room for cripples.

But Phezen's mother had hidden him and had kept the spindly deformed baby alive and had nursed him almost to adulthood, even though he had only one useless leg and the twisted stump of another. More importantly, he was lacking the flaps of skin that extended from wrist to ankle, and allowed a gliding flight in healthy adults. It wasn't real flight, that wasn't possible even on such a small planet, but it was enough to allow predatory swoops from tree to prey and also allowed the rapid gliding run along level ground made the Flyers the primary carnivore on the Main.

Conway could get no details, but the emotional content was clear and painful. Phezen had been confined to "Hole. Death. Rock." after his mother died, or was killed. There the cripple eked out a miserable life, probably on carrion or the blood of other discards like himself, until he had reached a desperate maturity. Conway imagined a chasm, or perhaps a tidal sinkhole with water at the bottom, and steep, unclimbable sides.

Somehow, with unbelievable tenacity, Phezen had survived and had amputated the poor remnants of his own twisted limbs. He had probably done this to increase his mobility in the depths of the deathhole, or perhaps his legs had become infected from being dragged through the rotting debris at the bottom of that foul pit. Conway was the tough child of a primitive planet, but even he was shocked and appalled at the picture he deciphered from more than a week's worth of hints, and halting words and torrents of flowing melody.

Probably there were others there, who survived for a time, down in that charnel pit. Perhaps even a few were humans, regular Mungians, although Conway could imagine no reason why they wouldn't have been immediately sucked dry and discarded. Perhaps there were seasons for prey, or perhaps they were diseased, or perhaps there was no sane reason. But Phezen had survived, and had learned whatever there was to learn, and had eventually fabricated his own shinbone into a flute, and then learned to master it, and had then done the even more impossible. He had somehow dragged his tiny body up and out of that Deathhole, and rejoined the society of the whole flyers, and had managed to convince them to let him live.

Perhaps they had thought him a ghost or returned spirit, or perhaps they had simply realized the incredible mental strength of the returned discard, and had allowed him to live, out of primitive awe.

His long, thin neck swelled with pride when he played the theme he had created to memorialize his dreadful climb, and his greenish eyes were bright, as he mimed that long, long struggle. Perhaps it had been his music that reprieved him, for surely Conway had never even imagined such a flautist, such an expressive musician, on any instrument.

Phezen's further career was even more mythical, and only the evidence of the migration of the flyers and the balloons gave it any credence at all. Somehow, over decades, Phezen had become, if not the leader, then the genius behind the Queen of the Flyers. He had learned to spy on the islands of the Pancreatic Sea, and had taken what knowledge he needed to insure the survival of his people, the people who had discarded him. He had learned fire and the smithing of metals, and the tanning of hides, and the workings of rope walks, all to one end, that he might fly, as his people did.

It had taken decades of intense work, and Conway became aware that Phezen must be far older than he appeared, but eventually he had achieved his impossible goal, and had lifted from the Main in Munge's first flying machine.

And just when all seemed well, everything had gone bad. Phezen had it as a chittering song that delineated millions of chitinous jaws destroying all his dreams and the most of his people. Conway had to turn to the spacers to fill in the details at this point. Feggio rarely come up out of his goship, but he was glad to converse for hours over the comm.

"We've dropped eyes to the Main, and it's obvious what happened. The beetles went Gould."

"And that means ?" Conway had developed dozens of ways to admit ignorance. It didn't matter if he was rude. The spacers never noticed.

"In every animal, every plant, is a…mechanism" Conway realized that the spacer was trying to simplify complex issues to a level that even a primitive could understand, and he was grateful. But he still didn't know exactly what a mechanism might be. Was it like a mill? How could a mill fit inside a person? But the comm continued; "That can turn on in the event of catastrophic change. It's called the Gould Gene. It makes the creature change to meet the new conditions. In this case it was a subtle change. The beetles simply changed their diets." Feggio seemed to think this was sufficient, but Conway needed more.

"Changed to what?"

"Oh….They started to eat meat. Live meat."

"They never…"

"They do now."

"If what you say is so, why don't the beetles here start eating us."

"They might. There are no guarantees." Feggio paused for a second, as he tried to translate his thought into simple terms. "But we think that the change was triggered by increased population among the Flyers. Something, or somebody, triggered an industrial revolution on Main that doubled the population several times over the last few decades. That's what led to the ecocrash. It happens almost every time. If the Murkans produce enough steam ships it might happen all over the Pancreatic Sea."

Conway could think of little to say to this that wasn't some variant of 'Why don't you just help us ?' He knew that it would be answered with some incomprehensible reference to some unbelievable rule or impossible regulation somewhere. But Feggio, as was his wont, continued with no regard for the possible emotions of any primitive.

"You must report some results soon. The season is advanced and the Blues are aware that they are leaderless, and are withdrawing back to Bluestem. The Ravels will probably attack the flyers on the Partchmon Peninsula soon."

"How do you know this?"

"My work here is based on the use of...eyes. They are tiny machines, that observe and report back to me, back to the goship. I edit these...reports and forward them to my superiors at Leo."

"What do these eyes look like ?"

"They are disguised as various insects."

"And so you send these eyes where ever you think they will be the most useful?"

"Naturally enough, we do. The hard part is deciding what is useful. There is so much data, and so few people to act upon it."

"So what am I supposed to do?"

"You must establish communication with your charge, and then travel with him to the Partchmon Peninsula and convince the flyers to emigrate to space. My superiors are most excited at the prospect of a whole new genetic heritage. And, of course, Hyacinth's father is anxious to be reunited with his lovely daughter."

Conway restrained several responses, some of which were simple gagging noises, and promised his utmost cooperation. Feggio urged diligence, and promised to send Badmash up with some delicacies for lunch. Conway was a little tired of never knowing what he was going to taste when he bit into something, and indeed found most spacer foods dry and over spiced, but it didn't seem to be worth arguing about. He could always roast some beetles or gather some fruits. In fact, that edibility made the plague of beetles on the Main seem not inequitable. Inconvenient, perhaps, but not inequitable.

Badmash soon joined them, bearing a plate of finger food and the inevitable bag of blood for Phezen. He was also eager for Conway to perfect communications with Phezen, so that he could finally get to space, and take up his new life. He would never say so directly, however, and so he attempted indirection. It was not an exercise he was comfortable with.

"Be rainy season soon."

"And?"

"It'll rain."

"Yes, it will."

"Hard to travel when it's wet out....Damp."

"Good thing you're going to space....No rain there." Conway had hurt Badmash's feelings by refusing to play along.

"Man....Why do you be like that? Didn't I help you, back on Angst?" Badmash wiped at an eye. "Did I ever ask you for anything?"

"Quaff."

"Outside of that?"

Conway relented. It was true. He had no reason to thwart Badmash. He felt unwilling and unworthy to be the agent of such a major change as the emigration of the Flyers, but he liked Phezen himself a lot, and was prepared to do almost anything to help the little cripple's survival. It was just that he had hated the Flyers so long, and feared them since birth, and the very idea that he, Conway the Inept, would be responsible for their preservation, filled him with emotions that were as indefinable as they were intense. Plus, he had gathered lot of inexpressible impressions concerning Phezen's relations with his people, and he was far from sure that the little monster had any desire to be reunited with his subjects. If that was the applicable word. Conway had an impression that captors might be the more accurate term. But there was obviously nothing to be done, but the doing, and there was little to be gained by putting off the inevitable.

"Phezen, we must go find your people, and save them from the Ravels. Do you understand me?"

"Yes. No. Dead. I." The words were barren rocks without the flowing water of melody around them, but Conway thought he got the meaning. He picked up his chuitar and strummed it, gentle chords without pattern.

"Yes, you understand me, no, you won't go."

"Yes. I."

"Why won't you go with me? They are all you have in all of Munge."

"Dead. I."

"You're not dead. You're right here with me, aren't you?"

"Dead."

"How can you be dead?" Conway pointed out, sensibly enough. "You're sitting in a hammock, drinking blood, just like a normal......" His mind finally realized what his mouth was babbling about and turned it off. But Phezen had gotten his drift.

"No. One. Dead." He lifted his flute and played a sad little dirge that perfectly expressed his aloneness. Conway, inspired and irritated, restated the melody in quick time and managed to fingerpick several harmonies around the little tune. He tried to express a multitude of other lonely Flyers, each yearning for their leader. But his torrent of notes had no effect on the basis melody. It just persevered, noble and sad, unbent by his histrionics. He stopped all the melodramatics and just returned to soft chords beneath Phezen's dirge. It was what he was feeling anyway. He was still alone, even though he was playing the best music he could have ever dreamed of hearing, much less playing. He was no nearer finding some one to love, and his plan of making chuitars was scarcely a tatter of a dream now.

He knew that Phezen understood everything that was said to him, and he also knew that Phezen was not cooperating for some very vital reason of his own. If he could not get the wretched creature to even admit he was alive....

"Badmash?"

"Do you have an idea?"

"Perhaps, I do. Do you....Can you get those pictures from the eyes up here so that Phezen can see them?"

Badmash's eyes glazed over for a moment, and his Adam's apple moved in his throat. "You mean the imputs from the anthroeyes?"

"If that's what you call them. I want Phezen to see his people. I want him to see that they are in danger. I want him to see what the spacers are offering them in space. Can you do that?"

"Man! Sure we can. This little comm can't handle full holos and sound, but there is plenty of equipment extant. We won't even have to nano up something."

"Well, then."

"I'll get right on it." Conway expected Badmash to hustle off down into the goship, but instead, he sank down on the nearest stool and picked up the comm. He pressed it to the netset necklace and closed his eyes. After a few moments there was a hum and a series of clicks and shiny platter thing flew up from out of the hut and landed on the packed ground, equidistant from the three of them. It had barely settled down on the ground, when the air above it seemed to curdle and jell, and then it was like a window opened in the commonplace air and suddenly they could see a rugged finger of land suspended in what must have been a dactyl eye view of the Partchmon Peninsula. The view swooped and enlarged as if the dactyl had found prey below the trees. Conway's stomach wanted to do tricks, but Phezen was totally engrossed with the picture. He even hopped from the hammock and handed himself over to the fireplace for a better look. Conway half expected him to try and touch the picture, but he didn't. In fact, he backed off a few hands to bring the view into better focus and then lowered himself onto the hard-packed earth and sat with wide eyes.

The view slowed down over a line of crags that jutted into the sea. This was obviously the utmost extremity of Ravelli and the Flyer's last refuge. Conway was reminded of the guano rock on Angst where he had been so badly belabored by the granny sagitary. There were less than a hundred Flyers visible and perhaps half that number of the great quetzals. They had scratched together nests of grasses and litter, and were fishing in the crashing surf below the cliffs. It looked as if they were surviving, but not thriving. Even Conway noticed many half-healed wounds among the Flyers, and the quetzals were bedraggled and looked thin. Phezen was making sad, quizzical noises deep in his throat, and kept peering from one familiar figure to another. Conway noticed that Badmash's Adam's apple kept moving, as did the picture, and he wondered if Badmash was controlling the insect eye so many flongs away. It didn't really matter, he supposed, but it was interesting in that it showed how facile Badmash was becoming in spacer magic.

As the eye neared the largest cluster of Flyers, Phezen became excited and reached out as if to touch one of the cluster. Badmash made the picture focus on the central figure, a large, very pale female. This Flyer was much more wrinkled that her companions and much better fed. Her breasts were great dependent orbs, and her wrinkled skin glowed with oils and attention. Conway suspected this was the Matriarch of the Flyers, and the obvious object of Phezen's attention, but he was gesturing towards one of the smaller females engaged in grooming the queen. Badmash muttered and the picture expanded to show a slight, dusky female, who seemed less wrinkled, perhaps younger, than those around her. Phezen pawed the air, trying to touch her, and when that failed, burst out with the longest vocalization Conway had yet heard from any Flyer.

Conway reached out and gently palmed Phezen's shoulder, suppressing a shudder as he always did at the feel of the fragile bones and the almost scorching body temperature of the semi-human person.

"Phezen…She can't hear you. If you want to talk to her, you will have to go to the Partchmon."

Phezen turned a burning look at him, and asked a single word. "Place?"

Conway looked a question at Badmash, and Badmash's throat moved. After a second, Badmash lifted a hand and pointed almost due west. Phezen slapped the flute tucked under his arm to assure himself it was there, and wheeled on one hand to clear the fireplace. Without farewell, he started off on his hands, a tiny, indomitable figure. Conway thought him so brave and ridiculous that he had to restrain himself from bursting out with laughter, or perhaps tears. Instead, he handed his chuitar to Badmash and picked up the small comm, and followed after the flyer. As he turned away from the picture, Conway thought he saw a human in the cluster of Flyers, but he didn't have time to make sure. Phezen was making good time. Conway caught up to him at the edge of a tongue of the purple woods and stepped in front of him.

"Are you leaving without a word?"

Phezen looked up at him with impatience in those gray-green eyes, but said nothing.

Conway tried again; "Wouldn't you rather fly there?" There was no mistaking the hurt in those huge eyes. Phezen turned to scuttle around Conway. Conway said, "Wait one moment. trust me." Then he lifted the comm to his lips and said; "Badmash, have Feggio fly the goship to the other side of the meadow, please."

Feggio must have been monitoring the situation, for no sooner were the words out of the boy's mouth than there was an immense throaty hissing noise, and the whole hill lifted up and unbelievable twenty feet and slid like a bubble on water around the two walkers in an arc to the other side of the trees they had been approaching. The hissing stopped, and the goship settled in a cloud of dust.

"Are you sure you really want to walk?"

Phezen looked from the goship to the boy and back to the goship several times. Then he spun on one hand and without any comment, started handing himself toward the goship.

Conway called after him; "Is that female your mate?"

Phezen didn't even look over his shoulder. "Child. I."

CHAPTER 15

▼

Feggio had consented to turn off the pictures in one small corner of the control room, and Conway kept his eyes wedged in that corner. He felt like a bad little boy, but at least he could keep his thoughts in order. Phezen and Badmash were huddled in one of the lounge chairs, Phezen pointing, and Badmash directing the pictures from the anthroeye. Feggio was apparently doing whatever Outers did to control their vehicles, although it looked as is if he was simply drowsing over a cup of chai. Attilina was in another corner of the huge room, battling monsters that only she could see. Her tunic was sweated to her small breasts and her katana was a silver blur in the multicolored lights that shone from the walls and decks of the goship. They had had to wait for dark before Feggio would consent to lift the goship the few hundred flongs to the Partchmon Peninsula. Conway never noticed when the goship lifted, and was just as glad. He was playing his chuitar and trying to discern any thread of logic that had led him here to this mad place. He could see no pattern, just a chaos of buffets that had cost him every thing he had ever known, and almost every thing he had ever earned on his journey. He still had Heoj's chuitar, and his knife and a few moneys in his spoan, but he knew that, at best, he would soon lose the only people he knew well on the whole of Munge.

His nuncle Bilbeau, was presumably still on Angst, and Woodie and Cynchie were probably still back in New Ahven, but they were scarcely more than acquaintances. LLord only knew where Gully might be, and

Conway was not such a fool as to expect any fond welcome from her. No, all he had in the world were Badmash, Phezen, and Attilina, and all three of them were bound off-planet as soon as possible. He had only one choice, and that was to go with them, but he could flog up no enthusiasm for the trip. From what little he had seen of spacer life, they were so rich, so incredibly gifted, that they were incapable of valuing anything. And what would he do in space ? How could he contribute, how could he feel like he mattered, when every person had access to thousands of years of music, and they didn't even have to crook a finger to sample any of it at any time. He had asked Badmash, and the old sailor had told him that there was no money, no work in space. All a person had to do was to prove a need for a given product or service, and it would be supplied to them. The only rule appeared to be that the larger a product might be, the more elaborate the proof needed must be. It had something to do with something called 'Grants' but, Conway was uninterested in the details.

He was interested in what his own, private life might be, and as far as he was concerned, his life had been blown off course ever since Attilina had come into his life. She had failed to kill Blundoor the first time they fought, and ever since his life had been a desperate series of improvisations, trying to survive the situations she had gotten them into. He tried to be fair, and supposed that she hadn't been responsible for the migration of the Flyers, but she had forced him to leave the security of the 'Grimshaw', for the desperate adventure in the balloon. He felt a certain grudging fondness for the warrior, but it was based on her strength of character, and stubbornness, rather than on her discretion or any respect for her judgment skills. He wondered what he could do next, friendless in a strange land, and the only float he could cling to was Captain's assertion that Lissa Ahven was probably full of abandoned shipping.

Well, it probably wasn't that bad, after all. Lissa was a decent sized city, and Hazlen wasn't that far away. He could stand to learn more about backing up a piper, and perhaps he could find somebody like

Gully to play with. Perhaps…A young Gully. Now there was a happy thought! Somewhat cheered by this imaginary goal, he was rising to look over Phezen's shoulder, when the goship gently thumped down, and everybody stood up to exit the goship. Everybody but Feggio, of course. He would have to remain at the helm, in case of emergency.

Attilina appointed herself leader, naturally enough, and everybody perforce followed her up the elevator. Conway bent down to pick up Phezen, and got a supremely dirty look for his trouble. The Flyer handed himself up to the platform, and then out of the imitation hut and down the hill to the real ground. Somewhere in this progress, he became the leader and Attilina became the guard. She scowled blackly, when she realized her demotion to sword carrier, but made no objection. Conway followed Phezen, and then Attilina, and then Badmash, who was attired in some one-piece suit of coppery Outer stuff.

The goship had landed at the base of the ultimate peninsula, just where the forest gave way to more or less bare rock. The path down the hill led directly to the Flyer Queen's rookery, and they had been awakened and frightened by the decent of the goship. Conway could not imagine what the Flyers could have thought of the huge flying hill, but they had no choice but to put on a brave front. They had no place to flee, except into the air, and there were not half enough quetzals to carry them all. There only other option was to jump off the edge of the cliff into the sea, and they were not quite ready for that, just yet. So they clustered together, males to the front, the few children inside a ring of mature females. A tattered few of the warriors were on their quetzals, waiting on the edge of the cliffs, to fly to the attack. This close, Conway could see that they were all battered and wounded and desperately thin. Many had mats of chewed leaves over their wounds. There was a spectacular silence when the Flyers recognized Phezen.

He stepped a few feet forward on his hands and then settled down on his stumps and waited, silently. Slowly, slowly, every Flyer face turned to their Queen, very like flowers turning to the sun. She stood like an elemental force, so sure she was of her powers, and waddled through her subjects to face Phezen. Her short legs and dragging wings should have been ludicrous, but Conway thought her vested in more majesty than Rosialindia ever had in all her cloth of gold.

The silence deepened, if that was possible, and the crash of sea on the rocks far below became painfully audible. Still, Phezen said nothing, and moved not a muscle. He seemed at his ease, perhaps all alone on his rock, and Conway began to understand the little creature's powers. The Queen kept striding up, until she towered over her adviser, and still the silence deepened, until it was a physical presence. Conway wanted to scream, to cry, to belch, anything to break that dreadful tension. The silence was grating on other nerves than his own, however, and suddenly a robed figure pushed through the crowd of Flyers and confronted the humans.

"Well, well, well, we meet again. The lovely and talented Attilina and the ever so clever young Mariner Conway. And in such distinguished company, too. A pleasure, a pleasure indeed to meet again, so unexpectedly."

"Mention. You survived!" Conway didn't want to speak, but he couldn't help himself.

Mention bowed and smirked a smile that bore very little good will. "Indeed my lad, Indeed. But, with little, as we might say, help from you. We noticed your presence on the 'liner, and your treachery. There might come a reckoning, young man, there might indeed."

"And Zharrissa?"

"Taken and slain, and to whose profit?"

"And what are you doing here?"

"We have become advisor to this noble band of refugees, indeed we have. In our past we were instrumental in the importation of certain valuables from The Contoax…And established contacts with the rulers of the Main. And now, they have come to depend on us. A small world, don't you agree?"

Mention preened himself and brushed invisible lint from his rich green robe. Then he turned and gestured to the Queen, with both hands. Conway decided that he was tired of maniacs who talked about themselves in the plural. He turned to ask Badmash to do something dramatic about the oily Mention, but Phezen beat him to it. He pulled his flute out from his armpit, and blew a single line of jagged melody. Then he lowered the instrument from his lips and ripped a single shriek from his lips. All the Flyer warriors in the front line took a single hopping step and launched themselves at the fat monk. It was like a single instant of nightmare there on that moonlit rock. There was a sweep of gray wings that converged on the confident criminal, and then there was a rolling a bundle of tangled leather that emitted a single bubbling moan, as from a throat full of blood, and then there was silence again. The bundle was soon still, and untangled itself into a line of Flyers and left a crumple of green cloth on the rock.

Phezen waited until the silence concealed again, and then he lifted his flute again. Conway had his chuitar on his back, as always, and unshipped it in time to follow the first notes of Phezen's song. It was a simple song, and Conway recognized the theme he had dubbed "The Flyer's Lullaby" and that he knew was Phezen's memory of his mother. But he had never heard it at such a slow, tempo, more of a dirge, a lachrement, and a sadness as massive as the planet beneath their feet. The music had an intense effect on the gathered Flyers, They all pressed forward, as if drawn against their will, and even the great golden dactyls turned back to land and carried their riders as close as the press would allow. They formed a living wall at the rear of the clustered Flyers, and it seemed that the Quetzals were as attentive as their riders were and as intelligent.

Phezen played the lullaby only a few rounds, but it was enough to make every eye sparkle with tears. Conway, blinking away tears of his own, realized that he had never thought the Flyers human enough to cry, but he saw that he had been wrong, and so seeing he thought himself a great beast. Even the quetzal's eyes were full, and their great, cruel heads were drooping. Then just as the pain and loss could be borne no longer, Phezen modulated in to the song that commemorated his escape from the Deathhole. It started in a low minor, and was scarcely faster than the lullaby, and as jagged as the lullaby was smooth. The theme built, and ascended the scale, as Phezen overblew notes, forcing them up, as it were to the light he had fought so fiercely, so long ago.

Finally the same theme became a paean of praise to the achieved sun. The jagged intervals smoothed out, and the legless Flyer played triumph and joy and freedom. Conway expected more music, and was ready with the "Chittering Beetles" chords, but Phezen stopped at the peak of triumph, and Conway was almost caught hanging. His tutelage under Woodie served him well, however, and he managed to stop himself from plunging over the musical edge and spoiling the mood Phezen had so masterfully created.

The Flyer left his statement hanging in the healing air, and turned to the human. He proved that Conway's intuition was right, and that Phezen had understood every word all along. He said "Tell where go."

Conway just pointed at the spangled quarter moon, and held the pose until every eye was fixed on the lights that sparkled and glittered, jewels on the dark of the orb. And as they looked, Conway felt that shift in his brain, and the moon turned from a coin at arm's length, to a huge rock, a vast world, and a very long way away. He could almost feel that same shift in all the minds around him, and he turned to Badmash, only to have his request die on his lips. There was a door, a door as big as any Faneportal in all of Smith, opening in the base of the hill, and a welcoming light shone out, and there stood Feggio in that opening, and beside him was a low trundle cart, and the trundle was all loaded with bags of warm blood. Phezen was the first to the trundle, and he lifted the first two bags of blood, and put them in his mouth and he handed himself back and gave the first bag to his queen, and the second to his daughter.

Attilina shrugged, looked at Conway for a long moment, shrugged again and walked into the open door. Badmash clasped Conway's hand, fought for words, and then just unclasped the netset from around his neck, and offered it to Conway. Conway looked at it for a moment, and then simply shook his head. Badmash nodded, as if he had expected no more and lumbered aboard the goship.

Phezen came up and stood by Conway, and they stood there in silence as the Flyers and their golden mounts filed on board the Outer ship. Conway couldn't believe it was all over, that an insoluble problem has been resolved with only one death, and he was waiting for some vast emotion to strike him. Nothing happened, and then his knees felt weak and he sank down to sit next to the Flyer. This brought their heads close together, and Phezen leaned over and whispered in his ear; "Give dart." It took a while for Conway to remember the bundle of darts he had in his spoan, but then he dug them out and offered them to Phezen. The legless Flyer daintily extracted one dart and deftly inserted it into the central bore of his flute. Then he tucked the flute under his arm in its accustomed place and followed the last of his people aboard the goship. He didn't turn or look back, and Conway finally felt the emotion he was expecting. It was his same old friend, loneliness, and he wanted to wrap it around him for warmth, like a blanket in rainy season. He thought he best get away from the ship before it took off, and tumbled him like a leaf in its hissing jets, and had just gotten to his feet, when Badmash came hurrying up with both arms full of leather.

"Conway, man...boy I'm glad you didn't leave. Are you sure you won't come with us, we could have such fun."

"Badmash, you old....I don't want to have fun. I want to live. I want to grow up. I want to make chuitars. You know."

"Yes, I know......Man, you're a stubborn one."

"You taught me everything I know. You're to blame. It's all your fault."

Badmash just laughed. "Here, I brought you our packs. Get in and we will drop you off outside of Lissa. It's a long walk."

"No tricks?"

"Not a single one. We owe you a lot. Not many people done what you done. You're a hero."

"I'm hungry, what I am."

"Man! There's an idea. C'mon, let's go."

C H A P T E R   16

▼

He supposed he should watch the goship hiss its way out of sight, but something about it's effortless transgression of all his boundaries irritated him. Its freedom wasn't his, as surely as Attilina wasn't his match. And all it proved was that mobies can't love axebeaks. And so it was. At least he still had his chuitar. It was beginning to resemble his heart; battered, but functional.

He found his feet wandering him back down to the docks, even though there would probably be no shipping until commerce reasserted itself after the war. But, in the event, he was proved wrong. A much-battered long liner was off shore of the Lissa, and its attendant shoal of bummers and coracles were ferrying casks of water to the big raft. It was earlier in the evening than he had thought, and the torches of the ships and boats were beautiful on the water.

Apparently the liner had been transporting mercenaries to the war, and was now at loose ends. A very motley crew of young men were idling or scrounging around the town of Lissa, and so Conway found a convenient shade tree and unslung his instrument. He strummed a few easy chords, and tried to play Kigney's Revanche. He found he was actually in the wrong key, but persevered, and the song forced itself into life, wrong key, wrong time and all, as if it itself wanted to be, to manifest itself right here, right now.

Conway could only stare at his own fingers, and let them do their worse. It was interesting enough, in a bemused sort of a way. At the beginning of the next round, he slapped the heel of his right hand down on the strings on the off beats, in the style of the Ogglanders of Southern Ravelli. Such an ornament was totally alien to the sparse Hazlen tune but it sounded well enough. A few passing sailors stopped to listen and one, a dark skinned lad from the far east, produced a clay triple pipe and skirled an esoteric accompaniment to Conway's whimsy. The crowd grew, and a few coppers hit the dirt before them. An old woman, a cook from her apron, squatted down on her heels and tapped out reverse rhythms on a Crippen triangle drum. An other, a one legged warrior from LLord knew where, had a transverse flute built into the back of his short sword, and he began to counter the piper's skirlings. Oddly enough, the intervals were not the same, but proved complementary.

Indeed, the wails and squirls and thumps all mingled into a sound that captured the tang of the leaves of the great bayn tree, and the salt taste of the air, and even the squalls of the sigils in the sky above the bay. A young lass, slight and fair, slipped through the crowd and stood foursquare in the midst of the musicians, and licked her pale lips once and began the refrain of the old revanche.

"And I'll not know, and I'll not care, and I will never be..."

And the crowd came in with the refrain, as if they had practiced all their lives for this moment;

"A stranger, no a stranger, never be, never be."

"And I'll not stay, and I'll not wait, and I will never be..."

The girl had a voice like mixed spices from far lands, sweet and pungent and musty all at once, till it seemed that her thin body could never contain all that sound, and it must burst out and be free. And the crowd sang

"A stranger, no a stranger, never be, never never never be."

And the three beats of chuitar and triangle drum and the warrior's single foot on the ground seemed to encompass the horizon, and the flute sword and the pipe and Conway's melody line soared and played in the sky like all the sigils and quetzals and drakes that ever might be, and the crowd grew and the coppers rained down on the hard earth and the girl rose on her toes and filled herself with the sweet sea air and sang the verses of the old revanche song from the far isle of Fortune.

"And when I a wanderer was, far did I roam
And all the waters of all the oceans were my home, sweet home.
And when I was a sailor, all the winds were fine,
And all the dactyls and all the fishes were mine, mine, mine.
And when I went a-rambling, the hills were my birthright,
And the mountains, and the valleys and the cities shining bright."

The band, for now it was a band, took a chorus, by mutual apprehension, and Conway dragged the syncopation down so far behind the beat, that he could feel the impulses travel down the audience's spinal chords until their feet began to move of their own accord, and the drummer was right there with him and a couple from Birdsley, perhaps, from their blue check kirtles, started a wild circling, stomping dance that fit the rhythm so well that Conway felt he was twitching their feet with his right hand, and then the girl looked him right in the eye, and winked and sang one last time

"And I'll not know and I'll not care and I will never be..."

The crowd roared out;

"A stranger, a stranger, no never be."

The spicy voice of the thin girl launched itself out of the crowd like a skipper coming out of a boat's bow wave.

"And I'll not stay, and I'll not wait, and I will never be..."

And the crowd replied like waves on a shore.

"A stranger, no a stranger, no never, never, no never never be."

Conway whipped them back in the chorus until the whole bay rang with the last line. And they danced the spangled moon down into the spangled bay and even though Conway knew that each spangle on the pocked moon was a city bigger than any on his little planet, he knew that they had something as precious as anything on all the far flung worlds of man and near man and not man at all. They had themselves and they had their music and they had their very lives. And that was all there was, that any being could have anywhere in the universe.

Much later, when it was graying, and they had sung their very own sun up again, Conway and the singer were gathering up the money that carpeted the beaten earth under the great bayn tree. Even as innocent as he was, Conway noticed that the girl was staying close enough to him that the hairs on their arms touched, and often enough their hands closed on the same coin.

After her silver hair swept his face for the second time, and he had gotten a full draft of her natural woman smell, spicy and musty as her voice, a joyous suspicion entered his heart and there became a certainty. He touched her shoulder in a way that was not quite casual. And she turned to him and looked him in the eye, and asked; "What kind of music do you suppose, that was, exactly?"

"That was our music."

"Does it have a name?"

He thought for a moment. "I suppose you could call it…blue green music. It's all of the ocean and all of the sky and all of the land music. It's ours."

"You talk like a poet."

"You sing like all the angels and all the devils in all the heavens."

They thought about these things for a minute, and then Conway boldly slipped his arm through hers, and shouldered his chuitar, and led her up the dirt street towards the town's best inn. She gave him one startled look, and then stepped off with him. As they left the shade of the giant tree, he turned to her and said, "I don't even know your name, dear."

"It's not important. I feel I need a new one anyway…What do you think it should be?"

"Spice? Venture? Spirit? Lissa?" They faced each other again. They shared a smile between four eyes. "This may be too much of a responsibility for a chuitar banger."

"It should be easy for a poet."

"This will require some thought, most certainly."

"Perhaps we could sleep on it."

Conway had no words, but perhaps something would come to him. He squeezed her arm and she squeezed back. Something would happen. He felt confident. The last glimmers of the spangled moon were fading into the blueing west and so he turned his face toward hers and kissed her lips and asked her;

"Do you think you could be called Abaraxis?"

She laughed with those pale lips. "Abby for short?"

"If it pleases you?"

"I am pleased"

"And myself, likewise."

"I will be Abby and the band will be Abaraxis." She said, as if it was all settled.

"What band?"

"Our band, love."

He looked at her. She looked at him. Two brains full of thoughts, and not a word to be said. They linked arms again, and walked off up the road from the Lissa docks toward the inn.

The Beginning

0-595-24185-9

Printed in the United States
23325LVS00008B/209